# The Games We Play
## Book One

# Cat and Mouse

This is a work of fiction. Names, characters, businesses, places, events and incidents are either the products of the author's imagination or used in a fictitious manner. Any resemblance to actual persons, living or dead, or actual events is purely coincidental.

Printed in the United States of America

ISBN-13: 978-0-692-76280-6

ISBN-10: 0-692-76280-9

First Edition

# Cat and Mouse

Book One of the *Games We Play* Series

Dear Reader,
　　Thank you. For your support. For your time. For your imagination. I hope you have fun taking this journey w/ Roxanne.

Written by Jacquelyn Phillips

*For Justin*
Love makes people do crazy things, doesn't it?

# Table Of Contents

# Chapter One

"DO YOU THINK my boobs look big enough in this?" Claire, my new housemate, and a girl I considered one of my best friends, asked from the backseat of the black Jetta.

I looked in the rearview mirror, watching as she adjusted her right breast, then the left, before shaking them both as if practicing a move for one of her dance performances.

Although I was driving, the Jetta didn't belong to me. It belonged to my other housemate, Shannon, who now sat in the front seat, trying to keep her silver eye-lined eyes open. I just happened to be the only one in the dorm—and probably the entire university—who didn't drink alcohol, and therefore, could drive the vehicle without worrying about arrest.

"You're asking the wrong person," Amber, my very well- endowed in the chest-area housemate, said from the seat behind Shannon as she gestured to her double-D cleavage. "Even Ds look like As next to me."

I snorted, squinting at each street sign we approached to make sure I was going in the right direction. Although it was my second year at Sonoma State University, I was still topsy-turvy when it came to the surrounding residential streets.

Shannon glanced over her shoulder, her vodka breath making me cringe. "They look bigger than they did earlier. They're definitely big enough." She then set her sights on Amber's chest. "I'm not gonna stand next to you at the party. You'll make me look like a twelve-year-old boy," she slurred.

Amber smiled and winked, her blue eyes sparkling in the headlights of passing cars. "I'd give my left tit to be as skinny as you."

Claire cleared her throat. "We're talking about me. Roxy, what do you think? Big tits? Be honest."

I shook my head. "I'm driving. I'm not about to crash the car to analyze whether or not that bra accentuates the size of your breasts." I paused, turning left when the streetlight turned green. "Besides, isn't it a little late to be asking that question? It's not like you have any other clothes to change into."

Claire's drunken gaze stared wide-eyed at me in the mirror. "You can take me back to the house and I can change."

I kept my eyes on the road, staying silent.

1

"It's my car," Shannon said, slurring. "And my gas."

"It's not that big of a deal," Claire asserted.

"Are we there yet?" Amber whined. "I really need to pee."

"Don't break the seal. You'll be peeing every five seconds," Shannon warned. "And you don't want to miss out on the cute boys."

I sat up straight. *Boys?* My armpits began to sweat. *Don't freak out. You knew boys are gonna be there. You can just stay in the corner so nobody will talk to you. It's not that hard.* I rubbed my palms on my jeans. *The girls are too drunk to notice whether I'm next to them anyway.* I then pressed down on my big, auburn curls hoping that my hairspray would keep the inevitable frizz at bay. *Don't sweat like a pig. Keep it together.* "Do you know these boys?"

"It's all the baseball boys. I know them from cheer." Amber uncapped her water bottle and sipped from her alcoholic concoction. "And I'm not impressed."

I wanted to tell Amber it was illegal to have opened bottles of alcohol in a car. I especially wanted to tell her it was illegal to *drink* alcohol in a car. My grip tightened on the steering wheel. *Don't be that girl, Roxy. Nobody likes a know it all.* "Not impressed?"

"I'll text Steven," Claire said, punching her fingers against the cell phone. "He's our way in."

"Steven?" Shannon asked.

"He's a baseball player—"

"Who fucked Danielle this summer," Amber interrupted. "Why are you still talking to him?"

*Danielle? Like—your friend Danielle? Danielle who helped you move in, Danielle?* I glanced in the rear-view mirror again, noticing that Claire's light brown eyes never left the phone.

"He's a *friend*," Claire scoffed. "And he's the reason why we can get in this party. Why don't you just chill?"

"He *fucked* Danielle—one of your *best* friends. Why are you talking to him again?"

"I don't like him like *that*. Danny can have him." Claire's phone vibrated, her pale skin neon against the screen's light. "If he knew I was a virgin, he would've had sex with me instead of her. Boys *love* that."

I bit the inside of my cheek. *Yeah, I'm not so sure about that, Claire.* As I pulled next to the curb, Shannon's head smacked against the headrest, neck lolling side to side, eyes closed tight. *Please don't throw up on me. Please don't throw up on me. Please don't throw up on me.* I put the car in park.

"Is he cute?" Shannon slurred.

I turned to look out my window, watching as students walked from house to house, parties awaiting behind closed doors. I also worried that Shannon wouldn't keep down her vodka, and any time she opened her mouth, I didn't know what would come out.

Claire shrugged. "He's alright."

"You weren't so nonchalant about it two months ago when you called me crying your eyes out."

I smiled to myself. *Talk yourself out of this. You don't have to go in. The girls won't care. I can pick them up when it's over.* "We probably shouldn't trust some guy who went behind your back and did something like that."

Claire opened her door. "He still loves me. He wouldn't have invited me here if he didn't."

*Oh great,* I thought when she stumbled. *Another night comforting you over the toilet. Just what I want.*

I followed the girls down the street, gazing at three of the four housemates I would be living with for the rest of the school year.

Shannon flaunted a skin-tight, black dress that exposed her skinny frame, long legs and olive skin. Her straight, dark brown hair was streaked with golden highlights, and hung just above her shoulder blades. Amber wore a V-neck red dress that displayed her extreme cleavage and hid her slightly plumper midsection. Her brunette hair fell in straight layers all the way down to the top of her round butt, her short dress hugging her muscular legs. Claire had converted an orange, strapless shirt into a tiny dress that was held upright by a wonder bra and looked vibrant against her pale skin. Her light brown hair, which she'd sworn she'd never touched with dye, was pulled half up with an orange clip, her bangs bobby-pinned to the side to make her forehead appear smaller.

It was strange that Claire and I got along like we did. We were nothing alike — I'd been forced to go to this party instead of staying at home and reading like I wanted to, while Claire downed shot after shot before she even put her party clothes on — but we'd met the previous year at a common friend's house and somehow clicked. Even now, as she tried to show off every inch of her skin, I was hiding beneath dark blue jeans and a baggy red t-shirt. While the girls buckled the straps of their high heels, I laced up my black and white Converse.

3

I didn't know if Amber, Claire's roommate from last year, or Shannon, a random student that fate decided to make Claire's roommate this year, would like me because I tended to shy away from the party scene. But I was willing to try to make an effort to get to know them better, hence why I was now pressing a button on the Jetta's keys to make sure the doors had locked behind us, instead of driving away like a mother would after dropping her teenagers off at the school dance.

As we approached the door, it swung open, releasing a cacophony of loud music, splashing water, clinking glasses and drunken conversations. I hadn't realized how nervous I was until I examined the massive amount of people cramped inside the tight confines of the house.

"Hurry up and get in here," a boy with buzzed blonde hair ordered as he ushered us through the doorframe. I shivered when the condensation from the beer in his hand dripped onto my arm. After inspecting the surrounding yards one more time, he closed the door behind us.

I had to admit, the boy, Steven I presumed, was cute. His light blue eyes and straight teeth would lure any girl into his bedroom. I blushed when he smiled at me, looking down at the white tips of my shoes.

"I'm Steven." His voice was raspy. He extended his hand out to me, and unfortunately, the manners my parents instilled in me from birth forced me to return the handshake.

"I'm Roxanne," I nearly whispered. My hands were clammy, but his smile didn't falter, nor did he pull away from me. I smiled at him shyly, hoping he didn't think I was some sort of freak. *Why do I care? He's a complete stranger. I'll probably never see him again.*

"You livin' with these party animals now?"

Amber was completely disinterested, her sapphire eyes scanning the crowds for some tall, dark and handsome man who would be able to provide her with free drinks. Claire giggled slightly and nodded as if Steven was talking to her, her prior comments about being disinterested completely forgotten.

I timidly took a step closer to him, the music making it difficult for me to hear him and nodded. "I didn't know they were party animals."

He laughed. "Then you don't know them at all."

Claire slapped his wrist. "Don't scare the girl, Steven. She's just getting used to us."

I shrugged. "I'm sure we'll be like sisters by the end of the weekend." *Or I can hide in my room for the rest of the year if we hate each other.*

4

I knew it wouldn't be appropriate to tell him the truth about my living situation, so again I bit the inside of my cheek, again growing nervous. It was obvious that Amber hated me for being Claire's new best friend, Shannon and I hadn't exchanged more than ten sentences with one another, and I had yet to engage in any real conversation with Elizabeth, the other housemate we were supposed to meet here. School began on Wednesday morning and I was already busy with Biology, Intro to Psychology, and Anatomy homework—and secretly flipping through the syllabus of my token English class, eager to delve into the poetry workshop component of the semester, dreading how my Anatomy textbook seemed to loom over me as I slept.

"Well, why don't we put your compatibility to the test?" He held the beer against my lower back and snapped the fingers of his free hand.

My back muscles stiffened, his too friendly touch catching me off guard. *Relax, Roxy. He's just trying to be nice. He's their friend. Try to fit in.* "Ladies, if you'll follow me please." Steven walked Claire, Amber, Shannon and I over to an elongated black table where ten red solo cups were placed near the edges of both sides in the shape of a pyramid. "Nothing like a game of Beer Pong to test the limits of true friendship."

*Dear Lord, get me out of here.* I shook my head and politely declined. "No drinking for me tonight. I'm driving." I also decided to omit that I didn't drink because I was scared to lose control of myself in public situations. The "I'm a great DD" card was always stacked at the top of my deck.

He frowned. "That's no fun. You can take a cab home."

"Oh, no we can't," Shannon interjected. "She's driving my car and it's not staying here."

Claire shrieked, waving her hand obnoxiously in the air. "I'll play!" She latched onto my arm and tugged me into her side, nearly dislocating my shoulder. "Roxy, you can be my partner. Shannon's car will be fine."

"No," Shannon said. "She promised she'd drive us home."

I wanted to throw my arms around her and kiss her cheek. *Thank you, Shannon. Greatest thing you've said to me, yet.*

"Well," Claire huffed. "Steven Can drink for you. Right, Steven?"

*Let it go, Claire. I don't want to play.* I pretended not to notice Amber's chortle when Claire shimmied her breasts side to side.

Steven ate it up. "I have no problem helping out such a pretty lady."

5

When he winked, Claire's grasp tightened around my forearm. I held back a wince. *I could sure use some help here, Amber. Before Claire rips off my arm and beats Steven with it.* Amber was too busy mentally throwing daggers at the back of Claire's head.

"But that would give you an unfair advantage," Steven continued. "And I don't cheat."

Claire released her Herculean grip, leaving behind red streaks on my white skin. She playfully slapped Steven's shoulder and wrapped her arms loosely around his neck. "You're being so difficult right now. Just say yes."

Steven smiled at me over Claire's shoulder and winked. "I'd do anything for a pretty lady," he repeated.

Rubbing my arm absentmindedly, I struggled to keep my sarcasm at bay. When he winked at Claire, I held back a gag. *You should really get that checked out. You might have something serious lodged in your eye.* "Really, thanks but no thanks. Amber or Shannon can play."

"C'mon Roxy," Claire spat turning to face me. "Stop being such a bitch and play one game. It's not going to kill you."

A sudden pang hit my eyes, making them water. *Now I remember why she and I never hung out when she'd been drinking.* I took a deep breath and smiled, despite the want to tell Claire that she could find another ride home. "I'm flattered, really, but *no thank you.* Ask someone else."

She sighed, glaring. "Fine. I'm gonna see if Lizzy's here. Danny's probably driving her crazy by now."

Once she stalked off, Steven scooted closer to me. "Danny's here?"

Amber crossed her arms over her chest. "What's it matter? You've already fucked her and fucked over Claire. You want to do it all over again?"

I winced. "So—" I chirped, hoping to ease the building tension. "Steven, where are you from?"

"The San Francisco area," he replied.

Shannon, whose hazel eyes barely hung open and whose cheeks shined, beamed at him. "Really? What part?"

I'd forgotten she was even there.

Steven smiled at her, his charm sucking her into Schmoozerville. When he winked, a giggle escaped her pale, pink lips.

*Another one bites the dust.*

6

I pulled away from her glowing complexion and studied the party around me. Girls and boys flirted shamelessly with one another, alcohol sloshed in plastic cups and shot glasses, and ping pong balls bounced off tables in every direction. The ratio of boys to girls was skewed heavily in the boys' direction, which was strange because Sonoma State was known for its larger female population, and the baseball team for its handsome players. The girls in attendance didn't seem to mind multiple boys vying for their attention.

I, on the other hand, had a difficult time interacting with any member of the human species, especially those that were expecting sexual favors at the end of the night.

I glanced at Amber, who was doing everything in her power to not look at me. Not wanting the rest of the school year to be awkward considering her bedroom door was directly across from mine, I flexed and unflexed my fingers, trying to dispel my nervous energy, and wondered what my older sister, Lucy, would do in this same situation. *Well, here goes nothing.* "Hey, Amber, you see all of the hunks mingling around here?"

Her scowl deepened at the sound of my voice, her eyes somehow looking even further away from me. "No. I'm too busy standing around watching idiots talk to one another."

I held back a flinch. *Try again. Let her know you aren't some weird freak who purposely stole her best friend.* "Why don't we try to change that?"

This time she looked at me, her usually light blue eyes nearing a shade of dark purple. "And how are *you* gonna do that?"

Determined to make Amber hate me less, I continued forward. I swallowed back the beer pong ball sized lump in my throat and said something that was completely out of character. "I do believe you ladies mentioned something about a dance party in the car earlier."

Her lips twitched. *A smile?* "Pretty sure that was Claire's idea."

"And I'm pretty sure Claire is off trying to make Steven jealous. "

Amber nodded. "What's your point?"

I shrugged. "My point is, either you can stand here and continue to be upset at her for ditching you, or me and you can start that dance party and have some real fun."

She blinked, just as surprised as I was—a dance party was the furthest thing from hiding in a dark corner, but the guilt I felt about Claire's behavior made me step out of my comfort zone to make Amber more comfortable. I really didn't want to live with someone who had the potential to make my life miserable for the rest of the school year.

"You're right." Amber's sapphire eyes sparkled with life, the angry purple long gone. "Let's go fucking dance." She grabbed the beer from Steven's hand, tilted her head back and downed the liquid before placing the bottle back in his grasp. "And then let's find some boys. I'm gonna need another drink soon."

She linked her elbow with mine and ushered me into the living room where a DJ was playing a top 40 list of music and drunken individuals mingled with one another, not a dancing body in sight.

I frowned. "Did I miss something?"

"What do you mean?" Amber asked.

I gestured to the empty circle in the middle of the room that people were consciously avoiding. "Why even bother paying someone to provide music if nobody's gonna utilize it?"

She shrugged. "People are too afraid to stand out."

I nodded. *Tell me about it. My plan was to stand in the corner the whole night.* Taking a deep breath, I began walking to the center of the crowd. "I guess it's up to us then." *You can do this. Do it for Amber. Do it because you want to make friends. Do it because you're tired of feeling so alone all of the time.*

"Are you really suggesting we start a dance party?"

*I can do this. If I can dance in front of the mirror at home, I can dance here. I don't know any of these people. They won't care. This is just to make Amber happy.* "Well, I don't think anybody else is gonna do it."

Amber grabbed my hand and sauntered over to the DJ's table, elbowing me hard so that I would smile at the two boys standing behind it. One was tall, muscular and clean-shaven, his beard and sideburns trimmed to perfection. His dark gold eyes trailed down the small V-neck that was held up by my above average sized breasts and back up to my face before he returned the smile. I bit the inside of my cheek to refrain from covering myself and backing out of the whole thing. When Amber squeezed my hand, reminding me that I wasn't alone, I arched my back and pushed my chest out further, hoping that some sort of false confidence exuded from my pores. *Say something sexy. Be like Claire, or Amber, or any other girl here.* I breathed in my nose and licked my lips. "How come no one's dancing? You boys aren't doing your jobs."

He shrugged, his dark black eyebrows rising high when he took note of my blue jeans — something he probably hadn't ever seen in a college party throughout his DJ career. "We play music, not dance."

His Latino accent made me blush.

Amber stared at the tall DJ's shorter friend. He had dark skin, emerald green eyes and blonde dreadlocks cascading down his wide shoulders. "That's a terrible excuse."

They raised their eyebrows at one another.

"What about the music?" Latino asked.

"Put it on shuffle," Amber said.

"Who'd we dance with?" Dreadlocks countered.

I tried not to stiffen when Amber hugged me close to her side. "I can think of two girls who might be interested."

*I can think of a million other things I'd be more interested in doing.* "How does that sound to you?" I tried to say flirtatiously.

Dreadlocks and Latino nodded once to one another, walked around their table, and grabbed our hands, leading us to the opening in the middle of the crowd. *Don't think about your sweaty palms. Don't think about what other people are thinking. This is gonna be fun. Look at Amber — she's happy. That's all you wanted. Breathe. Stop looking at your shoes and breathe.* Soon enough, other party patrons grouped together in a gyrating mob composed of whiskey breath, the stench of stale beer and raging hormones.

I watched as Amber bent forward and shook her butt against Dreadlocks, his face radiating pleasure as he pretended to slap her butt, the crowd cheering behind her. I, on the other hand, could taste blood on my tongue from biting the inside of my cheek so hard. Latino had his hands moving all over my hips and stomach and thighs, his erection poking against my jeans. *I shouldn't have come. I should just go home.* Amber grabbed onto my forearm and pulled me against her breasts, shaking them until my body moved along with her. Before I knew it, I was sandwiched between a stranger and a girl who I thought hated me, and my hips were moving in ways I never wanted anybody in public to see.

Strangely, after three songs passed, I realized I was actually having fun.

Amber wouldn't let go of my hand, Latino was making me feel things I'd only heard my older sister brag about, and the music allowed me to lose myself, forgetting about homework, about how embarrassed I'd be if anyone in my classes saw me dancing this way, and about being a constant disappointment to my parents.

I was dizzy and lightheaded and having the time of my life.

After two more songs ended, I told Amber I needed to get some fresh air. In reality, I needed to catch my breath because my cheek was beginning to hurt and my nerves were getting the best of me—I thanked the Latino, and blushed when some random boys raised their beers in my direction.

"Let's get outside before I embarrass myself further," I told Amber, hoping that my hair wasn't already a frizzy mess. "My hairspray will only last against sweat for so long."

She wiped the moisture from her forehead and nodded, leading me beyond two girls groping one another, boys gawking, and through the wooden front door. We closed out the noise and inhaled the crisp midnight air.

"I need a drink when we get back in there. My buzz is fading," Amber said fanning her face with her hand.

"How come you didn't bring your own?" I asked.

She grimaced. "Why would I do that?"

"Well—I—uh—because?"

"Oh, Roxy," Amber sighed, resting her hand on my shoulder as if I just admitted to her that I wanted to write poetry instead of curing cancer. "You have so much to learn about the capabilities of a woman's sexuality."

I cocked my head to the side. "You mean, like, exploitation?"

"I mean like showing a little cleavage and having the world give you everything you've ever asked for."

"And you're using that power for…"

She winked. "Alcohol, of course."

I couldn't help it—I laughed and laughed and laughed, until my stomach began to hurt, Amber's high-pitched and slightly hysteric laughter sounding pleasant to my ears. *I think I'm one step closer to having her not completely hate my guts.*

Nearly hidden by our laughter, footsteps crunched up the gravel driveway, a deep voice mumbling incoherently.

"I want whatever he's having," Amber snickered.

I nodded. "People are beginning to converse with themselves. It may be time to leave."

"He might just be the guy I'm looking for. I'm sure he'd give me his alcohol and not think twice about it."

10

An extremely tall boy came into view and shot a single wave in Amber's and my direction.

"Do you know him?"

She nodded and threw a hand up in the air. "Hey Lamont! Long time no see!"

Something strange overcame me. My heart did an Irish Jig against my chest; my palms grew clammy; my fingers numbed. Despite the chilly air, my cheeks burned a feverish pink.

With short black hair, tan skin, dark brown eyes and prime athletic height, he epitomized my expectations of tall, dark and handsome.

Really, *really* handsome.

His face was oval shaped, his black eyebrows bushy, the workings of a goatee hugging his chin. But it was his casual smile with those luscious, tan lips that made my jaw drop just long enough for the cold air to dry out my tongue. I tried to look away, but my muscles had forgotten how to function.

He ended his phone call and said, "Hey," in a deep voice so delicious, I wanted to eat it for breakfast, save a little for lunch and finish off the rest for dinner.

"You're running a little late," Amber said, pointing at an invisible watch on her wrist. "Pretty sure this thing started, like, three hours ago."

"Party doesn't start 'til I arrive," he replied.

Amber rolled her eyes. "I see you haven't changed a bit since last year."

"Then I'm still one hell of a fucking guy." He smiled again, miniature crescent moons forming on his cheeks. "What're you doing out here?"

I pushed my hands into my pockets, wondering what was going on with me. My heart was beginning to hurt my chest and whatever was floating around in my stomach was making me feel nauseous. I smiled at him when he glanced at me, growing very self-conscious when his smile faded. *Since when do you care about some stranger's attention? So what if his voice is so smooth, I'd like to drink a glass of it? That doesn't mean anything.*

"It's hot in there. Needed a break," Amber replied.

"Oh, good. I thought they'd already run out of beer. Want to grab one with me?"

His deep, deep voice vibrated through my core and filled my heart with warmth. *Maybe you're not drinking, but nod. Nod at the guy and make him think you're cool.* I stared at him—that awkward, silent stare shared between two strangers with a mutual friend. *Stop being an idiot. Remember what your sister told you: break out of your shell and meet some boys. Introduce yourself already!*

11

As his gaze moved from my hair to the pale-yellow painted toenails hidden inside of my shoes, I was consumed by a heavy wave of anxiety; I wished I'd dressed like the other girls instead of dressing in my usual simple ensemble. I steadied myself with a deep—yet silent—breath and brushed my auburn bangs lowlighted with dark brown streaks behind my ear.

"Hi," I managed, blushing foolishly.

Amber smacked her forehead. "Where are my manners? Lamont, this is Roxy, my new housemate." She pulled me against her side and squeezed. "She lives right down the hall from me."

He gave a slight nod. "Roxy, huh? Short for Roxanne?"

I swallowed back my anxiety and smiled. "Yeah. My parents had a thing for The Police."

"Clever. Smart parents. It suits you."

"Well, they are doctors, so they have to be sm—" When he cocked his head slightly to the side, I cleared my throat. "It's nice to finally meet you. I've heard so many things."

He turned to Amber. "Things, huh? What kind of *things*?"

Amber shook her head. "Don't flatter yourself."

"Trust me," I interjected. "They have nothing but phenomenal things to say about you." When I reached out to grab his arm for emphasis, his cell phone was knocked from his hand, falling toward the ground in painful slow motion.

It skipped down a cement stair with a crash.

"Oh my God." My cheeks flushed crimson. "I am so, *so sorry*! If it's broken, I'll buy you a new one."

Without thinking twice, I dropped my knees to the ground and snatched up the phone, hoping beyond all hope that I didn't destroy the thing. There were no visible scratches and the screen hadn't shattered. "Looks like everything is—" My face rose to meet his pant's zipper. *Oh my—get away from the crotch, away from the crotch.* I stepped back, stood erect, placed the phone forcefully into his palm and tried not to cry. "I'm sorry. I'm really sorry. Like, *really* sorry," I repeated, fingers fighting one another behind my back. "I can be a real klutz sometimes."

His dark eyes sparkled bright with curiosity. "You're not a klutz. I tend to make girls fall head over heels for me. It's not the first time I've brought a girl to her knees."

Amber laughed, completely oblivious to my sheer mortification.

12

I stared at the white tips of my shoes, curls dangling just over my breasts. *Way to go, Roxy. You really know how to make a great first impression.*

When a pair of white and black Nikes came into view, I shyly glanced up, surprised to find Lamont in such close proximity. "So," he asked. "How about that beer?"

#

LAMONT OPENED THE refrigerator door and handed out ice-cold beers as if he owned the place.

"Is he allowed to do that?" I whispered.

Amber shrugged. "He's on the baseball team. I'm sure it's fine."

"Here you are ladies."

I politely refused the beer he held toward me. "I'm the designated driver tonight," I said, not ready to admit I didn't drink regularly like everybody else. "Thanks, though. I appreciate it."

Before he could question me, Amber snatched the can from his hand. "I'll have it. Wouldn't want to waste it."

"Amber! Roxy!"

We turned around as Shannon walked toward us, her cheeks red, her fingers wound tightly with Steven's.

"Dude, Lamont! Didn't think you'd make it. You ready to fuck shit up at the beer pong table?" An intricate handshake-hug combination ensued.

"I take it they know each other?" I asked.

Amber nodded. "Best friends."

"Oh my God!" Shannon shrieked, startling all those who inhabited the kitchen. "You have a *Boobies* bracelet!"

Lamont glanced down at his wrist. "Doesn't everyone?"

"That's Shannon—our other housemate."

"Can I have it?" she asked, completely ignoring Amber's introduction. "I've always wanted one."

"It's like, three dollars from the mall. What's stopping you?"

The black, rubber bracelet had *I Love Boobies* engraved in white block letters, and it rested comfortably around Lamont's tan wrist.

Another strange feeling overwhelmed me—a feeling that I only got when the classmate sitting next me received a higher grade. *Is she flirting with him?*

"I want one *now*," she whined.

13

I wasn't one to engage in confrontation, but something deep within my gut told me that this behavior was not okay, *especially* when she was already holding the hand of another guy. I also knew better than to challenge someone as intoxicated as she was but seeing Lamont smile at her made me want to fight her—which was definitely different from my typical "run away and hide" technique. This was the first boy I was genuinely interested in getting to know since my junior year of high school, where the boy I fell in love with told me having a girlfriend would ruin his college experience. Part of me warned that I should ignore these feelings because nothing was worth the pain I'd experienced that year, but the other part of me said that I should stand up for myself and for my feelings.

I also had enjoyed his attention—which again, was unusual for me.

"Where did you get it from?" I asked, taking a small step toward him.

He looked down at me, lifting his arm just enough so I could see the bracelet at eye level. I fought the urge to rest my cheek against his forearm, wanting to permanently memorize the way his skin smelled. "Probably at Tilly's or something. They're super cheap." He raised an eyebrow when he saw me staring at the black and white rubber. "You wanna wear it?"

I smiled over his wrist at Shannon, who raised her hands up in frustration. "Are you kidding me? I asked you if I could wear it first!"

"She did ask first," I said. "It wouldn't be fair if I took it."

Lamont smiled, driving my pulse up to a dangerously high level. I felt a bead of sweat form between my shoulder blades and begin its descent down my spine.

Shannon held out her hand. "I promise I'll give it back."

I narrowed my eyes at her. *Just take it, Roxy. He offered it to you.* "But I mean, if you insisted, I wouldn't want to be rude."

Shannon swayed side to side, Steven holding her waist tight. "She doesn't even want it," she yelled, hiccupping slightly.

Lamont surveyed me, then Shannon, then me again. "How about I pick a number between one and twenty?"

My shoulders slumped forward. *You are so stupid sometimes. You should've just taken it when he offered it to you.* I clenched my jaw, fighting back unexpected tears. *Just guess the right number. That way, instead of thinking about Shannan all night long because she has his bracelet, he'll be forced to think about the curly haired girl instead.*

Shannon shook her head. "How do I know you won't change the number to match hers?"

Before Lamont could produce an answer, Claire ran up like a bat out of hell and threw her entire body around him. Her dress rose up around her hips, revealing her butt to all innocent bystanders. I watched mutely as she kissed the air beside his ears and pressed her nose against his cheek.

"Lamont, my love! I haven't seen you in forever!" she yelled, now *much more* intoxicated than when we first entered the party.

I glanced away, my body completely inundated by jealousy. *I've known Lamont for maybe fifteen minutes. We haven't even had any semblance of a conversation yet.* I pushed my bangs behind my ear and frowned at Amber.

She shrugged apologetically. "She does this when she's drunk. I hate to say this, but you will get used to it."

Shannon crossed her arms over her chest. "Why don't you give Claire the number? I know I can trust her."

"What're you talking about?" Claire asked still clinging to Lamont's neck.

"These girls both want my bracelet, so, they're picking numbers," he said.

*Actually, you offered me the bracelet.* I began fidgeting with the hem of my shirt, Claire's bare butt cheeks beginning to make me feel uncomfortable. *I don't get it. She made it quite obvious earlier today that she hates Lamont. Did I mishear her?* "Alright, Lamont. Pick a number," I croaked, my voice threatening to give away my true feelings.

When she climbed off him and beamed at me, my eye twitched. "I just love games! Turn around and I'll tell you when to guess."

Shannon and I turned our backs on them, but it didn't matter—I could hear every word of their exchange, which meant Shannon could too. It became quite apparent that drunk people didn't understand the meaning of the word "whisper" and Lamont basically announced his number to the entire room. My only hope was that Claire would ask me to pick a number first.

Instead, she smiled at Shannon. "Okay, you guess first."

She smirked at me and fluttered her eyelashes at Lamont. "Twelve."

He and Claire looked at one another and then at me. *You're really gonna make me guess?* "I don't care—nine." I frowned and blushed harder, hugging my elbows.

Lamont grabbed Claire's elbow and turned her to face him. Their noses were almost touching, but Lamont's rushed words were audible enough for me to understand. "Claire, help me. I really want Roxy to have it. I just don't want to piss off Shannon."

15

I blinked. *What?*

"She's hot and nice and funny. I like her. This is my chance to have her talk to me again. She'll have to give it back at some point—what should I do?"

Claire's flirty demeanor changed, her forehead wrinkling with annoyance. "Why don't I take it instead?"

I turned toward Amber. "What is she doing?" I hissed.

Amber readjusted her bra, her cleavage even more apparent than before. "She's being herself."

"But I thought she didn't even like Lamont."

"She doesn't," Amber said. "But she doesn't like when she's not the center of attention. God forbid anybody else get a chance."

"I just wanted to have a conversation with him."

Amber smiled. "Ohhh the little wallflower wants to bloom."

I shook my head. "No no no, that's not—"

"Well, what's the number?" Shannon asked, impatient.

Lamont glanced at Claire. "I can't remember."

"That's not fair." She glared at Lamont and shook her head. "You're being mean."

"Here—don't be like that—I'll put it behind my back—yeah—that's it. I'll put it behind my back. Shannon, you guess which hand you think it's in," Lamont said quickly, sliding the bracelet past his knuckles.

"It's a lousy three-dollar bracelet," Amber mumbled. "I have another one at home I could give you."

Lamont toyed with the rubber bracelet behind his back, his eyes darting nervously in my direction.

Shannon pointed to the right hand. "Amber, if I pick wrong, I want yours."

A sly smile crept onto Lamont's face. He slowly exposed the empty right hand in front of Shannon and then revealed the band resting on his left palm. I watched as he stretched it onto my wrist, feeling a spark ignite somewhere between his fingertips and my skin.

He pushed Claire to the side, wrapped his arms around my back and pulled me in tight. Although hesitant at first, I relaxed against him, allowing his embrace to comfort me. "I'm sorry I didn't just give it to you," he whispered. "I didn't want to hurt Shannon's feelings."

My heart seeped right through my ribcage, a puddle of pitiful mush. "I didn't really want it until you offered it, honestly."

16

He chuckled. "I just wanted another excuse to see you again."

I pulled away from him slightly, confused. "Me? Really?"

"Jesus you guys," Amber shouted. "If you're gonna have sex, at least get a room."

I closed my eyes, wondering why this guy had such a pull over me—his arms still held me tight, and for some reason, I didn't feel the need to push him away.

"Nobody asked you perverts to watch." He nuzzled my neck with his moistened lips.

My body shivered.

I was a goner.

#

THE RED AND blue lights flickered through the living room curtains. The music halted abruptly, the owners screamed at the attendees to shut up and those of underage status began to panic. I pushed my way through the crowd and found my housemates downing shots in the kitchen.

"Cops are here. We're leaving," I ordered grabbing each glass from their grasps and placing them on the counter.

"What? Are we in trouble?" Shannon slurred.

I shook my head and grabbed her elbow. "You will be if you don't follow me out of here. Just be careful and avoid eye contact."

Amber and Claire followed our lead.

As we walked through the front door, the police officers studied us suspiciously with flashlights in hand. I smiled at them, trying to appear calm and collected, when in reality, my heart fluttered like a hummingbird's wings. Once we made it to the car, we all took a collective deep breath.

I unlocked the doors. "I need all of your help." I slid into the driver's seat. "I do my best to avoid these sorts of situations—boys are really complicated. He hasn't stopped texting me." Each of the girls closed their doors. "I have this inkling that maybe he wants me to come over?"

"First of all, who says *an inkling*?" Shannon asked. "Are you drunk?"

Amber snickered. "No duh, he wants you to come over. *All over him.*"

I gulped. *That's not funny.* "I'm sure he just wants his bracelet back."

Claire grimaced. "Are you telling me you think he's cute?"

I shrugged, her accusatory tone filling me with shame. "Yeah—he's—he's okay. He's tall. He made me laugh. And—and—" I glanced at the bracelet. "I need to give his bracelet back."

17

"I'm down to go if they give us free booze," Amber chimed in.

"If you're *actually* gonna give him the bracelet after everything we went through, you might as well give it to me."

I smiled at Shannon. "I promise I'll go to the mall tomorrow and buy you a brand new one."

Claire snorted. "If you went through all that just to talk to him, you're pathetic."

"That's harsh," Amber said, defending me. "Besides, I've seen you do worse. She likes him. What's the big deal?"

I smiled in the rearview mirror. *Finally—someone who won't judge me. And to think she totally hated my guts only a few hours ago.*

"Firstly, he's fugly. Secondly, he has a girlfriend. She can't like him."

I chewed on my already raw cheek, again tasting blood on my tongue. *A girlfriend? What is she talking about?*

"If you think he's so ugly, why did you date him last semester?"

I slammed the breaks, nearly causing a collision with the headlights behind me. "Hang on just one freaking second."

Claire glared at Amber. "We did *not* date. We went on *one* date. Those are two *completely* different things."

"If you went on a date with him, you must have found him attractive."

Claire made a face. "It was out of pity. It was like, the fifth time he'd asked me. Besides, he took me to a hockey game. It was a free ticket."

"That's kinda mean, don'tcha think?" Shannon added.

"I think you guys are taking this all out of proportion," I said, signaling to get in the next lane over. "I need to give him this bracelet back—I promised. And besides, he seems like he'd be a good friend."

"A *friend* with *benefits*," Amber teased.

I waited for a snarky reply from Claire, but she remained uncharacteristically silent. She was texting away, a smile reflecting off the phone's backlight.

I furrowed my brow. "Everything okay, Claire?"

She didn't bother to look up. "His name's Chris. He's Lamont's roommate."

The wheels in my head began to squeal, a fresh drop of degreaser applied to the rusted gears. *Lamont's roommate. That's how I'll get to see Lamont again—make this all about Claire.*

"And...?" I prodded.

"He has a girlfriend," Amber laughed. "They've been together for like, three years or some shit."

The car rolled up to a red light.

I glanced over my shoulder. "What're you doing talking to him then?"

Her smile faded. "He does *not* have a girlfriend. They broke up last night. He told me all about it when we were playing beer pong."

Amber was skeptical. "You *actually* believe that?"

"They did! Lamont confirmed it."

"Oh, well, if he confirmed it, then it *must* be true."

Claire stuck her tongue out at Amber. "Stop being such a bitch."

"Has it even been officially over for twenty-four hours?"

Claire shrugged. "Who cares? He's single."

"Or so he says," Shannon mumbled.

"I wouldn't hook up with someone who has a girlfriend. I'm not that kind of girl."

*Join in on the conversation. Be their friend.* "If he just broke up with her, shouldn't you be worried about being the rebound?"

"So what? He obviously thinks I'm cute if he's already talking to me."

"No," Amber argued. "That means he thinks you have open legs and a ready vagina."

Shannon and I laughed, Claire's pout dropping to her knees.

"Shannon," I said. "This is your car, so you make the decision. What do you want to do?"

She looked over her shoulder and smiled. "Just how cute is he?"

That was the second time that night I wanted to throw my hands around her and kiss her to death. *God bless you Shannon. I'll buy you the entire Boobies bracelet factory.*

"He's adorable," Claire swooned.

"If it's just a kiss," I threw in, hoping I was beginning to fit in. "What's the harm in that?"

Shannon nodded against the headrest. "Let's do it."

"What do you think, Amber?"

She turned toward the window and shrugged. "I already told you. If they have free booze, I'm in."

My phone buzzed, an unknown number flashing on the screen. A number that had been sending me texts since we parted ways at the party. A number that was

19

already engrained into my memory forever. *This is it. It's now or never. Don't chicken out. This is your chance to really get to know him.* "Hey, Lamont?" I answered. "We're heading over now. Think you could give me some directions?"

#

WHEN WE FINALLY located the house, Lamont's tall and lanky frame came into view. He ushered us up the driveway asking what took so long.

"This place is a labyrinth," I admitted. "I may or may not have taken a couple wrong turns."

"You probably shouldn't be drinking and driving then," Lamont said opening the front door. "Cops'll hop all over that."

"Lamont, I'm sober."

He snorted. "Sure, you are. Everyone's in my room. To the right."

"No, really," Shannon countered. "I wouldn't let her drive my car otherwise."

"I was just giving her shit. I drink and drive all the time."

He followed us down the hallway and to the right into a room where boys were drinking, laughing and talking loudly. Some gathered around a laptop, others lounged on the two queen beds present, and two other boys mixed drinks at the bathroom sink. They all greeted us happily, but I felt my emotional balance begin to wobble.

*I don't know anybody here. I'm the only one not drinking. Claire says Lamont has a girlfriend. What if she's right? I don't belong here with these people. I belong at home, alone, with my books.* I fidgeted with the bracelet and wondered if everyone could hear my heartbeat. I sat on the bed beside Claire and smiled bashfully at Lamont when we made eye contact.

Claire nudged me. "Weren't you listening? He has a girlfriend back home. You don't even know him—stop pretending you do."

"I'm not trying to pretend anything. I'd like to get to know—"

She shook her head. "No, you really don't. I know I sound like a bitch but I'm looking out for you. Sonoma is a *tiny* school. Do you *really* want to have *home-wrecker* attached to your name?"

I began rubbing my palms up and down my thighs. "I know you say you're trying to look out for me, but I'm beginning to think you like Lamont."

Claire glared at me. "Are you crazy?"

I shrugged. "Like you said, I'm not trying to be a witch. It's just—I saw how you interacted with him at the party and—"

20

"He's disgusting, Roxy. How could you find him hot? Look at his face—okay, yeah, he's tall, but is that what you want to look at for the rest of your life?"

I clenched my jaw, my frustration reaching its peak. "Claire, could you please shut up?"

Her head snapped back, surprised. "What did you—"

"I said, please shut your mouth." I inhaled through my nose and out my mouth, trying to slow my pulse. "You don't have to think he's cute if you don't like him. But I'd like to get to know him, so, if you'd please excuse me, I'm going to find Lamont."

Before Claire could argue with me, I jumped off the bed and turned down the hallway in search of Mr. Tall, Dark and Handsome.

I spotted my target rummaging through the refrigerator in the small kitchen. He smiled when he closed the door, lifting a beer can in my direction. "You come looking for beer?"

*My, oh my, oh my. He is gorgeous.* Beads of sweat began to form beneath my breasts. "Actually, no. I came looking for you."

He raised his eyebrows. "Yeah, right. Let me grab you one."

"Lamont, no thank you. I'm not drinking."

He studied me carefully. "Really?"

My anxiety returned. "Yes, really." I rubbed my forearm and looked down. "I don't drink." I licked my lips, worried that he would find me some kind of a freak. "I'm sorry to bother you."

As I turned to leave, I heard the hiss and pop of a beer can opening. "You're not bothering me. Pretty girls don't talk to me unless they're hammered. I doubt a knockout like you actually wants to talk to me."

I blinked, surprised. "Me? A knockout?"

He sipped his beer. "Have you looked at yourself in the mirror? You're gorgeous."

I smiled, shaking my head. "You're very sweet." Resting my hand on the doorframe, I sucked in my stomach, hoping that my baggy shirt would hide some of the weight I'd gained over the summer. "I just wanted to talk."

His eyes burned a hole through my soul. "Why?"

"Honestly?" I shrugged, this whole confident façade beginning to exhaust me. *Why do I want to talk to him? Why didn't I just go home?* "Well, I didn't really get a chance to get to know you earlier. I thought I should know more about this mysterious Lamont."

21

He chuckled, holding out his free hand. "Come outside and we'll talk. I need fresh air."

I timidly put my hand in his. Our fingers laced together perfectly. *This—this is nothing like the chemistry I've studied my entire life. How is this even possible?* I tightened my grip and smiled when he did the same.

We made our way through the sliding glass door and stepped into the brisk, autumn air. "I should've brought a jacket. I didn't realize I'd be outside."

He scoffed. "You have a perfectly capable man standing next to you—you don't need a jacket."

"That's a little presumptuous of you."

"What?"

I shook my head and took in the scenery around me. "Never mind. It's not that cold," I lied, rubbing my hands up and down my arms. "I'm just saying I don't need you to keep me warm." *Even if just holding your hand made me feverish.* The backyard was medium sized, cigarette butts and beer cans strewn about the dead grass, the cement patio protected by a white, latticework covering, and giant wooden slats separating this property from the others around it. "You know, this is the perfect house for a dog."

"Dogs are too expensive."

Nodding, I took a step further, admiring the thick trunked trees sitting in the far corners of the yard. "I have a yellow lab at home. Molly. I would've brought her here with me, but sadly, pets are not allowed in the dorms."

Lamont smiled. "Molly, huh? Sounds sweet."

"Yeah, I miss her terribly and I've only been here for a week. My parents are gonna take care of her, but I still wish she were here. Sometimes, I feel like she's the only one who understands me."

After realizing how loudly the crickets were chirping, I faced Lamont and found him studying me quizzically. *Okay. How about we don't talk about family matters?*

"I've always wanted a dog, but they're way too much work. Puppies are the worst." He sat in a plastic patio chair and patted his thigh. "Care to join me?"

I hesitated, eyeing the chair beside him. "What do you want to talk about?"

He leaned forward, grabbed my waist and pulled me toward him. I struggled slightly before collapsing onto his lap. I straightened my back and tightened my stomach muscles. *Act cool. Pretend you sit on guys' laps all of the time.* "You know, there are plenty of other empty chairs here for me to sit on. I don't want your legs to fall asleep or anything."

"You weigh like two pounds, calm down." He placed one of his arms on the top of my thigh and wrapped the other around my back before resting his chin on my shoulder. "I like having you this close."

I tried to make my body relax, but my pounding heart was making it difficult for me to sit still. *If someone could explain what is happening to me right now, that'd be awesome.* "So," I squeaked. "W—what did you w—want to talk about?"

He connected his hands together and pulled me closer. The lack of distance was going to make my heart explode. His enlarge pupils flickered away from my lips reluctantly. "I lied," he whispered. "I just wanted to kiss you."

"You—what?" I asked, my lungs working overtime to try to get a grip on my breathing.

He smiled, his plump, tan lips enticing me to lean in toward him—to give up fighting what I was feeling and go with it. "You heard me," he breathed.

I had every intention of pushing him away because Claire's voice kept warning me about his potential girlfriend—but my voice remained hidden in the back of my throat. My muscles finally relaxed. The moment his lips touched mine, I knew something out of the ordinary had passed between us. I pulled away slowly, eyes closed, savoring the tingling sensation lingering on my lips.

I lifted my heavy lids and stared longingly into his chocolate brown eyes; a starry night sky gazed back at me. It had been quite some time since I felt this way—and it had been two long years since I allowed myself to succumb to my emotions. Lamont's kiss proved it was well worth the wait. I wrapped my arms around his neck, silently leaning in for a second taste, forgetting the questions that plagued me earlier. I pressed my lips hard against his, passion erupting beneath the moonlight. My world flipped upside down and right side up by a stranger I only met a few hours ago.

*I'm in way over my head.*

He nibbled on my bottom lip, his teeth teasing my senses, his fingers caressing my back. I swept my tongue against his upper lip—a seductive move I'd seen in millions of movies—and promised myself I would stop overthinking the situation.

*But what—what if—what if he really has a girlfriend?*

# Chapter Two

LAMONT WRAPPED HIS arms around me and rocked my body gently from side to side. "Your arms are freezing."

I rested my head on his chest and sighed happily, not caring that I had goose bumps in places I didn't know goose bumps could form. "I didn't even notice."

He smiled and kissed the top of my head. "Let's go back inside and see what everyone else is up to."

I nodded, staring unbelievingly when he locked his strong fingers with mine and pulled me through the hallway. Back in the room, we found pandemonium. Music blared through the laptop's speakers, Shannon was talking loudly to a boy named Trevor, Amber sat on Kevin's lap, her laughter bouncing through the hallway, and Claire relaxed on Chris's bed, her cleavage exposed for all to see. Two other boys, Hansen and Dylan, were playing some card game, a giant container of snack mix leaned on its side, crumbs smashed into the carpet. There were red cups in hands and liquid spilling over rims onto fingers and feet, chip crumbs littering laps and lips.

When Lamont let go of my hand, I slid beside him on his bed. Claire grimaced and shook her head when I smiled toothlessly at her.

I tried not to frown, wondering why my best friend wasn't happy for me. "Whatcha doin?" I asked, leaning into Lamont's shoulder, glancing down at the laptop on his thighs.

"Looking at porn." When my head turned toward him abruptly, he laughed. "I'm gonna put on some decent music."

"Don't change it!" Amber whined. "We're having a dance party."

"Nobody in this room is dancing." Lamont gestured around at his friends. "This is the worst dance party I've ever seen."

Amber wrapped her arms around Kevin's shoulders and attempted to move her hips back and forth. "What do you call this?"

"Being a whore."

Kevin chuckled. "Keep it up, girl. You might convince me to like dancing."

"Get a room—or just get out of mine."

Amber stuck her tongue out at Lamont and winked at me. "Keep your boy in check, Roxy."

25

Claire's eyes narrowed.

*My boy? What do you mean my boy?* "How about we take that walk? It's getting kinda stuffy in here," I whispered into Lamont's ear.

He smiled. "Should I grab you a coat?"

I shrugged. "Didn't you tell me earlier that you're a perfectly capable man who can keep me warm instead?"

"Oh, so now you're okay with that?" he teased.

I cleared my throat. "I never said I wasn't okay with it."

We stood and left the room despite Claire calling my name repeatedly. It wasn't typical of my doormat behavior, but something about Lamont's presence gave me the strength to walk through the front door and onto the sidewalk without feeling guilty about ignoring my best friend.

"Do you know why Claire is so pissed at me?"

I allowed him to put his arm around my shoulders. "What do you mean?"

He shrugged. "She keeps fucking glaring at me."

"She's kinda doing the same to me. I think she's afraid we're gonna have intercourse or something," I said. *Which means she knows nothing about me. I'm not that kind of person.*

His forehead wrinkled. "What the fuck? Why is that her fucking business?"

I slouched slightly, his arm almost slipping off my shoulders. *Why do you care so much? Because you have a girlfriend?* "Well, it doesn't matter because nothing is going to happen."

"I don't like people being in my business," he said, apparently not hearing me. "She should thinking about having sex with Chris."

The pebbles beneath my shoes crunched in the silence. "Why should she have sex with him?" I bit my lip. "Doesn't he have a girlfriend?" *Or do you?*

Lamont picked a leaf off a nearby bush and ripped it to pieces. "No—she broke up with him last night. They should have sex because they're attracted to one another. His ex-girlfriend is a bitch. Claire could get his mind off her."

I whistled a long, low, tune. "That's a little shallow, don't you think?"

He shrugged. "You can't always be an outstanding gentleman."

Although I didn't see eye-to-eye on the matter, I couldn't help but laugh. "I hate to be the bearer of bad news, but she won't sleep with him. She's keeping that V-card hidden deep inside her deck."

His neck snapped to the side. "You're fuckin' with me."

"What?"

"Claire's not a virgin."

It was my turn to pick a leaf off a nearby bush. "Yes, she actually is. She just told me in the car a few hours ago. Honestly, it caught me by surprise, too."

Lamont whistled. "Doesn't she hook up with guys all the time?"

"She does," I confirmed. "But never sex. Everything but sex, actually."

"Well, Chris needs to get it in, so she has to suck it up."

I snorted. *Why are you so focused on sex? Is that really the only way he's gonna get over his ex-girlfriend?* "I wouldn't hold my breath. It's not gonna happen."

Lamont stopped and turned to face me. I looked into his eyes, my heart thudding in my jugular. He made me feel strangely comfortable and uncomfortable all at once. *Please God. Just this once, let this be real. Let Claire be wrong. I don't want him to have a girlfriend.*

He smiled. "Can I kiss you again?"

Blushing, I nodded, my eyes transfixed on the smile lines running from his nose to the corners of his mouth. "I wouldn't mind."

Our lips met halfway for the kiss, his saliva both salty and sweet on my taste buds. His tongue didn't burrow into my throat but rather cuddled with my own, encouraging me to relax and bask in the affection. I nibbled on his bottom lip gently. I allowed my body to fall into his. *There's no way he has a girlfriend. Our chemistry is too perfect. He wouldn't kiss me like this if he had a girlfriend. And I wouldn't be kissing him like this if he had a girlfriend.*

When he pulled away from me, my eyes fluttered open to find him smiling. "How about we head back to your house before they send out a search party?"

"They're a bunch of haters."

"Yeah, but I'd rather not be pestered with questions." I walked by his side, our hands inseparable, my body in a trance. Trailing slightly behind him up the path to the front door, I licked my lips, the taste of his kiss lingering like cookie crumbs.

*I changed my mind. I don't want to go inside. I don't want this moment to end.*

When he stepped through the doorway, Lamont dropped my hand. Claire arrived out of nowhere, flinging her arms around my shoulders, wrapping one of her legs behind my waist.

"I missed you! Where've you been?" she screeched.

I winced, patting her back hesitantly. "Just needed some air. What've you been doing?"

She grabbed my wrist and yanked me into the bedroom. On the bathroom sink there were shot glasses, an opened handle of vodka and a variety of empty soda cans. "We all took shots. Hansen, Dylan and everyone else are in the living room playing some stupid video game. Trevor and Shannon won't stop making out—she's ho-ing it up tonight. I'm impressed. She should fit in with our dorm just fine. I've been trying to find you."

"Are you having fun?"

Looking over her shoulder, Claire noticed Lamont and Chris sitting close to one another speaking in hushed voices. "I'm bored," she whispered. "I don't want to hook up with Chris anymore. He won't stop talking about his ex-girlfriend and it's driving me crazy. Can we find a different room to talk or something? I want to get away from him."

"Why don't you try hooking up with Dylan? He seems nice."

She crinkled her nose. "Ew. I've known him for too long."

Having anticipated a full-blown lecture about how I'm a terrible person for pursuing Lamont, I was pleasantly surprised by her perky demeanor. *Maybe I shouldn't be so quick to judge the effects of alcohol. Clearly, Claire can go from brat to bundle of joy in the blink of an eye.* "I have an idea." The music rattling against the walls tickled my ears. *It worked with Amber. Maybe it'll work with Claire, too.* "How about we *actually* do that dance party thing you mentioned earlier?"

"I thought you'd never ask!" Claire basically yanked my arm clear out of its socket as she tugged me through the hallway. We followed the bass and pushed open the door to Kevin's room. He lay sprawled across his comforter, quite intoxicated, and on the verge of sleep.

"Jesus Christ," he moaned. "What the hell are you doing?"

Claire dropped my hand and flung her body onto the bed, her exposed thighs straddling Kevin's pelvis. "How are you sleeping at a time like this?" She wrapped her arms behind his neck and cuddled awkwardly beneath his chin. "We're having a dance party!"

I diverted my eyes from her bare rear end.

Kevin laughed and sat up, pushing Claire off in the process. The light glared off his bald head, his light green eyes clashing with the bright yellow polo he was wearing. "What's with you girls and dance parties?"

"What's not to like about a dance party?"

"You don't have enough people to start a dance party."

28

Claire winked at me. "Two girls. One boy. Sounds like enough people to me."

He sighed, scratching at the five o'clock shadow on his chin. "I don't have a choice, do I?"

"Nope."

"Oh, alright." He pointed towards his computer, which was currently blasting some awful techno beats. "Don't pick anything that sucks."

I sat down in the desk chair and turned my attention to the computer. After turning off his iTunes, I clicked the mouse a couple times, pulled up the Internet browser and searched for Pandora, typing "Top hip-hop hits" next to the magnifying glass graphic. When the first song started to play, Claire jumped off the bed shrieking and proceeded to grind her butt against the air. I giggled and watched as Kevin's eyes widened.

"C'mon Roxy!" Claire shouted, grabbing my hand and yanking me off the chair.

I stood there stupidly as she began to grind on me, her butt pushing against my pelvis, Kevin's whistles making me extremely uncomfortable. *I don't want to be a part of your strip show, Claire. This isn't what I had in mind when you said you wanted to dance.*

He placed his hands behind his head and nodded his approval, his cheeks flushed pink. "This is a great idea. Keep it up, girls."

"Roxanne, I'm doing all of the work," Claire complained. "You have nice hips—now use them!" She stood face to face with me, placed her hands on my hips and began making circles with her own, urging me to join.

I sighed and caved in, her light brown, almost yellow eyes pouting at me.

And then just as my body began to get into the rhythm of the loud bass, computer made instruments and extremely shallow lyrics, Lamont, Trevor and Shannon meandered into the bedroom. "What the hell is going on here?"

"What does it look like?" Kevin asked.

"We're having a dance party!" Claire shouted.

Shannon frowned. "Thanks for the invite."

Claire pulled her further into the room, sandwiching her between Claire and myself. I tried to shy away initially but eventually gave in to the girls' constant requests to keep dancing, their alcohol-induced nagging peer-pressuring me to act like an idiot. Lamont's presence made me nervous, so I purposely kept my eyes on anything except his.

29

The next song vibrated the speaker covers, the catchy beat pulsing through my veins. Claire smiled at me, grabbed my hand and began skipping backwards. I watched, shaking my head, too scared of making a fool out of myself in front of so many people. She slowed her skipping, showing me exactly how to move my legs and feet, the songs lyrics moving in time with her.

"I can't," I said, pulling my hand away from Claire's.

She stopped dancing and pouted. "Yes, you can. I'll show you one more time how to do it and you'll catch on."

I shook my head. "No, it's not that."

Before Claire could respond, Lamont tapped on my shoulder and began skipping backwards. It was Claire's shrieking and bouncing breasts that made me crawl out of my comfort zone and begin skipping backwards as well, the repetitive *You're a Jerk* keeping my feet in rhythm.

I glanced at Lamont who smiled at me and stumbled over himself, skipping no longer following the beat, his tall, lanky frame bent over slightly while he tried to concentrate on the beat again.

I couldn't help it—I laughed.

Lamont took hold of my shoulders and pulled me into a hug. "What're you laughing at?"

Suddenly nervous, I awkwardly pushed my bangs behind my ear. "I—I—uh—"

"I can't stop watching you," he breathed. "I want you—want to dance with you."

The lights dimmed to darkness and the song changed yet again. I turned my back to him, slowly swaying my hips from side to side. *He wants to be with me. But why?* His hands rested on my hipbones, his crotch hard against my lower back. *He asked Claire to go out with him. I'm nothing like her.* His hand moved down to my thighs, slowly inching up toward my zipper. Although I found myself becoming aroused, I grabbed his hands and lifted them over my head, trying to grind like Shannon and Claire. *I'm not that easy. If that's only what he wants, then why did that kiss feel so amazing earlier?*

Maybe it was because I was so intent on impressing Lamont, or maybe it was because I was lost in my own thoughts, but I didn't fight against him when he spun me around and hungrily pressed his mouth against mine.

Maybe that's why we didn't stop kissing when Dylan, Chris and Hansen walked into the room and turned on the lights.

Maybe that's why my body began shaking anxiously once Claire grabbed my shoulder and yanked me back to reality.

"What the fuck are you doing?" she snapped.

The jig was up. The secret was out.

And nobody in the room seemed very happy about it.

#

LAMONT TOLD EVERYONE to back off before leading me toward his bedroom, a desperate need for escape massaging our shoulders.

We craved privacy.

"I wouldn't have pegged you for someone who likes to dance."

Lamont shrugged. "Only when I'm drunk. Otherwise, I get bored."

I rested my head on his shoulder, our fingers playing with one another. "You weren't bored with me?"

"Anything but." He kissed my forehead.

*This isn't you,* I scolded myself. *You know better than to get close to him like this. And all alone. The smarter move would be to get up and leave. Now.*

"I'm having a lot of fun," he whispered.

Despite logic urging me to run away, I decided to make a move. "My lips are kinda cold. Think you could warm 'em up for me?"

Smirking, he pressed his lips against mine. I put my hands on his soft cheeks, his goatee scratching my palms, eager for his desire. However, when I saw said desire burning beneath his beer-heavy eyelids, my nerves scratched and clawed at my skin. The image of him on top of me was enticing but all too overwhelming. I took a deep breath, gave him a gentle kiss and gazed into the brown pools of disappointment and confusion.

"Is everything okay?" He motioned to maneuver me onto my back, but I resisted.

"I'm fine. I'm just—I dunno. Is this really a good idea?"

I let him kiss me then, the urge surging through my legs crippling my anxiety, allowing me to fall back, my curls splayed on the pillow behind me.

"You're going to get me in trouble," he breathed, his lips following the curve of my jawline to the nape of my neck.

*Roxy, stop. Stop this. Stop before it's too late. You just met him. You're not that kind of girl. Have some respect for yourself. Listen to the red flags.*

I placed a hand on his chest and firmly distanced myself from him. "Trouble? What are you talking about?"

He shook his head, sat back and rubbed his eyes with the palms of his hands.

31

Something inside of me broke down like a small child watching her fish go belly up in the fishbowl. *No. It can't be.*

When he glanced at his lap, I sighed.

I knew that look. *He thinks he's made a huge mistake.*

And I believed I had, too.

#

WHEN WE RETURNED home, I promptly excused myself to my bedroom. Elizabeth and Danielle never showed up to the party, preferring to drink with some of the basketball team players' house, but both of them were passed out drunk on the living room couches, snoring softly, not moving a muscle even when the lights were turned on. Shannon, Amber and Claire bid me goodnight and thanked me for driving before I walked up the stairs and closed my bedroom door.

After the awkward final exchange with Lamont, I'd gathered the troops together and informed them it was time to leave.

It was as if I'd been caught stealing the answers for a test off of the student next to me.

It left me feeling stupid and guilty.

I tried going to sleep, cuddling beneath my heavy comforter, snuggling with the stuffed dog that resembled Molly, but I couldn't rid myself of the anxiety leaving me uncomfortable and restless. I looked at the toy, wishing that it really were Molly, wishing that I could tell her my problems because she was unable to pass judgment. Turning on the little black light on my nightstand, I grabbed my phone and scrolled through my contacts.

Even though the clock read 3:37AM, I couldn't wait until morning to make the phone call.

"Do you know how late it is right now?" my sister moaned into the phone. "Unless you're physically hurt or have a test tomorrow and need help with a medical explanation, I don't want to hear it."

"Lucy, I'm sorry. I don't know what to do." I hesitated. Although she'd helped me with social issues and relationships in the past, she never understood why I struggled to be a normal girl my age. Have sex. Drink your heart out. Try drugs. Gossip. Just don't be an idiot and let your grades slip. It's not that hard.

I'd heard it all, but it never made trying those things any easier.

"You're not pregnant, are you?"

I pulled the phone away from my ear and glared at it. "Yeah, because I'm having so much wild sex."

"What?" Her voice sounded small in my hand.

32

"No, I'm not pregnant," I said into the receiver, monotone. "You've had me on birth control since I was sixteen. And since when do I have sex with strangers?"

"Then can it wait until morning? I have appointments to worry about and I'm trying to give up coffee. You're not helping."

"I think I kissed a guy who has a girlfriend."

A pause. "So?"

"What do you mean, 'so?' Did you hear what I just said?"

A yawn. "Is there a ring on his finger?"

"I didn't see one—"

"Then you're fine," she interrupted. "You're in college. Unless he's married, you shouldn't feel bad."

I didn't comprehend. "How can you say that? When James cheated on you, you lost fifty pounds and nearly drank yourself into a coma."

"And yet, I passed all of my exams."

"Lucy, please focus." I pressed my finger against my temple. "You were devastated. You swore off men."

"But that was eight years ago. Now that I'm married, I understand how fickle a relationship is without a diamond to seal the deal."

I sighed. "I think you're missing the point. Relationships and loyalty are important to me. Otherwise, what's dating for? If Roger cheated on you before you were married, would you still have married him?"

"God, no. I don't want to spend the rest of my life with a scumbag. That's why I broke up with James."

"Do you listen to yourself? Ever?"

She yawned again. "I get why you're upset, but don't lose sleep over it. You have more important things to worry about. Just use a condom. And maybe socialize with boys who don't have girlfriends."

"Thanks for that earth-shattering advice. I couldn't have deduced that on my own."

"Love you, sis. Get some sleep and move on. There's more than one penis in this world."

When she hung up, I stared at my lap. *Why do I even bother?*

#

WHAT THE HELL were you thinking?" Claire yelled the following morning. "I *told* you he had a girlfriend. But *no!* You just *had* to *completely* ignore me."

I stared at the muted television screen, a steaming bowl of oatmeal burning the pads of my fingers and the soft skin of my palms.

33

After falling asleep in tears, the stuffed dog doing little to bring me any comfort like it usually could, I had hoped the new day would bring me some sort of solace. *Lamont wants me to keep our kiss a secret. It would be bad if it got around. Pretend it never happened.*

That settled it for me—he had a girlfriend.

Then I woke up to a voicemail from Lucy apologizing about her attitude on the phone. "Really though, I'm sorry. If he actually has a girlfriend, stay away from him. I don't want anyone to have hurt feelings. That can be a really toxic situation." Of course, at the end, she added, "I'm proud of you for getting out of your room! Don't let this deter you from going out in the future. Not all boys are dickbags, I swear. Keep studying."

I blew the steam away from my breakfast. "Yeah, I know. We can drop it and never speak about it again. He wants nothing to do with me." My limbs felt weak, the spoon lead in my hands. "Happy? You were right about everything." I attempted to take a bite of the mush in the bowl. "Congratulations."

The oats tasted like ash, a rock landing in the pit of my stomach.

Claire stood in front of the TV, arms crossed, eyes narrowed. "I just don't understand you, Roxy. How do you not feel like shit right now? You're just sitting there as if you almost didn't ruin a perfectly good relationship—obviously, Lamont feels fucking terrible." She sighed and shook her head. "Put yourself in the girlfriend's shoes. What if a boy you loved cheated on you?"

"I do feel bad," I mumbled, growing angry.

She ignored me. "What if she found out? Do you know what that could do to a girl's sense of security?"

"I don't want her to find out," I hissed. *Calm down. She's trying to get a reaction out of you. Stay quiet. Just like you do around Mom.*

"You should've listened to me. It was pretty stupid of you, honestly."

Slowly, I lowered the unfinished oatmeal onto the coffee table. "You wanna know a funny thing about secrets? They don't get told. He's going home next weekend, they'll hook up and everyone will forget that anything ever happened. It'll be as if I don't even exist." *Like usual.*

Claire, unable to let it go, decided to pour acid over the open wounds covering my heart. "But you feel bad? And not for yourself, but for his girlfriend? Like— is this something you're used to? I'd feel so fucking guilty."

"Claire, stop," I snapped. "You don't know what's going on inside me right now. I feel awful. I wish I never even met the guy. I don't want her to be hurt. I just—I thought maybe—"

34

"You thought what?" she said, throwing her hands in the air. "That you could get away with it?"

I shook my head. "No. I thought that he and I had something."

"I *told* you about her. Don't try to sugar coat it. You are totally to blame. You were the *only* sober one last night. If you had just listened—"

"Jesus Christ, Claire," I sighed. "I already admitted you were right. Let's be real here. You don't care about the girlfriend. You're mad because I didn't do what you told me to do."

Her retaliation was interrupted by a knock at the door.

"Give it a rest, Claire," Tiffany—my *actual* best friend I met in the dorms freshman year—said through the cracked open window. "I can hear you from the other side of campus."

Claire welcomed her in. "You weren't there! She—"

"I know." Tiffany waltzed passed her, sat on the couch and rested her long legs on the coffee table. "I heard about it. Why do you think I'm here?" Claire stared angrily at my savior. The two had already met a few times during the week when Tiffany wanted to see what my room looked like, when we had a movie night and when she came over to complain about her boyfriend, Brian. I figured Claire was jealous of the friendship Tiffany and I shared, her not being my real best friend and all. I also figured she was jealous of Tiffany's naturally sun-tanned skin, her tiny waist, flat stomach and big hips. I knew I was.

"Everyone cheats in college at least once. Isn't that part of the whole 'college experience' thing we're paying for?"

I snorted, the knot in my stomach slowly untying itself. That's what I loved about Tiffany—she never beat around the bush.

Claire sat in the chair across from me. "Tiffany, he doesn't even want to *talk* to her ever again. Obviously, he regrets everything. Think about it—what if Brian cheated on you?"

"First of all," Tiffany began, holding up a manicured index finger. "I'm ninety-five percent positive he is cheating on me. I've been miserable because we do nothing but fight lately." She held up a second finger. "Two: why are you so upset? He didn't cheat on *you*, so unless you have a crush on him, I see no reason for you to be so damn angry." She held up a third finger. "Lastly, they just *kissed*. No fondling. No removing of clothes. No humping. Shit, Claire. You need to take a chill pill." She pulled her dark brown hair into a messy bun. "Let. It. Go."

I smiled. "Finally, *someone* who understands."

"But—"

"Let's drop it," Tiffany said. She smiled her big square teeth at me and reached for the remote. "Anything good on TV?"

#

A WEEK HAD painfully crept by before I found the courage to message Lamont about the bracelet.

*Your bracelet misses you. Want to take it home?*

I expected a witty response—something funny and sarcastic we could laugh about later when this situation was long forgotten. I saw no harm in remaining friends and wanted him to understand there were no hard feelings. He proved me wrong and made it more than obvious he wanted *nothing* to do with me. Three days later with no response, Claire barged into my room late one afternoon, telling me Lamont had texted her asking for the bracelet. "What do you want me to say?"

I groaned. "Nothing."

"You shouldn't have kissed him"

I sighed. "I know, Claire. I know."

Thankfully, Tiffany walked up the stairs at that very moment, coming to my rescue once again. "It's been over a week. I don't think you need to chide her for it anymore." She shooed Claire out of the room and closed the door. "Fill me in. What'd I miss?"

"Lamont won't have anything to do with me." I fiddled with the bracelet— *his bracelet*—on my wrist. "He's completely ignoring me. I'm sure he's blaming the kiss on the alcohol and not on the fact that we shared some serious chemistry. I study chemistry, Tiff. I *know* chemistry and I have no explanation for what happened between us."

"I wouldn't think about it so much," she suggested. "He probably feels really guilty."

I pushed the DVD player closed. "Danielle is one of his best friends and she said he's never cheated on a girlfriend before. She came over yesterday and cornered me when I was trying to study. She's terrifying. She might be 5'1 and have the prettiest blue eyes, but they turn grey when she's interrogating you. I had nowhere to hide. She told me he's really not a bad guy. As if that's supposed to make me feel better."

Tiffany popped a handful of popcorn into her mouth. "Well, then maybe the alcohol did partially affect his better judgment. Not saying it justifies anything, but he might feel bad about the whole thing. Maybe he really likes this girl of his."

I rested my head against the wall behind my bed. "This sucks, Tiff. I really like this guy. You know I don't go out much. And this was something that made

36

me feel so—different. Do you think he felt what I did? Or do you think I let my imagination get the best of me?"

She shrugged, another handful of popcorn leaving a greasy stain on her thin lips. "Maybe he did and now he's super confused. It makes sense—you might make him feel guilty. Or maybe he feels things he can't wrap his head around. Boys are stupid. Really, *really* stupid."

I nodded. "This is my luck."

"I'm sorry, Roxy. But you need to remember, he's not the only boy in this school. The male population may be small, but someone will sweep you off your feet in no time."

#

ANOTHER MONTH AND a half came and went without hearing a single word from Lamont—the bracelet remained on my wrist at all times, a painful reminder of the kiss that so quickly broke my heart. I shouldn't have worn it, but I felt naked without its rubbery texture slipping against my skin. I loved that bracelet for no other reason than it belonged to *him*.

The girls would go to parties every Thursday, Friday and Saturday while I studied for school and wrote poems about love gained and lost; a topic of which I knew nearly nothing but enjoyed moping about. I would accept an invitation to party once a week simply because I wanted to make sure my roommates arrived home safely. While boys slurred meaningless attempts at flirtation, I would fidget with the bracelet and wonder if I'd ever see Lamont again. As the girls recounted tales of hookups and drunken shenanigans, I would run the scientific names of body parts through my mind afraid that I wouldn't pass my Anatomy exams.

I cared less and less about bones and more and more about blank verse.

Oftentimes, I would lock myself in my room and ignore the girls' pleas to hang out with them. I tried talking to Lucy about it, but she brushed off my anxiety as something everyone goes through in college.

I didn't have the heart to tell her that I'd already failed my first three Anatomy quizzes.

Although I knew it wasn't likely to happen, I always waited for Lamont's text message to come. The more I pined over him, the more I hated him.

As I crumpled up my last pathetic poem into a ball and threw it on top of my opened Anatomy book, I scolded myself for crying.

*Stop it Roxy. You've let this go on for long enough. It's time to forget about Lamont Carwyn and that stupid kiss.*

37

# Chapter Three

"WELL, IT'S BEEN over a month since the fateful night," I told Tiffany over a bowl of chocolate chip ice cream. "This bracelet has fused to the skin of my wrist. I am officially and whole-heartedly pathetic."

We were sitting inside Baskin Robbins enjoying our weekly dollar-scoop-Tuesday ice cream, ignoring the piles of homework awaiting our tired eyes and catching up on the latest gossip. She had disappeared over the weekend to visit her boyfriend, Brian, at UC Davis, came home crying about the lack of intimacy after they had sex, about the fact that every girl at every party knew his name, and about how much she hated Sonoma State compared to the lifestyles of the students at UC Davis. I'd sympathized, agreed that men were pigs, that sex was overrated and unnecessary, and that Rohnert Park was not my favorite place in the world. As the small ice cream parlor filled with more and more bodies, my sweatshirt made me uncomfortable. I rolled up the sleeves, revealing the *Boobies* bracelet, and was immediately asked if I'd heard from Lamont.

After my morose response, Tiffany frowned. "Have you tried contacting him?"

"Sure haven't. We're friends on Facebook but it makes me feel worse about the whole thing. He goes home every weekend and posts pictures of the two of them *way too often*." I wrinkled my nose not liking how jealousy tasted on my tongue.

Tiffany licked her strawberry scoop and gave me a look that was something between pity and indifference. "At least you can stalk him without him knowing. Brian doesn't even have a Facebook, the prick." She shoved a loose, dark brown strand of hair behind her ear. "If I didn't have volleyball, I'd go home every weekend, so I don't blame Lamont. This place sucks." She sighed, wiped some melting ice cream off her fingers and smiled at me. "What's the bitch look like? Is she ugly? Fat? Deformed?"

I snorted, recalling Lamont's latest profile picture with the girlfriend snuggling against his chest, wrapped in his arms. "No. Unfortunately, she's *really pretty*. White. Blonde. Big breasts. Perfect smile. And she's skinny. She's in high school." I dropped my spoon in the small paper bowl, sighed and covered my face with my hands. "She's sixteen years old."

39

Tiffany laughed. "Oh, so what? You're only three years older. And you're beautiful."

I blushed. "Not as pretty as her."

She sighed. "Look, she had a five-month head start. I'm sure if he were single, he'd be all over your lady nuts right now."

"I don't want him all over my lady nuts," I said, poking my spoon at the bottom of a chocolate chip. "I just want him to not avoid me."

"Maybe you should wear something other than sweatshirts and sweatpants once in a while."

I glared. "You do that all of the time."

"Yeah, but I have a boyfriend. I don't need anyone else's attention."

I grumbled, placing my face in my hands. "I hate that I'm obsessing over him. I can't even take this bracelet off without feeling like I'm on the brink of a nervous breakdown." My ice cream began to melt around the pink, plastic spoon. "What's wrong with me? I have more important stuff to think about—like the Anatomy class I'm failing."

She waved away my worries. "You're playing mind games with yourself. She's the *hometown* girlfriend. Give it another month and he'll be over her—or hopefully *over you*." When she winked, I couldn't help but laugh. "As for your class, what's the problem? You're locked in your room studying *all the time*."

I thought about my Anatomy notebook, each body part marked with a rhyming word, every other page adorned in lines of poetry about what it feels like to be the failure of the family. Even the lecture notes I fought so hard to scribble down while the professor droned on were littered with lines of poetry that had come to mind when I should have been thinking about the various locations of different bones. "Yeah, but for some reason, the information isn't sticking. And we're just memorizing body parts. It shouldn't be this difficult. Once we really get into the nitty-gritty, I'm—as you would say—fucked." My ice cream no longer looked appetizing. "As for Lamont, I should just give up before it gets to the point of a restraining order—or a straitjacket. It's time I let him, and this bracelet, go."

She grinned. "My oh my. Did Roxanne Vaughn just cuss?"

"Please don't dwell on it."

"Well," she said leaning back in her chair. "Maybe, one day, Lamont'll ask for that bracelet and strike up a real conversation."

I raised my eyebrows. "And maybe, one day, you'll fall in love with Sonoma State."

"Point taken." She glanced around the ice cream parlor and grimaced. "Let's get out of here already. It's too crowded and those screaming kids are driving me crazy." Tiffany pushed back her chair and stood. "You done?"

I glanced down at my ice cream soup and followed her lead. "Another dollar wasted." I tossed my half-empty cup into the trashcan while Tiffany finished off the last bit of her sugar cone.

"How the hell are we supposed to get out of here?" Tiffany moved sideways to avoid collision with a small child in a floral romper. "It's like a fucking Chuck-E-Cheese."

"Just be polite. We'll scoot past the warzone with our Victorian-esqe manners."

Tiffany laughed. "Lead the way, Jane Austen."

"I'm proud that you know the reference."

She tapped my shoulder. "We've been best friends for a year now. Whether I like it or not, I'm stuck with this knowledge."

We struggled to dodge small clusters of unsupervised children, shouldered through the adults in the crowd and dove out the front doors into the fresh air. Finally, beyond the claustrophobia, my ears still ringing from the chaos, I heard a voice that made me trip over my own feet.

I elbowed Tiffany and frantically whispered, "Tiff, that's him." Her eyes followed my discreet pointing toward the end of the line. "What is he doing here?"

"I assume he's getting ice cream."

When she laughed, I glared at her. "You know what I mean."

"This place is a fucking Twilight Zone. You talk about someone and they're bound to appear out of thin air."

I hated my hands for shaking, my feet for feeling as if I was treading through wet cement, and my heart for thumping against my chest.

"You gonna make a move or what?"

*Stop freaking out. You decided you're gonna get over him, so just do it. Don't care about him.* "Yes. I'm gonna prove a point."

"Well, do it now because he totally just recognized you."

Looking back at Lamont, a wave of resentment crashed over my head. I wished the smile on my face was phony, but I was quite ecstatic to see him.

"Maybe if I just pretend I didn't see him, we can get out of here without confrontation."

41

Tiffany put her hand on my back and urged me forward. "Go give him a piece of your mind."

He gave me a single wave of the hand as I hesitantly made my way over to him. There were two girls in attendance, both of them looking at me as if I were a rodent chewing through their makeup bags. I fiddled with the bracelet, breathed in and then breathed out. "Hey Lamont."

He smiled uncomfortably, held up a finger and pointed to the phone.

I frowned and almost backed away, but when I realized it was probably his girlfriend on the phone, I grew angry. I nearly ripped the bracelet off of my wrist. "Oh, no need to say a word." I grabbed his forearm, slid the bracelet over his fist and tapped the back of his hand. "Good to see ya."

Walking away—somehow managing to refrain from looking over my shoulder—I linked elbows with Tiffany, the rocks of sorrow falling through the holes of my sneakers, allowing me to walk just a little bit lighter.

"I hope his girlfriend heard me. I know it was her on the phone."

Tiffany patted my forearm. "How did it feel?"

"Empowering." We clambered into her SUV.

"I'm proud of you, Rox. I didn't think you had it in you."

"To be honest, I didn't think I had it in me, either."

She patted my thigh. "Well, you did it! I have a feeling Lamont is gonna text you. It's like you gave his balls a nice grab and walked away."

I wrinkled my nose. "You really think he'll text me?"

My phone vibrated.

She nodded toward it. "Ten bucks says its him wondering why you left."

I read the text, snorted and held it up for her to see. "It's him. Asking why I left."

She laughed, shook her head and turned left out of the parking lot. "Sometimes, I'm a fucking genius."

I nodded, debating whether or not to respond to his text. *You text him back, you'll have to deal with the consequences.* "What do you think I should do?"

She shrugged. "Give that fucker hell."

#

LATER THAT NIGHT, I was scrolling through my sister's medical journal—she'd emailed it to me for inspiration, thinking that me "failing" meant I was struggling with a B—and writing down the latest techniques medical students should use when studying for exams.

42

"'Buy lots of instant coffee. If you find yourself getting more than four hours of sleep, you'll find your grades slipping.' You forgot to mention one must have sex to release natural endorphins. Or am I just the lucky one who gets that lecture?" I grumbled, quickly becoming uninterested. "'Even though many professors find the next statement controversial, I know how difficult lectures can be, especially early in the morning. Make a friend who has a prescription for Adderall. There's nothing against finding ways to remain focused.' Lucy, what is wrong with you? You don't encourage college students to take drugs. It's not right."

The bottom of the article had Lucy's picture beside her short biography. Her blonde, wavy hair was pulled back in a loose bun, just the right amount of hair falling next to her ears, tickling the bony shoulders hidden behind her white lab coat. Her green eyes sparkled against the camera's flash, her red lipsticked lips popping out of the photo as if I were wearing 3D glasses. And then, of course, her biography noted the success of the family—how Lucy hails from two prestigious doctors, the Vaughns, the best San Diego has to offer, who also attended medical school at USC. And how she married a very successful plastic surgeon—Roger Lovelace—whom she met while ordering a house coffee—fat free milk, one packet Sugar in the Raw—at the Starbucks medical students frequented, especially during final exams. He ordered the same exact drink, they accidentally touched hands when reaching for their sugar, and instantly fell in love.

"Nothing noted about her disappointing younger sister," I sighed. "What am I? A rejected liver?"

My Anatomy textbook stared at me from beneath the three-page poetry piece I had due for workshop tomorrow. "Why am I trying to be like them?"

A ping over the computer's speakers captured my attention. Exiting out of the journal's tab, I stared curiously at my Facebook homepage.

There, in the corner of the screen, was a message from someone who had wanted nothing to do with me for the past three years. The boy who broke my heart when I was in high school because he said being with me would ruin the college experience he'd always wanted.

Zachary Cameron.

My initial reaction was to close my computer and walk away, but the message box showed I'd read his greeting. "Why did I have to click the stupid box? Curiosity killed the cat, Roxanne." I hesitated before resting my fingers of the keyboard. *Hey Zach*, I typed slowly. *Long time no talk.*

This wasn't a guy I believed I could talk to—he wasn't someone who deserved my trust. I'd already made the mistake of falling in love with him once before. However, for some strange reason I couldn't quite pinpoint, he was being *friendly*. This was something uncharacteristic of him—at least towards me since he broke my heart and told me never to talk to him ever again.

*Just sitting here. Avoiding my homework.* My pinky twitched before pressing down on the return key. I knew that he wasn't to be trusted—boys always had motives behind their actions—but something was telling me to continue the conversation.

*What're you up to?* I tapped the keys, treading carefully.

While the speakers pinged once, twice, three times, with his responses, I stood and paced in small circles around the dirty t-shirts and sweatpants that littered my room. It was cordial enough but something in my gut was warning me to be weary. We didn't know one another anymore. High school seemed forever ago and his "all I want to do is get laid" behavior made me want to forget he was ever a part of my life.

I'd completely changed since our last interaction. Definitely for the worse.

Anxiety issues. Fighting depression. A cynical outlook on life. Loneliness. Social awkwardness. Zero self-esteem. Hating who I am as a person. Disappointing everyone around me. Wanting to write poetry instead of dissecting body parts.

I returned to my desk chair and rested my forehead on the wooden tabletop. "Wow. I really need to work on bettering myself. Or at least loving myself. I gotta change *something* because this is just sad.""

Staring at the computer, I wrung my hands together, wondering if I should just close the screen and ignore Zachary, pretending we never had this small exchange. After the hell he'd put me through, he more than deserved an ice-cold shoulder. *But remember, you want to change—and I'm pretty sure one of the first steps to change is letting go of the past. Maybe he's also changed. Maybe he needs a friend. Maybe he's lonely like I am.* I closed my eyes as my diaphragm expanded and retracted. *Maybe he wants to apologize for being a complete jerk.*

To help center my emotions—and in an attempt to slow my ever-racing thoughts—I clicked on my "classical music" playlist, the piano sweeping through the pores of my soul. The notes bounced against my anxiousness until my nerves hummed with a peaceful confidence.

My responses to his questions started to come quickly, less forced.

CHAPTER THREE

An unexpected knock and turn of a door handle announced Claire's arrival. She smiled as she welcomed herself in, a pint of Ben and Jerry's ice cream in hand. "Hope you're not busy! I thought we could watch a movie. Eat some ice cream. Be girls."

Rather than wait for an answer, she enthusiastically jumped on my bed, scooting my Molly stuffed animal onto the floor.

I glanced again at my Anatomy book, then at the clock in the computer screen's corner.

It was already 10:45. My poetry class was at two. My project was halfway done. *So much for going to bed early.*

"I already went to Baskin Robbins, but I'll put on a movie."

She beamed, ripping the lid off, melted ice cream droplets coming way too close to my bed spread. "Oh good. For a second there, I thought you were gonna kick me out."

*If you had any decency, you would realize how much work I have to do and excuse yourself.* "No, I was just making sure I had enough time to finish my project before class tomorrow." I closed my laptop and began fishing through the largest desk drawer for a romantic comedy. I figured that's the sort of DVD women watched when attempting to bond, but I didn't exactly know the protocol for a successful girls' night. I did, however, understand that part of bonding was talking about boys.

"Do you remember that story I told you about that guy who broke my heart when I was in high school? His name was Zach?"

She plopped a scoop of ice cream into her mouth. "It rings a bell, but I'm not really painting a full picture."

"Long story short," I began, stacking three movie choices beside me. "Met through mutual friends. He was drunk at the time—an arrogant prick, really. Initially, I didn't like the guy. But the more we spent time together, the more he grew on me. Nerdy. Socially awkward. Poor self-esteem."

Claire slid off the bed and hovered behind my chair. "What's he look like?"

I smiled shyly at her. "He's a swimmer. Strong body. Handsome face. Short hair. But not so good on the teeth front."

"Just shut up and show me a picture already."

Hesitantly, I reopened my computer, clicked on his Facebook and scrolled through his seven, rather unflattering, profile pictures. His non-photographic self was still as handsome as I remembered—only he had more manly features having grown out of his baby face and lean muscle.

45

"It's weird looking at him. I haven't seen him in years. He deleted me off Facebook a long time ago. I still don't know why he asked me to be his friend again tonight."

*I did forget just how handsome the guy was. Why didn't he get uglier?* With his high cheekbones, prominent French nose, sharp jaw leading to a round chin, and green eyes alive with emotion, I found it difficult to look away. His sandy brown hair was cut close to his scalp now, a habit probably developed from his short-lived training stint with the military.

My stomach leapt unexpectedly. *Oh, please. Am I really that lonely? After all this time, a stupid picture can make me feel this way?*

Claire purred beside my ear. "Damn, he's hot. Look at that body—those arms. He is *gorgeous*. Invite him up. I wouldn't mind taking him out of your hands—and putting mine all over him."

I slammed down the laptop screen harder than I'd intended. "How about that movie? Take your pick. I couldn't decide between these three."

Although slightly taken aback, Claire lifted the DVD off the top of the pile and handed it to me.

I sighed, disappointed with the irrational annoyance building inside my chest. *Who cares if she thinks he's good looking? Everyone with eyes can see that. He's not yours to protect so get over it. This isn't you.* "The last thing I want to do is invite up an old lover to visit." *And the last thing I want is to hand him over to a slutty roommate.* "Especially one that left me in the dust because he 'realized' having a girlfriend during his first year in college would 'ruin' his overall experience. I hated him, Claire. It took me forever to get over him." I scooted my chair away from the desk, picked up the stuffed dog and cradled it to my chest.

"You sure you're over him?"

I nodded, although the nervous jitters in my stomach would say otherwise. "Not that it matters. He has a girlfriend. Or did, last time I heard."

Claire returned to her post on the bed and sighed. "Another guy with a girlfriend? Sweet Jesus, Roxy. You're a fucking magnet."

I glared. "Hey, don't pin this on me. I wasn't the one who engaged the conversation so don't start with that again, please."

"Just do me a favor and don't overthink it. I'm sure it's nothing to worry about. A waste of your time."

But try as I may, I couldn't stop dwelling on the possible reasons for his sudden interest in rekindling—what—a friendship? Even as Claire began tearing up at the most romantic scene in the movie, I couldn't draw myself into the storyline. *There's no way he messaged me for no reason. He's way too shy to reach out just because he's bored.* An unnerving sensation began to crawl up my spine, small spidery legs making contact with each of my vertebrae.

My phone vibrated in my sweatshirt pocket, my bones nearly jumping through my skin. I took a silent breath while Claire blew her nose into a wrinkled tissue. Being careful to avoid Claire's peripherals, I read the message from Lamont.

I quickly calculated that the movie would be over in half an hour. *I'll just respond once Claire leaves. Practice playing hard to get.*

"How are you not crying right now?"

I stealthily slid the phone beneath my thigh hoping that Claire didn't notice. "I'm not big on crying during movies. No judgment, just not my thing." Which totally wasn't true. I cried all of the time during movies, even during scenes where tears made no sense.

She blew her nose again, her mascara smearing beneath her eyes. "Don't lie. You're overanalyzing the Zach thing, aren't you?"

I laughed. "No, I'm actually not. Just thinking about the poem I have due tomorrow."

It wasn't a total lie. I wasn't really worrying about the Zachary conundrum. There was another problem I had to deal with.

A taller problem.

#

SHANNON, ELIZABETH AND I clambered over the benches scaling the light blue and white walls of the gymnasium.

"I can't believe people actually came to this," I said, watching my step carefully so I wouldn't trip over my two-year-old skater shoes. "I thought nobody cared about sports at this school. We don't even have a football team."

"Well, the athletic department has to do something to promote their terrible sports program. That's why there are prizes being given out this year."

Glancing around the dense crowd, I laughed with Shannon. *He already told you he wasn't gonna be here. Pay attention to the girls.*

"It's Sonoma State. This place is just another version of high school," Elizabeth said. "The players were all getting wasted together beforehand— Danielle was with them. Even the athletes aren't taking any of this pep-rally stuff seriously."

47

"Claire and Amber are lucky we're such good friends. If they weren't performing, I'd be at home watching TV. I can already hear my pajamas calling my name."

Elizabeth snorted. "Real Housewives reruns?"

"Don't judge me." Shannon playfully slapped Elizabeth's shoulder. "I know damn well you'd be doing the same thing."

"*Actually*, I have class in the morning unlike *some* people. Right, Roxy?"

"Don't drag me into this," I said smiling, even though, deep down, I was suffering from extreme panic. My Anatomy lecture was at 7:15 every Thursday morning and it began with a quiz that was impossible to prepare for. *Unless, according to Lucy, you inject coffee into your veins and pop a few pills beforehand.* "I have to memorize all the different bones in the body, match them on a diagram and spell them correctly. One misplaced letter and you get that entire answer wrong. No pity points."

Elizabeth and Shannon grimaced. "And you want to be a doctor because?"

I shrugged. "I don't really want to be a doctor but my dad's a plastic surgeon, my mom's a gynecologist and my sister's a gastroenterologist. And then Lucy married a plastic surgeon, so it's kind of expected." I paused, reflecting back on my Friday morning trepidation. "I'm not gonna lie, though. The other day during my Anatomy lab, we had to dissect frogs and I gagged a little. This Friday, we're supposed to get started on cats—matching bones and knowing the names of their innards. I love cats. I don't know what I'm going to do." I sighed, wishing I didn't have to think about it. "I'll need to find a way to get over it. I don't really have much of a choice in the matter."

"You can't force yourself to do something that won't make you happy." Shannon patted my thigh. "Roxy, you always have a choice. Trust me. It's your life, not theirs."

My phone pinged as the chatter around us grew to an unbearable pitch. "Yeah, well, tell that to my parents and sister." I pulled the phone out of my jean pocket and felt my lungs constrict.

*Where are you?*

I swallowed, my mouth dry, palms moist. My eyes instinctively darted to the entryway.

There he was in all his tall, dark and handsome glory, wearing a black and orange baseball cap, a black shirt and white basketball shorts. I grew dizzy. *Breathe. Just breathe.* I closed my eyes as the temperature in the gymnasium skyrocketed. *How can he already have this effect on me? Maybe I just have a temperature*. But I knew better—the only reason I felt so warm was because of his presence. I opened my eyes again, studying his movements, the confident manner in which he interacted with those around him. *Look at me. Please just look at me.*

"Hello! Earth to Roxanne. Are you there?" Shannon asked, waving her hand in front of my face.

I tore my eyes way from Lamont and smiled at the girls. "Sorry. Totally spaced out."

Shannon looked at the court and found Lamont conversing with his fellow baseball players. She smirked and shook her head. "You're helpless, you know that? Didn't your mother ever tell you that staring is rude?"

"No. She always told me I could look, just not touch." When the girls laughed, I shook my head. "I'm being serious. She's told me that ever since I was old enough to walk."

Elizabeth raised an eyebrow. "So that's who you've been talking to all day. No wonder you've been in such a good mood. When did that start up again?"

I turned back to Lamont and watched him take a seat at the bottom of the bleachers. He was looking around the gym for something—or someone. *Should I text him back? Maybe he's looking for me.* Resisting the possibility of making a complete fool out of myself, I shoved the phone back into my pocket. *Who am I kidding?*

"Nothing 'started up again.' I just happened to look at the door when he walked in."

Elizabeth roughly snatched my wrist—my newly naked wrist. "What happened to your bracelet? Shannon, did you notice it was missing?"

"You never take that off," Shannon noted, glaring.

"C'mon you guys. You're acting as if I've been snorting cocaine or something."

"You're hiding something from us." Elizabeth dropped my hand and frowned. Her dirty blonde hair fell in front of her shoulders, her golden eyes baring into my soul.

I began to squirm. "I dunno. Last time I said anything, I was judged really heavily."

Both girls furrowed their eyebrows sympathetically. "Roxy, we're not gonna judge you. We're your friends. You should know that we care."

I rubbed my sweaty palms on the side of my jeans. *If I can't trust the girls I live with, then what's the point of living with them? Open up a little and let them in. You heard them. Friends.* "Okay—honestly, I haven't been hiding anything. Last night, I ran into Lamont at Baskin Robbins and gave back the bracelet. He's texted me on and off since."

"But you loved that bracelet."

I shrugged. "Yeah, well, I had a point to prove. He was on the phone when I gave it back, so I didn't give him a chance to say anything."

Elizabeth nodded. "Girl, you are totally playing hard to get."

"No, I swear I'm not. He has a girlfriend. There's no point playing stupid games."

The girls stared at me skeptically.

"What?" I threw my hands in the air. "I don't have time to worry about him. Anatomy is killing me, Psychology feels like a waste of time, Biology is nothing but busy work and all I want to do is write poetry—" My face reddened when I noticed the girls glance at one another. "What I mean is that him texting me is no big deal. You can read my text messages if you don't believe me."

"I hate to tell you this, but I think you're in denial."

"Yeah," Elizabeth agreed. "With the way you were staring at him, I'd say this situation is more important than you'd like us to think."

Before I could argue the obvious truth, the announcer spoke into the microphone to capture the audience's attention.

"Don't think you're off the hook," Shannon hissed. "We *will* continue this later."

I fumbled with my phone before reading Lamont's text over again. Rather than inform him I'd spotted him the instant his Nike's crossed the gym's threshold, I decided to play coy.

*I told you, I'm at the sports thing. Why?*

His response vibrated against my palms instantly. My fingers shook as I flipped open the keyboard. *I'm here. Where are you? I want to see you later.*

Shannon looked at my screen and nudged my shoulder. "So, not a big deal, huh?"

I smiled even though my legs began to tremble. "What should I do?"

She chuckled. "Just don't do anything tonight that you'll for sure regret tomorrow."

#

"YOU REALLY WON'T go with me?" I asked Elizabeth and Shannon later that night. "I can't go over there alone."

50

Once the pep-rally festivities began to simmer down, the three of us decided to leave before any other students had the same idea. Upon returning to the dorm, the girls changed into their pajamas and plopped on the couch to indulge in a mini Real Housewives marathon. I, on the other hand, paced nervously from the kitchen counter to the backdoor, creating a worn path in the cheap, blue carpet.

"I really can't do this by myself."

Shannon sipped her decaf coffee and smiled. "You'll be fine. He probably wants to hook-up with you. It'll just get awkward with me and Lizzy there."

The panic intensified. "Don't say that. Last time we kissed, he refused to speak with me." I pushed my hair away from my face. "No—he has a girlfriend. I'm not gonna be an idiot." My pacing slowed to a stop in front of the TV. "Please, *please* come with me," I pleaded. "Even bring your coffee and your magazine with you. I'm sure there will be a TV. You can watch Housewives there."

Elizabeth glanced over her *Cosmopolitan.* "If you don't want to hook-up with him, then why go? You have a quiz to study for. And it's after midnight. Sounds a bit like a booty call."

The front door flew open exposing Amber all dolled up in her cheer outfit. The skirt accentuated her round bottom, and the tight top crushed her breasts together. "Booty call? Who?" She tossed her light blue sports bag by the stairs and sat beside Elizabeth.

"Lamont and Roxy," Shannon said.

Amber studied me quizzically. "Say what?"

"No, that's not true." I shook my head. "He asked if we could hang out. Nothing else."

"It's after midnight. That's a booty call."

Elizabeth laughed. "I told you."

"He's at a friend's house playing beer pong and he invited me to play. Nothing about booties or calls were involved."

"You're delusional. He obviously wants a piece of dat ass."

As the girls laughed, I slumped into one of the dining room chairs, exhausted. "Oh my God, stop. I'm already freaking out. I've never not studied for a quiz before—should I just tell him I'm busy?"

"Honestly, you should go."

Amber nodded with Elizabeth. "Jokes aside, you should live a little. What's one little F in the greater scheme of things?"

51

*Just another paper to add to my stack of failures accumulating in my Anatomy binder.*

"Why don't you talk to Claire?" Shannon suggested. "She owes you for last weekend."

I put my face into my hands.

Last Saturday night, I went to bed early. Declining multiple invites to go out with the girls, I'd read the Edgar Allen Poe printouts for poetry class, read through the three chapters concerning cardiac, smooth and skeletal muscle tissue for Anatomy, and enjoyed a handful of double stuffed Oreos, crumbs littering my comforter. During my REM cycle of sleep, I was rudely awoken by multiple pings shattering through my dreams at three-thirty in the morning.

Claire was wondering if I could give her a ride home because the guy she was drinking with had been pressuring her to have sex. Dazed and concerned, I threw my mangled curls into a makeshift ponytail, stumbled out of the back door and drove recklessly over to the apartment complex highlighted on my GPS.

There, inside the unlocked apartment, leaning against the kitchen counter, were Shannon and Trevor—the boy she met the first night I kissed Lamont, her go-to cuddle buddy that she swore she wasn't having sex with—drinking glasses of water from the sink.

"What're you doing here?" she asked.

"Claire said she needed a ride home."

Trevor laughed. "She told us the same thing twenty minutes ago."

"If you're here, why did she text me?"

Shannon shrugged. "Trevor told her he'd give her a ride home when he took me home. I've been ready to go to bed for a while now."

Beyond frustrated and more than exhausted, I marched to the end of the hallway and pounded on the closed bedroom door. "You have ten minutes before I break this down! Get your butt out here or you're sleeping here. It's four in the morning, Claire!"

Twelve minutes later, a boy emerged from the room like a rodeo champion, Claire's giggles bouncing off the walls, hurting my ears.

She promised me they didn't have sex, but she did do unmentionable things to him.

Having to think about it all over again made me want to strangle her. "I don't know. What if she does that again?"

Amber snorted. "Is that a chance you're willing to take?"

"You're right. I deserve a night of fun." I began pacing again. "It'll be good to get out of my room. I won't stay long. Where is she?"

"You plan on coming home?" Elizabeth smiled.

Amber cooed. "Better not be alone."

"Oh, goodie!" Shannon clapped her hands together. "We can ask him how the sex was over coffee and bagels."

As the girls laughed, my face flushed bright pink. "Seriously, you guys. I don't want to have sex with him. More importantly, he has a *girlfriend*. Why don't any of you believe me?"

"Maybe because your cheeks are bright red and whenever you talk about him, your voice goes up like a boy going through puberty," Elizabeth joked.

I flushed a deep purple. "Now you're being cruel."

They laughed again just as Claire opened the front door, dropping her bag beside Amber's. Still dressed in spandex, jazz shoes and a sports jacket, she smiled at us. "What'd I miss?" She walked into the kitchen to pour herself a glass of milk.

"Nothing. Something on TV was funny," I said quickly, hoping she didn't notice the TV was on silent. "You wanna go out for a little bit tonight?"

She eyed me over her glass. "*You* want to go out?"

"Well," I began.

The laughing turned into hushed giggles.

My confidence waivered. *C'mon you guys. Give me a break. I'm trying.*

"One of Lamont's friends has a beer pong table set up and is having a party or something. We were all invited but the other girls are being lame."

As an eerie silence filled the room, I dropped my shoulders.

Claire slowly lowered her glass until it clinked on the granite. "Are you drinking?"

I shook my head. "I do think I'll buy myself a Slurpee to keep myself awake, though."

My mom's voice nagged me about unnecessary sugar intake late at night and how it would sit on my thighs because my metabolism slowed during those late hours when I should be sleeping. *Shut up. I'm an adult and can do whatever I want. One Slurpee isn't gonna give me diabetes or make me gain any weight.*

Claire crossed her arms, foot tapping. "How long you wanna be there?"

"Maybe an hour or so? I have class early tomorrow."

She studied my green long sleeved shirt and faded black jeans and looked down at her dance attire. "Can I wear this?"

53

I smiled, happiness lifting me atop a puffy pile of clouds. I tried not to think about the fact that she only had a sports bra under her jacket and her spandex showed off the dimples beneath her butt. "You mean—you'll come?" I didn't want to have to bring up the following weekend myself, so I hoped she knew she owed me one on her own.

She sighed, staring at her empty milk glass. "Yeah, I'll go. But I swear to God, if you come home crying because of something Lamont did, I'm not going to hold your hand."

"I know he has a girlfriend—so, no, I won't be kissing him."

The girls laughed again, Claire shaking her head. "Right. I'm not holding my breath."

#

WHEN WE ARRIVED at the dorms across campus, Lamont introduced us to his friend, Robert, and a blonde girl named Angelica. I may have had the ability to analyze the most difficult multiple-choice questions and had a knack for uncovering the most difficult themes in the most bizarrely written poems, yet I so often interpreted text messages incorrectly.

When Lamont said his friend was having a "couple people" over, and when he said, "I'd like you to join," I thought that meant his friend was having a party and he was inviting all of us girls. Apparently, he was being quite literal and there was no need to find an underlying message.

Claire was officially the fifth wheel, and by the look she shot me, it was obvious she was not happy about it.

"I'm sorry," I whispered to her. "I swear. I thought it was gonna be a party."

She sighed. "If you're happy, I'll be happy. I owe you for saving me last weekend, anyway."

*She's your friend for a reason. She does care about you in her own way.* "Thank you, really. I appreciate it."

I wrapped my arms around Lamont when he approached me, finding unexplainable comfort in how much I missed him. As I pressed my cheek against his warm chest, I felt myself begin to lift off the ground, my happiness defying gravity.

"It's good to see you," I mumbled beneath his chin.

"Alright girls," Robert said impatiently. "Which of you is gonna play first?"

I pulled away from Lamont and linked elbows with Claire. "We're a package deal."

Maybe it was stupid of me to care—usually when we went out together, Claire would disappear with whatever guy captured her fancy—but I felt guilty about the entire misunderstanding. The last thing I wanted to do was make Claire feel left out or uncomfortable, even if she did owe me big for everything I'd done for her.

Claire half-smiled and squeezed my forearm. "We can take turns throwing the ball."

"Does that mean you'll be taking turns drinking?" Lamont wondered.

Before I could lie and say there was vodka in my Slurpee, Claire shook her head. "We can't stay long because we both have class tomorrow morning. You, my lucky friend, get to drink it all."

Focusing on my faded shoes, I awkwardly nibbled on my Slurpee's straw. *Just this once, could you let me do the talking? He's going to think I'm a loser. This is the second time we get to hang out and again, he knows I'm sober. How's that supposed to look?* I thought, liquid sugar washing over my taste buds, my body relishing in the instant metabolism spike.

"You're kidding. I have to drive home."

"Then pour water in some of the cups and only drink from the ones that have beer," Claire snapped.

Lamont ignored her, cracked open the beer can and began pouring the light brown liquid into the red cups on the table.

"I can drive you home if that'll help," I added.

"I need my truck."

"You don't have to be such a—"

I shook my head at Claire. "That's fine. I'll pick you up in the morning and bring you back."

He glanced at me and shrugged. "I can drive my truck home. Don't worry about it."

Again, I shook my head. "I'll drive you. It's not worth taking that chance."

"Are you losers ready to play yet? Angelica and me are getting sober," Robert complained. "Let's fucking play already." Robert was the exact opposite of Lamont. About my height and a bit chubby, his stomach hung out over his cargo shorts. His dirty blonde hair was sticking up in different directions as if a cow had just licked him, and his beard was unkempt, as if a cat had spit up a hairball on his chin. His eyes, however, were a beautiful swirl of blue and green, kindness overwhelming me despite his attempt to act like a jerk in front of Angelica.

Lamont finished pouring the rest of the second beer into the remaining empty cups and then picked up a Ping-Pong ball. "Let's see if you can play as good as you talk shit."

Claire stood on his left and I on his right, completely aware of the warmth radiating between the hairs on our arms.

Watching him throw the ball across the table, I realized just how handsome he was. Those high cheekbones yearned for me to touch them, those lips teasing me, and those long eyelashes making me slightly jealous because I had to wear expensive mascara in order to achieve volume like that. I scooted closer, the burst of energy from the sugar providing me with a pinch of confidence.

"You're lucky we're on the same team. I'm pretty good at this game. It can get rather intimidating."

His eyebrows rose. "A lot of shit talking from the girl who doesn't even drink."

I reached into the water cup for the second ball. "That doesn't mean I don't know how to play." Lobbing the ball across the table, I waited for it to land straight in the middle of the cup.

I missed my mark entirely, the ball hitting Robert's thick thigh.

Everybody laughed, my confidence backing into its defensive, insecure shell.

"Oh yeah, your skills are terrifying. You better watch out, Rob. We have a real professional over here." He nudged me playfully.

I smiled to mask my uncertainty. *They're joking around. Don't take it personally. Have fun. You're with Lamont. And he's still wearing the bracelet. Relax. So, you have to wake up and take a quiz in five hours. When is the next time Lamont will be drunk enough to want to hang out with you? It's time to live in the moment. Just let loose for once.*

I nudged him back. "That was just a warm up."

"Watch a *real* pro at work. If you're gonna talk shit, you better be able to back it up." He tossed another ball and nodded when it splashed inside of the front cup.

"Whatever—you're like, seventeen feet tall. That's an unfair advantage."

Claire laughed. "Leave it to the med student to analyze a game of beer pong like that."

I cringed. *Please shut up, Claire. I don't need him thinking I'm a nerd.*

"You sure you can bring me to my truck in the morning? You have class. I won't drink anymore if you can't," he mentioned while Robert threw the ball in our direction.

I smiled, completely obsessed with his big, brown eyes. "I promise. My class is over around ten. You'll probably still be sleeping."

He nodded. "It's an excuse for me to see you again."

"You know," I mumbled. "You don't need an excuse."

He cocked his head to the side. "You know I do."

*The girlfriend*, I thought, my Slurpee feeling like sand in my stomach. *It'll make him feel less guilty about talking to me.* I pretended to not hear him. Instead, I glanced down at his wrist and smiled. "I've missed wearing that bracelet. Think I can borrow it for the night?"

He shook his head. "No way. Last time I fell for that, one night turned into one month."

Gently lifting his arm, I began rubbing circles around the back of his hand. "You know that wasn't my fault."

He followed the motion of my hand silently.

"Oh, come on. I promise I'll give it back." I said.

"We could make a game out of it," he suggested.

Claire let loose an obvious sigh of disgust, nonchalantly making her shot land in a cup in front of Angelica. "What is it with you two and that stupid bracelet? You can buy one like every other normal person for three dollars at Tilly's."

I stared into his eyes. "What kind of game?"

"You're both pathetic."

He grinned at Claire. "Just shoot the ball."

"I did. It's your turn."

"What kind of game?" I asked again, wishing Claire would stop interfering when it came to me attempting to flirt with Lamont.

He slid the bracelet over his knuckles. "We trade off any time we see one another."

"And just how often do you plan on seeing me?"

Lamont put the bracelet on my wrist. "Guess we'll have to find out, won't we?"

"Hey! Love birds!" Angelica shouted impatiently. Her white shirt hung loosely off her bony shoulders, a lime green bra covering her breasts. "Are you in the game or what?"

I handed the Ping-Pong ball to Lamont repeatedly reminding myself not to blush. With the bracelet safely in my possession once more, I knew he and I were finally on good terms.

The thought of seeing him again—of him wanting to see me—made me woozy.

It was more than a little overwhelming.

As the night continued, my skills not showing any hope of improvement, I told Claire to take over the remainder of the game. Standing in the kitchen, searching through the refrigerator for a bottle of water, Robert decided to strike up polite conversation with me.

It was small talk, questions about Claire—somewhere between the second and third game, Angelica had excused herself to go throw up in the bathroom, so Robert was determined to try to convince Claire to join him in the bedroom—and general inquiries about school. Trying to take Robert's attention away from getting into Claire's pants, I decided to ask how he and Lamont met.

That was my mistake.

"We played baseball together last year—both injured—and talked on the bench a lot during the games."

"What happened?"

He took his phone out of his cargo shorts and began swiping through pictures. "I slid into second base and hit it too hard. One of the players stepped on my knee—all kinds of messed up shit. Bone sticking through my skin and everything. Crazy, huh?"

"Oh my. That sounds like it would hurt." Not thinking much of it, I looked at the multiple X-Ray photos he turned in my direction. He wasn't joking—the bone was shattered in half, something straight out of a badly directed medical soap opera.

Placing my water on the table, I swallowed back the flood of anxiety that had swiftly washed over me. All of a sudden, I didn't feel so good—slightly feverish.

*It's just a broken bone. Even if it is severed completely in half.*

He continued to talk, describing the pain, the surgery process, scrolling through zoomed-in images. I wanted to look away but continued to stare for fear of appearing rude. Steadying myself on the beer pong table, sucking in quiet, deep breaths, I wished I could nicely ask him to stop. *This isn't an owl bone. This is a human bone. Oh my God.* My stomach pain intensified, immediately followed by the familiar taste of metal in my mouth. *No. Don't do this here.*

*Fight it. Try to fight it.* The room began to spin within the shrinking diameters of a black tunnel. *Run. Get out. Now. Get air. Fresh air.*

"Just a moment, please," I managed to whisper before my ears started ringing.

I raced to the front door, knowing that if I could just hold on for one more second, I would be okay. But as my hand turned the knob, the door slightly opening, I lost consciousness and fell back on the tile in front of everyone.

# Chapter Four

UPON OPENING MY eyes, I found four frightened faces frozen above me. At some point between me falling flat on my back and me regaining consciousness, Angelica had made her way into the kitchen once more. *Did I do what I think I did?* Feeling miserable, I closed my eyes wanting to fade away from my mortification. *Did I really faint from looking at a picture of a broken bone?* My ears were ringing, my mouth felt like it was stuffed with cotton balls and my stomach churned round and round, much like the ceiling I'd been staring at very briefly. *This can't be happening.*

"Roxy!" Claire shouted above the pounding in my head. "Don't die on me, Roxy. Please don't die on me." She placed her hands on my shoulders and shook vigorously. "Please, open your eyes!"

Although fatigued and wanting to fall asleep, I grabbed her arm and fluttered my eyelids. "Stop." My brain rattled and acid threatened to burn the back of my mouth. I swallowed and reminded myself to breathe. "Don't do that ever again or I'll make it a point to throw up on you." *Do not cry. Be a big girl and keep your composure.*

Claire frowned. "Are you okay?"

*No, I'm not okay. I feel like I'm going to die of embarrassment.* "Could someone get me a drink? Juice, maybe?" I croaked.

Robert bolted to the refrigerator, bottles soon clinking against one another. "Sorry, but no juice. Soda? Milk? Water?"

"Water. Please. Yes."

My eyes closed again. I wanted to sleep—nobody here knew what they were doing. *Amateurs.* They were only succeeding in making me feel worse. *Can't you all leave me alone?*

Someone gently took my hand and placed the water bottle in my weak grasp. I looked at Claire and offered her a not-so-sincere smile. It didn't seem to lessen any of her terror. *Hasn't anyone seen a girl faint before?*

"Does your head hurt? Should I call an ambulance? How's your back? Can you see me? How many fingers am I holding up?" Claire rocketed through her questions frantically. "Somebody call 9-1-1!"

*Apparently not.* "No, Claire. Don't call an ambulance," I managed. "I fainted. I'm not dying."

I lifted my head and awkwardly sipped some water. The ringing in my ears subsided, the water filling my mouth with fresh saliva, the spinning room having, thankfully, abated. "My tummy just hurts."

My body went rigid when a hand began to rub my stomach tenderly. Glancing to my left, I found Lamont on the ground next to me, his eyes staring into mine with so much love and concern that I thought I might lose consciousness again. "I've never seen that happen before," he began, breaking eye contact. "Your eyes rolled back, and you wouldn't respond, and you really scared the living shit out of me—uh—us."

I wanted to smile to prove that I was fine, but my strong resolve was beginning to falter. *Again, with the great impression.* "Yeah, I'm sorry I scared all of you. Kinda snuck up on me too."

"No, I'm the one who should be sorry," Robert interjected. "I had no idea you couldn't look at pictures like that." Guilt washed over his face. "I feel really bad."

*Neither did I. A doctor who faints at the sight of a broken bone. I'm sure that'd make national news. Bring shame to prestigious Vaughn family.* I shuddered, suddenly frigid. Waving a hand in the air, I attempted to appear perfectly content. "You did nothing wrong. Really. Guess I have a vivid imagination. Fresh air would've helped." I chuckled and patted the tile floor. "I just didn't make it that far."

My peers laughed nervously, their shoulders finally relaxing. I, on the other hand, was trying to use any remaining strength to hide the anxiety wracking through my nervous system. Even my mother's nagging voice—*I told you ingesting sugar this late at night would lead to nothing but disaster*—was drowning beneath my legitimate worry that Lamont thought I was a freak and would never want to see me again.

To make matters worse, I was upset for being so weak. *What kind of doctor can't look at an X-Ray?* I sighed, again wishing I was alone so I could cry. *I'll never be a doctor.*

"Well, this is one way to sober everyone up." Claire knelt beside me and rested a comforting hand on my shoulder. "God forbid you fell on the carpet—no—you had to run to the *one* place in this *entire* apartment where there's tile."

I shrugged. "Could've fallen in the kitchen, cracked my head on the counter and bled to death."

"Not funny, Roxy."

"Hey, at least you fell gracefully." Lamont interlaced his fingers with mine and squeezed. "You even got the door open. Only a pro could do that."

"This may come as a surprise to you, but I don't pride myself for falling unconscious in front of a group of people—ballerina-like or not. Probably not something I would add to my list of accomplishments." *Or my list of un-accomplishments.* Lip trembling, I sniffled and focused on the blood making its way back to my brain. "Thanks for noticing, though." *Lamont is here holding your hand. He cares about your well-being.*

Lamont smiled and kissed my knuckles. "It was impressive, really."

The room spun again, my heart pumping air from one half of my body to the other too quickly. *Stop making me dizzy. I can't handle it anymore.*

"You think you can get up?" Claire asked.

I struggled to scoot my body up and rested on my elbows. When my stomach turned itself upside down, I shook my head and returned to my original position. "I need a few more minutes. Could you maybe get my car ready? Keys should be on the coffee table."

"Of course, Sweetie. Don't faint again, please."

As she grabbed my keys, I nodded. "I'll try my best. I think I've already ruined the night enough as it is."

"I'll be right back." Claire sprinted through the still-opened front door and nearly hopped the seven cement stairs leading down to the courtyard.

"Please, continue doing your own thing. Just pretend I'm not here. I find it's not difficult for my peers to do."

Robert chuckled. "Let me know if you need anything, okay? Again, I'm sorry."

He and Angelica began clearing off the beer pong table, leaving me to reflect on my embarrassment. To my surprise, Lamont remained seated on the ground beside me.

Although my body still tingled and my heart clenched into a fist of anxiety, taking note of the sincere worry burning through Lamont's eyes made my lungs swell full of the fresh air I needed earlier.

A few moments passed before the silence—and the tile—made me extremely uncomfortable. Ready or not, it was time I mustered the strength to move. "Can you help me lean against the wall really quick? I need to sit up if I have any intention of walking out of here without fainting again."

63

He nodded and moved out of the way, resting one hand on my lower back once I sat up, keeping the other tightly wound with mine. Smiling, I rested my head against the wall. *Maybe I'm an idiot, but at least he's still sitting with me.*

"You sure you're alright?" he asked. "Maybe you need a beer."

I laughed. "Somehow, I doubt that'll raise my blood sugar levels."

His shoulder touched mine when he joined me against the wall. "Have you ever tried it?"

"Yeah, no, not gonna happen. Besides, I have orange juice at home just waiting to spike my energy." I paused, gulped a large sip of water. "I'm sorry I ruined your night."

He squeezed my hand. "Shit happens. But didn't Claire say something earlier about you being a med—"

At that moment, Claire barreled through the front door, nearly trampling over Lamont and me. "You ready to walk? Car's here," she wheezed, breathing heavily.

I nodded, thankful Lamont wouldn't question my obvious lack of doctor material and shifted my body to stand. However, I was quickly stopped when he hopped up and pushed down on my shoulders.

"You're not walking outta here on your own. I'm gonna carry you."

My panic flared, heightening the nausea floating through my intestines. "No, I'm fine," I argued. "It's no big deal. You don't have to—"

I attempted to pry his hands from my shoulders, but he held firm. "Stop. Just let me help you."

"Look," I sighed. "That's really nice of you but you're drunk."

He glared at me. "Fine. Stand up then."

"I will." Stubbornly, I pushed myself into an upright position, trying to ignore my wobbly legs. "See? I told you. I'm—"

Lamont must've seen the weariness come to life in my eyes because he swiftly moved one arm beneath my knees and one arm behind my back, hoisting me close to his chest effortlessly. "I'm sorry. Were you going to say you're fine? Because I can feel you shaking."

Tears rose to my eyes and drowned my vocal chords. I tightened my grip and snuggled closer, refusing to let my crush see me cry. The smell of beer and tobacco tantalized the hairs of my nose, the comfort of his body surrounding mine and bringing peace to my nerves. "Thank you, Lamont," I whispered.

Once we made it safely down the stairs and to the street, he gingerly lowered me to my feet and held my arm as I unsteadily clambered into the car's passenger seat. "Just want to make sure you're alright." He kissed me on the forehead. "Claire's driving home. At least it's only across campus."

I smiled, my heart moving too fast, grateful for his sympathy.

When the door closed, I lowered my eyelids, absorbing the silence around me. Completely drained of energy, I was eager to get home where I could lock myself in my bedroom and cry without prying eyes judging me. As I inhaled a deep, calming breath, the driver's side door opened, the car shook, and the scent of beer and tobacco wafted through my nasal passages once again. Opening my eyes, I watched as Lamont pushed the driver's seat forward and somehow twisted his lanky limbs into the nearly nonexistent back seat.

Before I could ask what he was doing, he rested his palm on my left shoulder. "You promised me a ride home, remember? Besides, I wanna make sure you get inside your room safely. That way, if you feel weak again, I'll be there to hold you."

Claire sat down heavily, switching the car into drive.

I hazily watched the parking lot lights creep by. *Is this really happening? I must be dreaming. Lamont cares?* I fiddled with the bracelet absent-mindedly. *In what universe would that be true? I'm dreaming. It's only logical.* Except, Lamont twirled one of my curls around his finger and lightly brushed the skin of his hand against my cheek. *It's not a dream. I can feel it. He's feeling me.* My lungs hungrily devoured a balloon of air. *Maybe I should get out more often.*

"I'm so glad you came to see me tonight," Lamont breathed into my ear, his voice barely audible over Claire's mindless chatter.

I felt dizzy.

And all at once, I thought I might faint again.

#

IT TURNED OUT Lamont and Claire didn't have to walk me up the stairs because my energy had returned just in time for me to hug both of them and tiptoe into my room without waking the other girls.

Even though it was two-thirty in the morning, and I had to wake up for class in a few hours, I needed to talk to my best friend.

Tiffany answered the phone so loudly, I had to yank it away from my ear. "Where are you?"

She laughed. "The basketball team's house. They had a party after that sports thing. The volleyball girls are here."

I shook my head. "Be careful."

She laughed again. "Oh, puh-lease. I'm not an idiot. I know how to use a condom."

"Tiffany, you're drunk. Think about Brian."

"He cheats on me all the time. Why can't I?"

"Two wrongs don't make a right." Music began playing behind her, a mish-mash of voices making it difficult to focus. "You don't want to do that, Tiff. Those basketball boys are all just players—no pun intended."

"I already have a boyfriend. I need a good fuck."

More laughing ensued, followed by a boy's voice asking her to get off the phone.

"Fuck off. I'm talking to my best friend. You can wait," she shouted, her words rolling together into one giant syllable. "Roxy, what're you doing awake? Don't you have a quiz to fail first thing in the morning?"

I smiled. "That's why I called! I went over to one of Lamont's friend's dorms to hang out with him."

"No fucking way! You went out *and* saw Lamont? That's big night for you."

"And his friend showed me X-Rays of a broken bone and I fainted."

She laughed and laughed and laughed. "Are you kidding? Tell me you're kidding."

"I wish I were."

"Dude, Roxy, you have the worst luck. Are you okay?"

"Physically, yes. Emotionally, no."

Voices began shouting at Tiffany again, only louder this time. "I'm sorry, Roxy. I gotta go. Tell me when you're outta class and I'll come over. I miss you!"

She hung up the phone before I could reply. Shaking my head, I stood to change into my pajamas. "This is why I don't like to go out. You can faint, or you can cheat on your boyfriend, or you can fall in love with someone you barely know." I sighed. "She's gonna sleep with one of those guys. I just know it."

#

"WHAT WERE YOU doing drinking a Slurpee at some stranger's house on a Wednesday night?"

I instantly regretted calling my mother. Seeking comfort after having a miniature emotional breakdown, cradling the little stuffed dog until I thought its head might pop off, I realized that I was craving real love from the woman who brought me into this world. However, instead of receiving a virtual hug, I'd gotten a slap to the face.

"How many times have I told you not to intake sugar after eight at night?"

"I know Mom, but—"

"No buts little Missy. You know better. You're studying pre-med. You need to take care of your body."

"Yeah Mom, I know, but—"

"Do you know how late it is? I have patients at seven-thirty. I have to wake up in three hours. You know I don't drink caffeine. I can't afford to lose any sleep."

"I'm sorry Mom, I just—"

"Vaginas won't check themselves, you know. You have no idea what sorts of issues I have to look at every day. Do you know how heartbreaking it is to see a fifteen-year-old receive her first examination only to realize she's got Chlamydia? Her first time having sex. No condom. You use condoms, right?"

"Mother! Isn't Dad sleeping right next to you?"

A slight pause. "Oh, he's snoring like a bear."

I shook my head, my cheeks burning. "I'm gonna go. I'm sorry I called you so late. But first, how's Molly? I miss the little polar bear."

I could almost feel my mom's smile. The dog was the one thing we ever seemed to agree on. "She's doing great. Your father put her on a diet because she's getting a little thick. I would say fat, but I swear she understands me when I say that, and she just winds up moping around the rest of the day. I'm sure she misses you."

*Yeah…I know the feeling.* "I'm glad she's doing good. It's okay if she's fat. She's getting old—she deserves to eat whatever she wants."

My mom chuckled. "And that's why obesity is running rampant through America. People think because they 'only live once' they can eat like cows."

I snorted. "Again, I'm sorry I called you this late. Thank you for answering."

"How's school going?"

*Horribly. I'm going to fail.* "Fine."

"No more shenanigans. We're paying for you to go to school to get a degree in Biology, not in Boys."

I didn't have the heart to tell her that her daughter was knocked out cold because of a picture of an X-Ray, not because she drank a small Slurpee at an ungodly hour. "Yes, Mother. I know, Mother."

*I can't be a doctor. I can't even look at a picture of a broken bone. I'm gonna disappoint my parents. I'm gonna taint the Vaughn name.*

Claire walked into my room and found me lying on my bed staring at the small cracks in the ceiling, my spirits beaten and bruised.

She sat down beside me, my mattress tilting slightly. "Roxy, do me a favor and *never* do that *ever* again," she said, brushing a stray hair away from my face. "I think I've suffered from a minor heart attack. Do you think you could check my vitals?"

"Sorry, but I might faint again," I mumbled bitterly.

She frowned. "Hey, hey, hey—I was kidding. What's going on?"

"In a stupid moment of weakness, I called my mother. I was hoping she'd make me feel better, but she beat me into the ground. I'm a failure, Claire. I'm training to be a doctor and I fainted tonight. That's inexcusable."

"Don't let her get to you." She patted my arm. "You live your own life. You're just getting into this whole 'doctor' thing. Maybe you gotta desensitize yourself. It was just a rough night."

I shrugged. "The one night I decide to blow off studying, I screw up. It's just so typical."

"Before you beat yourself up—" Claire rose from the bed and began pacing across the cheaply carpeted floor. "I just—do you—you really like Lamont, huh?"

"Why do you care?"

"Just answer the question."

I looked at her, startled. "You want the honest answer?"

Claire opened her mouth, closed it, and continued to pace.

"Is there something bothering you?"

Turning to face me, she collapsed melodramatically into my computer chair. "I don't know. He has a girlfriend."

I sighed. "If you're going to lecture me—"

"No," she said. "It's not that. He just—he had *a lot* to say about you on the way home."

My body jerked upright, my hands instinctively wrapping around my knees in an attempt to protect my feelings. "What are you talking about?"

She hesitated. "Do you promise you won't freak out?"

Although I knew it was a lie, I nodded. "I promise."

"He *really* likes you. Roxy, I'm serious. He wouldn't stop telling me how beautiful you are—how funny—how sweet—how fun—God. He wouldn't shut up. It was actually kind of annoying."

My hands began to shake. "He—he—he—no. You're lying. After everything that happened? There's no way."

Claire looked away and bit her lip. "Just remember that he's drunk—don't let him get into your head."

*My head? It's way too late for that. I'm worried about him completely commandeering my heart.* "I'm just sitting here. Listening."

She nodded. "As bad as this is, he even mentioned that he thinks about you when he's with the girlfriend. It was hard to understand because he kept mumbling and jumbling his words together, but I thought he said something about a break up."

I rolled my head from side to side and attempted to relax my shoulders. *Don't freak out. Don't freak out.* "You're for real? He doesn't think I'm a freak?"

She shook her head. "He's worried about you. He also wanted me to remind you to bring him back to his truck after class."

*Worried? About me?* "Well, I have to wake up in—what—three hours? Hopefully, I won't fall asleep at the wheel."

Claire stood to leave. "Don't joke. I just saw you fall to the floor." She paused and leaned against the doorframe. "Roxy, Lamont said some *really* sweet things about you. Don't get me wrong—I'm glad he cares about my friend—but *please* be careful. He's drunk. And he might just be saying those things because the beer's talking."

"But—but what—" I bit my nail. "What if he's telling the truth?"

"Only time will tell." She sighed. "Look, it would break my heart if he hurt you. I told you because he wouldn't shut up and I'd feel bad hiding it from you."

After she closed the door, I released the grip I had on my knees and lay back.

"So what if I'm in a family of doctors and I fainted?"

Endorphins flooded my body with happiness.

"Roses are red, violets are blue—"

My cheek muscles twitched, a smile plastered to my face.

"I like Lamont and he likes me too!"

My eyes fluttered closed. *He wants to break up with her. He thinks about me. When he's with her.* I fell asleep not worried about my quiz, about fainting or about my awkward behavior in most social situations.

Cloud nine kept me warm.

I dreamt I was snuggled beside Lamont, a book of poetry clasped tightly against my chest.

#

"I'M GOING HOME to see my girlfriend," Lamont informed me the following morning. "I need to get laid."

A scalpel pierced through my aorta. My legs twitched from lack of blood flow. My hands involuntarily tightened around the steering wheel. Even my teeth began to grow tender from clenching my jaw. *No tears. No tears. No tears.* "That should be fun," I managed without sounding uninterested or unkind. Or like he'd just opened the car door and watched me roll across the asphalt, laughing and pointing at my inevitable death. *No tears. No tears. No tears.*

He leaned back in his chair and mumbled, "Sex is the only good thing—if she'll even put out. She cries if I don't come visit every weekend and cries when I leave. I hate when girls cry."

*No tears. No tears. No tears.*

Glancing over, I noticed just how hungover he was. Sunglasses, a wrinkled t-shirt, basketball shorts with a tear at the hem and two socks that were completely mismatched—one grey and one red, one ankle and one crew.

A complete mess.

I, on the other hand, had taken the time to race home after class to cover the bags under my eyes with makeup, spritz myself with perfume and throw my curls into a purposefully messy ponytail, even though my fingers had gotten stuck in the knots and tangles I hadn't been able to comb out due to my lack of shower.

I'd taken my Anatomy quiz half-asleep and accepted the fact that I was destined to fail.

Except the professor returned last week's quiz and I'd somehow managed to get a D.

I drove to Lamont's house feeling as if I'd smoked a blunt—high and completely carefree, and ready to take a nap.

And then Lamont had to go and ruin everything. *I hate you right now.* "How much did you drink last night? You barely played two games?"

He burped and rolled down the window. "I puked when I woke up, so that made me feel better."

70

I wrinkled my nose. "Please spare me those details."

"A bunch of guys got together before the pep rally. We drank Sailor Jerry. Then I drank before you showed up to Robert's." He shrugged. "I blacked in and out." He pulled a small, round container from his pocket and tapped it against his palm. "Do you have a water bottle?"

I reached behind my chair and found the bottle I'd thrown into the back in a last-minute attempt to clean out the trash from the floor of my front seat—something I'd ignored the previous night because I was too busy attempting to look okay when I clearly was anything but.

"That's unnerving. You carried me down a flight of stairs and to the street. What if you fell?"

He snorted, unscrewing the container's lid. "Seeing you faint sobered me up enough to make sure you were alive."

I watched him place a brown substance behind his bottom lip. "That stuff is awful for your health."

He smiled at me. "Better than chewing tobacco."

"Dip will still give you cancer."

"Everything gives you cancer."

I resisted making a snide comment. *Stop sounding like your mother. Boys don't like being told what to or what not to do. Let it slide. You're not his girlfriend. What you say doesn't matter.*

"Besides," Lamont continued, spitting a black substance into the bottle. "I know you think it's sexy."

"Right," I laughed, not liking the tingling sensation making my lower half squirm in my seat. "Does your girlfriend?"

He shrugged, oblivious to the crack in my voice. "She doesn't care. If she asked me to quit, I probably would."

*Of course, you would. I'm sure you're just the perfect boyfriend. Just not when you're with me.* "Sounds like you're both happy together."

He yawned loudly, stretching both arms out until they touched the dashboard. "Yeah. I've known Melanie for a while now."

I cringed. *She has a name.* Hearing the three syllables roll off his tongue made her existence painfully real. Even seeing her picture on Facebook hadn't crystalized her reality like this. "That's good." Words escaped me. I wanted to sit in an uncomfortable silence, turn on the radio—*anything* except talk about *Melanie* any longer.

"At least I get sex every weekend. Except when she's on her period. I stay here and prefer to masturbate than deal with her crying every time she feels an emotion."

I hit the brakes harder than intended. "Well, when you can have the real thing, why settle for less?"

His laughter lifted the pressure wrapped around my lungs. Usually, I kept my sassy remarks to myself, afraid that nobody would laugh. This was a bad sign—I was getting too *comfortable* around him despite the underlying anxiety swimming in my stomach. And that meant my feelings for him had intensified— which was not good because he had a *girlfriend* named *Melanie* and they have sex *every weekend*. We sat in silence for a few minutes, his frequent spits creating an easy and unforced way to break any remaining tension tugging on my vocal chords. His statement lingered in my ears, plaguing my brain with vivid images of them in bed together: her on top, him behind, her wearing a lacy bra, his face when he climaxed, her groaning and shouting his name.

I bit the inside of my cheek. "So, I wanted to thank you for helping me last night. I hope I didn't embarrass you in front of Robert or anything."

We pulled into the deserted parking lot beside his giant, white truck.

"I wasn't the one who fainted. I have nothing to be embarrassed about." He opened the passenger side door and closed it roughly.

"Right. Thanks for that." I followed suit and stood awkwardly in front of him, hoping my jeans and tank top looked great without seeming like I changed my outfit six times before settling on something overtly simple. "As if I wasn't already completely mortified by the entire situation."

He smirked. "Shit happens. Glad I could help."

After he gave me a half-hearted hug, he grabbed my wrist. "I do believe it's my turn to wear this."

I glared. "That's not fair. I've barely even worn it."

"Rules state that we switch whenever we see each other." He held out his hand, palm up. "So, hand it over."

Reluctantly, I gave it back, my wrist feeling far too light and my heart far too heavy. "Have fun this weekend." *I hope you think about me whenever you look down at your wrist.*

I ducked back into the car and drove the short distance to the parking lot behind my dorm. I couldn't get a solid grasp of Lamont's character—it was as if he were two different people.

The previous night, he'd swept me off my feet and later proclaimed his love for me to my roommate.

And now, he reluctantly gave me a hug, making it a point to bring his girlfriend to life.

I placed my forehead on the steering wheel and finally allowed the tears to fall.

*I should hate him. Why can't I hate him?*

#

I WAS ALMOST positive that life couldn't get worse, but a phone call from my sister proved me wrong.

"I have news," she squealed into my ear. "Roger and I are pregnant. Sissy, I'm gonna have a baby!"

The normal reaction of any good sister would've been genuine excitement. I, on the other hand, foresaw the cradle's shadow looming over me, my family oohing and awing over another child prodigy while I slept in a cardboard box in the alley. *Maybe I missed the memo that sex is the new thing to do on weekends.*

"That's great!" I feigned excitement. "About time you guys stopped caring about yourselves and start caring about someone else."

She didn't seem to hear me. "We're so excited! Mom'll be the one who delivers the baby and hopefully, Dad can get rid of any stretch marks I might develop during the whole process."

As Lucy continued to ramble on and on about how she was gonna be a cute pregnant woman and "not one of those beached whales who succumbs to their disgusting pregnancy cravings," I wondered if I should tell her that her living and breathing younger sister was thinking about straying away from the family fame to become something that didn't involve hospitals or clinics or scrubs or white lab coats.

"Lucy, there's something I really need to tell you."

She stopped talking. "I swear to God if you're pregnant, I'll kill you. This is my moment."

*Who are you kidding? Your entire life has been your moment.* "You have to have sex in order to get pregnant, if I remember correctly."

My door opened. "And lord knows you're too busy studying to have sex."

I looked up to find Tiffany smiling at me. Silently motioning for her to sit down and mouthing, "my sister" as I pointed to the phone, I barely caught the end of Lucy's sentence.

"...sex without a condom. What's the problem?"

73

"I don't think I can be a doctor anymore."

That produced a gasp from both Tiffany and my sister—only, Lucy's was filled with a tad more judgment, while Tiffany's was coated with a thick layer of shock.

"You've got to be kidding me."

I leaned against the wall. "Nope. I fainted when looking at an X-Ray last night."

"So. The fuck. What?" Anger and disappointment rang shrill in her normally angelic voice. "You're studying premed. You're in a family of doctors. Find a way to desensitize yourself and get over it."

"But what if I'm just not cut out for it?"

I could almost see her perfectly sculpted eyebrows furrowed so far down her face that they were resting on the bridge of her nose. "You're gonna give me fucking wrinkles. Stop being such a baby and get over it. Read the article I posted about facing your fears of medical school. I think it might help."

"That reminds me. Your last article had a ton of grammatical errors and typos. You should probably have someone—"

She laughed. "What're you? An English major? Talk to me when you own your own practice. Anyway, stop psyching yourself out. It was probably a fluke thing. I gotta call Mom and Dad to tell them the news. Love you, Sis!"

Per usual, she hung up before I could respond.

Tiffany whistled. "Are you sure you two are related?"

I shrugged. "I'm beginning to believe I was adopted despite the fact that I obviously share traits from both my parents' gene pools."

She shook her head. "Well, I have news that might make you feel less shitty."

"Yeah? And what's that?"

Her eyes watered slightly. "I cheated on Brian."

I sighed, realizing that we both needed a pizza and a really sad movie to make the pain go away. I still had to tell her about Claire's and Lamont's conversation, and my brief encounter with the devil himself this morning. "And how is this supposed to make me feel better?"

A half-smile and a shrug. "Misery loves company?"

I couldn't help but laugh. "You pick a movie out of my stash and I'll order the pizza."

"Thanks Roxy. You really are my best friend."

I nodded, already standing to hold her while she cried. "You tell me about what happened. Everything is going to be okay."

But even I had a hard time believing that.

#

IT WAS A Tuesday like any other. I spent part of my day in class, managed to workout at the gym with Tiffany in an attempt to be healthy, and avoided studying for my Anatomy quiz like a small child avoids the dentist.

It was ordinary, that is, until my phone buzzed, pulling me out of my desk chair and away from the poetry of William Blake.

I ran to Claire's room hoping for some advice. She was sprawled out across her bed reading from a large textbook. However, I didn't feel guilty for my interruption because she never hesitated to barge into my room and distract me.

Closed doors had become a rare find in our household.

"Sorry to be a bother, Claire, but I am in urgent need of your help," I said, abruptly sitting cross-legged on the floor.

"I'm studying for a test," she replied, clearly flustered. "Can't this wait?"

"No, it can't. I wouldn't have said it was urgent if I thought we could discuss it tonight over dinner." Again, my sass surprised me. *What's wrong with me? It's like my filter is on the fritz.* "I'll only take ten minutes away from your study time. Ten minutes *tops*." I was desperate. Even though I believed Claire was a little too flirtatious for my liking, she could help me when it came to boys. Or, at least, I could deduce certain information and figure out the rest with some careful analysis and planning—sometimes a quick Google search could do the trick. "Seriously, Claire. Just one answer and I'll be out of your hair."

"About what?" Amber asked from the doorway. "I could use a study break."

Claire slammed her book down at the foot of her bed. "Apparently, she needs help."

Amber rolled her eyes. "I figured out that much, thanks for clearing it up."

"It's about a boy," I mumbled, fidgeting with my fingers.

"A boy, huh?" Amber smiled. "Lizzy! Shannon! Get your asses up here, now! We have an emergency—Roxy needs boy advice," she shouted down the stairs.

After a minor stampede and a quick impromptu game of musical chairs, I found myself surrounded by my four roommates, each focusing their undivided attention on me.

75

"Now this is a day I didn't think would come any time soon," Elizabeth said, hands wrapped around her ankles.

"Yeah," Shannon agreed. "I didn't even know you talked to boys."

I rolled my eyes. "Are you gonna help me or make fun of me?"

They giggled, urging me to continue.

"I'd like to preface this by letting you *all know* this has *nothing* to do with Lamont. So, you shouldn't be that excited."

They all heaved heavy sighs, whether in relief or disappointment, I couldn't decipher.

"Honestly, until the girlfriend is out of the picture, you should probably avoid any contact with him," Elizabeth suggested.

"Well, since that will never happen," I spat bitterly, "I'm doing my best to ignore him completely."

"If this isn't about Lamont—"

"Then who have you been talking to?" Amber interrupted Claire.

Again, I fidgeted with my fingers, wishing I had the bracelet on my wrist to keep my nervous ticks at ease. "We haven't been *talking* in the way you all define *talking*. We text here and there—"

"Yeah, yeah, yeah," Shannon said, waving her hand in the air, completely dismissing me. "Just tell us who."

"Zachary Cameron."

"Ohhh. The hunky swimmer?" Amber asked.

I looked at Claire. "I see you've taken the liberty of filling everybody in on my life."

She shrugged. "We gossip sometimes. He's hot. I have no other explanations."

"Oh, who cares? What did the text say?" Elizabeth asked.

I pulled out my cellphone and read aloud from the latest text on the screen: "Hey. I'm gonna be in Nor Cal visiting a friend in a few weeks. I thought I should tell you I'm only gonna be two hours away."

The girls were beaming at me obnoxiously.

I glanced down at the pale pink bottoms of my bare feet and blushed.

"Do you think he wants to come visit?" Amber questioned.

"Of course, he wants to visit!" Shannon shouted. "Why else would he say that?"

I shrugged. "No—I don't know. He probably felt obligated to tell me because it would be—awkward if he didn't? Or something?"

76

Claire shook her head. "Get your head out of your ass. He obviously likes you."

"Well, should I invite him over? Ask him what his plans are? Completely ignore the text and pretend I never read it?"

Shannon frowned.

"Don't look at me like that," I countered. "This is why I need help. I suck at this stuff. Help me stop overthinking this."

Amber smirked. "I know what the *real* question is lurking in the back of your mind." She elbowed Elizabeth's ribs and giggled. "You're wondering if you should have sex with him."

"No. Nononono," I argued aggressively. "That's the last thing on my mind. I just don't know what to think or how to feel. The last time we talked was heartbreaking. Like—the last time we tried having something romantic. Texting is one thing. Seeing him in person is something *totally* different. I'm scared."

"What are you scared about?" Claire stretched out her legs.

"Looking like an idiot. Taking this whole situation completely out of context. Falling for him all over again only to have him tell me he's no longer interested."

The girls slyly glanced at one another and then smiled at me.

I began to lose my patience. "You guys, please. I'm not going to sleep with him. We thought about doing it once and it was bad—he couldn't unhook my bra." I sighed. "You would've thought it was our first time ever seeing another person naked. I couldn't go through with that again."

When their smiles widened, I threw my hands in the air. "You know I don't sleep around. What would make this any different?"

Elizabeth laughed. "Maybe he wants to prove he knows how to have sex now."

"I doubt that. He hates me. He broke my heart and got another girlfriend right away. You don't do that to someone you care about."

"Sweetie," Amber cooed softly. "If he hated you, he wouldn't text you. He wouldn't tell you he's gonna be within driving distance. He's obviously trying to fix things."

"Yeah, he's willing to drive up the state to see you. That has to mean something, right?" Shannon chipped in.

"You should invite him to visit. You don't *have* to hook up with him. Maybe seeing him will be fun," Claire suggested.

"Just be ready to drink." Elizabeth winked.

"I don't like to drink," I admitted. "I'm way too afraid of losing control. What if I do or say something I'm going to regret?"

"It's not that bad, I promise," Shannon said. "It might help you loosen up a bit."

"Yeah," Claire agreed. "You'll get over your fears. Just ease yourself into it."

"You should probably get started as soon as possible. Zach isn't even here yet and I can see your hands shaking."

"I don't want to drink. And I don't want to sleep with him."

Shannon sighed. "I know I can be pretty shy, but Roxy, I've really come out of my shell. You need to let yourself live. Be spontaneous."

"Stop thinking with the logical side of your brain and embrace the irrational," Elizabeth said.

*The girls are right. Live a little. Let some of the control go. Invite Zach to spend the night.* I gulped, my stomach knotting and unknotting with every breath I failed to slow. "So," I coughed, my voice suddenly strained. "Now that I've distracted all of you from your studies, any vodka suggestions?"

#

DESPITE MY SHEER exhaustion, I had somehow managed to keep my heavy eyelids open while my white-haired professor spoke passionately about William Blake. I hadn't managed to read all of the poems assigned for class discussion, but I gazed admirably at the wrinkled woman who so clearly loved her job—who so clearly loved the written word and shared her knowledge with those who secretly wished they were born into a family that wasn't so demanding and condescending.

I flipped through the pages as the professor discussed potential themes present within the selected poems that had been assigned. My pen wiggled from one side of the notebook to the other, trying to jot down every word that came from the professor's pale, chapped lips.

I hated that the students around me were uninterested when nothing but beauty was scrawled across the pages in front of them. They were texting, doodling pictures in the corners of their books, drooling all over the wonderful images written from the brilliant poets of the past.

And that's when the realization hit me like a blacksmith's hammer atop an anvil.

# Chapter Four

*This is how everyone sees me in Anatomy. I'm just taking up space in a class where some sad students hadn't been able to register in time, setting them back in their medical studies.*

I stopped writing and reread the words printed on the PDF documents covered in notes—they were much different from the stark pages found in my Anatomy binder. Something inside my gut was telling me to prepare for an unexpected change; the missing puzzle pieces to my happiness were slowly being put into place. The solution was hidden somewhere in the rhyme and meter of Blake's work.

I just hoped that the Lamb, the Tiger, and the Chimney Sweeper would give me the courage to stray off the path I was destined and discover what it is, exactly, that would finally take away the darkness poisoning my soul, allow me to live— outside of the shadow of my sister—and to make me understand what it means to actually be alive.

#

COMPLETELY IGNORING THE voice of reason that usually aided in my decision making, I ran outside, my soft feet being scathed by the rough cement and asphalt—I'd been so nervous, shoes hadn't come to mind—and made my way to the parking lot.

Even for someone as socially uncomfortable as me, I'd reached an all-time low. Creeping stealthily over the pebble covered black top, I peeked inside the windows of every big, white truck that came into view.

Not only were bystanders giving me suspicious glances once they noticed me prowling around unattended vehicles, but I felt guilty for sneaking around because I was afraid of running into any of my roommates.

Lamont had texted me, wondering if we could hang out before his class.

Rather than weigh the pros and cons of the situation, I'd wordlessly left the dorm, quickly responding that we should meet up in the parking lot. Although highly unlikely, I wanted to sneak him up the stairs and through my bedroom door without any of the girls noticing. Hiding a 6'5 athlete would take skill, but I was determined not to expose my true feelings to my roommates, especially because they'd told me to be weary of Lamont countless times.

But there was a flaw that prevented me from executing this clever plan.

I couldn't find Lamont.

Not anywhere.

*How is it that 75% of the students at this school drive big white trucks?*

As my embarrassment, anxiety and general frustration intensified, I did the unthinkable.

I called him.

"Where on earth are you?" I asked haughtily. "I'm running around the parking lot looking for you. Are you aware of the ridiculous population of large white trucks that park on campus during weekdays?"

"Why are you in the parking lot?"

I pulled the phone away from my ear and stared at it incredulously. *Because I like looking like an idiot, obviously.* "Lamont, I'm looking for you. I told you to meet me in the parking lot."

"Well, I'm in your living room with Claire. So, you should probably come home."

"You're with—you're what?"

"I'm with Claire in your—"

I hung up the phone and ran, not caring that people were laughing at me and not caring that my feet felt like they've been worn down to the bone.

*Stupid. Stupid stupid stupid. This is bad. Bad bad bad.* I slowed my pace as I rounded the corner and tried to steady my breathing when I reached the front door. *Oh man. I really need Tiffany to force me to go to the gym and get me in shape.* Before making my grand entrance, I tried to pat down any frizzy hairs, wiped dried saliva from the corners of my mouth and straightened out my white and blue striped t-shirt. *Play it cool.*

Claire was in the kitchen making a sandwich and Lamont was lounging on the couch as if he lived there.

"You didn't mention anything about Lamont coming over," she said, spreading mayonnaise on her bread a little too aggressively.

*That's because I didn't want to face the Spanish Inquisition.*

I smiled at Lamont who stood to greet me. "This wasn't planned," I mumbled, my cheek smashed into Lamont's chest. "He asked if he could stop by before class because he had to bring Chris to campus earlier than usual."

"Well, isn't that convenient." The way she was twisting the lid made me feel sorry for the innocent condiment jar.

Lamont released me and sat back on the couch. "Claire found me wandering around on her way home from dance."

"Why didn't you wait in the parking lot?"

He shrugged. "I found a parking spot by the dumpster outside. And your dorm was right here. Guess I got lucky."

"Of course, you did. Thanks for making my manhunt futile."

Claire threw the knife into the sink. "What're you gonna do?"

Lamont patted the cushion beside him. "Roxy said she has a movie that's *so great*. I want to see just how *great* it is."

Instead of sitting where his hand was inviting me, I separated myself from his touch, afraid that any remaining rational behavior would go by the wayside if we even made the subtlest of contact.

"Claire, did you want to watch it with us?'

She slammed the refrigerator door closed and turned to glare at me. "Thanks, but no thanks. I have a test to study for. You kids have fun. Don't do anything I wouldn't do."

I couldn't help but feel guilty. *I'll study for my quiz when he leaves. He has class in two hours. I could use a break from school.* "Good luck studying! Feel free to come down if you change your mind."

When she continued up the stairs, I pushed play and smiled at Lamont. "You just wait. I know good movies."

He scooted closer. "I'm excited to see what I've been missing all this time."

The scent of Copenhagen wafted through my nose and into the crevices of my brain. His voice was too sexy, his body too warm. I could feel the little better judgment hanging on for dear life quickly losing its grip. Thankfully, before I experienced a full-fledged panic attack, Elizabeth emerged through the back door. Though slightly taken aback from Lamont's unexpected presence, she swiftly raised and lowered her eyebrows before extending him a warm welcome.

"Mind if I join?"

"The more, the merrier," I chirped, relieved.

She sat in the chair, opened her laptop and quietly stared at me over the top of her screen.

#

"YOU GONNA FOLLOW him or sit here as awkwardly as possible?" Elizabeth asked after Lamont excused himself to use the restroom.

The movie was almost over, and I'd ignored every attempt Lamont had made to get close to me. Of course, I wanted to hold his hand, but I was too afraid that my palms would be sweaty, my fingers squeezing too tight, or that it would lead to something I was too awkward to follow through with.

Mainly, I didn't want to be a complete ignoramus.

Again.

He was still dating Melanie, so this had been intended as a friendly get together.

But every time he laughed, my heart would urge my brain to stop fighting my true feelings and simply kiss the guy.

"You're talking crazy," I replied coolly. "Following him to the bathroom would be more awkward than awkwardly sitting here. That's pretty unsanitary if you ask me."

She snorted. "You're not good at playing dumb."

My shoulders slumped forward. "Lizzy, he has a girlfriend. We're just friends."

"Roxanne, you need to get your head out of your ass and open your eyes." She looked at the clock. "If I'm not mistaken, his class starts in—oh wait—it started over an hour ago, and yet, he's still here. *With you.* What do you think that means?"

"It means that he was really into the movie?"

"Girl, stop. I know you're shy when it comes to this kind of stuff, but you need to learn how to take a chance. The tension in this room is making me horny. Go up there and tell me all the dirty details later. If anyone deserves to get laid in this house, it's you."

I gulped. "Don't say it like that. You're making me even more nervous."

She smiled. "Sweetie, go. People always say there's no time like the present—or some shit, right? We both know you'll regret it if you don't."

Nodding, I stood and stiffly walked over to the staircase. When I took the first step, I heard Lamont making his way back down. My heart thudded against my lungs. *Don't back down. You can do this. Lizzy's right. Take a chance. This is an opportunity to live.* I found it difficult to breathe, but I continued to step up those stairs, continued moving forward.

Lamont and I met halfway.

I looked up into those eyes, those brown beauties stopping time around me. Unsure of my ability to be seductive, and even more unsure of how he'd react, I took two hesitant steps toward him. He wrapped his arms behind my lower back and pulled me against his body.

He'd made his move.

Now, it was my turn. *If I walk away, that'll be it. I can pretend nothing ever happened and continue hiding in my room—always wondering what if, busying myself with school. But, is that what I want?* I angled my face upward and smiled. Despite the fact that I feared rejection and heartbreak, when he returned a lazy grin, nothing else mattered. *It's just him and me. Right here. Right now.*

Standing on my tippy-toes, I dangled my arms over his shoulders, daring him to—praying, really—make the next move.

A slight eyebrow arch followed by a sly smirk—a slight lean forward, eyes closed.

And then a kiss, so tender, you could cut it with a plastic spoon.

Rationality and logic were quickly replaced by a desire I only studied in romance novels. I became fully aware of every minute detail: his soft hold on my hips, the spicy tang of Copenhagen rolling over my taste buds, the feathery texture of his hair, and his hard presence slowly pushing against my belly.

Even though I was extremely nervous, I didn't want the moment to stop.

"How about we finish that movie in your room?" he whispered against my lips.

Until he said that.

*My room? Alone?* "The girls might get suspicious," I mumbled, struggling to let my inhibitions go.

"I don't care what they think."

"I have a quiz to study for."

He blinked once. "That can wait."

"Well," I whispered, biting my lip. "What about your class?"

His brown eyes bore into mine. "Fuck class. I need to be here. With you."

Breathless and eager, I nodded, my body yearning for him. I slowly wrapped my fingers around his and led him to the bedroom.

Lamont silently followed and closed the door behind us.

# Chapter Five

I DID EXACTLY what everyone had been engraining into my brain—I was embracing spontaneity and letting go of rationality. Lamont and I were merely experiencing a spur-of-the-moment reaction to two friends having a great time together.

Lamont's hot breath made my spine shiver. When he wrapped his arms around me, spooning my body flawlessly alongside his, I couldn't help but question my present state of being. *Am I really awake or have I been dreaming this whole time?*

I spotted his bracelet, almost forgetting the game we'd made at Robert's dorm. Smiling, I wiggled my arm free from his embrace and slowly crept my fingers up his hand, firmly grasping onto the black rubber band. "I do believe it's my turn to take that bracelet."

He chuckled. "I was more focused on you."

I pulled the bracelet off his wrist and moved it over to my own. "I have a hard time believing that."

"Are you kidding?"

I shrugged. "No, not at all. I'm nothing special."

He snuggled me closer. "Roxy, you're beyond special." Lamont's heart raced against my back, keeping pace with mine. It was as if no clothes were between us, just our skin, muscle and bone coming together as one.

Thinking like one of my roommates, I tried to play off my insecurities as a flirtation device. "Well, if I'm so special, you should just let me keep the bracelet forever."

His right leg covered mine. "Where's the fun in that?"

I rubbed my fingers up and down his arm, trying and failing to fight against my jitters. We were fully clothed, but we were in my room.

With the door locked.

On my bed.

All alone.

After taking a steady breath, I focused my attention on the tiny television screen, the images blurring behind the questions plaguing my mind.

*What about Melanie?*

*What if roles were reversed and she were doing this to me?*

*Why am I even here?*

*Why do I think I can trust him?*

I shivered involuntarily, my anxiety beginning to compromise the cool and collected façade I was trying to portray. *He has a girlfriend. Melanie is a real person with real feelings. This is wrong.* But being encased in his arms felt so right.

"Guess we're not gonna finish that movie, huh?" Lamont mumbled.

*Guess I'm not gonna get any studying done for my quiz tonight, huh?* "I didn't really get the chance to go get it, did I? I could go grab it really quick."

He interlaced his fingers with mine, pulling me even tighter against his chest. "No. I like cuddling with you. Screw the movie."

When I felt his hard response against my butt, my muscles stiffened, and my heart ceased to pump blood to my brain. *Being drunk and kissing me is one thing. I understand how he can forgive himself for that. But to really cheat on Melanie—sober and completely in control of the situation? Did something happen over the weekend? Did they fight? Is she on her period? Does any of that matter?*

"But it's a really good movie," I argued weakly, making a final attempt to be a decent human being.

"I doubt it's better than this."

My selfish feelings had stomped all over the want to respect Lamont's relationship with Melanie—love trumped shame on all costs. *The girls are gonna kill me. But it's been so long since I've felt like this. Since I've cuddled with someone like this.* As the emotional hemisphere of my brain raged against the logical one, the need to make a moral choice fell lower and lower on my list of priorities. *I don't want to be the other woman. I don't want to be second best.*

Lamont shifted behind me, interrupting my thoughts. He released my hand and began to trace the contours of my body with the pads of his fingertips. From the seam on the shoulder of my shirt to the pocket of my sweatpants, his delicate touch left my hair standing upright. When he moved my shirt and made direct contact with the skin of my hips, the sensuality disappeared.

My body ached to squirm, giggles beginning to rise up my throat. The *last* thing I wanted to do was ruin the moment. But his gentle caress was *tickling* me. I grabbed onto his hand and squeezed, hoping that the action appeared flirtatious rather than aggressive. "I'm sorry," I said sweetly. "But I can't have you do that."

He propped himself onto his elbow and looked at me quizzically. "Are you ticklish?"

The wicked grin on his face ignited my stubborn flame. "No," I spat, turning my back to him. "I'm not ticklish."

"Well then," he said, uninterested. "I see no problem doing—*this*."

Pulling his hand free of my grasp, he forced me onto my back and began to tickle the sweet spots beneath my ribcage mercilessly.

My sides began to cramp from laughter. *Why didn't I see that coming?* Trying and failing multiple times to grab his hands, my frustration and the pain threshold of my abs had reached its peak. "Lamont, please—" I begged, nearly out of breath. "Please—st—stop." I feared my face was turning purple, unable to hide behind the extra foundation I'd applied when I escaped to the bathroom the moment the movie first began. "I—I can't—no—no—no more."

The stupid grin of triumph on his face morphed into a nervous smile. His hands now rested beside both of my arms and his lips were hovering directly above mine.

*Look at you, Casanova. Touché.* "I see what you did there."

The chemistry that had been bubbling in the beaker of sexual desire exploded between us, our bodies gravitating closer and closer to one another.

"Are you impressed?"

I nodded mutely, afraid that talking would waste what little air remained in the room. Lightheaded and shaky, I feared that I would faint from overwhelming surrealism. *Why am I worth putting a wrench in his relationship with Melanie?* But before I could ask him any questions and ruin any chance of being intimate with him, Lamont dropped his mouth onto mine. My brain cautioned me against this behavior, but my heart burst out through my fingertips, gripping onto his hoodie, begging him not to stop.

As he lifted my shirt over my head, I prayed he wouldn't struggle with my bra and promised myself—no matter the outcome—that this would *not* leave the bedroom.

*I'm not this girl. This isn't okay.*

He moved down to my sweatpants.

*Oh my God. Don't stop.*

He kissed the inside of my thigh.

*I shouldn't be doing this. This isn't who I am. He's going to break my heart.*

He reached his hand up my stomach and cupped my breast.

*But you feel so, so good.*

I decided right then and there, that this would remain our little secret.

#

LAMONT NEEDED TO leave my room as quickly as possible. I was embarrassed by my behavior, and I was even more embarrassed about the fact that I wanted Lamont to spend the night because I didn't want to feel like a cheap hooker. However, before I could even consider how to sneak him past my roommates in the morning, Lamont sat up, swung his legs off the bed and pulled his clothes on silently. Covering my exposed breasts with the flimsy white sheet, I promptly wondered if I'd done something wrong.

As he laced up his shoes, he shot a quick glance in my direction.

My lungs inhaled a hushed gasp.

*Oh my God. He regrets it. He wants nothing to do with me anymore. I gave him what he wanted—he doesn't need me.*

I grabbed my shirt off the lampshade and shyly shuffled through the wrinkled comforter to find my sweatpants. After awkwardly maneuvering my body into my clothes, I sat on the bed beside him and hesitated before resting my hand on his thigh.

"Is everything okay?"

He subtly shook his head before thinking better of it and shrugged. "I need to get home."

Tears leapt to my eyes. "Did I do something?"

Lamont brushed my hand from his thigh and walked over to the door.

My limp limb fell onto the cold sheet.

"No, you didn't. I'm tired and my contacts hurt."

"You wear contacts? I didn't know that."

He nodded. "You don't know a lot about me."

"Oh." I didn't know what else to say, my heart pounding with a mixture of shame and anger. *Yeah, well there's a lot you don't know about me, either.* "You should probably take them out if they're bothering you. Contacts can hurt your eyes if they're too old."

He nodded again, not speaking.

*Why did I believe he would care?* There was no pillow talk, no cuddling or kissing. *Why did I believe I'd be pretty enough for him?* It felt as if he refused to be near me now that he'd seen what was hidden beneath the lid of the cookie car. *He doesn't want me.* My ego clawed at my insides in a desperate attempt to save itself. *I'm just another mistake.* When I sniffled, he turned to look at me. Even in the dim glow of the television, I could tell that he was unsure of what to do next. I shook my head. I was sad, confused, ashamed and flustered.

"Please try to be quiet on the way out." I walked over to him and wrapped my arms around his back. "I'm sure the girls are all asleep right now. I'd prefer you not wake them."

He didn't hesitate to return the hug and nodded his chin against my head.

But he still didn't say anything.

*Please tell me you think I'm beautiful. Please tell me I'm not some stupid mistake. Please tell me that I'm not an idiot for trusting you.*

I glanced up shyly and surprisingly, received a hard kiss—a small reminder that there was a spark between us, that there was a reason we shared our bodies.

A small hope flickered beyond my doubt. *Maybe he doesn't regret it.*

"Goodnight, Roxanne," he mumbled deeply.

*And maybe he'll never speak to me ever again.*

"Goodnight, Lamont."

After closing the door behind him, I pushed aside the stuffed dog that had been cradled between the pillow and the wall and crawled beneath the covers, unsure of how to analyze the multitude of feelings buzzing through me.

It had been difficult to connect our bodies together at first. He hadn't struggled to remove my clothes, which was pleasant, but he'd struggled to remain fully—alert. However, I was so intent on trying to get him to *see me* on an emotional level that the situation didn't make me feel awkward or uncomfortable. I coaxed him—*relax, don't be nervous*—in the hope that he'd get hard and I wouldn't shy away and cry for feeling inadequate.

Fat. Ugly.

I coaxed him to coax myself.

Because I was the one who was nervous.

My heart and body wanted him to become a part of me.

"But that's not okay. He has Melanie. Maybe he told Claire he likes me, but the girlfriend is *still* in the picture." I wanted to give myself wholly to Lamont to prove my true feelings for him. "But does he *actually* have feelings for me? Or am I just easy access to intercourse when Melanie's on her period?"

While I drifted into an uneasy sleep, I wondered why I dropped all of my barriers, allowing myself to fall so irrationally in love with a boy like Lamont Carwyn.

#

"YOU TWO HAD sex, didn't you?" Tiffany asked the following morning.

89

It was eleven. I'd woken up at five-thirty to study for my Anatomy quiz, pretending that I'd slept for the recommended eight hours instead of the realistic four and a half hours, received a C on last week's quiz, and now found myself sitting at a round table at the coffee shop across the street from the dorms.

Celebration coffee was a must.

And since Tiffany didn't have class until two, I invited her to join me.

We'd barely sat down at the table when she noticed the bracelet was back in my possession and nosily asked what I did last night.

I mentioned a movie and she jumped to her own—aggravatingly correct—assumption.

I choked back my mocha. "Wow," I managed after a brief coughing fit. "Do you even know me?"

She smiled. "Your hair is a fucking mess and you're wearing a white bra under a black shirt."

"And? What's that mean?"

"That you're a mess."

I snorted. "I was up late, and he was helping me study."

"You didn't shower this morning."

"Are you even listening?"

Tiffany nodded. "No matter how busy you are, you *always* shower because you don't like how knotted your hair gets when you sleep. You also *hate* when your bra shows beneath your shirts, and white shows through black. So, something happened that shook your routine. I'm assuming that would mean you engaged in some fuckery last night."

I flushed so red, my skin burned as if I'd walked into a radiation lab without proper protection. "If I tell you what happened, you can't tell anybody."

"Roxy," Tiffany said, reaching out to comfort me with her free hand. "I'm your best friend. You know you can tell me anything."

I rubbed my arm, watching my hair stand straight and lay against my skin over and over again. "It's not a pretty story."

She frowned. "Was he any good?"

"As much as I would love to weave a tale of passionate romance and phenomenal love making, I can't lie to you. Tiffany, it wasn't good. Not that I'm a veteran or anything, but the physical stuff didn't necessarily go as anticipated." I sipped my mocha, patiently awaiting her response.

"So," Tiffany drawled. "You mean to tell me that your expectations fell flat?"

"Not so much flat." I shrugged. "More like—limp."

She laughed so hard, she spit out green tea onto the ground beside us. "Oh my God. Oh my fucking God. I *cannot* handle this right now."

I attempted to disappear behind my coffee, my face a strawberry in a field of lemons. "Now, hang on," I argued defensively, filled with embarrassment. "It wasn't the *worst* sex I've ever had. Not that I'm a pro. You know—things happen. Maybe he was having a bad night or something."

A giant smirk spread across her face. "Does he—well—you know. How's he hanging down there?" She giggled.

The corner of my lip twitched. "You're asking too many questions."

"Oh, C'mon Roxy. I told you about the guy at the basketball house."

"Yeah. And I'm still emotionally scarred from the details."

She tapped her fingernails on the table. "We're not leaving here until you tell me."

We stared at one another in painful silence until my awkward meter began to overheat. "God—fine. Let's just say—how can I put this poetically? He's not what one might compare to a horse."

Tiffany slammed her hand on the table, face flushed with amusement. "I fucking knew it!"

Other café patrons swiveled in their chairs to look at us. "Sweet Jesus, Tiff. Can you take the volume down a notch? You're making a scene."

"I'm sorry but I fucking knew it."

"How can you even say that? You've never met the guy."

She shook her head. "There's no need. His hands were tiny in those Facebook pictures you showed me."

I frowned. "Who on earth pays attention to that kind of detail?"

"I do," she stated proudly. "I don't mess around. Small dicks are a waste of time and a serious waste of my energy."

"Can you stop before I jump into oncoming traffic?"

She sneered. "I'm just saying. Those are details you *need* to pay attention to. You study anatomy. You should know better than anyone."

"Tiffany, I am training to be a professional. Besides, if you're looking for a guy that resembles an elephant from the waist down, you're bound to have a disappointing sex life. Studies show that average—"

"So far, my methods have worked for the better."

"Can you be quiet and let me explain the situation before you continue to be obnoxious?"

She nodded, sipping her tea. "You've already gotten this far so don't leave out any details from here on out. I'll know if you're lying."

"Well, first off, he's *not* tiny, so just shut up about that." I then started from the beginning: running through the parking lot, Claire's suspicions, his attempts at showing me affection during the movie and Elizabeth's order to stop being such a coward. I described my feelings during our kiss shared on the stairs and the way we wound up cuddling together in my bed.

"And then he tickled me."

"You're kidding!" Tiffany cackled.

"Hey," I hissed. "What did I say about making a scene? Self-control."

"I'm sorry but I can't help it. That was his big move?"

I shrugged. "You know, technically, it worked."

She took a moment to reflect. "True. But you're a sucker for any attention he's willing to give you. Any move made in your direction would've charmed your pants off."

"Can't you give me the benefit of the doubt?"

"I don't mean any offense, but it's the truth. I calls 'em as I sees 'em."

I held up my hands, begging her to stop. "Tiff, I need you to listen. This is more than physical attraction. I think I love the guy."

She sipped her tea in a pensive silence. "Even after the awful sex?"

I nodded gravely. "Not that I go out and get wild every weekend, but even I know that what we shared would rank high on the scale of disappointment. I just—I don't care. Somehow, I still *want* to have sex with him. There was a real connection there—like, something surreal happened. Physically though, we struggled. Maybe the first time was a fluke. I wish I could try again."

A skeptical stare.

"He told me, straight up, he was nervous. I thought he had a problem because I wasn't attractive eno—"

"Stop right there. If you're gonna dis the way you look, I don't want to hear it."

I morosely sipped my coffee. *But it's happened before. Why else would a guy struggle to get an erection? Either you want to have sex, or you don't.*

"Look, if he wants to continue these rendezvous with you, he better get over his 'nervous' bullshit. There is no excuse if he's sober and under the age of sixty-five. Either he can get it up or get the fuck out."

I sighed, resting my forearms on the table. "He has a girlfriend. Shouldn't I feel guilty about that and not about the difficulty we had connecting physically?"

She wiggled her eyebrows. "How's it feel to be the other woman?"

"You're not helping."

She laughed. "Have him buy you a vibrator."

"This is why I don't talk about sex. Nobody takes me seriously."

"I'm only laughing to keep from crying."

I fiddled with the bracelet. "Shouldn't I feel like a terrible person?"

She shrugged. "He's made an impression on you. That's nothing to be ashamed of."

My stomach flipped around the coffee I swallowed. "I think I'm missing class today. I'd much rather wallow in self-pity."

She nodded. "You're suffering from a case of bad sex. Shit happens."

I smiled. "Thank you for not judging me."

"You're my best friend. There's nothing to judge."

#

MY LAB PARTNER held back my hair as I vomited into the trashcan located conveniently outside the laboratory's double doors. Tears streamed down my cheeks and mixed with the pastel colored cereal my body hadn't yet gotten the opportunity to fully digest.

"I'm sorry," I sobbed before another heave.

Andrew, my overtly homosexual, diva of a lab partner—and the only friend I'd been able to make in my classes this semester—rubbed my back.

"You didn't look hungover when you first walked in this morning."

I shook my head. "I'm not hungover."

When my stomach stopped caving in on itself, I fell into Andrew's chest. He basically dragged me through the hallway and shoved me into the girl's bathroom.

"Being gay doesn't mean you're allowed to waltz right into the lady's restroom."

Andrew scoffed at me. "It's a Friday. Nobody comes to class on Friday. Unless you're a slave to the requirements of premed."

I turned on the faucet and splashed cool water in my face. "I can't do this. I just can't."

"If anybody walks in, they'll take one look at me and know we're not engaging in coitus. You don't need to freak out."

I laughed. "No, not that."

He handed me a paper towel, gesturing to my mouth. "What are you talking about?"

93

"Anatomy." I swiped at my tears. "I just ran out of the lab because I watched you run a knife through a dead cat's stomach."

Andrew shrugged. "Do you like cats?"

"I love cats."

"Then your reaction makes sense."

I shook my head. "And what happens if I need to work on a human being and I vomit all over the patient? And then they die."

Andrew laughed. "Roxanne, that's ridiculous. You're overthinking."

"But I'm not. I can't do this. Physically, I can't."

"Don't you quit on me. I have the hottest lab partner in class. What else can I brag about?"

I half-smiled. "Your 4.0 and perfect hair?"

He ran his fingers through his black locks while checking out his pale skin, green eyes and muscular frame in the mirror. "It's a real shame you don't have a penis."

"It's a real shame you aren't interested in women," I joked.

"Seriously, Honey. What's wrong? Not to rush you but I do have a pussy to dissect."

"How long have you been waiting to say that?"

He beamed. "It just came to me."

"Looks and laughs. You're the whole package, aren't you?"

Andrew grabbed my shoulders and turned me to face him. "Stop ignoring me. We've been lab partners for a couple months now. You can talk to me."

My lip trembled. "Andy, I don't think I'm meant to be a doctor."

"Okay. And?"

"I'm wasting your time and I'm taking up class space. I'm throwing up outside. I get queasy just thinking about physically tearing apart an animal."

"What if you imagined it was a stuffed animal?"

I shook my head.

"What if we pretend it was a game of Operation, Kitty Edition?"

I snorted.

"What if we give you a scarf to put over your nose and you write whatever I tell you to put on the paper?"

I nodded. "I can do that."

He pulled the flowy, lime green scarf from his neck and dangled it before my nose. "This is Chanel. If you throw up on it, I will be forced to kill you."

"I can't make you any promises."

"Well, do your best. I don't want to request a new lab partner."

"Will you still love me even if I'm not a doctor?"

Andrew wrapped my body in his and kissed my forehead. "Who would be stupid enough to hate you for something like that?"

I inhaled his scent of peaches and hand sanitizer, trying to steady my uneasy stomach. *Why don't you tell my family that? Because they're going to hate me more than they do now.*

#

SOMETIME THE FOLLOWING week, I wound up sitting at a local diner, sharing a booth with Lamont, Steven and Tiffany. I had a stack of papers waiting in my dorm room that needed to be read for poetry class and a study guide to memorize for my Psychology class, but the girls had urged me to get out of the house and Tiffany offered to come along as moral support.

Instead of participating in the witty repertoire bouncing from mouth to mouth, I remained dreadfully silent. I'd just introduced Tiffany to these boys no more than fifteen minutes ago and they were hitting it off as if they played in the sandbox together as small children. *My best friend likes the boy I love, and he likes her right back. This is good news. This is something I should be happy about.* The uncomfortable feeling lingering in my gut left me wanting to bury myself alive. *Of course, this would happen to me. Tiffany is beautiful. No wonder Lamont likes her. He likes her more than he likes me.* He hadn't taken his eyes off Tiffany since they exchanged greetings.

I'd attempted to play it cool and smooth by sliding onto the cloth covered booth seat beside Lamont, entertaining the idea that we could hold hands beneath the table. However, my oh-so-suave move failed the instant Tiffany chose the seat across from him.

His hands remained atop the table in plain sight for all restaurant attendees to see.

I tried not to notice how small they were in relation to his height.

Tiffany's skin glowed in the diner's light, her teal eyes intently studying Lamont's face, her own beautifully manicured hands fiddling with the condensation surrounding her water glass.

*You're supposed to be my best friend. Why are you doing this? Look at his hands! Remember what you said about his hands?*

Tiffany told a joke that made Lamont throw his head back in laughter, shaking the bench he and I shared. When he reached across the table and touched the tips of her fingers, my own hands cold and lonely beneath the cheaply constructed booth, I was forced to look away.

*Stupid. Why do I continue to be so stupid? Why did I think he would like me?* As jealousy and betrayal gripped at my sanity, I regretted inviting Tiffany. Regretted opening up to her. Regretted calling her my best friend. Regretted sharing my soul with Lamont. Regretted falling in love with him. *What would Lucy tell me to do? How could I play this game?*

I targeted the oblivious individual sitting in front of me.

Steven.

The waitress brought out the food, providing a slight lull in the conversation.

I smiled as Steven talked to me, nodded between bites, giggled at his sarcasm and even slapped his hand playfully when he turned up his sleazy charm.

It was exhausting.

I crawled further back into my shell, wishing I could go home, no longer caring about the food on my plate or the soda in my cup. The three of them left the restaurant laughing and having a grand time. *This is your fault. You opened the floodgates of cheating. He's not looking for a girlfriend. He has one of those already. He just wants someone in the same zip code who will have unattached intercourse with him.*

I barely said good-bye, quietly handed Lamont his bracelet, didn't make eye contact with my best friend, and realized I should've just stayed home to study.

Tiffany wrapped me in a bear hug, the joy emitting off her skin smothering my smug attitude. "Thanks for inviting me! That was really fun. Let's do it again soon."

I absent-mindedly patted her back. "Yeah, for sure." *Over my dead body. Fuck you, Tiffany,* I thought angrily, not caring about cursing any longer. *Fuck you. Best friends my ass. I hate you. I really fucking hate you.*

#

I WAS DESPERATE for human interaction from someone who I could trust, no matter how painful the truth may be. So, I made a phone call seeking some reassurance.

"Sis! Long time no talk! How are you, Little One?"

I smiled at Lucy's enthusiasm, grateful that no matter how out-of-control life became, my sister would never change.

"Not doing so good but we'll get into that later if there's time. How goes the pregnancy?"

"Roger may say otherwise, but I think it's going great. One day I want to eat the house and the next day, I refuse to eat anything Roger offers me. Cravings are no joke."

"How far along are you now?" I asked.

"Six weeks."

I snorted. "Cravings my ass. You're just using the pregnancy as an excuse to be a picky pain in the butt."

"Hey!" She pouted. "I resent that. Pregnant or not, Roger always caters to me."

*He's your husband, not your slave.* "Yeah, but now that you're pregnant, he's probably afraid to call you out on your crap."

Lucy laughed, a beautiful sound like wind chimes dancing in the breeze. "Roxanne, did you just say something funny?"

"Yeah, so?"

"Oh. My. God."

My pulse picked up. "What?"

"You had sex, didn't you?"

Although nervous, I laughed. "Those two situations are not correlated to one another. You've lost me."

"You've come out of your box! I've known you for twenty years and you don't have a funny bone in your body."

"Actually, I do," I corrected. "It's located in the elbow region."

Lucy laughed again, my lips curling into a satisfied smirk.

"So, how was it?"

"Lucy, I didn't do anything," I lied. "I'm just trying to take your advice and release the reins a bit. I've always been funny, I just kept my hilarity to myself."

"Well, when you do have sex, make sure to use a condom. I know that unprotected sex *feels so much better*, but then you'll wind up preggers like me."

"Lucy. Stop. I'm not having sex."

"Seriously, Roxy, I'm proud of you. You're finally making friends!"

I shook my head in the ensuing silence.

"So, how's school going?"

And then my happy bubble popped. "I threw up in lab last week."

"You—what? Why?"

"We were dissecting cats—"

"They're dead."

"Yeah, but—"

"No, stop," Lucy scolded. "I'm tired of your excuses. I told you last time we talked that you need to get over this nonsensical behavior."

I grew frustrated, again wishing I hadn't felt the need to call her, somehow always forgetting she knew how to make my night that much more unpleasant. "Maybe I'm not meant to be a doctor. Maybe my body is trying to tell me something."

"Or maybe you're being a big baby. You're still an undergraduate. You should have nothing to complain about. It's not that hard."

Angry tears raged through the cracks of the emotional dam I'd been attempting—and failing—to repair since Lamont and I first kissed. "Why do I have to be a doctor? What if I'm destined to be something else?"

Lucy sighed. "You're upsetting me, which means you're upsetting the baby. I'm getting off the phone. Roger and I have to work in the morning and it's already late. Love you, Sis."

I hung up without responding.

"Can't I get a break? Just this once?"

My Anatomy notebook fell off the desk, my loose-leaf attempts at poetry flying across the carpet in disarray. I sighed, placed my face in my palms and sobbed. "No, I guess not."

#

"WHY NOT START from the beginning?" Shannon suggested, breaking the silence. "I'm not gonna lie, you've confused the shit out of me."

Claire, Amber, Shannon, Elizabeth and I had gathered together in the living room on a particularly cold Friday afternoon. They'd attended a party the night before, bummed that I'd denied their invitations, but determined to drink a stressful week away. Tired of being forced to socialize with people I didn't know and emotionally exhausted from no longer knowing who I could trust, I intended on crawling beneath my comforter and falling off the radar for the rest of the weekend.

I'd already contacted Andrew, informing him I'd rather not study the innards of an owl alongside my own spilled innards, threatening to make scientific discoveries about evolution based on the shared diet of owls and humans. He'd sent me a "lol, bitch" before calling me and making sure I was okay. Once we'd gotten off the phone, me assuring him that everything was fine, I just needed the day off and was fine with the fail I was bound to receive anyway, I prepared a bubble bath to calm my body before climbing into bed.

Unfortunately, my night hadn't gone as planned.

98

"Well, what do you consider the beginning? I've pretty much lost track of it all."

"We know that cuddling was involved."

*Minus the fact that we had coitus.*

"You said didn't ignore your text messages, for once."

*Minus the fact that I had contacted him first.*

"So, why don't we start with dinner?" Amber suggested.

I swallowed the uncertainty burning at the back of my throat. *You've already fed them lies. Maybe it's time to start telling them the truth—or at least, enough truth to take some pressure off your chest. Be careful. You trusted Tiffany and look what she did.*

I'd refused to see Tiffany since an exchange we'd shared at the gym the night after the dinner I wished I could forget. Sweating profusely on the elliptical, I listened while Tiffany blabbered on about wanting a tighter butt so Brian wouldn't continue cheating on her week in and week out. I wanted to make a snide comment about her definition of loyalty but nodded instead.

"Thanks again for dinner last night. I had more fun than I thought I would."

I produced another nod, unable to construct a literate sentence without profane language and accusations.

"The funniest thing happened after class tonight," she continued. "I ran into Lamont."

I stumbled slightly, struggling to regain my steady pace. "Really? Where at?"

"Apparently, our Thursday classes are right next to one another. What're the odds?"

*Clearly, pretty in your freaking favor.* "You hadn't seen him before?"

She shook her head, two drops of sweat falling to her shoulder. "I wouldn't have noticed him, but he flagged me down. We exchanged numbers so we could walk together. We've decided we're basically the same person. Like distant cousins."

*Yeah. Right. Kissing cousins.* "I just remembered I have studying to do. Thanks for convincing me to try and work out. Let's do this again. I'll text you." And I'd run home, my adrenaline still pounding, my feelings scraping raw on the ground beneath me. *She's not my friend anymore. A real friend wouldn't do this.*

"Long story short, he ignored me the whole time. Tiffany became the center of his attention." I paused, recalling how devastated I'd been for the rest of the night, the phone call to Lucy making things that much more disagreeable.

Questioning my weight, my appearance, my personality, my inability to judge character properly, my naivety, my life choices—I'd ripped off the mascara stained pillowcase in the morning in an attempt to pretend the night never existed.

"He hadn't even remembered it was his turn to take the bracelet from me. I basically shoved it on him while he was busy ogling Tiffany's perfect model body—"

"Now stop right there," Amber ordered. "You don't think she's prettier than you, do you?"

I shrugged. "He only looks at me like that when he's drunk. She's tall, skinny, tan—"

Claire snorted. "Roxy, you need to stop. If you think like that, you'll drive yourself crazy."

"You don't understand. She told me they exchanged numbers the following night because they have class right next to one another. He never asks to see me on weekdays. It's literally only happened that *one time*."

"No fucking way," Shannon gasped.

I nodded. "Just my luck. After all this nonsense, I figured everything between us was done."

"Okay," Elizabeth sounded out slowly. "Then what happened?"

I hesitated, studying the ends of a particularly unkempt curl. "Something happened last night."

"Oh no," Claire groaned. "What did you do?"

"If I actually tell you what happened," I mumbled. "Then none of you can pass judgment. A lot went down, and I can't handle feeling anymore emotionally distraught."

They eyed one another before nodding curtly. "We promise."

"Let me just preface this by letting you know how devastated I was at dinner that night. He *ignored* me. I swear I thought I saw drool pooling at the corners of his lips—he was admiring everything about her directly *in front* of me. And I know it'll upset you guys, but she's obviously *beautiful*. She's basically a model. And he chose *her*. He freaking chose her!"

The girls frowned, Amber and Elizabeth beginning to rub my back.

"He broke my heart. And yet, when he texted me last night, I jumped at the opportunity. I *needed* to talk to him and find out about his feelings."

However, I refused to speak my insecurities out loud—how I had planned on finding a way to seduce him in the hope of getting him to notice me more than

Tiffany. Melanie didn't even cross my mind. It was clear that that relationship had sailed, even if they weren't officially split in two.

"I take it you didn't go to bed early then, huh?" Shannon joked.

"Unfortunately not. We were talking until, like, one or something. I probably crawled into bed right before you all came home."

I hated myself for lying but I'd trusted Tiffany and that backfired. I wasn't ready to let these girls know the complexities of my messed up social life. *They'd just jump to unnecessary conclusions if you told them he was over until three.*

"How did it go? Get the info you needed?" Elizabeth asked.

Amber laughed. "Oh, please. Do you *really* care about their conversation? Tell us the juicy stuff!"

"Juicy stuff?"

"Yeah, like, how big is he?"

I rolled my eyes. *Does an emotional connection with a guy not mean anything these days?* "I wouldn't know," I lied.

"Nobody wants to know that!" Claire whined.

"I said I wouldn't know."

"That question was hovering around here like a white elephant. Speaking of elephants…"

As the girls giggled, I managed to remain composed. *Don't blush. Don't give anything away. Don't let them see in.*

"You need to start listening. We kissed." *Lie lie lie.* "And cuddled. Fully clothed." *Lie lie lie.* "But if I ever get the opportunity to measure him, I'll report my findings to you immediately." *Lie lie lie.*

Amber winked. "I'll admit it, I was hoping you'd been having secret sex with him."

A whole new fit of laughter erupted around me. *Yeah. Secret sex. It's secret for a reason. That reason being, it's my business and nobody else's.*

"Alright, let's get back to business," Elizabeth said. "What could you possibly talk about for how ever many hours?"

"I grew a pair and asked him about Tiffany."

"What'd he say?"

"Some crap. They're just friends. She's funny. She's pretty, but he's not attracted to her. I dunno. I don't believe him. He also dropped Melanie's name. I'm beginning to think he's using her as an excuse to not get emotionally attached to me."

Claire scowled. "Or maybe he actually loves her, and you shouldn't continue to interfere."

I breathed in. *Don't say anything.*

"You've been in a relationship where your boyfriend cheated on you."

I breathed out. *Not one word.*

"Out of everyone in this room, you should respect their relationship and stop trying to get his attention."

*Let it go.* I ground my teeth together.

"We all know he's never going to break up with her and if you have sex with him, that's all you'll be to him. An easy lay."

"Claire, you need to stop," I spat, hands trembling. "You don't know anything about me if that's really what you believe."

Shannon, Elizabeth and Amber looked back and forth between us, their eyes travelling like spectators at a tennis match.

"I've had enough," I continued. "You are so aggressive toward me and I don't understand why. I'm not gonna sit back and let you walk all over me like this. I fucking love Lamont! This isn't a fucking joke!"

The girls' eyes widened.

"He rejects me day in and day out. He has the hots for a girl who is supposed to be my *best friend*. If I thought our connection wasn't real, do you think I'd let him put me through this bullshit?"

Silence. A strong and shocked silence.

I closed my eyes in an attempt to gather my composure. "You have *no idea* what I'm going through right now."

"Did you actually cuss?" Amber asked.

"Is that really all you got out of that?"

She apologized. "It just caught me off guard."

"You—you—love him? Are you sure?" Shannon asked timidly.

I shrugged. "I dunno. Maybe. Yes. It feels like it."

Claire glared. "You said it yourself. He keeps hurting you. And as long as he's with Melanie, he can string you along and not feel bad. I'm just trying to help you from getting hurt. He's a bad guy, Roxy."

I couldn't help but think about Lamont's broken promise of texting me once he returned home, of the rushed way he snuck out of the dorm, and the annoyed look on his face when my voice broke, small tears exposing themselves at the wrong time. *Claire, you don't know the half of it.* Lamont and I had been intimate with one another, despite the insecure and depressing conversation we'd had only moments before he pressed his mouth hungrily against my neck. And while Lamont rested his head on my pillow, I spoke up, my heart reaching for any hint of adoration.

"What're we doing?"

His eyes fluttered open. "Having sex?"

"That's it? That's all this is?"

He sighed. "What do you want from me?"

*Everything you give Melanie. Everything you see in Tiffany. I want you to love me.* "I don't know. I don't want to be the other woman."

"I'm not going to break up with Melanie. I love her."

My heart screamed, a knife cutting through the thin tissue. "Then we can't do this."

"Why're you making such a big deal out of it? We're having fun. I thought that's what you wanted, too?"

"Fun? We're having fun?"

"Yeah, two *friends* having a good time together. Relieving stress. No strings attached."

"You can't play me like some stupid toy, Lamont. This isn't what I want. This isn't what I asked you for. Get out and leave me alone."

He nodded, not arguing, not pretending he cared. I watched him leave, dropping the black bracelet on my computer desk before he closed the door softly. I stared into the darkness, where the bracelet stared back. *How have I fallen so in love with someone who will never have the capacity to love me back?*

#

I STUDIED THE outfit on the frowning girl in the mirror, analyzing the dress she'd impulsively purchased a little over an hour ago. First turning left, then right, the girl prayed this would be sexy enough to make a phenomenal impression. Red was a color that people often told her she looked good in, but she was hesitant about wearing a strapless ensemble on account of her broad shoulders. Even the faux-diamond necklace falling down her chest and the heavily hairsprayed curls cascading around the middle of her back did little to ease her anxiety. The big, black leopard print belt cinched above her waist made her appear slimmer while simultaneously pushing up her breasts. The short length flattered her long legs and the four-inch, cheetah-print high heels flexed her leg muscles in all the right places.

And even though that girl was my reflection, I had a hard time believing it was actually me standing there. I didn't wear short dresses, I didn't wear high heels, and I most certainly wasn't the type to dress up in order to try to make someone like me. But somewhere, deep down below the shame of succumbing to peer pressure, I actually liked what I saw. That girl was—pretty, and that was an adjective I hadn't used when looking in the mirror before.

The only thing I hated was the stupid black bracelet weighing heavily on my wrist. I couldn't find the strength to rip it off—I needed its presence to make me feel whole, a habit I hoped to break later in the night. *This is my chance to forget about Lamont.* "Lipstick and eye-shadow aughta do the trick," I mumbled, curling my lashes with thick, black mascara. "I really hope I don't make a fool out of myself tonight." I swiftly applied the rest of my makeup, adding finishing touches with bronze and blush that lifted my cheekbones even higher.

When I grabbed the flavored vodka from my mini-fridge, my reflection stared at me, plucked eyebrows furrowed, red lips pouting. "Is this really me? A girl who drinks to gain confidence and dresses like a hooker for attention?" I glanced at the vodka bottle and sighed. "I can do this. I can be a normal girl." My Anatomy lab book had begun to grow spider webs having remained untouched for the last two weeks on top of my desk. "Since when is it okay to drink the night before class?" I shook my head and walked down to the kitchen, not entirely sure how to begin. I pulled soda out of the community refrigerator and tapped my poorly painted fingernails on the granite countertop wondering if I should back out.

"Amber! I don't know if I can do this!" I shouted up the stairs.

"What?" she called over the railing.

"Taking shots. I don't know if I can do it."

She chuckled. "You silly girl! You don't have to start yet. It's barely eight-thirty! I'm not even ready yet."

"I'm not talking about that," I replied. "I don't know if I should even go tonight." I looked at the vodka and soda and felt my eyes beginning to sting. "I'm so stupid. I should've never invited Zach. He's gonna be here in a matter of hours and I'm dressed like a hooker and I can't take this stupid bracelet off my wrist."

Elizabeth's head peaked out from behind her bedroom door and two sets of footsteps descended from above me. I was then surrounded by three half-naked girls wrapping me in a group hug, commanding me to relax.

"What if this is a huge mistake?" I admitted pathetically.

Shannon rubbed my arm. "You have nothing to be afraid of."

My shoulders slumped. "I don't like losing control. I don't want to do anything I'm gonna regret tomorrow morning."

"You don't have to sleep with him," Elizabeth reminded me.

"I know that—but look at me. This isn't me." I glanced at the ground. "He already broke my heart once before. Why shouldn't he do it again?"

"Roxy, you're changing—coming out of your shell. Stop giving yourself such a hard time. It's not a bad thing you're acting out of character."

"Besides, that was years ago," Amber reassured me. "You guys were both young and stupid and he obviously didn't know any better."

I gulped. "Yeah, but—"

"Let's get that first shot out of the way," Shannon suggested. "Don't think about what might happen later. Live a little. You look hot. And let's be real, that's what really matters."

My heart raced. "I'm kinda nervous about *this*." I gestured to the vodka taunting me, begging me to untwist the cap.

Elizabeth patted my shoulder. "That's what it's for, silly—to calm your nerves."

They rummaged through the cabinets and produced four shot glasses. "How about a toast?"

We smiled at Shannon, lifting our glasses into the air.

"To new friends," I cheered weakly.

Amber winked. "To old lovers."

After I threw back the vodka, washing it down with the soda dramatically, I gagged, shaking my head with disgust. "Good Lord," I choked. "Do you ever get used to that?"

Elizabeth grabbed the liter from my hand. "No," she sighed, wiping her chin. "But the more you drink, the easier it gets."

I nodded, poured another shot and held it up to my pleasantly surprised housemates. "As you all say: go big or go home, right?"

# Chapter Six

"IT'S TIME I meet this bitch face to face," I slurred, stepping past the house's screen door. "I know she's here. Let's ask Lamont who's the better kisser."

Shannon grabbed my elbow. "Roxy, that's not a good idea."

"Oh, you're right. I should ask who he'd rather fuck." I tried to yank away, nearly breaking my ankle just above my too-tall cheetah pumps. "It's time she and I settled this."

"This is not what I expected." Amber laughed, patting my shoulder. "I like shit-faced Roxy. She's sassy as fuck."

I smiled, my vision thinning between intoxicated eyelids. "I usually keep my thoughts to myself. They're precious motherfuckers. Get me in a lot of trouble."

Elizabeth stumbled beside me. "Before you yell at Lamont—"

"Not Lamont. His stupid girlfriend. *Melanie.*"

"Whatever. Before we do *anything* else, we need to find Claire."

"And then I'm gonna give that bitch a piece of my mind," I declared, ignoring the glares from the scantily clad hobags outlining the hallway leading to the kitchen.

Tiffany had been the one to warn me of Melanie's unwelcomed presence in Rohnert Park. Back in my dorm, she pulled me away from the positive energy buzzing through the radio's speakers and whispered the unfortunate news with a toothy smile embodying the entirety of her stupidly beautiful face. To keep my hands from accidentally clamping around her throat, I wrapped my fingers around a double-shot of Vodka and swallowed the burning liquid, hoping it would dispel the jealousy still managing to swim through the waves of misplaced confidence already sloshing against the lining of my stomach.

Initially, it hadn't bothered me that Melanie was visiting. She *was* Lamont's girlfriend, and I understood her appearance was bound to happen. No, what *really* infuriated me was that the information was delivered from Tiffany.

And she said it as if this was something I should be excited about.

Lamont *still* hadn't contacted me since our "talk" we shared the week before. Discovering that he and Tiffany spoke so often that he would open up

107

about the girlfriend's visit was like rubbing an extremely juicy lime all over a canyon-deep wound.

I downed another shot to prevent myself from screaming and ripping her eyes out. *Don't freak out. They haven't slept together. It's only a matter of time, but don't dwell on it. Maybe they are just friends. Maybe if you keep telling yourself that, you'll eventually believe it.*

"What'll you do if we run into her?" Tiffany asked, somehow still unaware that she was no longer my best friend—that she could no longer group us together as a "we."

*Throw her—and you—straight in front of a freight train.* "Probably ask how she has sex with someone whose dick is *maybe* the size of my pinky," I said, instead.

She laughed, but it was nothing like the obnoxious bellow she'd let loose at the coffee shop. It was *forced*, and that led me to believe there was *something* really happening between the two—something that *just friends* wouldn't be caught doing together.

And I had to blame myself because I'd introduced them to one another in the first place.

"That's one way to get her to break up with him."

I nodded, moving into the living room to rid myself of the negativity swarming around Tiffany's perfectly straightened hair. "Yeah. And then vultures like you can dig right in."

Amber had been the first to notice my bitter aura. "You alright?"

I'd sighed, nodding weakly. "Let's discuss it later. I'm ready to have a good time—preferably without Tiffany shoving her nose straight up my rectum."

Usually, the curious stares of Amber, Elizabeth and Shannon would have frightened me into silence, but this time, I needed to vent—and I loved that they were more than willing to listen, nodding their heads and gasping when necessary. I told them what Tiffany said and pointed out how she remained glued to her phone screen, Lamont's name constantly popping up in the little square message box, and admitted that killing her may have crossed my foggy mind.

Maybe the bonding was alcohol induced, but it helped me break down my barriers, and become more comfortable with my roommates—girls who I wanted to consider friends. The vodka even made my filter disappear, the control I wielded dissolving along with the bread I'd consumed during dinner in an attempt to absorb the toxins I was pouring willingly into my body.

We'd arrived at the party house—belonging to Claire's friends on the dance team—close to eleven, music vibrating the window panes, the front lawn littered with boys peeing on the hedge and girls smoking cigarettes, coughing when they inhaled too hard. I'd already lost count of the drinks I'd consumed and was amused by the tingling sensation tickling my lips.

That's when I asked where Melanie was.

And that's when Elizabeth suggested we find Claire.

"Easy there, Rambo," Amber warned. "Melanie hasn't done anything wrong. If you need to hurt someone, aim for Lamont."

"Look, the sooner we find Claire to wish her happy birthday, the sooner we can get back to drinking," Shannon said.

"She's probably in the kitchen licking up herpes from some guy who'll never call her back."

Elizabeth frowned at Amber. "Claire may not always pick winners, but tonight, give her the benefit of the doubt."

"Oh, whatever Lizzy. I know her too well to feel bad. After what she's been doing to Adam? She deserves herpes."

"Don't say that," Elizabeth scolded. "She invited him out tonight, so she obviously wants him here."

"Right. And I'm sure he wants to see her eating some frat boy's dick."

"We have to be nice. It's her birthday. Please?" Elizabeth pleaded.

"Maybe we should warn her to be on her best behavior, especially when Adam arrives," Shannon suggested.

"A warning?" Amber asked. "He should see Claire for who she *really* is. She's pretending to be in love with him and then hooking up with random guys behind his back."

"Ohhhh yeah. And the blowjobs," I garbled. "She gives lots and lots of blowjobs."

Amber and Shannon laughed, Elizabeth shaking her head sternly. "It's her birthday. If she wants to give a random guy a blowjob, she's allowed to give said random guy said blowjob."

"Girls!" A high-pitched male's voice shouted. "How are you? Whatchu talking about?"

Shannon and Amber snickered.

Elizabeth glared at them nervously.

Adam's short, black hair was freshly buzzed, round chin newly shaven, brown eyes squinting through an intoxicated gaze, crooked—but absolutely charming—smile stretched from ear to ear. He wrapped his arm around my shoulders and leaned onto me. Already unsteady in my heels, I felt my body begin to descend to the side, Amber's strong arms saving me from collapsing in front of everybody.

"We're on the lookout for the birthday girl," I said, attempting to shove him off me. "Dude," I breathed. "Get off me or we're both going to collapse and sustain some pretty gnarly muscle tissue injuries when we hit the ground."

Adam laughed, straightened himself, and slapped my shoulder as if I scored a touchdown. "Doctors, man. Even when drinking, your brain never quits."

I nodded, my good mood deflating slightly. *Too bad I'm a poet, not a fucking doctor.* "Have you seen Claire?"

"I'm looking for her. I was hoping you all knew where she was."

Screams erupted from the kitchen door, Claire's laughter beckoning us to see what was going on. After a hesitant pause, the five of us ran to the doorframe and peaked in, completely unprepared for what was happening. A prince-charming-haired, beefy armed, strong backed frat boy stood atop the counter pouring vodka all over the girls standing within his vicinity.

Claire, clearly more drunk than the others, climbed atop the counter— eighteen-inch-high high heels and all—with the assistance of her friends and positioned herself beside him. After a moment where everyone secretly questioned if she would slip off and break her neck, we all watched her tilt back her head and open her mouth, her skinny, pink tongue falling over her bottom lip.

The boy's eyes widened. "Oh—I think the birthday girl is asking for a shot!" he shouted.

I watched, dumbfounded, as he tilted the vodka bottle, poured the alcohol into her mouth, dribbled it down her chin, and nodded as it pooled at the top of her exaggerated cleavage. I cringed when the boy bent at the waist, tongue out, slowly and methodically licking at the liquid glistening over her skin.

"Anyone else feel like we're watching a cheaply budgeted porno?" I asked, hoping to ease the uncomfortable tension swirling around us.

Nobody responded, too busy staring at the full-blown make-out session that had proceeded to take place, girls screaming their consent, emptying their red cups onto the birthday girl, the ceiling, the counter and the floor.

"Oh shit," Elizabeth sighed.

"Well, it *is* her birthday. Technically she can do whatever she wants to," Shannon finally said before calmly sipping from her own cup.

"I just spent fifty fucking dollars on that dress," I realized. "That alcohol is gunna ruin it. At least a seamen stain would've come out with some Zout."

Shannon spit her drink all over Adam's face, snorty laughter flaring through her nose.

Elizabeth elbowed me.

I shrugged. "What? Fifty dollars is a lot of money. That's a week's worth of groceries."

Elizabeth placed her palm over her face. "What happened to your filter?"

"I think she left it at home," Amber said, clapping her hands together. "Who knew she had it in her?"

Adam stood immobile, Shannon's vodka and cranberry mixture dripping off his face.

"Aren't you glad you're not up there making a fool out of yourself?" I asked Adam, my ability to provide comfort hindered by my haze of intoxication.

He hiccupped once, turned to the side and projectile vomited all over the kitchen floor.

I closed my eyes and covered my nose, refusing to embarrass myself by growing queasy and following suit. However, the hacking that sounded from the kitchen showed that other unsuspecting bystanders hadn't been as fortunate.

That's when Claire noticed us hiding by the doorframe, disgust painted collectively on our faces.

I completely blamed myself for causing the following series of unfortunate events: Claire's heaving sobs of "my party is ruined." Bath towels from the house's linen cabinet being covered in vomit, thrown into plastic bags and tossed into the backyard trashcan. Amber cursing like a sailor because her favorite heels were now caked in Adam's intestines. And, most importantly, two frat boys heaving Adam up by his skinny arms and, literally, throwing him out the door and onto the grassy front yard, his tail bone hitting the mud, his jeans stained green and brown, his face contorted in something akin to a teenage girl about to throw a temper tantrum.

Any normal human being would've felt bad about all of this, but I was far too drunk to feel anything except the warmth spreading from my stomach to the tips of my fingers and toes. In fact, I believed the situation could've been improved if Tiffany had waltzed into the kitchen, slipped on vomit and died when her face collided with the white kitchen tile. Yet, she'd managed to avoid the chaos by having disappeared the moment we entered the party.

So, when she shoved her ridiculously beautiful face in the middle of a conversation between Shannon, Amber, Elizabeth, Steven and myself, it took whatever self-control that had managed to escape the tidal wave of inebriation to *not* throw my drink at her, melting the flawlessly executed makeup off her face.

"What's so funny?" she asked, giggling.

The plastic cup in my hand crinkled in my grasp. *Bitch, if you hadn't ditched us, maybe you'd know.*

"Amber's shoes are ruined," Shannon said.

"What? How?"

I huffed. *Nobody asked you to be here.*

"Throw up. Everywhere."

Elizabeth nodded. "The kitchen was destroyed. How'd you miss it?"

Tiffany coughed hesitantly and shrugged. "I was talking to some old friends out front. Hadn't seen them since last year."

I nodded, skeptically. *Right. Old friends named Lamont.*

"Well, we went into the bathroom to clean her shoes and accidentally walked in on some guy peeing," Shannon continued.

"And Amber got a good look at his penis," I said, narrowing my eyes.

Elizabeth raised a subtle eyebrow. "One thing led to another and now they're macking. Hard."

"We're hoping she's gonna get it in," Shannon chirped.

Tiffany laughed, resting her elbow on my shoulder. "Knowing Amber, I'm sure she'll succeed."

*Too bad you don't know her,* I thought before shrugging her off, pretending that I was waving at someone standing across the room.

Unfortunately, from that point forward, Tiffany took it upon herself to constantly inform me of Lamont's whereabouts—information I had no desire to know. And as the night continued forward, she'd become glued to my side, interrupting conversations, forcing shots into my hands, and giggling at the phone reflecting off her mesmerizing, teal colored eyes.

I vaguely remembered her saying something about Lamont and Melanie going to a movie instead of attending the party.

And then she disappeared.

Shortly after, the phone call came.

I answered happily, my vision too blurry to focus on the name flashing across the screen. "Why, hello there. How might I help you?"

112

When he laughed, my heart rate soared beyond the moon and the stars. *What the hell happened to the time?*

"I'm excited too," I responded sincerely. "I'll meet you outside."

*Oh my God. He's right down the street. He's here. He's fucking here.* It was too late to fix any loose strands of hair, too late to reapply any lipstick and far too late to get the sour taste of vodka off my breath.

"Well," I said, stumbling out the front door. "Here goes nothing."

Two headlights shined on me when I wobbled like a baby deer into the middle of the street. I smiled and waved, incredibly thankful for the amount of alcohol I'd consumed.

Sober me would've called a taxi and gone home.

Intoxicated me played it cool.

He honked his horn and made a U-turn to parallel park his car.

*Alright. This is it. This is what you've been preparing for.*

Zachary Cameron had finally arrived.

#

WHEN HE STEPPED out of his beat up and bird poop-stained Honda Civic, I wondered if I'd ingested enough alcohol to begin hallucinating. Zachary lived over five hundred miles away, attended college classes at San Diego State University, had a job as a local lifeguard and friendships that required dedication and focus.

He had a *life*—one that wasn't easily left behind, even for one weekend. And yet, there he stood in front of me, beaming as if nothing else in the world mattered.

The instant he opened his arms wide for a hug, I found myself falling under his spell all over again.

"Holy shit. Is it really you?" His voice swirled around me, making me feel as light as a piece of computer paper.

I took five ungraceful strides and leaped, wrapping my legs around his back, squeezing my arms behind his neck. "Me? Is it really *you*? What the *fuck* are *you* doing here?"

He spun me around in three circles, squeals of fear and delight escaping from my throat. His laughter embraced my heart while he placed my heels on the ground, his hands remaining firmly grasped on my sides. "Since when do you cuss?"

I blushed. "I may have drank a large amount of vodka tonight."

He laughed. "And since when do you drink?"

"To be honest with you, this is a new thing for me."

We stared at one another for what felt like hours, absorbing each other's facial features as if one of us was about to disappear into thin air. The world was tilting right and left around him, but nothing could take away from his beautiful face. Dark green eyes crinkled into Cheshire cat smiles, tan skin accentuating the shadows beneath his high cheekbones and the bleached tips of his sun-kissed hair, and lips curved into an eager grin, purposefully hiding the yellow, crooked teeth that lined his mouth.

My heart pumped blood into my cheeks, my balance beginning to falter. I rested my hands on his shoulders to steady myself, consciously avoiding the rock-hard biceps and washboard abs that were pushing against his *very* well fitted blue shirt. He was no longer the scrawny swimmer I remembered from high school. Physically, he'd matured into a young man that sent a totally inappropriate and uncalled-for sensation rippling through my spine.

"You look beautiful," he said, squeezing my sides.

My knees weakened. *He's always been charming. Don't let his sweet demeanor fool you again. That's how he hooked you the first time.* I wrapped him in another hug to hide from his gaze, inhaling the scent of his laundry detergent at the same time. *I guess I didn't realize I've missed him this whole time.* "You look great, too. Have you been working out?"

When he laughed, I blushed from my hairspray to my heels. *Filter. I must use my filter.*

"It's all a part of the job—swimming, saving lives. You know, the usual."

I chuckled, pulling slowly away from his body. "Now I understand what people mean when they say it's the alcohol talking."

He placed his hand over mine. "Relax. It's just me."

I smiled. "Well, the party's died down, but I do have beer hidden in the fridge."

He squeezed my hand and shrugged. "Don't worry about the party. I drove all this way to—well—to see you."

I turned and had him follow me into the house, face so red, I was too afraid to look at him. The party had subsided more than I thought. The living room was no longer the center for mingling guests, the kitchen was void of screaming girls and the few remaining boys had moved their intoxicated conversations onto the back patio.

"I have no idea where my girlfriends went, but you can meet Claire—the birthday girl."

We found her playing a card game at the kitchen table with the frat boy from the counter incident and some girls from the dance team. Even though Claire jumped out of her seat and hugged Zachary over-affectionately, I didn't allow myself to feel threatened or self-conscious.

Maybe it was the alcohol, but I wasn't questioning his intentions or wondering if Claire was going to pop out a tit to steal away his attention. *He told me he was here for me.* In fact, I was so oddly confident about the situation, I told the boy I was attracted to and my slutty roommate that I didn't trust as far as I could throw, that I was going to look for the other girls and would be right back.

However, after searching through the various bedrooms and bathrooms to no avail, scanning the porch without any better luck, I returned to the living room to call Shannon and find out where everybody went. I threw pillows onto the floor, got on my hands and knees to search beneath tables, and groaned with frustration. *Where is my phone? It was here no more than five minutes ago.* I hugged my knees, my stomach seeming to debate whether or not to rid itself of the poison I'd been drinking all night. *Who the fuck steals a phone? Like, honestly?* Trying to ignore the panic inching closer, I chose to busy myself by looking around the house for my girlfriends one last time. Having endured the shouts of two naked strangers, washing away the tears of some girl with her cheek plastered to the toilet seat, and pretending to listen while some pot-smoker endorsed the importance of Marijuana, I felt abandoned and exhausted.

The empty living room brought unexplained tears to my eyes. "Where is everybody? What happened to my phone? What am I doing?"

Plopping myself onto a green ottoman, I tried to think critically about the last moment all of us were together but failed miserably. The entire night was already blurring into a timeless warp of nothingness. The one image I could visualize with some cohesiveness was of Shannon, Amber and Elizabeth saying something to one another when Tiffany walked by, whispering into the phone. *Why can't I remember what they were talking about?* Worry soon grasped at my drunken calm. *What if I blacked out when they told me where they went? What if they invited me and I argued with them?* As the world quickly spun like a carousal out of control, I closed my eyes in the hope of steadying my nerves. Not only had I lost track of time, but I'd lost track of my roommates. *I knew vodka was a stupid idea. I'm a fucking idiot.* My stomach churned and burned, leaving a sickening sensation boiling against my organs. I placed my face into my palms and moaned, the sense of loneliness pushing fearful tears to the corners of my eyes.

I felt a comforting hand squeeze my shoulder gently. "Hey, you left me hanging in there. Are you doing alright?"

Opening my eyes stung, a single drop of water perched on my mascara-covered eyelashes.

Zachary stared, those beautiful green oceans bursting with sincerity and concern. "Do you want me to drive you home?"

I sighed. "No, I'm okay. I just—I'm struggling to remember where my girlfriends went, and I can't call them because my fucking phone has disappeared." I paused, glancing at the beer in his hand. "You found a drink. I take it whatever game you were playing went well?"

He shrugged. "Would've been better if you were playing it with me."

"I'm sorry. I wasn't trying to ditch you. I just feel really—unsettled."

Zachary waved the bottle in my face. "Would this help you?"

I grimaced. "Might make it worse. What'd you think about Claire?"

"She's nice. She kept giving me shots."

I nodded. "That's good. Did she hit on you?"

Zachary laughed whole-heartedly. "Not that I'm aware of, but maybe I missed something. She seemed pretty invested in that blonde guy sitting across from her."

I suddenly felt the need to hide behind my insecurities. "Bummer. I bet you wanted her attention."

"Hey, hey, hey," he said, smile gone, voice serious. "You're the one who left me in there to fend for myself. I didn't drive eight hours to see her." He plopped on the chair in front of me. "I'm here to see *you*."

"Yeah, right."

"What's going on? Do you want me to leave?"

*Stop it. You're gonna ruin everything. Stop pushing him away.* I glanced at the bracelet settled loosely on my wrist. *He's not Lamont. He's not here to play games with you.* I shook my head, my frizzy curls bouncing against my cheeks. "No, don't leave. I'm sorry. Everybody loves Claire. I figured you would too."

"Well, I don't. If I wanted to meet some slutty girl, I wouldn't have wasted six hundred miles worth of gas."

I laughed, fingers fiddling with the black rubber bracelet, my feet bouncing up and down in my heels. *Come up with something sexy. Be creative and clever. Knock his argyle socks off.* "I could give you some gas money if you need it."

He laughed, his cheeks turning red, crooked teeth exposed from their chapped cage. "Man, I missed you. I forgot how funny you could be."

116

I sorted through an infinite amount of possibilities, hesitant to decide on a course of action. *Maybe he's not just here to reignite that old flame. Maybe he's not trying to makeup for that failed sex attempt. Is it possible he really cares about me? No. There's no way. We're just friends. And we're barely friends at that.* I convinced myself I didn't want him to care about me in any romantic capacity what-so-ever. *Having him back in my life would just lead to heartbreak again.* My pulse refused to slow. *C'mon Roxy. There's no point thinking about this. It's way too complicated.*

I noticed the gold sparkles shimmering around his pupils. He wasn't using pick-up lines. He wasn't being a schmoozer. He wasn't trying to impress me with how much he could drink. Most importantly, he wasn't making any moves on me—no pressure to kiss, to touch, to make idle conversation.

My logic was slipping straight through the fingers of spontaneity.

Leaning forward, I rested my elbows on my knees and fluttered my eyelashes. "That makes me *really* happy. Like, stupidly happy."

His goofy smile instilled me with a pinch of bravery. I uncharacteristically held out my hand and motioned for him to move closer with my index finger.

He glanced at my extended limb, shock swimming across his slightly opened mouth, a twitch tugging at the corner of his lips. He leaned forward hesitantly.

Eyelids closed, my body began to tremble with anticipation. *Don't appear too desperate for his affection. Try to look confident and semi-uninterested.*

I waited. I grew nervous. I squirmed.

*Maybe I'm completely off—*

The hairs on my neck, legs and arms stood at attention. His lips brushed against mine so delicately, I briefly wondered if I'd imagined it. Slowly, I lifted my lids, quivering beneath the intensity of his stare. He touched my cheek, his hand icy cold from the beer bottle, spider-walked his fingers down my jaw and rested his thumb and forefinger on the rounded edge of my chin.

I didn't know what to expect.

But what I received was something akin to magic.

Stars tattooed the inside of my eyelids. The rhythm of my heart slowed to match the choir of angles harmonizing in my soul. Memories—sweet, delectable memories—flashed quickly through my mind.

Our first kisses enveloped with youth and innocence.

The love notes I'd find hidden beneath the doormat on the front porch.

The poem I'd written, hinting at my true feelings for him.

Then the memories darkened.

Watching him walk away.

The screened phone calls.

His denial of any emotional attachment.

*Don't cry. Not here. Not now.*

His hands covered mine, calloused and shaking.

*He's just as nervous as I am.*

My anxiety lifted slightly, his passion providing a safety net beneath my feet, his arms ready to catch me if I fell.

*He's here for me. Nobody else. Just me.*

When we eventually moved away from one another, I kept my eyes closed in an attempt to harness our shared electricity, not quite ready to break the connection. *This isn't supposed to happen. I'm not supposed to feel anything. The girls said the alcohol would prevent this from happening. It's supposed to be sex. Mind numbing, don't give two shits about one another, sex.* A pulse pounded against my panties. *This is one of those moments where I'm supposed to take a chance. Be risky. Do something just for fun. No logic. No emotion. Purely physical.* I squeezed my thighs together, stood abruptly and yanked my hand from his. *This is too much for me. I don't know if I can do it.* "I think I could use another drink. What about you?"

He maneuvered his gaze from my feet to my face, tenderly grabbed hold of my wrist and urged me to sit down again.

I lowered my body slowly to the ottoman, keeping my eyes on my feet.

"Why don't we get that drink back at your place?"

I began to breathe hard, as if I'd just run around the block. Although I was buzzing with fear, the alcohol pushed me past the safety of my socially awkward box, giving me the strength to make the next move. "That actually sounds great. I'd love to."

#

IF I WERE the one who had to worry about losing my erection, the situation would've been beyond awkward. I was already socially inept when it came to talking about easy topics like the weather. I wasn't qualified to brush off his words and continue working my hips without the uncomfortable pause of uncertainty.

*Am I supposed to pretend he didn't say anything? Is he expecting me to say it back?* I let out a moan and raked my freshly clipped nails across his tense, muscular back. *Maybe I heard him incorrectly.* I inhaled the salty scent of his

118

skin and prayed he hadn't really breathed those completely malicious words into my ear.

He rolled off me, sweat beads glittering across his forehead, his chest heaving up and down. A smile produced dimples in his cheeks, dimples I had found adorable until he dropped the bomb on me.

Resting my cheek on the pillow beside him, I blew out a sigh. My focus slipping and my initial desire to get naked and be intimate with Zachary was wavering. *I can't do this anymore. Why did I think I could do this?* As the alcohol began to escape through my sweat glands, questions mercilessly ate away at my drunken high. *Was this a mistake?* I scooted closer, our bodies burning to the touch. *Am I emotionally equipped to handle this?* Climbing on top, I placed my lips on his chest, pheromones recharging my low battery. *I don't understand why I thought casual sex was a good idea. Why'd I listen to the girls?* I smiled when he groaned, slowly rocking my hips back and forth. *He's enjoying it. Get out of your head.* I allowed my body to relax, wanting to understand the beauty of drunken sex and experience that bed-breaking orgasm the girls believed I so rightly deserved.

Except, when I finally got into a steady groove, he moaned the words again—and there was no mistake. He'd meant for me to hear them.

*I love you.*

My muscles tensed, but not in the way a woman would want them to tense during sex. No—I immediately grew self-conscious and yearned to hide beneath the safety of the covers. *I waited so long to hear those words, and you're gonna say them now? After you decided to completely ignore me for three years?* The clock on the nightstand winked mockingly at me. It was already four-thirty. We'd gone through three different types of condoms and five bottles of water in the two and a half hours we'd been fooling around with one another.

Thanks to my alcohol-induced trance, I'd been un-fatigable. Also, thanks go my alcohol-induced trance, I was unable to reach that point of elation I'd read about in the naughty poems I'd found on the Internet. I was beginning to get antsy, wanting to fall asleep and pretend this was all some alcohol-induced dream. I had my Anatomy lab first thing in the morning, but I hadn't intended on telling him that until I was forced to roll over his naked body when the sun came up. *After all this fucking time. I don't love you anymore. I can't say it back.*

Vulnerable and awkward, I patted his chest. "I need a break."

Zachary flashed his crooked teeth. "How long of a break?"

My legs were beginning to ache. "I don't know. Three minutes?"

He effortlessly lifted me off him, his biceps flexing in the moonlight shining through the open window. Our bodies were slicked with sweat and my hair was a frizzy nightmare. I reached over Zachary's well-defined pecks and grabbed the water bottle off the nightstand, desperately in need of hydration. *Two and a half hours. I don't think I've ever done that before. Is that why people drink?* I glanced up and down his strong body, allowing myself a moment to pause at his hardy package. *Is this what would've happened if he took my bra off the first time?* I placed my head on my pillow and stared at the ceiling, not wanting to believe what Zachary had said.

He loved me.

*He doesn't love me. He's drunk and hasn't had sex in a while or something. He doesn't even know me.* I moved my hand over his chest, down his stomach, his body shuddering at my touch. *Sure, we've been texting one another. But you can't fall in love with someone over text messaging.* I twirled my finger in small circles around his heart. And then Lamont's face smiled at me, shaking me out of my trance. *Who the fuck am I kidding?* My heart began to ache. *Why am I doing this? My heart isn't in it. This isn't right.* He kissed my forehead and pulled me closer to his side. His fingers idly traced the back of my hand and his breaths began to slow. I pulled the blanket over our naked bodies before kissing him on the lips.

His eyes fluttered open. "What do you think you're doing?"

I cocked an eyebrow. "Getting ready to go to sleep?"

He smiled slyly. "It's been four minutes. Your break was over sixty seconds ago."

#

"GOOD LORD ROXY," Andrew said when I stumbled into my seat just as the professor began writing the lab instructions on the whiteboard.

I shook my head at him. "Don't you say a word."

"I'm curious. Did you look in a mirror before you decided to leave your room?"

"At least I'm here and my face isn't in the trashcan outside."

He nodded. "Little Missy, are you hungover?"

I raised an eyebrow at him. "No. I always wear overly large sunglasses indoors, skip out on taking a shower and forget to pull my hair into a ponytail. I also decided that wearing two different types of shoes across campus would make a fashion statement."

"Your t-shirt is tucked into your hot-pink thong."

I lowered the sunglasses to the tip of my nose. "I have to bring my lab grade up somehow. Is that a problem?"

Andrew snorted so loudly, the professor coughed and pointed at the board. "Is there something funny about owl bones that I am unaware of?"

"No sir," Andrew said, shaking his head, the tips of his ears shining a bright shade of red. "I was just clearing my sinuses."

"Please take care of such personal issues before class."

When the professor turned away, I leaned in closer to my lab partner. "Haven't you heard about the bones in the owl's wing? Apparently, they're pretty humerus."

Andrew snickered, his shoulders shaking up and down beneath his light orange, Lacoste polo. "Bitch stop," he hissed, his eyes watering. "You're gonna get me in trouble."

Suddenly feeling nauseous, I placed my face on the cool lab table. "What're we doing today?"

"Apparently, washing your greasy ass makeup off my immaculate work station."

I smiled at him and shrugged. "It's either this or I throw up the dry piece of toast I barely managed to choke down all over your overly-priced designer jeans."

"You wouldn't dare," he gasped, his hand rising to his chest.

The professor gestured to the stack of brown boxes lined up on the tables crowding the back of the classroom. "Please gather the bones you dissected last week and put them in their proper position with the proper name labeled beside each appendage."

"Can you remain here unsupervised for five seconds?" Andrew asked before getting off the stool to gather his work from the last class I missed.

I nodded, my cheek sticking to the refreshing, metal surface. "Don't mind me. I'll just be lying here regretting last night's horrible decisions."

When he returned to the table, he tapped his boat shoes on the tile floor impatiently. "Should I rearrange these bones on your face?"

"You know how I feel about bone on my face."

He threw back his head and laughed, his unkempt hair swaying over his ears.

"Dude, get your act together and stop drawing attention to us." As I slowly lifted my head, a crick in my neck shot down my back. "The professor is gonna forbid me from returning to class if you keep this up." I rubbed my shoulder and grimaced.

Andrew slapped my shoulder before pushing the lab book in front of me. "You slutbag. You totally did the nasty-nasty last night."

I uncapped my pen and wrote the date on the top corner of a fresh page. "Where did that come from?"

"You're cracking jokes left and right."

"Was there some scientific study I missed out on? Since when do sex and being funny relate to one another?"

"Make sure you put everything in the proper place," the professor droned. "This will be graded at the end of class."

"Sex and laughter are always related," Andrew whispered. "Endorphins are released and all that weird, neuron-type shit."

I shook my head.

"C'mon," he begged. "Give me the details. I haven't had sex in ages."

"Since when does heterosexual sex turn you on?"

He winked. "So, how big was he?"

"It is far too early and there is far too little coffee in my system for this topic of conversation." I sighed and pointed at the plain, brown box filled with owl bones. "How about we just focus on the owl bones and not worry about the anatomical configuration of the boy I tried to have unattached intercourse with last night?"

#

"HE SAID WHAT?" Amber shrieked, nearly knocking her smoothie off the table.

Upon returning home from class, I found Zachary making my bed, the smell of his manly soap wafting out of the open bathroom door. He was dressed in dark jeans and a green t-shirt, hair still wet, small droplets rolling down his temples. He apologized for having to leave—his friend was planning on Zachary arriving around lunch time—but promised to call as soon as he got home. I'd walked him to his car and kissed him good-bye, thanked him for visiting and sent him on his way, apologizing one last time for having my Anatomy lab interfere with our time together.

I'd watched him drive out of the parking lot, thankful he hadn't mentioned anything about what he'd said last night, images of our sexual endeavors making me extremely embarrassed.

Now, the girls and I sat in the strip mall five minutes from campus, each of us in need of nourishment and hydration.

"Please tell me you're joking," Shannon said, digging into a bag of potato chips.

I shook my head. "I wish I were. He told me he *loved* me. And he didn't say it once—he repeated it any time the—well, you know—started getting good." My cheeks flushed.

"Ohhh, Roxy," Elizabeth teased. "Getting into detail? I like this!"

I tried to hide behind a large bite of blueberry scone. "No, I shouldn't—"

Amber patted my forearm. "No, you *should*. Let me live vicariously through you."

"My life isn't that exciting," I mumbled.

"At least you're getting a good amount of dick," Amber said. "I'm proud of you."

Shannon grinned. "You've been hiding this side of you from us."

I shook my head vigorously. "No, I don't think you understand. None of it should've happened. It was that stupid vodka."

Elizabeth lifted an eyebrow. "Blaming the alcohol already?"

I sipped my coffee, nearly burning off my tongue. "Can we focus, please? You guys are making me feel worse."

Amber shrugged. "Maybe you should drink more often."

"Look, I'm extremely confused," I admitted, ignoring her. "Didn't you tell me this would be easy if alcohol was involved?"

"More like *you* should be easy if alcohol is involved."

I glared at Claire as the girls laughed. "I don't want to talk about this anymore."

Elizabeth frowned. "Oh, c'mon Roxy. We're only kidding around. You know, trying to take the edge off of this whole situation."

"I mean, did I do something wrong?"

"Well," Amber said, smirking. "Technically, if he said he loved you, you're probably doing something *very* right."

More laughter from the girls made me contemplate eating my entire coffee cup. "This was a huge mistake. I shouldn't have listened to you guys. I should've told him I was too busy."

"Did you have fun?" Elizabeth asked.

I nodded half-heartedly. "Kind of. I kind of feel really silly, though. Thinking I would be able to do this."

"You need to just let go," Shannon said sternly. "Drinking that vodka was the best thing that ever happened to you."

123

"You had great sex with an old lover, and you didn't throw up even though you drank a shit ton. You should be happy." Amber patted my hand. "You're growing up."

I rolled my eyes. "I don't know if I can ever talk to him again. He told me he *loved* me. Like—why?"

"Roxy, I think you're overreacting," Claire added. "You both were drunk. He probably got caught up in the moment and thought that was what you wanted to hear."

"And even if he does love you, you should have *no* inclination to love him back," Amber said. "Remember, this was meant to be a liberating experience. Another way for you to break out of the safety of your little box. Not to be a total bitch, but who cares how he feels?" She stroked my arm for reassurance. "This is about you and your feelings, Love."

"Now, let's talk about the matter at hand." Shannon smiled.

I eyed her curiously. "What am I missing?"

Then I noticed Elizabeth, Claire and Amber sitting doe-eyed and antsy. I sighed and shook my head. "I swear to God. Is penis size all people care about these days?"

Amber nudged me with her shoulder. "It's just an important factor that you shouldn't keep secret from your best friends."

"You know what else is an important factor?" I asked, sarcastically. "Telling your best friend where the heck all of you disappeared to last night, leaving me drunk and alone and questioning whether or not I blacked out, when in the cruel reality I live, I was actually *ditched*."

Almost instantly, their eagerness was replaced with guilt.

I fiddled with the cardboard protecting my hands from burning on my coffee cup. "And clearly, those expressions indicate you planned on hiding something from me."

"That's not true," Elizabeth argued. "We were just waiting for the right moment."

"And we didn't want to leave you." Shannon pushed her lettuce leaves from one side of the plate to another. "But you were so excited about seeing Zach—we didn't want to ruin that."

"You see, Tiffany and Lamont were texting all night—"

I interrupted Elizabeth with a wave of my blueberry scone. "Don't remind me. She made it a point to keep me up to date on Lamont and Melanie's whereabouts all night."

The three glanced at one another nervously.

"You're killing me." I placed my food down, no longer hungry. "What's going on?"

"She lied to you," Amber spat. "Melanie isn't in town. Tiffany had planned on seeing him and ditching you the entire time."

I gawked. "W—she—I don't understand."

"What better excuse to wear a skanky, black dress than to attend a birthday party? Think about it. If you believed she was at the party, you wouldn't ask her what she did last night, and she wouldn't feel guilty lying to you about it."

"And then she wouldn't have to remember the lie later on."

"And have to cover her tracks if you asked any questions about the party."

I didn't like the direction this was headed. "So, are you trying to tell me that—that she—she went over to—to—Lamont's house?"

Elizabeth frowned. "The baseball boys had a party last night, but they didn't tell many people because they didn't want the police to show up."

"And Tiffany didn't tell you about it because she wanted alone time with Lamont."

I stared at Shannon, dumbfounded. *Not only did Tiffany keep the party a secret, Lamont didn't invite me. Neither of them wanted me there.*

"We only found out about it because Danny told us where she was headed when she was leaving Claire's party. You know how close she is to Lamont and those baseball boys. Since we didn't want your night to be ruined, and since Claire had forgotten we were there anyway, we asked if we could join her."

A new anger flared in my chest, burning against my aching heart. "This whole time—" My words faltered. *No. No, this can't be happening.*

"Tiffany and Lamont have been *talking*. And not just as *cousins*," Shannon said.

Amber nodded. "Even Danny was confused when we walked in and saw Tiffany clinging to Lamont. Her dress was hiked up her ass and her makeup was smeared all over her face. We initially went to scope out Melanie so we could report back to you, but Danny told us Melanie wasn't here. That her and Lamont had gotten into a fight during the week, and that he had refused to visit her back at home because of it."

Shannon fingered the water droplets running down her soda cup. "And I'm glad we walked in when we did."

My body temperature dropped. "Why do you say that?"

125

"Well, she was being really touchy-feely. Not only did we see them interact as beer pong partners, but she was constantly grabbing at his elbows, his hands, his chest, his pants pockets, his belt—everything."

"But," Amber added. "When she saw us, she ran straight over to her group of volleyball friends and kept her distance from him the rest of the night. And he was busy texting—most likely Melanie—so we don't know whether they hooked up later on or not."

I gulped. "You don't think something happened, do you?"

The three girls shrugged. "You say there's a sensitive side to Lamont, and Danielle swears he treats his girlfriends well—your situation aside—but I've known him for over a year. If a girl throws herself at him, I have a hard time believing he's going to refuse her advances. Especially if he's blacked out."

"If it means anything," Shannon chimed in. "You looked really happy with Zach this morning. And Lamont is a fool for missing out on the chance to be with you."

I wondered if the girls noticed the steam clouds rising from my ears. I wanted to punch something, throw up and jump in front of a bus all at the same time. I wasn't mad at my friends for leaving me alone at the party—they had the best of intentions.

They actually had my back.

I was mad because the one girl I believed I could trust had betrayed me. The girl who had the nerve to call me her best friend while she was trying to throw herself at the guy I was in love with.

"Now wait just one fucking minute," Claire snapped. The four of us flinched, surprised. I'd totally forgotten she'd been sitting in attendance the entire time. "You bitches left my party? Are you fucking kidding me?"

"Oh, please," Amber replied. "Like you even fucking noticed we were there."

I shook my head, stood up and excused myself to the restroom.

"We're really sorry," Elizabeth said sincerely.

I closed the heavy door, shutting out the argument that was bound to ensue. I collapsed onto the toilet seat and stared at the graffiti littering the stall walls. My body was shaking, my stomach hurt, and I was sore from my sexcapades—three very different emotions were tugging me in three very different directions.

*My best friend lied to me.*

*The boy I once loved apparently now loves me.*

126

*The boy I am completely infatuated with is still in his hometown relationship, wants nothing to do with me, and is probably sleeping with a girl more beautiful than me.*

*I had casual intercourse with Zachary Cameron.*

Rolling the toilet paper out of its container, I couldn't help but stare at myself in the metal reflection in front of me. I bunched the toilet paper together, my hands trembling. *Who are you and what have you done with the real Roxanne Vaughn?*

# Chapter Seven

TWO WEEKS HAD passed since Zachary and I shared that intoxicated night in one another's arms. Two weeks since he moaned *I love you* into my ears. Two weeks since I decided to keep Tiffany as an ally, despite the fact that she was a backstabbing whore.

During those two weeks, I remained locked in my room, refusing to attend parties where Lamont and Tiffany could potentially be spotted together, losing myself in the poetry of Elizabeth Barrett Browning, crying over the jumbled lecture notes from my Anatomy class, and hugging my stuffed version of Molly while heartbreaking movies looped on my television screen. I hadn't called my sister or my parents, I remained quiet when my roommates idly gossiped with one another, and I attended gym sessions with Tiffany, constantly bringing up her relationship with Brian in my subtle attempt to make her feel like the horrible person she was.

Maybe the act of casual sex had altered the state of my mind, but I'd begun to care less and less about the opinions of others.

The one person I focused on was the one person I wasn't supposed to care about. Zachary was slowly mending the void Lamont had so easily torn in my heart. We would text throughout the day, him Facebook messaging me while he was in class, me writing countless poems about two very different people falling in love. Then, at night, we'd crawl into our separate beds five hundred miles away, whispering into the phone until one of us began to drift into a peaceful sleep.

The atomic L-bomb was never dropped again, but his love was present in his constant attention and affection. I couldn't help but count down the days until Thanksgiving break. Although my parents had suggested I remain in the empty dormitory for the four days everyone else would be home so that I could study in peace, I begged them to buy me a round-trip plane ticket, promising that I would lock myself away to study during the day as long as I could experience real life at night. They'd only agreed because Lucy and Roger would be joining them for Thanksgiving dinner and in order to avoid the need for a rental car, I would be responsible for driving them too and from the airport—they would be sleeping in Lucy's old room during their stay in San Diego.

129

We'd be one big, happy family, just like the days before Lucy left for college—and, as always, I'd be the designated driver for a family who could "hold their liquor." I decided not to mention that Lucy was pregnant and could drive just fine, or that the two didn't need to take a commuter plane from L.A. to San Diego, completely capable of driving their own luxury vehicle the few hours it would take via the freeway. I didn't need my mother complaining about what a smartass I'd become in the few short months since school had started.

I didn't look forward to being surrounded by people who often forgot the same blood ran through our veins, but I had grown weary of my surroundings in Rohnert Park. Everything reminded me of the love I stupidly couldn't let go, and it was time for me to get as far away from Lamont as physically possible.

#

"EXCUSE ME, MISS? We're preparing to land. Could you please put your table in its upright position?" the flight attendant asked, her acrylic nails resting on the chair in front of me.

I pulled the headphones from my ears and nodded apologetically, frantically shoving my poetry notebook into the backpack sitting beside my faded Vans, and securing the table safely into its nook on the back of the blue and white chair directly in front of me. The plane ride was only an hour and a half, but my heart hadn't taken this opportunity to relax—my anxiety revolving around flights had left my body shaking like a rat knowing it was being tested for the safety of a new, highly chemical, hair product.

My mind, too, was restless.

I was finally able to admit to myself that Zachary was an important figure in my life, but my heart and mind were currently in the middle of a duel, large swords and shields clanking violently against one another. *Zach is the same guy you knew in high school. There's really nothing stopping him from breaking your heart all over again.* I breathed in and out as the plane tilted forward, speeding straight for the runway. *So what? That's what life is all about, right? Taking chances and putting yourself out there—falling in love with the risk of being hurt at the end of it all.* The wheels contacted the runway abruptly, my heartbeat finally reaching a steady rhythm, my logic and emotion blending together as the pilot announced it was safe to unfasten our seatbelts.

My mind continued to highlight the awful memories that had, at one point in my dramatic young life, haunted my dreams every night. The drunken phone calls filled with obscenities and insults. The day he was kicked out of the dorms because he'd blacked out and woken up naked in his neighbor's bed when she

130

wasn't home—the roommate had walked in and screamed, waking him out of his stupor. The time he scolded me because I'd made fun of his girlfriend in front of our mutual friends. And the fact that he stripped into nearly nothing any chance he could in order to show off his body and bask in the attention given by random onlookers.

I tried convincing myself we were both different people now, but I still didn't know Zachary that well. There was still so much to learn about this new man who drove five hundred miles to see me.

I breathed in the sterile air, stood up and struggled to swim through the other sardines canned in the airplane. My new replacement phone slowly powered on while I made my way passed the other terminals, fast food kiosks and overly crowded restrooms. The small ping vibrated through my phone's speakers and against my fingers, stealing my attention away from someone holding flowers near the baggage claim. I scrolled through my contacts, stopping once I came upon my mother's name, and fleetingly smiled at the man in a plaid shirt while I put my phone to my ear.

When the man made eye contact with me, my voice caught in my throat and the phone slipped from my fingers. The clattering of metal against cement startled those around me, but nothing could pull my attention away from those green pastures of sunshine and bliss. I bent down to pick up my phone, my heart believing that my mind was playing a cruel trick on me, only to be met by his handsome face when I stood.

I brushed my bangs behind my now red-tipped ears and looked at my feet. *Say hi. Open your big, stupid mouth.* I fussed with my sweatpants and ran my hand over my sloppy ponytail. *I wish I listened to my mother and put on some lipstick before I got on the plane. I must look like a total mess.*

"What're you doing here?" I blurted.

At his frown, I wished I could shove my foot straight into my mouth.

"Oh, shoot. I didn't mean it like that."

He handed me the bouquet of fragrant flowers and began rolling from his toes to his heels. "I wanted to surprise you."

"Well, you succeeded. I didn't even recognize you at first."

Another frown.

I cringed, attempting to hide behind the sunflowers. "Thank you. These flowers are absolutely beautiful. I'm sorry I suck at spontaneous conversation. How are you?"

He opened his arms wide. "I'll be better as soon as this pretty girl I'm talking to decides that it's socially acceptable to give me a hug in public."

*Me? I'm pretty?* All of those negative thoughts suffocating me on the airplane finally released their hold on me. Zachary smelled of pool water and Old Spice deodorant. I inhaled his masculinity and squeezed hard before letting go. "This is *really* a wonderful surprise," I said.

His cheeks flushed scarlet. "I think the sweetest girl in the world deserves to go home with flowers in hand."

My heart swelled like the body of a small child allergic to peanuts biting into a peanut butter and jelly sandwich, only to deflate once the child was stuck with an EpiPen. *My mother is picking me up. How am I supposed to explain this to her? She didn't approve of Zach the first time around.* "Thank you, Zach. This is—this is just—thank you. I'm at a loss for words."

"I'm glad you like them," he mumbled.

We walked side-by-side for two steps before he took my massive suitcase away from me and interlaced his fingers with mine. Rather than see it as a sincere and heartwarming gesture, I panicked. *Okay, so obviously, he cares about me. That's a good thing, isn't it?* He kissed my cheek, a small dab of saliva sticking to my skin. *No. No, this is not a good thing. Not only do I have to explain that I plan on changing majors when I return to school, I have to explain that I've won over the heart of a history major. Not a doctor.* I half-smiled at Zachary and rested my head on his shoulder, trying not to show any of my distress. *At least he has a major, and is on his way to graduating on time. Lamont's already switched majors three times and he's only a sophomore.* I swallowed.

"You're awfully quiet," Zachary noted.

I cleared my throat. "It just feels really good to see you. I'm kind of basking in it all."

He nodded. "I haven't stopped thinking about you since I left Sonoma. Honestly, I've been counting down the moons until I'd see you again."

*I've been thinking about my supposed best friend screwing the other guy I'm still in love with.* "Moons? What do you mean?"

"I've been counting down the moons. I'd stare at the moon and think of you every night before bed because nights are shorter when we sleep. Therefore, the time it would take to see you would be less. If I counted the suns, the days would drag by—like a man thirsting for water in the desert."

I nearly tripped on the mat located in front of the automatic sliding doors. *Cheesy or romantic? Gag or smile?* "So, these flowers aren't some ploy to get into my pants?"

He laughed and shook his head. "Roxanne, I'm being serious. I wake up every morning and wonder if it was all just a dream."

I was blushing red hot despite the cool, evening air. "Zach, I—"

He stopped walking and dropped my hand, his eyes burning their love straight through my undecided heart. "If you're free tomorrow night, I'd like to take you on a real date. Do things the way you're supposed to."

I sniffed the flowers. *A date? A real date?* "I'll text you tonight after I've consulted with my parents. How does that sound?"

He walked me over to the silver Lexus parked beside the curb—the one that had been honking obnoxiously during our brief exchange. "Sounds wonderful. I look forward to hearing from you." He placed my suitcase into the opened trunk before giving me another hug. "Six o' clock. Tomorrow. Let your dad know I'll have you home by eleven."

And before I could shoo him away, he opened the front door and greeted my mother. "Mrs. Vaughn, so nice to see you."

The shock on her face stirred up my heartburn.

"Zachary, was it?" My mother nodded curtly. "It's been quite some time. Didn't think I'd see you ever again."

I cringed. "Thanks again, Zach. The flowers are beautiful."

He smiled, but I could see the hurt pushing through that optimistic glimmer always present in his eyes. "You're truly a breath of fresh air. I'm really glad you're home."

"Roxanne, I will leave you standing on this curb if you do not sit your ass down, now."

"Good-bye, Zach. I'll text you."

He closed the door once I drew my foot into the expensive vehicle, the leather squeaking beneath the slightest move—as if my mother had added one too many coats of Armor All only minutes before her departure. The radio wasn't on and the crinkle of the plastic covering the flowers exploded through my ears.

"Hey Mom. Thanks for—"

"If I had known Zachary would've been here to see you, I wouldn't have taken the time out of my busy schedule to be here and wait for you."

Her voice irked me. "I didn't know he'd be here. If I did, I wouldn't have inconvenienced you."

"Excuse me? Are you majoring in bad attitude and minoring in ungratefulness?"

I snorted. "Mom, please. I don't mean to be rude but you're making me feel like a nuisance." My heart pounded nervously. *You better hold your tongue or she's gonna kill you.*

"Well, why was he there? And why did he bring you flowers?" She pushed her straight, blonde hair behind her ear.

I shrugged. "We've kinda been talking."

Her eyes glanced over in my direction, but her focus remained on the road. "What do you mean *talking*?"

While I wanted to spout off the definition of "talking", I bit down on the inside of my cheek. "I mean, like, we're romantically interested in one another."

My mother turned onto the freeway a little too sharply. "With Zach? Didn't you try that once before? And look how well that turned out."

I bit my lip. "Mom, please. People change."

"Oh, *right*. What—what does he *do*, exactly?"

"He's a student. And a lifeguard."

"That sounds promising," she mumbled loudly enough just to get beneath my skin. "And what is he majoring in?"

My fingers twitched with the sudden urge to turn up the volume on the radio, to roll down the window, to act like a child and cover my ears. Anything to stop the conversation from continuing. "H—h—history. He wants to be a te— te—teacher. Or a professor."

My mother laughed. "Oh, okay. As long as you realize you'll be the one bringing home the money."

"Mom, please stop. We're *just* talking. Nothing that serious. He wants to take me on a date tomorrow night."

"A date?"

I smelled the flowers, their fragrance bringing me comfort and confidence. "Yes. A date. With romance and chivalry."

"Who's going to pay for said date?"

The demeaning tone of her voice did nothing but make me even angrier. "He is. He has a job, Mother. He saves lives, much like doctors do."

She took her hand off the wheel and twisted the volume knob up just enough to tell me she'd had enough. "Your sister will be arriving tomorrow afternoon with Roger. You are responsible for picking them up. Your father and I have respectable jobs to work."

I sighed and glanced out the window. *Welcome home, Roxy. Now do you remember why you didn't miss it?*

#

FOR SOMEONE WHO hailed from a family of doctors, a crisis would typically be a situation where the patient's life was a lost cause—where no amount of electricity or surgery could bring an individual back to consciousness. For a twenty-year-old girl about to embark on a *real* date with a *really* handsome boy she once loved, this was most definitely a code blue.

With only thirty minutes left before Zachary was scheduled to pick me up, I still had nothing suitable to wear—nothing that would impress him while also showing him how good I could look without putting in too much effort. *Stop freaking out. You're sweating. You don't have time to take another shower. Get it together.*

My hands wouldn't quit shaking.

As I held different outfits in front of my body, I decided it was of utmost importance for me to impress Zachary to make up for my God-awful appearance in the airport. *Prove to him that you know how to look nice. No sweatpants, no smeared makeup, no drunk sex. Just me—looking natural and effortlessly stunning.*

I threw the dress in my hands on the ground and released a frustrated sigh. "Why do you care so much, Roxy? He knew you in high school. He knows you don't have cute clothes. Stop trying to be someone you're not."

Twenty-five minutes and Zachary would be knocking at the front door.

"Lucy!" I yelled, flinging open the bedroom door. "Can you help me, please? I don't know what to wear!"

"So what?" she shouted back down the stairs. "He's studying to be a teacher. I'm sure you'd impress him in your flannel pajamas!"

She and Roger laughed.

"Lucy, please? You're my older sister. You're supposed to help me with things like this."

"Oh really?" she drawled. "Since when do you take my advice? I told you to talk to boys, but not to boys who have no hopes of a decent future."

Faint whispers trailed down the stairs, Roger's voice sounding stern, but not loud enough for me to distinguish exactly what they were saying.

"Oh, whatever," Lucy replied. "I give it two weeks, tops."

"She's getting out of the house. You're always urging her to live her life."

"Not with someone studying to be a *teacher*."

135

I slammed the door, tears threatening to smudge the eyeliner that took me fifteen minutes per eye to perfect. "Why do you even bother with her? She's never gonna change."

The clock burned red on my nightstand. *Great. Just freaking great. I've wasted three more minutes.* "Why did I say yes? Why did I even come home?"

At a loss, I tore through my suitcase, settling on a pair of dark blue jeans with heart pockets on the back, and a red, long-sleeved shirt that hung down just enough to show a smidge of cleavage. "Maybe I shouldn't tell them about switching majors. I just might give Mom another unwanted wrinkle and upset my sister so much, she'll hide her anger behind a quart of chocolate ice cream."

I studied myself in the mirror, turning from right, to left, to right. The outfit was simple, but somehow, I felt sexy. My curves were hugged in all the right places and the red shirt brought out the natural strawberry highlights in my hair, which contrasted with the dark brown ones I had asked my hair stylist to create. I added a lightweight black sweater and some black flats to finish off the ensemble. Although I didn't feel like myself, I liked who I saw in my reflection—someone with confidence. It may have been feigned, but Zachary didn't need to know that.

The doorbell rang just as I finished hair-spraying my curls. After nearly choking to death on the spray's fumes, I splashed some perfume on my neck and raced up the stairs. Zachary was receiving the third-degree from Lucy, Roger sipping a beer and watching from the sidelines.

"Have you ever thought about pursuing a career in the medical field?"

My foot hit the last step before Zachary had a chance to answer, our eyes meeting and stopping the world around us. Our chemistry exploded, electricity zapping all of the molecules floating between us. I silently thanked myself for using that extra spritz of hairspray, certain my hair would be sticking straight out as if I'd been rubbed down with balloons. Blushing, I stared at my purple painted toenails peeking through my flats.

"He wouldn't be able to have any older patients. One look at him and those old ladies would be on the list for a heart transplant." I said.

Lucy snickered, shaking her head. "Get out of here before you make Roger choke on his beer."

"Since when does Roxy tell jokes?" he asked Lucy as if I wasn't standing right in front of him. "And since when does she wear makeup?"

"I'll explain later," Lucy said, studying me quizzically. "Alright kids, you two have fun."

When I summoned the courage, I gazed at the handsome boy smiling at me. With his brown hair slicked back, his face clean-shaven, and that swimmer's physique flattered by a tight, grey polo, I felt my knees wobble.

Crawling down the stairs and hiding beneath the blankets suddenly seemed like a better idea. *What am I thinking? I can't do this. Why would someone like him want to date a loser like me?* But before I had the chance to cancel on account of flu-like symptoms, Zachary held out his elbow for me, waved good-bye to Lucy and Roger, and closed the heavy, front door behind us.

"Thanks for saving me back there," he said, finally giving me the hug we were both too scared to exchange in the presence of any family members.

"I'm really sorry," I replied, loving how strong his body felt. "They can be real jerks."

He shrugged. "They just care about you a lot."

I snorted. "Yeah, and pigs can fly."

"Well, now that we're out of there, are you ready for the best date of your life?" He walked over to his car and opened the passenger side door for me.

I stared at him, a smile tugging at the corners of my lips. "That's a pretty brave assumption."

After I slid into the car, he closed the door and jogged over to his side. I couldn't help but giggle. "I know this place in Hillcrest that has amazing sushi."

"And if I don't like sushi?" I asked.

He buckled his seatbelt slowly, his shoulders hunching forward sadly. "Then this is the beginning of a *really* uncomfortable date."

Sensing his uneasiness, I frowned. *You can like sushi for him. It's just fish and rice. He doesn't have to know.* I rested my palm on his thigh and squeezed. "Lucky for you, I just so happen to *love* sushi."

He focused on my hand for one long moment before turning toward me. "You have *no idea* just how lucky I am."

#

THE ONE THING I desperately needed wouldn't stop running away from me, my thoughts and feelings frightening the poor thing into a dead sprint. Sleep. A no-nagging family, free from decision making, chamomile tea induced sleep.

An hour of incessant tossing and turning passed by at a snail's pace, frustration forcing me to kick off my blankets and sigh angrily into my beige pillow case. "Who cares what your parents say? Lucy approves of his grown-up good looks, you approve of the way he treats you, and Dad didn't greet him at the door with a pistol when he dropped me off. That's all great. So, what's the problem?"

I tossed twice more before sliding off my dark green comforter, my one true source of comfort slumbering on the carpet at the foot of the bed. The yellow lab was snoring, her legs twitching from whatever crazy dog dream she was experiencing. I lay down beside her and rested my head on her plump ribs. She responded with a quick stretch of her legs, a long groan and a loud sigh.

"I'm sorry Molly, but I can't sleep. I really wish you could talk to me. You're the only one who'd give me decent advice—no sarcasm layered with a thick coat of disappointment. I'm afraid I'm in some trouble and I need your help."

She shifted her neck to face me and licked my nose, a giggle escaping from my lips.

"If only it were that simple."

Molly returned to her original position, the silver nametag clinking against her pink collar. I closed my eyes, breathing in the scent of oatmeal shampoo and dirt. "I had so much fun on my date with Zach, but I'm *really* confused about the way I feel."

The date was simple, yet influential. Dinner and a movie followed by a shameless make-out session in the mall's parking lot. Unfortunately, Lamont remained a persistent nuisance hovering just above my forehead. Whenever Zachary would reach for my hand, put a piece of food in his mouth, tell a story, or even laugh, I would compare the two boys. The most annoying part was that my lips were constantly analyzing the technique, the amount of pressure exchanged, and the pressure applied to that of Lamont's deliciously flawless kisses. I was hopeful this line of thinking would help to clarify what I liked and disliked about each of them, positive that my heart would pick one over the other. But rather than produce any encouraging results, my feelings for them became entangled in a mess of unstable emotions. One minute, Zachary would whisper something to me that would make me laugh, and the next, I'd hear Lamont's monotone voice caressing my ear, urging me to come back to Rohnert Park.

I pat Molly's head and scratched gently behind her ears. "I think I like Zach, a lot. But Lamont—there's something I can't quite explain. I don't know why I still love him. Besides, Zach lives in San Diego and I live in Rohnert Park. Wouldn't it be stupid to fall for someone so far away? But he's *such* a gentleman. Lamont would spontaneously combust before opening a car door for me. But he and I have this *chemistry* together." I paused, listening to the beat of Molly's heart. "What should I do?"

She grunted and sneezed.

I turned onto my back and stared into the darkness. "It's so much better to be here with you. Maybe I can sneak you back to school in my suitcase." Her tail thumped three times against the thick carpet. "Who would you choose?"

Another grunt.

"Zach is so handsome and he's such a sweetheart. He knows how to make me laugh. He's a kind soul—the *epitome* of a good guy. He didn't push me to do anything even though we were alone, he paid for dinner, and he *actually* listened to me when I was talking. Oh, and have I mentioned that his kisses are so very *delightful*."

She shifted her body, squirming and wiggling to force me off her side. I giggled, moved and lay beside her, face to face. After licking my nose, Molly curled her paws just enough so I could snuggle with one arm around her. Sleep began to swirl throughout the room, pulling down my eyelids, blocking out the moonlight shining through the window.

"His kisses are nothing compared to yours, Molly." I felt her warm breath touch my cheek. "I think I'm falling for this guy. It's scary. He hurt me so badly before. What if this is just another stupid mistake? I've already made so many in these past few months. Is it worth it? Should I take the risk?"

A yawn escaped me, my eyes like lead curtains.

Molly whined and placed her head beneath my chin.

I nodded lazily. "You're right. Maybe he deserves a second chance."

#

LAUGHTER RANG THROUGHOUT the Vaughn's dining room on Thanksgiving evening. Lucy was the only other one not drinking alcohol, sparkling apple cider bubbling in our individually monogrammed wine glasses. My parents were each on their fourth glass of Pinot Grigio and Roger was working on his sixth glass of Riesling. The good white china had been removed from storage for dinner, each plate scraped clean, and the napkins had been pressed at the local dry cleaners a few hours earlier.

Holidays were the only occasion where an individual in the Vaughn's household could eat until one's stomach bloated over his or her jeans without judgment. Except, of course, me. A second helping of mashed potatoes and gravy earned me a narrow glare from my mother, who proceeded to make a snide comment about the fact that I was wearing sweatpants.

"Do any of your jeans fit you anymore?"

Everyone else laughed, believing she was making a joke. I, on the other hand, stayed quiet for the rest of the meal, my fingers resting on my overly stuffed belly. *You know she's just being obnoxious. You've lost ten pounds this semester. Don't let her get to you. If only she knew that throwing up every Friday during lab is weekly exercise.*

"Roxanne, clear the table," Lucy ordered. "The baby wants some pumpkin pie."

I sighed, pushed the chair back and began stacking plates, my hands shaking slightly.

"Better steady those hands of yours," Mother teased. "Unless you get your act together and stop throwing up in class, you'll be stacking dishes for a living."

*Ah. I am mistaken. Of course, she knows that I get sick every week. Why would I think I could trust my sister to keep her mouth shut for one freaking second?* My eyebrows dropped close to my eyelids. "Lucy, what the heck? I told you that in confidence."

She shrugged. "I thought Mom would be able to help."

"Yeah, mocking me is the sure-fire way to get me to pass my classes."

"Roxy," Mother snapped. "Again, with that attitude of yours."

I placed the dishes beside the sink, my teeth biting down on my cheek so hard, I could taste blood.

"Honey, why didn't you say something?" my father asked in his annoyingly calm demeanor. "We—your mother and I—know methods of desensitization. We're here to help."

"Sissy, the pie?" Lucy interjected.

I opened the refrigerator and grabbed the pie with one hand, a tub of low-fat Cool Whip in the other. "Right. Maybe it's my body telling me I'm supposed to be doing something else with my life. Ever thought that might be the case?"

When I turned around, four exasperated faces stared at me. I dropped the pie and the topping onto the table, the four of them bouncing slightly in their seats. "Eat up."

"You're not going to warm up the pie?" Lucy asked.

"What do you mean, 'something else?' We're all doctors. Do you want to be a *nurse?*"

I rolled my eyes at my mother. "I'm thinking about becoming a poet."

"Guess that's a no," Lucy sighed. She served herself two pieces of pie, smothering the dessert in two scoops of Cool Whip. "Again, with this poetry nonsense. What will you do as a poet? Besides starve and live on the streets?"

"Roxanne, how long have you been thinking like this?" Father asked.

I shrugged. "I don't know. A while. I'm still taking all of my science classes, but I think I'm going to change majors."

"You can't be serious?"

I turned to my mother. "As serious as a fatal heart attack."

She pointed at the stairs. "You go to your room young lady. I refuse to have you ruin my dessert."

"I thought you'd never ask," I mumbled, attempting to ignore their mean remarks as I trudged down the stairs.

"At least you're pregnant," I heard my mother say to Lucy. "You'll makeup for the piss poor job your father and I did raising your sister."

#

"ROXANNE, I CAN'T hold back anymore. I love you."

It was my last night in San Diego. Since my parents weren't talking to me anyway, I'd escaped my room, snuck out through the garage and gave Molly a kiss on the nose before hopping into Zachary's running car. He'd taken me to a play at Balboa Park, followed by a trip to the nearest ice cream parlor. The best part was that he'd managed to light a fire in the living room's fireplace—my parents sound asleep in their bedroom downstairs, earplugs and eye-masks sure to keep them dreaming—and we ate our melting dessert while whispering to one another, Molly snoozing at our feet. Even when Zachary informed me he was leaving so I could get some sleep before my flight tomorrow morning, I didn't feel the slightest bit disappointed. He'd been the reason why I didn't experience a complete meltdown every time I overheard my parents questioning what they did to deserve such a disappointing daughter.

I'd walked him up to the door wishing my trip had been a few days longer. My time with Zachary had been both emotionally draining and mentally stimulating, my feelings evolving at an alarming rate, and I wasn't sure this short trip had provided me with ample time to weigh the pros and cons of the two men in my life. I wrapped my arms around Zachary, my body relaxing once he returned the gesture. Standing there, my cheek nestled comfortably against his collarbone, I smiled. *I'm glad I'm giving him a second chance. People really can change for the better.*

141

Unfortunately, my muscles stiffened when he murmured those three words, and I wanted to push away from him, close the door and never contact him again. *No, you don't love me. You can't love me. We're still getting to know one another.*

"Look, Zach—"

He placed his fingers against my lips. "No, you look. That's how I feel. And these past few days have solidified that for me."

I pulled away from his magnetic gaze. *I need to sit down. I don't feel good.* My stomach cramped. My legs numbed. *I'm leaving in the morning. Why would he say that?* I shook my head and bit my cheek. "You don't even know me anymore," I mumbled.

He shifted the weight on his feet, concern wrinkled on his forehead. "I know you don't want to hear it. I know that's why you never mentioned what happened in Sonoma. I'm not gonna lie to you—I've loved you ever since that day you brought me that poem." He grabbed a hold of my hands desperately. "I know I was in another relationship for quite some time, but Roxy, you've always held a place in my heart. And seeing you made all of those feelings erupt—as if my heart had been dormant these past few years. Roxy, you're the *sweetest* girl in the world. You've given me so much happiness. And I need you to know that."

"Zach, I'm not that person anymore."

He smiled. "You've grown into a beautiful woman, Roxanne. I know you're not the same person—hell, when I saw you stumble into the road, I couldn't believe it. I know you don't drink. I know you don't sleep with someone if you don't care about them. But I also know you have this sassy side to you that you're embracing, and I think this new you is amazing."

I took my hands away from his and placed them firmly on his chest. *Yeah, but you don't know about my anxiety. About how sad I am all the time. About how I hate myself.* "I'm sorry, Zach. I just don't feel that way."

He shrugged. "I'm not expecting you to. But I needed you to understand why I'm so drawn to you."

I nodded. "I do care about you. I really do. But, you—you broke—I just—"

He kissed my cheek. "I was a real asshole, I know," he whispered. "But I'm going to wait for you. My feelings won't waiver—I promise, I'm not going anywhere this time."

As our lips touched, my heart tore in two. *Waiting for me is a mistake*, I wanted to scream. *I don't even know what I'll want for breakfast tomorrow. How*

142

*will I know when I'm ready for a relationship?* "I'm gonna miss you," I whispered into his lips, afraid of anything else I might say.

"I already miss you." He placed his hands on my lower back and pulled my body into his. "I can't wait to see you again. Three weeks won't go by quickly enough. I'll be counting the moons until I get you back in my arms."

I watched him walk across the street before closing the door and biting my lip. *Maybe he'll help me forget about Lamont. Maybe he is good for me.* I closed my eyes and placed my forehead against the wooden door. *And maybe I'm gonna be the one to break his heart this time around.* "Why did I ever listen to my sister? I should've just stayed in my room. Everything would've been less complicated that way."

#

AFTER A QUICK plane ride where I drank two Sprites and ate two bags of peanuts, where I wrote three pages of poetry about the loyalty of a dog and ignored the Anatomy textbook burning a hole through my backpack, I found myself paying the cab driver far too much money for the forty-five minute, traffic free trip from Oakland to Rohnert Park. It was around noon when I entered through the back door of the dormitory and yet, I found all of my roommates lounging in the living room—still clad in their pajamas—watching some trashy show on the television.

I was so excited to see them that I shrieked when I slammed the door behind me, eliciting obnoxious greetings from my friends. We exchanged bear hugs and "I missed you's" before settling comfortably on the couches—it was as if we hadn't been on break at all, easily able to fall back into our usual morning routine.

"Guys, I have a story to tell you," I said placing a green throw pillow over my stomach.

Amber crossed her legs and tapped her foot against the chair. "Do tell! We were all hoping you'd have some juicy stuff to share."

*Well, my parents hate me and my sister thinks I'm a quitter, but other than that, break was quite eventful.* Deciding to omit any details pertaining to my family, I regaled them with the details of last night, beginning with my outfit and ending with Zachary's emotional good-bye. They all gasped, filling my body with relief. *Thank God they understand.*

"No way!" Claire shrieked.

I nodded. "He told me he loved me."

Shannon gripped my forearm. "Had you two been drinking?"

"Not this time."

143

"And you weren't having sex?" Elizabeth asked.

I shook my head. "We didn't have sex the entire time I was home."

"So, you're telling me—"

"Yes." I smiled at Amber. "He said it to me while we were *hugging* good-bye. He meant it. He freaking meant it."

Elizabeth awed and sighed. "Oh, Roxy. This is amazing. Did you say it back?"

I laughed at the girls' expectant stares. "Sorry to disappoint, but no, I didn't. I was honest. You know, explained that I'm not ready for an emotional commitment of that caliber. He just said he couldn't hold it in anymore—he wanted me to know the truth."

"Just don't dwell on it too much."

The snarky tone of Claire's voice forced me to turn toward her slowly. "And what's that supposed to mean?"

"Look, I'm not trying to be a bitch. I'm actually proud you told him you don't love him. But just because he loves you *doesn't* mean you need to love him back. You have this tendency to fall for guys who admit they have feelings for you."

"So, you're saying that you think I only like guys when they say they like me?"

"Well—I—yeah, kind of. Zach lives in San Diego. You're up here. Don't jump into a relationship with him because you guys are experiencing some long overdue honeymoon stage."

I glared. "Will you ever approve of anyone I choose? Lamont lives up here and you have a problem with that relationship opportunity as well."

"*He has a girlfriend.* You guys don't have much of a relationship anymore, either."

*Like you know so much more about relationships Ms. Blowjob and Run.*

"Speaking of the devil himself. What're you gonna do about Lamont?" Shannon asked.

The tension in the room thickened. I cleared my throat and rolled my neck to relax my shoulders. "Haven't heard a word in three weeks. If he misses me, he'll contact me."

"You really think you can resist contacting him first?" Elizabeth wondered.

I nodded firmly. "Me and Zach have something. And I don't want to play second fiddle to Melanie anymore."

144

In the following lull, I heard Amber clicking away on her computer. "You're surprisingly quiet," I noted. "You normally have a lot to say when we talk about Lamont and Zach."

She laughed—a laugh so boisterous, it eased the tension and brought smiles to all of our faces. "You bitches will never believe what just happened."

"Share the gossip, Slutbag," Claire teased. "What's so funny?"

"Lamont's relationship status."

I grunted. "Are they finally engaged?"

Amber shook her head. "Lamont Carwyn has gone from 'in a relationship' to 'single.'"

The smile fell straight off my face and landed with a splat near my toes. "What? He—single? No more—what happen—he's not with Melanie?"

"As of about a minute ago. Guess the happy couple went through some tough shit over break."

"Give me that." I snatched the computer off her lap and tried not to throw up when the words floated, in bold type and twelve-point font, in cyber space. *Lamont Carwyn has gone from in a relationship to single.* "He even changed his profile picture."

Claire sighed. "Amber, you couldn't have kept that to yourself?"

"You're the one who told me to talk." Amber shrugged. "She was bound to find out."

"Wow," Shannon whistled. "Lamont is single."

Elizabeth chuckled. "So, Roxy. You still gonna avoid him?"

I closed the laptop and put my face in my hands. "I'm going to give it the good ol' college try."

Amber grinned. "You're a goner."

I looked at her, crestfallen. "No—I'm an idiot."

#

ANDREW PATTED MY back encouragingly while I heaved my oatmeal into the trashcan located outside of the girl's restroom. I'd barely made it to the door before the remains of apple and cinnamon came back up my throat and coated the hallway tile.

"Who the hell moves a trashcan?" I cried. "It's outside the lab for a reason— for people with weak stomachs like me."

Andrew tucked a strand of loose hair behind my ear. "At least you were smart enough to tie your hair back prior to class this time."

145

"I'm mortified." I wiped the tears with the back of my hand. "I couldn't even make it to the trashcan."

"That's why we have a janitorial service. Our tuition has to pay for something."

I half-smiled. "You mean the school isn't providing you with those snake-skin boots and that matching belt?"

He shrugged. "They should. If you were touring this place and saw me walking by, wouldn't you tear up your other acceptance letters and attend Sonoma State in a heartbeat?"

We walked through the bathroom doors so I could wash out my mouth. "Your modesty really knows no bounds, does it?"

He gripped my elbow and lead me to the sinks. "I'm merely making my argument for my next attempt at a scholarship."

I shook my head. "Andy, I'm so mad at myself. I was doing *so good*. Why did the professor have to bring cadavers into class *today*?"

Andrew tilted back his leather hat slightly, switching his bangs from the left of his forehead to the right. "Well, we are studying to be doctors. If we didn't work on human bodies, we wouldn't stand a chance in the medical world."

"I'm going to be sick again. I'll have to accept an F for the day." I held my hands under the poorly running water, let it pool and splashed it into my mouth, attempting to get the taste of acid out of my mouth.

He reached into his pocket and pulled out some gum. "Chew this. You're repulsive."

After I spit the water back into the sink, I slapped his shoulder. "I can't help it." I unwrapped a stick of gum and shoved it into my mouth. "How was break?"

Andrew sighed. "My brothers played football together while I drank mimosas with my sisters. My parents still don't believe I'm gay."

"Have they looked at you lately?"

He fussed with his bangs again. "They're in denial. Even if I had breast implants and danced topless for a living, they would continue to pester me about marrying a nice, Jewish girl."

I splashed some cool water onto my face. "Can I ask you something personal?"

"Not if you continue to drip your nasty ass face-water so close to my three-hundred-dollar boots."

I flicked my hands at him and giggled when he gasped. "I'm being serious. I need help. I'm at a crossroads and a homosexual outlook might be enlightening."

Andrew crossed his arms. "What's the problem?"

"I'm in love with a guy who doesn't love me and developing feelings for a guy who does love me."

"Well, it's a no brainer."

I threw the paper towel into the trash bin. "I should pick the one who loves me?"

He laughed and shook his head. "No, silly. Who cares about love at our age? Who has the bigger ding-a-ling?"

"What is it with people obsessing about size every time I talk about a boy?"

Andrew pulled up his light green jeans, a bulge protruding next to his zipper. When he gestured toward it, I blushed. "Because it matters. In both the gay and straight communities."

I opened the paper towel dispenser and tugged on the roll until it came free. "You are no help what-so-ever. I don't know why I bother asking you anything."

"It's because you love me."

We returned to the hallway where my breakfast had already begun to dry on the cracked tile. I unrolled the paper towels and held my breath, the remaining contents in my stomach beginning to tumble in lopsided circles.

"Wow. That's your brilliant idea? To leave a giant ass layer of paper towels over your bowels?"

I frowned. "You suggested I do nothing. At least I'm attempting to cover it from plain sight so that nobody else gets sick."

He smirked. "It's a wonder you have the ability to be charming enough to win over anybody's heart."

"The only heart that matters to me is yours, Andy."

"Well shucks." He wrapped his arm around my shoulders. "There's that charm. Spread on thick just like chunky peanut butter on white bread."

"Who needs a boyfriend when you have a best gay friend?"

"Well, even though you'll have my heart forever—despite your lack of prestige and food when you become a homeless poet—you are lacking what I need to keep me physically happy."

I squeezed myself closer to his side. "You could cheat on me. But at least I'd have a man to come home to at night—maybe two. How would your parents feel about you marrying me?"

He sighed. "Unfortunately, that'd be worse than me coming out of the closet. I can't marry a Catholic. My mother has very high standards."

I laughed. "What would I do if I never met you?"

He kissed my forehead. "You'd be throwing up alone every Friday morning. And nobody deserves to throw up alone that often."

#

AFTER BEING HOME for a week and still not hearing a single word from Lamont, I told myself it was over. Sitting alone in my room watching some sappy Chick-Flick about finding happily ever after with a man who had originally been a jerk throughout the film but wound up being a knight in shining armor at the end, I caved and texted him first.

I didn't think he'd respond, so when he asked me to come over, I didn't think twice—didn't think at all.

I wanted to kick myself for being so weak willed, but I needed to see him. I needed to know if everything between us had been a lie. I needed to know if it was time to force myself to forget about him entirely.

I parked behind his big white truck, pushed my bangs behind my ear and breathed slowly to try to steady my racing heart. I hated to admit it, so I didn't say it out loud. But I missed him. His deep voice, his handsome face, his warm embrace and his sincere smile. I missed the way he looked at me as if I was the center of his world, even if it only lasted for three seconds.

This was my first time back in the house since the first night we kissed. After letting myself through the front door, I glanced at the living room and kitchen, wondering if he and Tiffany preferred the privacy of his bedroom, or flaunted their sex life by doing it on the communal couch. *None of that matters. Lamont invited you here. He obviously missed you.* I blinked, the glare of sunlight reflecting from the plastic porch furniture hurting my eyes. I couldn't help but to remember the way I initially felt when Lamont first held me; before I knew about his girlfriend and he'd made me believe we had something special.

"Lamont?" I called out shyly.

"Come into my room."

His deep voice made me dizzy, the hallway now stretching miles ahead of me as if I'd walked into a house of mirrors. When I turned into his bedroom, I found him snuggled in his bed watching TV. He peered at me over the blankets and smiled. My heart skipped like a little girl playing hopscotch.

"Well, don't you look cozy?" I sat at the foot of his bed, focusing on the TV. "What're you watching?"

148

"Animal Planet." He paused. "You're not gonna say hi?"

I looked over my shoulder and shrugged. "Hi."

He shook his head and smirked. "It's been weeks since we've seen each other and that's all I get?"

I nodded once. "You're the one who's made no effort to contact me."

"It's a two-way street."

"Yeah, you're right. It is. And I drove down my side of the street when I invited you over a month ago. Looks like it was your turn."

He remained silent, his gaze hungrily fixed on mine.

I gulped. "So, Animal Planet, huh?"

"Yes. I like animals." Lamont sat with his back now propped against the wall and patted the bed next to him. "Get that big butt of yours over here and give me a fucking hug."

I hesitantly walked over to him, bent down and went in for a friendly hug. "You know, that's not necessarily considered a compliment."

He wrapped his arms around me and pulled me onto the bed with him. "Come cuddle with me," he murmured into my neck.

I ignored the voice in my head telling me to abort the mission immediately. "So, does that mean you've missed me?"

He snuggled behind me and kissed the skin exposed just above the neckline of my sweatshirt. "You know I have," he purred.

My stomach caved in on itself and my head spun like a vortex. I even tasted metal in my mouth. I wove my fingers through his and pulled his hands tightly to my chest, forcing back the panic attack making its way up my spine. *We're both single. Nothing to feel guilty about anymore. I'm allowed to do whatever I want, and he's allowed to do whatever he wants.* I smiled at him.

"It's a little hot, don't you think? Why not take that clunky sweatshirt off?"

I nodded silently, moving my body to pull the hoodie over my head, listening while it landed quietly on the floor.

"That's much better. Now I can feel you."

And with his body so close to mine, I too, felt his hard erection pressed against me—straight through his flimsy sweatpants and my thin yoga pants. He began kissing my shoulder blades, the cotton of my shirt not thick enough to keep goose bumps from erupting over every inch of my body. He moved up to my neck, pushing my hair to the side, biting gently near my jaw and finally stopping to nuzzle my ear. My body trembling, I turned toward him, eagerly meeting his lips with my own. I didn't realize how much I desired his touch. I couldn't get enough of him: the tobacco taste in his mouth, the scruff of his chin, the way his hands decisively moved beneath my clothing, caressing my body possessively. I gripped my hands behind his head, his black hair tickling my fingertips. He moved on top of me, my breath rushing from my lungs. However, when Lamont's hand made it down my pants—*Think about what you're doing. What about Zach? What would he think about this? And what about Tiffany? How manh times have they done this here in the same spot?*

I grabbed his hand, a flurry of emotions overwhelming me.

He shifted his arms, holding himself above me. "What's wrong?"

I moved from beneath him, the blood rushing from my head. Panic tingled at the end of my fingertips. "I can't do this."

He began kissing me again, fully taking advantage of my vulnerability. I allowed his lips to dance with mine, our tongues seducing one another in a provocative tango. I grasped onto his shirt and pulled his body closer to mine. His hands surrounded my breasts, slowly making their way down my stomach, easing beneath my pants once again. I stopped kissing him and pushed his hand away.

"Lamont, I'm sorry, but I don't want to do that right now."

His eyes lost focused. "Are you on your period or something?"

Caught off guard, I stared at him silently, my brain trying to process what I just heard. *This is all I am to him. A glorified hand.* "Yeah. I am."

After studying me for a moment, he rolled onto his side of the bed, his attention back on the TV screen. The silence grew to an agonizing volume, my pulse banging heavy drumsticks against my eardrums. I tried to cuddle behind him, only to feel his body stiffen and arch away from mine.

Hurt and angry—and refusing to let him see me break down into a million little pieces—I climbed over Lamont and showed myself out the door; no kiss, no good-bye, no nothing.

Tears warmed my cheeks as I walked down the driveway.

I had gotten the clarity I needed.

I no longer wanted to have Lamont Carwyn in my life.

# Chapter Eight

ON THE SATURDAY morning before finals week, I was surprised to open my bedroom door and see Tiffany standing there, two cups of coffee in her hands.

"You look terrible," I said, welcoming her into the dungeon I called a room.

She smiled. "I went out last night. What's your excuse?"

I patted my hair down and brushed off the cookie crumbs sticking to my overly large, unflattering t-shirt. I'd fallen asleep sitting up the night before and had completely neglected to look at a mirror since my alarm went off, a horrible pain in my neck, and smudged chocolate chips all over my anatomy notebook.

"Anatomy. I need to do really well on this final in order to get an A. I'm close to it and I refuse to get any lower—especially when I finally got the hang of those stupid quizzes."

She handed me the coffee, pushed some crumpled up papers off my desk chair and sat down. "I won't stay long, but I need to tell you something that I think you'll find important."

I sat on my bed, ignoring the crinkling of notes beneath me. *This is it. She's gonna tell me that her and Lamont are in a relationship.* "What's up?" I managed to ask before sipping on the steaming peppermint mocha.

"Claire and Adam have a thing going on, right?"

"If by *thing* you mean she kisses him one day and hates him the next, all the while leading him to believe that she will eventually give into a real relationship, then yes, they have a thing. He's head-over-heels in love with her. They text all day, every day."

She nodded and sipped from the plastic lid covering the paper cup. "Well, why didn't Claire go out with the other girls last night?"

The coffee felt warm against my hands, the bitter taste making my tongue sing. "She had some dance thing out of town. She'll be home sometime this afternoon. She left on Thursday." I paused and raised an eyebrow. "Is something wrong with Adam?"

"I was at the same party as Shannon, Amber, Danielle and Elizabeth last night. "

I nodded.

"Well, as the night wound down, Lizzy, Danny, Amber, Shannon and Adam decided to sit on the couch. Put their feet up. Relax."

I nodded again.

"Adam and Shannon had a blanket over them, which both pairs of both hands were under. And her head was resting on his shoulder and they were touching noses together. They didn't kiss, but there was definitely something going on beneath that blanket."

A moan escaped me. *Shannon and Adam? No. She wouldn't do that. Her and Claire share a bedroom.* "You must be mistaken. Adam worships the ground Claire walks on. I find it hard to believe he'd do anything to ruin his chances with her."

Tiffany shrugged. "I swear on my life. I know what I saw, and it raised some red flags."

I shook my head, frustrated. "Why would you tell me this? I have to tell Claire now. Do you realize the position you just put me in?"

Tiffany stood, her sweats hanging down low enough that I could see the edges of her polka dot G-string. "Well, Claire deserves to know what's going on before her and Adam get serious. It wouldn't be fair to keep her in the dark."

*And you couldn't tell her yourself?* "She's kinda been toying with his emotions, though. Maybe he's moved on."

"She may not be the best person in the world, but nobody deserves to be fucked over by one of their best friends—especially when it comes to love."

I stared at the back of her head. *Oh, right. But it's okay to go behind my back and not tell me the truth about Lamont?* "Hey, thanks for the coffee, Tiff."

She smiled over her shoulder. "Anytime. Good luck on your finals! I'm sure you'll do a fantastic job. You're a smart cookie."

When she made her way down to the kitchen, I placed the coffee on my nightstand and collapsed onto my paper-covered bed. "Claire's not gonna believe me. Tiffany did this on purpose. But there's no way I can't tell her, right? She does deserve to know. Just like he deserves to know how she sees different guys over the weekend and lies to him about it." I covered my eyes with my arm. "I hate this. I really hate this."

Although not sure I was doing the right thing, the instant Claire stepped through the front door, I invited her up to my bedroom, asked her how the competition went, and offered her the leftover cookies I'd been too exhausted to finish. At first, Claire didn't suspect a thing, but while I blabbered on about nothing—my anxiety taking control of the reigns and making easy conversation nearly impossible—her eyebrows began to arch higher and higher.

"Did you sleep with Lamont or something?" she asked.

I started. "What? God no."

She placed her hands on her hips. "Well then, spit it out. You obviously have something to tell me. I know you. I can tell when your anxiety acts up."

I sighed. "Okay, I do, but I don't really know how to begin."

"Just tell me. You're making me nervous."

Even though Claire wasn't much of a friend anymore and hadn't been there for me throughout the semester, I knew hiding this information from her would leave me restless. I fiddled with my fingers, wishing that Tiffany hadn't mentioned anything; she could have informed Claire of the news herself. *I hate being in the middle. Why is she doing everything to ruin my life? First Lamont, now my friends? I wish I could just lie. It would be so much easier.* After taking a deep breath, I reached out for my stuffed Molly and held it tight against my chest. "Tiffany came over this morning and told me some suspicious news from last night. About Adam. And Shannon."

The color drained from her face and she swayed slightly. I grabbed her hand and forced her to sit on the bed beside me. As I repeated the information Tiffany gave me, Claire's cheeks grew pink, her eyes narrowing near the tip of her nose. And then the shouts came—obscenities, insults and profanities, some of which I'd never heard before. Once the storm clouds of anger blew over, the rain clouds pouring down dark despair took shape, Claire's eyes a faucet leaking big, betrayal filled tears. I knew where she was coming from, so, I offered her tissues and wrapped her in a hug to ease the pain.

When she ran down the stairs to confront Shannon, I cringed. *Why didn't she just leave it alone? Why can't she just stay quiet?* Shouts climbed up the stairs and swirled around me, the voices of Amber and Elizabeth joining in on the debacle. *Oh man. They're gonna blame me. Nonono I didn't do anything.*

"You treat him like shit. Why do you care?" Amber asked.

"You don't know anything about me and him, so shut your fucking mouth. You all know damn well we talk every day."

"Claire, think logically here. You've told us a million times that the two of you are *just friends*. You kissed Adam once, like, a month ago and told us you regretted it. You brought some other guy home last weekend and locked Shannon out of the room. It doesn't really seem like you care much about Adam," Elizabeth pointed out rationally.

153

I could hear Shannon sobbing beneath the high octaves of Claire and Amber's shrieks.

"You're only scared of losing him because you need a male's attention 24/7, otherwise you don't feel adequate. And let's be real, without him, you'd have *nobody*. People are beginning to see through your big boobs and fake smile, and that's why they only talk to you if they want a blowjob—not if they want a real connection with somebody."

"You're just jealous because I get attention, you bitch!"

I closed my door and stared at my Anatomy notes. Their voices still penetrated my walls, but I had finals to study for. "Everyone around here is a liar. I'm never leaving my room ever again. Books don't hurt people. People hurt people." I sighed, patting the yellow stuffed animal still resting against my chest. "I can't wait to go home. I can't deal with all the drama anymore."

Just as I grabbed my poetry notebook, the banshees opened my door, their voices piling atop one another, their angry tears burning holes through my carpet.

"What the fuck did you tell her, Roxy?" Amber yelled.

My body swelled with guilt and discomfort. Although I'd become better at escaping the safety of my box, their accusatory stares had me diving back in, headfirst. Taking a deep breath, I crossed my hands in my lap and looked each girl directly in the eye. "I told her the truth about Adam and Shannon."

It was at that moment a civil war broke out in the dorm with Shannon and Amber as the North, Claire and me as the South, and Elizabeth remaining a neutral third party, too torn up about the situation to pick a side.

And it was at that moment when I realized how fickle relationships could be, even between a group of girls who considered themselves the best of friends.

#

"JUST BREATHE, ROXY. This is your last final and then you'll never have to worry about looking inside a human being ever again."

Andrew and I stood outside the laboratory doors, my hands shaking, his hands stroking my arms methodically. The rest of the class had gathered at their stations inside, but a sudden burst of panic had left me running for the exit.

"Well, unless you become a lesbian."

I gagged, my stomach beginning to hurt. "That's not funny."

"Look, you're already in your lab coat. The gloves are already on your hands. Once you put the goggles on, you're pretty much done. And you haven't thrown up yet! Bonus points."

I shook my head, my heart thumping too loudly against my skull. "I can't. I'm going to be sick. The sight. The smell." I wrapped my arms around my stomach. "No. I don't think I'm going to be sick—I *am* going to be sick. I can feel it coming up."

He grabbed my shoulders roughly and forced me to look him in the eye. "God damn it, Roxy. You've made it this far. I refuse to see you fail. We can come up with a way to get you through this. I just need a minute to think."

While he paced back and forth, I wrung my latex gloved hands together. "Look, Andy, I appreciate you trying to help me and all, but I just can't—"

"Shut up," he ordered. "I have a plan. Stop being so fucking stubborn and listen to me."

I froze, lips quivering.

"We're gonna get you to pass this exam. Grab a mask, put on some sunglasses and keep a pen glued to your hand. You say you want to be a writer? Well, I'm gonna make you fucking write. Spray a splash of perfume on your mask, keep your eyes averted from the cadaver and write down *every single word* that comes out of my mouth. Do you hear me? You and me—we're in this shit together. I will not let you quit."

"Are you sure?"

He nodded. "You stay here, and I'll go get you a mask. I have Lady Gaga's latest perfume in my bag. And here are my sunglasses. They're Dolce and Gabbana. Don't you dare fucking break them."

I wrapped him in a huge hug. "You are my guardian angel. Seriously, Andy. You're a real friend. Probably the only person I can trust in this town."

He kissed the top of my head and slid the sunglasses onto my face. "I love you, Roxy. You made this semester bearable. Make sure you visit me in the science department when you're off writing beautiful poems and stories. Don't forget about us lowly doctors being forced to work on dead and decaying people."

I tried not to gag, chuckling when he winked at me. "I'm still going to see you, Andy. I'll force you to attend a party with me one of these nights."

"Let's not say good-bye just yet. We have a final to pass, and I can't afford to cry and smear my eyeliner."

#

EIGHT HOURS OF driving alone in the car gave me more than enough time to think about how much my life had changed in the past four months. I'd learned how to somewhat socialize like a normal human being. I acted crazy after drinking too much vodka. I'd tried my hand at casual sex and failed miserably.

I'd made a true friend in the one class I was certain would've been the death of me. I'd learned how to be a fake friend in order to gather information from someone who deserved everything but my attention. I'd even found myself in the middle of a heated girl fight—one that lasted precisely four days and twelve hours before everyone decided it was all just one big misunderstanding. We concluded that Tiffany was just stirring up unnecessary drama to take my attention away from her and Lamont.

Most importantly, I learned how to stand up for myself and take charge of my own life. I'd switched my major to English and Comparative Literature.

A poet among a family of doctors.

I came to realize, if I could survive the ups and downs of my first semester as a sophomore, then I could handle anything life threw at me.

The sign for San Diego—only ten miles more—reflected against my headlights.

I smiled. "Good-bye to the old Roxanne. There's a new girl in town."

#

"HOW DID YOUR finals go?" my father asked over dinner.

I'd spent the day watching TV with Molly sitting on the couch beside me, her head resting comfortably on my thigh. It was a peaceful first day home because my parents were in Los Angeles visiting Lucy and they weren't planning on returning home until early evening. Lucy was officially fifteen weeks along in her pregnancy and wanted our parents present for her sonogram.

I shrugged, pushing around the peas on my plate. "They went fine. I studied really hard for all of them." *And I managed to survive the anatomy lab with only puking twice.*

My mother sipped her white wine. "I'm sure your English class didn't require that much preparation."

"Honey," my father said sternly. "Just because certain classes can be more challenging than others, doesn't mean—"

"Dad, I know this is your attempt at being helpful, but it's not really working."

"Roxanne. Think logically. You can't compare science and English. That would be like trying to compare bananas to watermelons."

I sliced through the grilled chicken breast with my parents' newly sharpened knives. "I'm not even trying to compare them. I know they're different subjects, but English class isn't *easy*. It's difficult in its own way."

My mother scoffed. "Oh, really? And what way is that?"

156

"Have you read and analyzed all the major British works of literature? And had to summarize said analysis into a twenty-page paper with ten outside scholarly sources?"

"And have you looked inside of a vagina while it's fully dilated only to help deliver a child that you know is going straight into foster care because the irresponsible mother is only sixteen years old?"

My father slowly lowered his silverware to the table. "My dear, what have I said about vagina talk at the dinner table?"

"I was making a point."

"Mom, I understand you're upset with me, but I want to be happy and being a doctor wouldn't have done that for me."

Both of my parents sipped their wine and ignored me.

I sighed. "So, how's Lucy?"

My mom's eyes lit up like the fluorescent lightning at the hospital. "She's beautiful—pregnancy suits her. That ivory skin of hers is simply glowing."

*I hate you.*

"She's already in her second trimester," my father added. "The baby is developing just as it should—healthy heartbeat and all."

I smiled despite the fact that I could care less. *Just more attention given to the prodigy child. Could I be any more invisible?* "I'm really happy for her. Have you guys discovered if it's a boy or a girl yet?"

My mother patted her perfectly lipsticked mouth with her pearl colored, cloth napkin. "Yes, your father and I know, but Roger and Lucy want it to be a surprise. So, we had the sonogram technician take us outside the room and whisper it to us." She paused. "Roxanne, why not find out what it takes to become a sonogram technician? I could use one in my practice."

I glared at her. "No." Then I turned to my father. "Dad, boy or a girl?"

He dabbed the napkin against the corners of his now moistened blue eyes. "She's having a girl."

The chicken in my mouth grew unchewable in my suddenly dry palate. "That's great," I squeaked.

"Make sure you don't say a word to your sister about it."

I nodded, squeezing the napkin on my lap in my fists. *A girl. Of course, she's having a girl. Just what they need—a granddaughter to replace me.*

"You do know that your father and I won't be paying for your tuition as long as you're not studying to join the medical field, right?"

I pushed back my chair and brought my dish over to the sink. "Guess that means I better start filling out my Fafsa form."

My mother threw her napkin on the table. "Roxanne, stop being ridiculous."

"You're the one who isn't accepting who I am as a person. If I have to pay for my own education, then I will. I just wish you'd support the decision that makes me happy."

"You won't be happy when you're starving in the streets and sleeping beneath the Want Ads page of the newspaper."

*I'll find someone who loves me for me. And I'll be the most successful poet to ever live. I'll show you. I'll show everyone.*

#

I WALKED THROUGH the front door of my friend's apartment and found myself surrounded by faces I hadn't seen since high school. Electronic Dance Music blared through the speakers, alcohol poured from glass bottles, ping pong balls bounced into red cups and weed burned in handheld, glass pipes. Luke, my best friend I hadn't seen since summer, welcomed me into the party, his arms creating a comforting bubble around me. His skinny frame was familiar in a place that had become strangely unfamiliar to me.

"Wow, Luke! I missed you so much," I breathed, my cheek pressed against his soft, designer, button-up shirt.

He held me away at arms length, his straight teeth shining bright between thin, tan lips. "I missed you too. How the hell are you?"

"I've been alright," I said, glancing around me. There were kids I hadn't seen in years, and their curious smiles were making me nervous. "Did you invite the whole world here?"

"Oh, don't worry about it. They're just staring because you're beautiful."

I snorted. "Yeah, right." The vodka in the plastic bag hanging from my arm was beginning to weigh me down, the need to take some shots extremely overwhelming. "How about we start drinking?"

His jet-black hair was spiked in every direction, his round chin coated in the beginnings of five o' clock shadow, and his dark brown eyes were bloodshot from the marijuana that he, undoubtedly, smoked earlier. "What?" he asked. "Since when do you drink?"

I slipped the plastic bag off my shoulder, removing a fifth of vodka. "I don't," I replied. "I tried it once and regretted it."

"So, why did you bring a bottle of vodka?"

"I thought I'd give it another try."

158

He slid his hand into mine, tugging me into the kitchen. "Believe me, Roxy. I won't let you do anything stupid."

*Where have you been the entire semester?* "And don't let me drink too much, okay? I don't want to lose control."

"What have you done with my best friend?" Luke joked, pouring the alcohol into two shot glasses. "I mean seriously. What has college done to you?"

I searched through the plastic bag again, grabbing hold of the two soda cans remaining. "I don't know. It's weird. I stand up for myself, too."

He smiled, nudging me with his elbow. "And that's how it should be. I think Sonoma State might be the best thing that's ever happened to you." He handed me one of the glasses.

I threw back the bitter drink, cracked open the soda and gulped hungrily. "I don't know about the best thing," I choked. "Does it get any easier to drink this stuff?"

Luke laughed and poured each of us another shot. "Not exactly 'easier.' I just think once you've hit that point of drunk, you don't give a shit anymore."

I resisted the urge to gag when the scent of Vodka caught my nose. "I don't know why I started drinking this. It's revolting."

"It may be disgusting but it makes you feel like a fucking God, doesn't it?"

We both tilted our necks back and grimaced before drinking greedily from our soda cans. "You mean people don't think I'm a God without this elixir breaking down my liver?"

Luke slammed his can on the counter and burped. "Sassy. Very sassy indeed. But no—a turtle maybe. A very awkward turtle. There's no such thing as an awkward God. Could you imagine Zeus blushing and hiding behind a cloud every time someone worshipped him? Because that's how you react whenever someone so much as compliments your shoes."

I elbowed him, cuddled against his chest and wondered how I'd survived so long without Luke's comforting presence. "You know, I have a friend up north who reminds me of you. He was my lab partner. Has great taste and is extremely handsome."

"That's unacceptable. I refuse to lose my best friend to another—another— well—me."

"Is someone jealous of my newfound friendship?"

"I'm just saying you should come back to San Diego for school. I'm not digging this whole 'distance' thing that's happening between us," he said before kissing the part in my hair.

"Or you could move up to Rohnert Park. We sure would benefit from some good-looking fellas like you."

The front door opened, a cold gust of wind chilling my skin, and when I turned my head to see who joined the party, Zachary walked through the doorframe behind his two best friends. "I didn't know he was invited," I muttered.

Luke pulled away. "What'd you say down there?"

That was the moment I should've told Luke about Zachary, but something held me back. The two boys never got along, and I didn't want to endure any of Luke's lectures regarding the kind of men I tended to gravitate toward. Zachary also hadn't texted me much since I'd returned home, so I was confused about his intentions. I shook my head, trying to ignore the anxiety clawing its way up my stomach. "Just because you're gorgeously tall doesn't mean you can look down upon us shorter members of the species."

"Actually, it does. I have no other choice."

I quickly hid in Luke's shadow. "Do you want to do me a favor?"

"What kind of favor?"

"Can you hide me?" A prickling sensation burned on the back of my neck. Zachary's voice grew louder—he was moving closer. I'd be face to face with him shortly and that made me want crawl under the dinner table before Zachary could see me. My insecurities were strangling me; when he and I were alone in Sonoma or at my parents' house, that was one thing, but I wasn't confident enough to believe he would still find me attractive standing amidst girls who didn't believe in leaving things to the imagination.

For the first time in my life, I'd squeezed my curves into a black corset, light blue jeans and black, knee-high, high-heeled boots. In my room, I'd felt sexy; my mother had been the one who urged me to buy new clothes and pushed me up to the salesman to buy the boots—and if she approved, then I knew it didn't make me look fat.

Now, I imagined myself as a beached whale, stranded on the sand amidst anorexic sea lions, mocking me for my inability to slip back into the ocean—or my inability to slide into a size three pair of pants. *I can't watch Zach hit on other girls. It's going to kill me.*

He eyed me suspiciously. "Why?"

"Zach," I whispered. "He and I have been talking."

He rolled his eyes, reaching for the vodka bottle again. "How long has this been happening?"

160

I shrugged. "A few months."

"Then why are you scared?"

Reaching for the Coke can, I played with the tab, trying to ease my discomfort. "Look at me compared to the other girls here. They're sticks and I'm a redwood."

"Girl, I don't know what mirror you're looking at. You're hot."

I put the soda to my lips to hide my bashfulness, but nearly spit out the sugary liquid when a pair of hands, not attached to Luke's arms, rested on my hips. "You hiding from me or something?"

His calm voice caused my blood pressure to spike, trapping the soda in my throat. *So much for hiding from him to gain some time to gather my thoughts.* "Hi Zach," I barely managed, the soda sloshing between my vocal chords. "Why—why would I be hiding?" I glanced at Luke who shook his head. "I have nothing to hide."

He pulled me into a hug—gentle, but firm. "I'm only playing around. Wanna take a shot with me?"

"Um—" I began playing with a loose curl, feeling just as nervous as I was when he visited me in Sonoma. "Yeah. In a little bit, if that's cool?"

"Sure. I'll wait for you." He wrapped me in another hug, my boobs nearly falling out of my corset when his chest pressed against me. "Why didn't you tell me you were gonna be here?"

*Stop blushing like an idiot. And stop comparing yourself to those girls.* I shrugged. "It was a last-minute thing. I asked Luke to hang out because I haven't seen him in forever and he invited me to join him here. Is that okay?" *Why did you ask his permission? Why does it matter what he thinks? He's the one who hasn't asked you to hang out with him.*

I hadn't wanted to come to the party, but I didn't have a choice. Luke pressured me into attending, promising me it would be a good time and that he would drive me home. I hadn't even intended to drink, but the thought of having to see a bunch of strangers while wearing a corset made me nervous enough to steal a bottle of vodka from my dad's liquor cabinet.

He chuckled. "Why wouldn't it be?"

"I don't know—there's a lot of other girls here I'm sure you know well."

His frown made me frown. "Roxanne—"

"Hey, can I have my best friend back?" Luke snapped. "We were kinda busy catching up with one another."

Zachary nodded, patted my shoulder and wandered over to drink with his friends.

Luke aggressively turned me to face him. "Are you gonna fill me in on what's going on with you two?"

"I'm not entirely sure what's going on. We've been talking."

He crossed his arms across his chest. "Then why are you acting so weird?"

"Because I don't know how I'm supposed to act. We're surrounded by a bunch of people he's good friends with. We haven't exactly determined what we're doing together."

"There's no time like the present."

When he nudged me, I smiled. "Presently, I'm interested in hanging out with you."

After two more painful shots that Luke insisted I drink so he wouldn't feel like an alcoholic by himself, I interlaced my fingers with his, loving the warmth of his palm and the smoothness of his skin. "You ready to play some Pong?"

We walked into the living room together, taking our place at the left end of the table. "I'm ready to put these losers to shame." He picked up a ball and sunk it into a cup on the other side with ease.

A small flutter in my chest surprised me, Luke's effortless toss reminding me of the night I fainted—the night I stupidly believed Lamont would leave Melanie for me. That already felt like years ago. A different lifetime with a different Roxanne.

"How did you like them apples?" he asked.

On my tippy-toes, I planted a kiss on his cheek. The vodka was beginning to kick in, my social anxiety filtering straight through my liver. "Thank God you're my best friend. I'm always guaranteed a great Pong partner."

He chuckled. "But do you suck?"

A flirtatious smile spread across my face. His eyebrows rose when I fingered the ball in my hand. "Watch and learn." The ball sailed across the table and splashed into the same cup that Luke's hit. "You impressed yet?" I asked, nudging his ribs.

He scoffed. "You sure that wasn't just a lucky shot?"

The sound of a ball splashing into a cup beside my arm snapped me out of my Deja-Vu-like-trance. There, on the opposite side of the table, stood Zachary and some short, skinny, slutty brunette smiling at one another.

Jealousy nipped at my insides, my hands squeezing into fists by my side.

162

"Looks like we've got ourselves a game," Luke drawled lazily, sprawling his arms across my shoulders.

I leaned into his side and glared at Zachary, who was flirting so openly with the tiny girl, I secretly hoped she'd giggle herself out of the window and in the middle of on-coming traffic.

When he looked at me, I nuzzled Luke's chest, resting my hand softly on his cheek. The vodka was now taking control of my central nervous system, alcohol replacing all sense of responsibility and regret. *Two can play this game.*

"I'll do my best not to let you down, Luke."

#

I DIDN'T THINK losing to Zachary and the busty brunette could've gotten any worse, but then I found myself sitting beneath the table right next to the boy I thought, at one time, had real feelings for me. He'd played just as poorly as I did, and I was being forced to share the tiny space beneath the table beside him—as if embarrassing myself in front of everyone wasn't punishment enough. I kept my back to him. Throughout the entire forty-five-minute time span it took for the brunette and Luke to finish off the last cup of our game, I watched Zach put his arms around the anorexic girl, fake tits nearly popping out of her child's-sized tank top. He complimented her talents with hugs and high-fives, offered to drink all of her beers, and blushed when the whore placed a kiss on his cheek.

I nearly vomited when he kissed hers back.

Now, Luke and the busty brunette were playing on the same team, and by the sounds of the feet surrounding me, they were winning. I sighed, shifted my legs and rested my chin on my knees.

"Funny meeting you here," Zachary slurred behind me.

My body stiffened.

"Roxanne, are you upset with me?" he asked almost too softly.

I turned around. His hair was disheveled, eyes blood-shot, shirt stained with beer. *What happened to that man I've been falling for? This is the same guy I knew in high school. I don't like it.* "Upset isn't a strong enough word to explain what I'm feeling."

His face dropped. "What did I do wrong?"

I crossed my arms around my legs, trying desperately to hide my body. "You mean you really don't know?" I took note of the hurt penetrating his eyes. *I don't want to deal with this right now.* "You know what? Don't even worry about it."

He bit his lip. "I'd rather you be honest with me."

163

I shrugged. "I don't like losing." It wasn't a lie, but it wasn't the whole truth, either.

"Well, at least you have company, right?" His crooked smile—the one that usually warmed my heart—aggravated me. "It could be worse."

"You're totally right. I could've watched a boy I *really* like hand fuck an extremely skinny, slutty and straight-haired girl directly in front of me." I hiccupped, my eyelids heavy. "Lucky fucking me.

Pain and confusion distorted his usually handsome facial features. "Roxy, your body is absolutely bea—"

"Game over! C'mon and take a shot with me," Luke said, grabbing my hand and pulling me out from beneath the table. "Someone just brought in a bottle of Grey Goose!"

To my dismay, Zachary crawled out after me and followed Luke and I into the kitchen. Glancing over my shoulder, I took note of his bowed head, his dragging feet and his bitten nails. *Why didn't I just stay home?*

Luke glanced at Zachary, furrowed his eyebrows and poured two shots before tapping the bottle with his index finger. "Guess this'll be my shot glass since he decided to join us."

I looked at Luke skeptically. "You can have mine then. You promised to take me home tonight."

"We're gonna be here for a few more hours. That's plenty of time for me to sober up."

Zachary grunted. "You're not staying here?"

"Never mind, Luke. Cheers." I tapped my glass against Luke's bottle, swallowed the burning liquid with difficulty and yanked an orange juice carton off the counter before jamming it to my lips.

"Now, Little Woman, answer my question," Zachary said after wiping his lips on his sleeve.

I snorted. "Do you really think I'm the kind of person to spend the night at a stranger's house? Especially in a house full of drunk assholes?"

He put his arm around my waist and pulled me into his side. "I'd protect you from the stupid boys around here."

*Yeah, but who would protect me from you?* Clenching my teeth together, I struggled to relax my muscles. *The last thing I want to see is you getting cozy with that skank, again.* "I appreciate the offer," I said before slowly removing his hand from the skin between my top and my jeans. "But I'd rather not sleep in a corset—you can imagine how constricting that would be."

"You could always take it off."

Irrational anger tugged at my vocal chords. "Or I could always leave it on and go home as planned."

His lids began to drop heavily, his body lightly swaying left to right. "What did I do, Roxy? You're all over Luke and completely ignoring me, but as soon as I so much as speak to another girl, you lose your shit."

"Firstly, Luke is my best friend. Secondly, I was not *all over him*. I didn't know you were gonna be here, so yeah, it made me uncomfortable. We haven't seen each other yet, and you haven't made any effort to make plans to see me. I didn't know if you even wanted to see me again. Plus, you and Luke don't like each other, and I didn't have the chance to tell him what's been going on between us lately."

The music from the living room grew to a deafening level, drunk boys and girls pressing their bodies aggressively onto one another.

"You only texted me that you'd gotten home a few days ago. You didn't seem interested in doing anything with me." When I shook my head, Zachary glared at me. "You're embarrassed to tell Luke about us, aren't you?"

"No, I'm not embarrassed. I don't even know what *this* is right now. I have to tell people on my own time," I countered.

His green eyes turned a dark shade of gray, his anger suddenly morphing into sadness. "What am I doing wrong? Why don't you love me?"

My heart lurched forward. *We're both too drunk to be talking about this right now. We're supposed to be having fun, not questioning each other.*

"Zach, I think it would be beneficial if you stopped drinking."

"Oh, you think so?" He grabbed an unopened beer bottle from the counter, twisted off the lid and chugged it directly in front of me. After he burped and placed the bottle down, he glared. "I wasn't gonna drink anything else, but now that you mention it, I'm *really* fucking thirsty."

"And here I thought you'd changed." Shaking my head, I walked away. *He really had me fooled. I actually believed he'd learned how to control himself.* I wandered over to the couch and sat down, suddenly too exhausted to join in on the impromptu dance floor. *This isn't the Zach I've developed feelings for. This is the Zach from my past.*

And I never wanted to see him again.

#

I STOOD STARING, arms crossed, foot tapping the carpet, disappointment and cheap beer leaving a bitter taste in my mouth. My lips were tingling, cheeks numb, body pleasantly warm. I'd reached that embarrassing point of intoxication where forgiving Zachary for his less than desirable behavior was inevitable.

I was ready to make-out with the guy as if that awful exchange earlier never happened.

Unfortunately, Zachary—having ignored my previous request to stop drinking—was presently passed out on the couch. I shook his left shoulder until his eyelashes wiggled and he smiled drunkenly at me.

Sitting beside him, I ran a hand through his mussed hair. "You gonna wake up or what?"

He mumbled something indecipherable and turned away from me. I sighed impatiently and shook his shoulder again.

No response.

"God. You are such an asshole."

Still no response.

Frustrated and angry, I plopped my butt onto the coffee table, busying myself by changing TV channels, wishing I could go home and sleep.

Luke sat beside me reeking of weed. "You alright? You seem pretty fucking down."

I shrugged. "Am I really that obvious?"

"You flipped right past three reality TV shows. Roxy, you're my best friend—you wouldn't pass up trashy television unless something serious was bothering you."

My body began to relax beside him. "I dunno. I'm just drunk and stupid and tired."

He spread his arm across my shoulders, my head naturally cuddling against his chest. Maybe it was the exchange Zach and I shared earlier, maybe it was loneliness, or maybe it was because I'd ingested too much alcohol, but I found my lips smashed against Luke's, our tongues wrestling with one another. His mouth was moist and warm, his hands cool against my cheek. The desire that thickened my blood coated my pale skin in goose bumps. I broke off the kiss and blushed fiercely.

"Well," Luke whispered, his raspy voice sending an electric shock straight through my spine. "That was interesting."

"I'm sorry. I don't know what came over me."

"Just look at me. I don't blame you."

I slapped his thigh playfully. "Your modesty is really something else."

"I only speak the truth."

"Okay, Honest Abe. Have you sobered up enough to drive me home?"

He smiled. "If I say yes, will you give me another one of those?"

Blushing slightly more, I looked away from him. The guilt biting at my ankles nearly brought tears to my eyes. *I just kissed my best friend and Zach is sleeping right behind me.* I rubbed my elbows. *Why should I feel bad? Zach's the one who laughed at me when I asked him to stop drinking. He's the jerk here.*

Luke brushed his fingers against the bare skin of my arm. "Earth to Roxy. You still there?"

Absorbed by the sheer sincerity glowing in his eyes, I gave him a quick peck on the lips. "Take me home."

"It would be my pleasure."

In truth, I was too drunk to care about common sense. When Luke helped me stand, the TV tilted from side to side, my high-heeled boots making my ankles wobble like a new born foal. I thought of my friends up North and remembered their orders to live spontaneously, and all I could think of was what it might be like to have casual sex with my best friend.

We left the apartment without saying good-bye to anybody, Luke's hand keeping mine warm. The dark street in front of my parents' house was the perfect location for a drunken rendezvous in the backseat of Luke's car. The problem was, the combination of beer and vodka hit me like a cartoon anvil, and before I could so much as step out of the front seat, I vomited all over the sidewalk next to the car. It hurt, my body trying to purge itself of guilt, anger, excitement, betrayal, confusion. Luke leaned over the center consul and rubbed my back.

Crying and ashamed, I ran into the house and straight into my bedroom, chills threatening to break my spine in half. My throat burned, my knees throbbed, and my heart ached. No longer drunk and now very alone, the reality of the situation hurt worse than the hangover I knew I was going to have tomorrow.

"Why is this happening to me?" I cried, hating myself.

I threw up once more before brushing my teeth and crawled beneath my comforter, wishing I could rewind to the morning and change the series of events that took place.

"Someone please help me," I whispered into the darkness. "I don't know who I am anymore. Please, someone—anyone—help me figure out what the heck is happening to me."

#

"LUCY, I REALLY need you to help me right now. I'm in the midst of a crisis," I said into the cell phone's receiver, my computer opened before me.

167

Zachary was online, the conversation box blinking at the bottom of the Internet window, the speakers pinging each time he sent me a new message. With my heart still unsure of how I should feel about the events of the previous night, I had yet to read what he had to say.

Lucy sighed. "Sis, I love you and everything, but it's nine o' clock on Saturday morning. What have I told you about calling me on weekends?"

"That I'm supposed to wait until noon, but you're pregnant. You can't go out and drink until all hours of the night anymore. There's no need for you to sleep in."

"No, but I'm trying to get as much sleep as possible before this baby comes and puts bags under my eyes."

"You're only, like, three months pregnant. You have plenty of time to sleep. I, on the other hand, do not have plenty of time to figure out what I should do."

"Okay, fine. What's wrong this time?"

Another ping from the computer's speakers. "I think I made a mistake last night."

"You hook up with another guy who has a girlfriend?"

Even though she was teasing, I grew defensive. "No. I kissed Luke."

"Sweet Jesus, Sis. First you kiss someone who's taken. Then you kiss someone who has no real future ahead of him. And now, you're kissing gays? What is going on with your self-esteem? You need to start thinking highly of yourself."

I held up my fingers as if we were talking in person. "First, I didn't know Lamont had a girlfriend. Second, a history teacher is a completely reasonable job. Third, Luke is totally not gay."

"Oh, please. He's about as a straight as a circle."

"You've met him once. How can you say that?"

"It only takes meeting him once to know that kid's sexual orientation."

"There is such a thing as a man being metrosexual."

Lucy laughed. "He's gay, Roxy. Hillcrest, rainbow flag, gay."

I shook my head. "*Anyway,* Zach was sleeping on the couch and I kissed Luke sitting two feet away from him. Does that make me a horrible person?"

She snorted. "Roxy, I think the real problem is you."

"What do you mean?"

"You're getting in your head. I know that coming out of your room can be scary, but you have to push through your anxiety. I'm gonna call in a prescription

168

of Lexapro for you. Start taking five milligrams every night before bed. It'll help you."

Another ping. Closing the computer, I laid back on my bed. "So, I shouldn't feel bad?"

"God, no. You're not even doing anything wrong. Until you have a diamond sealing the deal, you're a free agent."

"But what do I do about Luke? And Zach? And their feelings? And my feelings?"

"Absolutely nothing. Do nothing. Say nothing. Pretend nothing ever happened. You're living your life. Stop beating yourself up for it."

I smiled. "Thanks Lucy. I really appreciate it."

"And I'm serious about this prescription. We need to do something to help you stop being such a weird little freak. Life is too short for you to hide in your room all the time."

Even though part of me wanted to argue, the other part of me knew she was right. I needed something to help control the anxiety that had been plaguing me more than usual. "I'll pick it up later today."

"I am *such* a good sister." I could feel Lucy's smile. "Now that we have a hold on your social life, why don't we talk about the mistake you're making in your professional one?"

#

DESPITE ALL OF my conflicting emotions, Zachary had managed to massage my heart until it snuggled back into his hands. Five days had passed since the party. In that five-day period, I'd convinced myself there was no reason to overthink the situation. Since we were both single, Zach and I were allowed to partake in whatever behavior suited our moods. I loved Luke and trusted him with my life—and since we never did engage in coitus, our friendship wouldn't suffer from any awkward side effects of a one-night-stand. Although Zachary's behavior at the party was a complete turn off and made me rethink my decision to give him a second chance, I was currently sitting on the couch next to him with a fire crackling in front of us.

He'd showed up on my doorstep unannounced after I'd ignored his messages, texts and phone calls, with a bouquet of red roses in hand. Not only did he admit he'd been a complete jerk at the party, he apologized for his outrageous actions and pleaded for my forgiveness. With my arms crossed, I leaned my back against the doorframe, my heart beating far too quickly, my brain continually telling me to send Zachary on his way. He handed me the flowers and invited me

169

into his car, claiming that he had a date planned to make it up to me. Unable to resist his green eyes—and hating to admit that I cried every night into Molly's fur because I missed talking to him—I'd accepted the offer.

But I insisted he pick me up the following night because my parents would be out of town, visiting Lucy and Roger in Los Angeles.

He'd arrived at seven o' clock sharp—looking dashing in a yellow polo and beige Dickies—opened my door and drove us to the nearest mall to watch the Chick-Flick I'd been wanting to see for weeks. Initially, I feared things would be painfully awkward between us, but conversation came easily, soft rock music serving as background noise during the fifteen minutes it took to get to Grossmont Center Mall. He reached for my hand while we walked through the crowded mall, we kissed slowly in the back row of the movie theatre like timid teenagers and whispered our opinions to one another throughout the ending credits, not rising from our seats until the staff entered with cleaning supplies. Afterwards, Zachary purchased me an ice cream cone at the nearest sweet shop, scoffing when I'd pulled out my wallet, insisting he could afford a two-dollar dessert. He'd made me laugh, opened doors for me, shrugged off his jacket to shelter me from the chilly air, and held me close as we walked from store window to store window.

Upon arriving back at the house, I asked Zach to add some wood to the fireplace while I called Molly inside. I bent down to kiss her nose and pat her ears until her fur was no longer cold. She sat by my feet when I sank onto the couch, where I watched Zachary work with newspapers and a lighter, the shadows dancing on his face, a tingling sensation rising to the area between my thighs. When he joined me, his arm casually stretched across my shoulders, easing me into his side.

A strange case of Deja-Vu hit me hard.

"Isn't this kind of weird to you?' I asked, tracing my thumb on the back of his hand.

"Isn't what weird to me?"

"This." I gestured to him, then me. "Us, sitting together on the couch watching a fire. I mean, we *hated* each other not too long ago."

His body shifted, muscles by my neck twitching. "I'm so, *so sorry* for all the pain I've caused you. For the other night, too." He sighed and kissed the top of my head. "I never *hated* you though. I just did whatever I could to push you away. It's a pathetic excuse, but I wasn't ready to be in a relationship with you. I was young and stupid; you would've hated me even more than you did. I had some immature shit to work out of my system."

170

My throat constricted as if a snake was attempting to suffocate me. *Roxy, it's time to let these things go. The past is the past. This is now.* "So, that night in your dorm," I began, palms growing moist, tongue feeling thick and mossy. I cleared my throat. "That night in your dorm when we didn't have sex—do you regret not pressing forward?"

Another shift and a quick adjustment of his shirt collar. "I don't think 'regret' is the right word. At the time, I would've loved to. But it's better the night didn't work out that way. Our relationship at the time was already complicated enough."

I smiled slyly. *Live in the moment. Make a move.* "Do you think it would complicate the situation now?"

His eyes widened at the husky shift in the tone of my voice. I pressed my lips against his, basking in the lust that washed over my body. Zachary's hands reached for my waist and tugged. Although my heart was skipping unsteadily, my bodily instincts controlled my every move, legs straddling his thighs, hands raking up and down his chest.

My nervous system short-circuited when he kissed the tender spot right beneath my jaw. "Are you sure about this?" he whispered.

*No. I'm not sure about anything.* I kissed his forehead, his left cheek, his right, and finished with a tender nibble on his upper lip. "I'm sitting like this because I want to discuss politics." My hands traced down his shirt to the brass button of his pants. "Are *you* sure about this?"

Zachary lowered his gaze, stopping only when we both took note of his tenting pants. "What do you think?"

I giggled, softening the tension building on top of my diaphragm. "I think we should do less talking and more doing."

"Since when are you so funny," he mumbled, pulling my head toward his lips, passion and desire overcoming the shy demeanor both of us usually embraced. He slid his hand under my shirt and over my breast.

I inhaled and moaned, savoring the warmth of his touch. "Apparently, since we've had sex." When he chuckled, I wanted to tell him I loved him. I wanted to admit that he was someone I could see myself with. I wanted to kiss him forever and ever and ever. Because I loved that he made me feel wanted.

I didn't feel used.

Or guilty.

Or insecure.

I felt the love that Zach had for me.

And for the first time since I decided it was necessary to give Zach a second chance, I wasn't afraid.

Quite the contrary, I wanted more.

#

A FEW DAYS later, after sitting through a painfully awkward dinner with my parents and Zachary, I found myself unsuccessfully sorting through my feelings. My mom and dad questioned him about his intentions, about his major and about his future. They'd insinuated that he wasn't good enough for their daughter. They didn't laugh at his jokes. But when he went to use the restroom after helping clear the plates off of the table, my parents smiled at one another, the slightest indication that they *actually* liked him. We said goodbye at the front door, his kiss still lingering on my lips.

Once I closed the heavy, white, wooden door, I leaned my back against it, my legs beginning to feel like those of a land-lover on a boat. *He doesn't want to be in a relationship with me. He said he loved me, but he said I should really think about what I'm doing. He said I would be happier single because he wants me to enjoy the college experience.* I breathed in and out, my eyes staring into darkness. Unlike him three years ago, I didn't believe the "college experience" included hooking up with everyone and everything just because I could. *Maybe he's right. Maybe it's stupid. Maybe I'm getting ahead of myself.* I ran my fingers through my curls, the sweat from our hushed, yet extremely passionate, moment of intimacy straightening the ringlets around my scalp into frizz.

"Is this what I want? To remain single? To spend countless hours in my room alone?"

Even though Lamont did make an appearance in my mind more often than I cared to admit, I had promised myself he was no longer a part of my life, and I meant it.

As the cool wood of the door produced bumps all over my exposed skin, I realized it was time for me to take action; if I remained idle on the sidelines, a golden opportunity would pass me by. And the thought of "what if" nagging at me gave me the courage to open the front door. *It's time to make your choice.* I bit my lip, my feet freezing cold on the front porch's tile. *If you don't say anything, you're gonna lose Zach. Move your feet before it's too late.*

I ran, my feet stinging on the rocky asphalt, eyes watering from the midnight air. "Zach!" I shouted, hoping I hadn't missed him. "Zach?" I'd forgotten about dreaming neighbors, about the possibility of waking everyone at such an unforgivably early hour.

172

A car door slammed shut.

Startling me, heart now sprinting in my chest, I turned left. There stood Zachary, confusion and worry etched onto his face. I smiled and ran in his direction. I jumped and wrapped my legs around his waist, my arms probably suffocating him. "Zach! Thank God!"

"Are you okay?' he murmured into my shoulder. "Are you hurt?"

"I don't need time to think."

He raised an eyebrow. "What're you talking about?"

I unhooked my arms and legs, gingerly returning my bare toes to the street. "You know darn well what I'm talking about. Me and you. Us. I don't want to analyze the pros and cons anymore."

He shook his head solemnly. "This is when you're supposed to live your life and get everything out of your system. You've just crawled away from that safety net of yours and you should experience college just like everyone else does. Recklessly."

"Zach, do you know me at all? I'm not that person and never will be."

"I'm five hundred miles away. The last thing you need is an anchor weighing you down. You should live your life."

"You keep saying that!" I yelled, throwing my arms above my head. "What *life* are you talking about? The one where I sit in my room day in and day out studying? I go out with the girls every once in a while. What are you so scared of?"

"I don't want you to resent me later on when you wonder why you didn't party with your girlfriends," he said, his voice filled with a mix of hopefulness and hopelessness.

"I'm not your ex-girlfriend, and I'm not who you were when you started college," I growled, losing patience. "This is about us—nobody else matters—just *you* and *me* right here, right now."

When he didn't answer, I sighed and stared at my feet, the bottoms blackened from the asphalt. To my surprise, he cupped my chin with his thumb and forefinger, tilting my face to meet his. I smiled half-heartedly, the adrenaline and cold turning my body numb. "Roxanne Vaughn, will you please be my girlfriend?"

And just like that, the mouse was officially off the market.

# Chapter Nine

FIVE MILLION YEARS ago when I was a hopeless high schooler swooning over a soon-to-be college freshman, this had been my dream. I was finally in a relationship with the boy who had been so unbelievably unavailable at a time when love seemed less complicated—although everything still felt surreal, I was happily camped out on cloud nine, those old feelings beginning to take shape in my heart once again. Each day Zachary and I spent together increased the emotions I'd originally told myself to ignore. No longer was I concerned about Zachary running away with my heart, preparing to chuck it off the Coronado bridge. He'd convinced me that this relationship was serious and that meant he'd do anything in his power to keep me safe, healthy and happy.

However, no amount of my boyfriend's love and adoration could ease the pressure expanding in my stomach; an uncomfortable sensation one might attribute to gas but was really a side effect of panic.

A single text message made me wonder if I'd been rash in my decision to make things official with Zachary: *I'm in San Diego. Why don't we meet up?*

Zachary had managed to save me from being alone the night before, but he wasn't here to keep me plastered to the couch—to keep me from driving across the freeway and into the arms of the boy I'd come home in order to escape. *What is he doing here?* As I buckled my seatbelt and turned up the radio to drown out my conscience, I told myself there was no reason to feel so anxious. "Lamont's my *friend*. It's okay if I go visit a *friend*—even if I'd sell my soul to hear him say he loved me."

There was a little voice screaming at the back of my head to turn around and ignore the texts making my phone buzz, but it wasn't loud enough to prevent me from driving forward, my eyes moistening when I saw the big white truck that frequented my nightmares. My heart fiercely thrashed against my chest, hands shaking as I pulled my keys out of the ignition, street spinning around me as I closed the car door. Zachary was at work and couldn't answer his phone, so I didn't bother to text him about seeing Lamont—he'd only assume the worst and I'd have to come up with an explanation even I wouldn't have believed.

I walked through the multiple hallways, a maze of concrete floors, puke stains, broken bottles and cracked walls. "Maybe he realized what a jerk he's been and wants to apologize." The apartment number captured my attention because it was hanging haphazardly to the side and there was a floral welcome mat awaiting the dirty soles of my beat-up tennis shoes. Mustering up the courage that shouldn't have been missing in the first place, I knocked on the door softly. *C'mon Roxanne. There's no need to be nervous. You have the greatest boyfriend in the whole wide world.*

When Lamont opened the eggshell colored door, his lazy smile made all confident thoughts about my relationship fly straight to the moon. I smiled in return. *Your boyfriend, whom adores you, is Zach. He is currently at work saving lives. He is not standing before you, tall, dark and irritatingly handsome.*

"Hey, You," I said coolly, trying to mask my uncertainty. "Long time, no see, huh?"

He nodded. "Been a few weeks."

"And of all places, I see you here, in my territory."

"Well, you talked so highly of San Diego. I had to see it myself."

I leaned against the doorframe and readjusted my purse strap. "And what do you think?"

He shrugged. "Just another city. Ain't got nothing on the country life."

"I'm a city girl. What can I say?"

An awkward pause ensued, where I briefly wondered why he invited me over if we were going to remain standing in the hallway having a pointless conversation. He shuffled his feet while I twirled a curl around my finger.

"You want to come in?" he finally asked.

*No*, I thought sarcastically, *I just want to stand here and stare at you.* "That would be great. Thank you."

He closed the door behind me. "I'm glad you found the place alright. Chris came down with me. Him and his girl are in a fight or some shit."

"Oh, they're back together?" I asked.

He shrugged. "I think they just fuck occasionally. I really don't care, honestly."

The place was filthy. His cousin had to race to work—still hungover and looking tired as hell—briefly requesting that Lamont and Chris clean up the place before she got home so she could cook dinner. Red plastic cups littered the floor, beer bottles lined counter tops, mysterious marks stained the beige carpets, empty liquor bottles were strewn beside shot glasses, and a lamp lay broken in multiple pieces on top of the cheaply made coffee table. Chris was sprawled out on the couch, his shirt wrinkled, pants crumpled on the floor in front of him. He waved absentmindedly when I smiled at him, lazily returning his dazed gaze to the television. Lamont sat at the kitchen table and unwrapped one of the three McDonald's breakfast sandwiches placed in front of him and pointed to the plastic chair across from him.

"Feel free to sit."

I nodded and plopped down, wondering how long Lamont had been in town and why he hadn't invited me to the party. "Looks like you guys had a great party last night."

"Wasn't my party. It was my cousin's." He took a bite of his sandwich and continued talking between chews. "I can't remember very much—Pong and Sailor Jerry. Probably had fun." He swallowed. "I'm gonna clean but I need to wait until my head stops spinning. Otherwise, I'll throw up."

"Is that why you didn't invite me?"

He shrugged. "Not really. There's something else I need to—"

"Oh my God, Roxy? Is that you? I thought I recognized your voice!"

The room temperature dropped below freezing with a negative forty-five degree wind-chill. My eyes remained glued to the bread crumb resting on Lamont's upper lip, my heart dropping to a dangerously low pace—one that would frighten even the most well-practiced cardiologist. "Is that who I think it is?" I whispered.

Lamont chewed slowly, unable to meet my fiery gaze.

I forced a smile and turned around to greet the *last* person I expected to find in San Diego—and she was wearing the red and black flannel Lamont had worn the night I first introduced the two at dinner. "Tiffany!" I stood and opened my arms for a hug. "What brings you to Southern California?"

She squeezed me tight, oblivious to my hesitation. That's when I realized, there was nothing else covering this girl's body—except for a pair of tan Ugg Boots. *They slept together. They slept together and she hasn't showered yet. She's getting their sex sweat all over me.* I tried not to cringe—to excuse myself to the bathroom and scrub my hands until they bled. "Lamont told me he was coming down for a few days and I thought—well, you know—I could see you."

Her stutter angered me for no reason other than she was obviously lying. *Don't cry, Roxy. Don't even sniffle.* "That's great!" I shrieked. "Did you just get down here yesterday?"

Tiffany glanced at Lamont so briefly, only one with a heightened sense of rage, such as myself, would notice. *Tell me the truth you filthy whore.* "Um— no—like, three days ago or something."

My cheeks began to burn from the fake smile melded onto my face. "Oh! I would just assume if you were here to—you know, *see me*—you would've contacted me a lot sooner."

The uncertainty encompassing Tiffany's beautiful, teal eyes brought me too close to tears. *Don't let either of them know how much this hurts.* She frowned, tugging at the sleeve of Lamont's shirt. "I know, I suck. Lots of things going on—the drive and the party."

*I hate you.*

"But," she continued. "I think Lamont's cousin mentioned something about another party tonight. Consider this your official invitation."

I shrugged and stole a quick glance at Lamont, who was conveniently glued to his phone, his fingers quickly tapping against the screen. *Is this what you had to tell me? That you're screwing Tiffany? That you never loved me? That you lied to me the whole time?* "I would love to, but my boyfriend and I have dinner plans tonight."

Overwhelming satisfaction surged through me when Lamont's head jerked up. "Your what?"

Tiffany clapped her hands together and tried to scoot Chris off the couch, despite his protests. I glanced at my shoes when the shirt bounced around her thighs, the bottom of her butt exposed for all innocent bystanders to see. "Oh my God! Why didn't you tell me sooner?"

*Because you're the last person I want to tell anything anymore.* "Must have slipped my mind."

"How long have you been together? Where'd you meet him? Is he cute?" She tapped the seat beside her, inviting me to chat. "Details!"

*Oh, so you can steal him away, too?* I politely declined. "We'll talk about it some other time. Maybe when school starts, or something."

Tiffany frowned. "I guess now's the time to tell you I'm not going back to Sonoma. I'm moving back home, permanently. This whole breakup with Brian just made me realize how unhappy I was."

*Oh, so you just decided to steal away the boy I told you I loved? I don't care how unhappy you are. You deserve it. I hope you never find happiness again.* I forced myself to look sad. "Wow, really? It's the end of an era."

She placed her hands in her lap and nodded. "I'll still see you and all of my other friends, though! The drive is maybe an hour. We can party together, still. Maybe we can get lunch when the semester starts, and you can tell me all about this new boyfriend of yours!'"

I didn't mention how we never partied together anymore. I also bit the inside of my cheek instead of telling her I'd sooner die than go to a party with her. *Good riddance. I'm glad you'll be gone. Maybe Lamont will follow suit.* "Yeah, of course."

The silence that followed was painful, the fake smile plastered on my face beginning to give me a headache. "Well, I better get going. Don't want to take up any more time away from—" I gazed down at Tiffany's bare thighs. "Whatever it was you were doing. It was nice seeing you all. Enjoy the rest of your stay here in sunny San Diego."

Before either of them could respond, I let myself out of the apartment and slammed the door behind me, needing to forget what I just saw. *They're together. They're actually together. My roommates tried to warn me. Why did I think I stood a chance against someone who looks like her? I'm an idiot.* I hugged my arms around my chest, something deep inside threatening to burst through the faucet connected to my eyes. Betrayal and satisfaction battled within the recesses of my heart. When I placed my shaking, pale hand on the car's door handle, a steady, tan hand covered it. Goose bumps scattered up and down my arms and legs, the curly hairs on the back of my neck scared straight.

"You really think I'm gonna let you leave without an explanation?" Lamont asked, the demanding tone kindling the fire crackling in my lower belly.

I turned to face him, hating how small I felt beneath his glare. "Oh, I'm sorry. You believe you deserve an explanation? I have *nothing* to say to you."

He pressed both palms against my car, pinning me between cold metal and his warm body. "Yes, you have a lot to say to me. A boyfriend? Were you gonna tell me about him?"

"Maybe if you checked Facebook every once in a while, you'd see it was official not too long ago."

He looked away. "You really hadn't planned on telling me yourself?"

"Did you plan on telling me about you and Tiffany?"

"There's nothing to tell."

I tried to push his arms away from me. "Fuck off, Lamont."

My aggressiveness startled us both.

"She's the one who started talking to me. It's nothing. We're not dating. She's the most beautiful woman I've ever met, and I just couldn't stop myself form responding to her. That's all it is."

It was my turn to look away, stunned. "Did you not hear what you just said to me?" My voice cracked and my nose began to run. "I'm not doing this with you anymore. I'm done playing these games."

"Fuck," Lamont sighed under his breath. "I didn't mean it like that. Roxy, you know you're beautiful—"

I shook my head, tears blurring my vision. "You already said it—now, I know how you *really* feel about her. The most *beautiful* woman you've ever met. Glad I hooked you two up. Sorry I wasn't up to your fucking beauty standards."

"Roxanne," he grumbled. "Why do you have a boyfriend?"

"Why do you care so much?"

"Because I—because—just tell me why."

I threw my hands up in frustration. "Because he doesn't play these fucking mind games with me like you do! Just listen to yourself! Do you even know what you want? Do you even notice what you've done to me? Do you hear the things you say? I'm not letting you treat me like this anymore."

He looked away, clearly wanting to argue, but instead said, "You don't have to cuss at me." He was quiet. When I didn't say anything, he decided to look at me again. "What's his name?"

"Zach. He's a good guy. A *really* good guy." *Better than you'll ever be.*

Lamont stepped back, opened his mouth to speak, only to close it when nothing would come out. I leaned against the car and closed my eyes, afraid that looking into his brown ones would suck the soul straight from my body. "Out of every girl that crossed your path, why did you pick Tiffany?"

"Does it *really* bother you that much?"

When I opened my eyes, I realized I'd actually said that out loud, which made me blush. "She was my best friend. I introduced you two."

He shrugged. "It's not like we're in a relationship. She and I are just friends."

*Does that mean I haven't been lying when I tell the girls that we're just friends? That there's nothing to worry about? That we mean nothing to each other?* "You knew how I felt—" I sighed. "After everything I've told—" I paused again, afraid to give away too much. *They're fucking. Just what he wanted.* "It doesn't matter, Lamont. I need to go. Zach is getting off work soon and we're supposed to hang out together."

And then I saw it: Sadness. Confusion. Hurt.

Even though I knew he didn't deserve it, I felt guilty for being so mean to him. I pushed my butt off the car and gently touched Lamont's forearm, the contact shocking my fingers. "Look—it was nice to see you. But things are different. Tiffany is waiting for you and Zach, well, he makes me happy. You're wasting your time."

His gaze fell to my hand. It melted some of my resolve to note his hurt because I understood what he was experiencing; his struggle with words tore me to pieces. And then when he sighed, his nonchalant façade returned as if the sadness was just part of his game. A way for me to feel bad and fall right back into his embrace because he knew how much I cared about him. "Does this mean we can't have sex anymore?"

Something inside of me snapped. Maybe it was my patience or maybe my kind spirit. Maybe it was the last straw. But either way, I no longer worried about hurting his feelings. "You have to be fully erect in order to *actually* have intercourse, in case you weren't aware. Maybe you can use that information next time you decide to go fuck yourself." I opened my door and slid into my seat, driving away from Lamont's shocked stare, my tears burning hot on my cheeks.

#

LATER THAT EVENING, Zachary and I were walking Molly up and down the hills that made up the ritzy neighborhood my parents lived in. I'd been debating whether or not to tell him about my encounter with the devil and his mistress. I cried into my pillows as soon as I got home but pulled it together by the time Zachary texted me that he was leaving work. I refused to have a meltdown in front of him. I worried he might realize the true feelings I held for Lamont, so I washed my face, re-applied my makeup and threw my mascara stained pillowcase into the washing machine before he pulled up outside of the house.

He'd noticed something was amiss when we were sitting on the couch together, but he didn't push me on it, suggesting we get some fresh air and bring Molly with us. He told me about his slow day at work, the fight he had with his father about the price of tuition and mentioned he would be going out with a couple of his buddies later. Once the easy topics were exhausted, I knew it was my turn to tell him about my day, but I still hesitated.

"You doing alright?" he finally asked.

I tightened my grip on the leash, causing Molly to glance over her shoulder. *He's your boyfriend. You should be able to tell him anything. Except that maybe you still have feelings for someone who is totally wrong for you. Or that he's in San Diego right now. Or that you've never felt so hurt in your entire life.* "I had a weird day. Remember my friend, Tiffany?"

181

He nodded. "I remember you vaguely telling me about her. Didn't you two have a falling out of some sort?"

I shrugged. *More like she went against all of girl code without so much as an apology.* "You could say that. Well, apparently she's been in town these past few days and she—um—she invited me to her hotel because she wanted to see me." *It's just a little lie. Don't feel guilty about it. You're talking about your feelings. No need to bring up Lamont. Ever. Again.*

Molly stopped on a small patch of grass and squatted.

"Wow. What's she doing in SoCal?"

*Having sex with my tall, dark and handsome dreamboat.* "Visiting some friends. It was weird. Things are tense between us. She did mention she wasn't coming back to Sonoma though. Not even to finish this next semester."

"And is this a good or a bad thing?"

*If she doesn't show her backstabbing face ever again, a fantastic thing.* "Eh. Indifferent. Kinda good though. Hopefully, things will be less awkward for me without the prospect of running into her. I don't like being fake, you know?" The silence that followed was soothing. Zachary's arm remained tight around my waist and the jingling of Molly's tags eased my nervousness. "Zach? Can I ask you something?"

He kissed my temple. "You can ask me anything, Little Woman."

"Will you come up to Sonoma with me for a few days before you start school? I think having you there will make me feel better about going back."

"I see no harm in that."

"And will you not mention it to my parents? I don't want them freaking out."

"You want me to lie to your parents?" When I gave him my cheesiest smile, he shook his head and sighed. "Fine. But I'm not okay with lying to them. I'm afraid your dad will come home one day with one of his doctor tools and kill me."

I giggled and leaned into his chest, Molly's slow pace allowing for ample displays of affection. "You're the best, do you know that?"

And despite the events that occurred earlier in the day, I meant it. I believed Zachary would be the one to eventually save me from Lamont. I just hoped that day would come sooner rather than later.

#

THE NINE-HOUR, dangerously foggy and extremely exhausting road trip to Rohnert Park was not as fun as I'd originally anticipated. Although Zachary had been kind enough to drive the first three hours, navigating through the fog made him skittish, which made me suggest we pull over so I could drive. I thought we would chat non-stop, shamelessly sing along to every song, and play a few rounds of "I spy," but after forty-five minutes, Zachary's head rolled to the side and heavy breathing escaped his mouth. I turned up the radio and kept myself awake, trying not to focus on the disappointment bubbling up inside.

Strangely, I was enthusiastic about my return to the usually dismal little town. It would give Zachary the chance to have some *real* privacy and allow us to see what it would be like to play House together for a few days. Now that four weeks had passed by, I knew the drama that had plagued the house before break would have dissipated completely, no more hard feelings or sarcastic comments that made me question how we'd all been friends in the first place. I wondered how the girls would treat Zachary now that we were official—a big part of me hoped they wouldn't judge me for not being able to have casual sex. Although they knew Zachary and I spoke on the phone nightly, being in an official relationship was different.

When I pulled up to the dorms on campus, I realized I actually had no idea what to expect and was nervous about seeing the girls again.

So, when I threw open the back door and found Elizabeth, Claire, Amber and Shannon sitting together in the living room, I dropped my luggage and greeted them with an enthusiastic screech. They joined in, wrapping me in their arms, telling me how much they missed me. I told them I missed them too, squeezing them even tighter when I realized I was telling them the truth.

"Zach," I said, ushering him in the door. "You remember the girls. And girls, you remember Zach, my *boyfriend*."

They giggled excitedly, embracing him without taking note of his embarrassed blush.

"Nice to see you ladies again," he mumbled shyly.

"Alright. That drive took a lot out of me. I gotta take a quick power snooze and then I want to hear about everyone's break," I said, heaving my bags over my shoulders.

"Right—a *nap*," Amber joked, winking at Zachary, who chuckled as his face grew a deeper shade of scarlet.

"That's not what I'm talking about!" I shouted down the stairs, wanting nothing more than to lie down and sleep.

But even nestled in the warmth and safety of Zachary's arms on my tiny twin bed, I was unable to surrender to my fatigue. The red numbers on my clock switched slowly, Zachary's breaths becoming deeper and less frequent. *He sleeps in the car and can fall asleep right away here. How is that fair?* I scooted away from him, careful not to disturb his slumber, and tiptoed down the stairs to make myself a cup of tea. *No need to be mad. He is who he is. Just let it go.*

"Fuck girl. That must have been one serious power nap," Amber said looking up from her self-pedicure.

"I wish. I couldn't fall asleep, so I'm gonna make myself some tea. I must be too tired or something."

"Well, while you're waiting for it to cool, you can join us." Elizabeth smiled and patted the couch.

"Yeah," Shannon agreed. "Zach had you during break. It's our turn."

I smiled, a strange feeling of happiness gathering in my chest. *They missed me.* After a quick two and a half minutes watching the microwave plate spin in agonizingly slow circles, I had my steaming mug of tea on the coffee table and my butt sitting on the middle cushion of the couch.

"So, things are official with Zach?"

I shrugged at Claire. "It would seem so."

"You seem rather nonchalant about it," Shannon mumbled.

They all exchanged concerned glances.

"If you're with Zach, that must mean Lamont is completely out of the picture, now?" Elizabeth asked.

"Yes."

The girls shared surprised glances before looking at me again.

"Did something happen over break you're not telling us?"

I opened my mouth to answer but Amber hushed me with a wave of her hand. "We don't want some bullshit answer. Tell us the truth."

My shoulders hunched forward. "He came to San Diego. Zach doesn't know about it, so this doesn't leave this circle. He brought Tiffany with him."

The girls gasped.

I nodded solemnly, the memory still making my heart ache. "She was in his flannel with *nothing* underneath it. *His flannel.* She lied straight to my face."

"Oh, I'm so sorry," Shannon whispered. "I can't imagine how that felt."

"Like shoving a hot iron against my chest."

Claire rolled her eyes. "Well, you knew there was something going on between them since my birthday party. The girls told you they saw them together. You really can't be this surprised."

Amber glared at Claire before shaking her head. "That doesn't make it any easier. Give her a break, Claire."

"I've been telling her he's bad news since day one. It's her own fault for not listening to me in the first place."

"Can we not do this again?" I asked, feeling myself getting angry. "This has *nothing* to do with you, Claire. How would you feel if one of your best friends hooked up with a guy you had feelings for?"

Claire looked down at the floor, Shannon and Elizabeth hesitantly looking at one another. Considering how Claire reacted when I told her Shannon *allegedly* gave Adam a handjob, I knew I'd hit a nerve. "Yeah. That's what I thought."

Amber smirked at me, approval glinting in her sapphire eyes.

*Yeah, I know. I stand up for myself now. Weird, huh?* Not wanting to ruin the cease fire that had been put into place before winter break began, I stood up and stretched. "You know, I'm suddenly exhausted. I think I'm actually gonna try to take that nap, now. So, if you'll all excuse me, I have a handsome man to cuddle."

"Behave you married woman, you," Amber called after me.

"Let's not make jokes like that," I hollered back. "I'm barely socially capable of being in a low-key relationship."

Walking into my room, I found Zachary snuggled beneath my blankets, my stuffed Molly pressed against his chest, my pillow covered in drool. I climbed in next to him, kissed his jaw and smiled. *Who cares about Lamont and Tiffany? What Zach and I have is real. I'd take this over a friend with benefits any day.*

#

I FELT LIKE a five-year-old returning for the first day of school: backpack stuffed with fresh notebooks, sharpened pencils, a bottle of vanilla hand sanitizer, a folder with *The Great Gatsby* book cover on the front, and a handful of colorful pens. I knew it was overzealous, but I arrived at class thirty minutes ahead of time and sat directly in the middle of the room, covering my desk with the required anthology and a shiny, blue notebook. My legs were bouncing beneath the desk, my sweatpants hanging over my light brown moccasins, and even though it was silly to be nervous, I was.

This would be my first semester without a science class—American Literature, American History, Art History and Creative Writing—and I never felt so eager to learn. Although not a fan of history, I was ready to delve into the text so I could understand Zachary's passion more fully, and I figured a class where any sort of art was involved would help flush out my creative energy. American Literature had always left a sour taste in my mouth in high school, but it was a requirement for the major, so I hoped it would help me with my own writing—or I hoped it would change my feelings about how dull I found the classics. This would also be the first time ever showing my work to anybody other than Molly, forcing myself to share my innermost feelings with complete strangers—and it wasn't just poetry; half of the semester in Creative Writing would be dedicated to fiction.

That was more terrifying than the night I told my parents I switched majors and expected them to kick me out on the streets.

I began scribbling lines of poetry on the crisp lined paper, handwriting resembling a doctor's signature because my hands wouldn't stop shaking. I wrote about the intimate moments I'd shared with Zachary, about the tears I'd scrubbed from my face in the shower because I still couldn't shake the guilt brought on by the cruel last words I'd said to Lamont, and about the struggle of living with five extremely different girls who were best friends.

Once students began to file into the room—nobody sitting anywhere near me, making me feel like I reeked of science—I ripped out the paper, crumpled it up and shoved it deep into the darkness of my backpack, fearful that my fellow students may find even the slightest hint of my vulnerability.

And when the ancient, black professor shuffled through the door with a leather satchel slung over his shoulder, I allowed myself to breathe. *This isn't the class you need to worry about. You don't have to spill out your soul here—academic papers are easy. They're nothing but research. Stop freaking out. You're officially an English major.*

The professor wrote his name on the board and began passing out the syllabus, which outlined the guidelines that would be enforced throughout the semester. I fingered the photocopied papers still hot from the copy machine and finally felt my body relax. *Now this is where I'm meant to be.*

\#

I SLOUCHED AGAINST the counter regretting the amount of alcohol I'd consumed throughout the night. I hadn't the slightest intention of going out—there was a quart of ice cream and a pile of Disney movies calling my name—but when Elizabeth, Shannon and Amber nearly knocked my door off its hinges, I agreed to join them. They pointed out that Claire was at a dance competition three hours away, providing the four of us with the opportunity to be together without any drama. I'd dressed in a navy-blue jumpsuit, a silver belt around my waist, silver flats on my feet, my hair pulled into a loose ponytail and minimal makeup adorning my face, ready for a fun night.

However, once the four of us made it home from the basketball house party, the laughter stopped, and the tears began to flow. The four of us stood in the kitchen, water glasses filled to the brim and a bag of chips opened on the counter behind us. I hadn't realized how little I knew about the girls I'd been living with for the entire semester until Amber slammed her glass onto the granite and sobbed into her hands.

"I feel like you guys are leaving me out and nobody cares about me being all alone." Amber's big, blue eyes dropped big, blue tears. "I'm *always* alone in my room and *nobody* knocks to see if I'm okay. I don't remember the last time *any of you* asked me about my day." She grabbed a paper towel and blew her nose. "Lizzy, we *lived* together last year. You should know something is wrong if I'm not in the living room with you guys."

"How can you believe we don't care?" Elizabeth wondered, her voice drowning in sadness. "You push me away whenever I try to talk to you. I'm not a mind reader—if you ask to be left alone, I'm gonna leave you alone."

Amber was on the verge of hysterics. "You were braiding each other's hair watching TV—I walked right by all of you and *nobody* bothered to say anything."

My stomach bubbled uncomfortably, the vodka and Sprite I'd ingested earlier sloshing against my liver. "You and your friend didn't say hi to us."

"You're all too busy spending time with *Claire* now," she said as if she hadn't heard me.

Shannon crossed her arms and shook her head, anger spilling through her golden eyes. "*Really?* That's your argument?"

"Is that an actual concern?" I asked.

"Because that's bullshit," Shannon continued, ignoring me. "We *did* invite you to join us, but you and your cheer friend practically sprinted past us."

"That's right!" Elizabeth slurred. "*You* were the one who ignored *us*."

*That's what I said*, I thought bitterly.

Amber brushed at the black streaks on her cheeks with the back of her hand. Her blue eye shadow smeared around her nose, so she now resembled a raccoon and her fire engine red lipstick was smudged on her chin. "Why would I want to be around Claire? Why would *any of you* want to spend time with Claire? You all hang out with her everyday and forget about me. Don't you see she's trying to get you on her side? To turn you against me?"

Shannon snorted, eyes glazing over. "Amber, you can't be serious."

"Ever since she accused you of hooking up with Adam, this house has been torn in half. None of you took my side. You're all believing whatever lies she's feeding you."

"You're being ridiculous," I added.

Amber sniffed. "Shannon, I fought for you"

Again, I was ignored, the girls making me feel stupid for choosing Claire's side during the great divide. *This is between them. Get out of here.*

"I took your side," Amber continued. "And ruined whatever remained me and Claire's friendship. I'm the one who told her she was a slut! How could you be her friend after I said that for you? How can you forgive all of the mean things she said about you?"

"I don't have a choice!" Shannon cried. "Me and her share a room. I sleep there. My clothes are there. You can't get mad at me for trying to keep the peace."

When I took a small step toward the stairs so I could escape to my comfortable bed, the girls all turned on me. I began to sweat under their glossy gazes. "What?"

"Where do you think you're going?"

I shrugged at Amber. "To my room?"

Shannon sighed. "Roxy, you're a part of this. Claire is your best friend."

"That's not true."

"Then why did you take her side?" Amber inquired.

I threw my hands in the air. "Because Tiffany told me it happened! Claire cried to me—Tiffany put me in the middle of some bullshit rumor, and I didn't know what to do."

"But I *told* you the truth and you still didn't believe me," Shannon said, defending herself. "You know I'm not that kind of person."

"Obviously I know that now! But people do stupid shit when they're drunk, and I stupidly believed that Tiffany wouldn't lie to me about something like that." They stared at me, unbelieving. "What do you guys want me to say? That Claire drives me fucking nuts?" I blurted. I felt cornered by three hungry bears, their ravenous red eyes eating away at my soul. "You guys have no idea—I fucking hate her. If I have to hear one more story about her blowing some guy, or if she comes crying to me because Adam's mad at her, I swear I'm going to shoot myself. That bitch only cares about herself and I'm done listening to her judge me when she's the one whoring herself out. I can't put up with her fake bullshit anymore."

188

The girls remained silent for three excruciating long minutes, their mouths caught open in surprise.

"I don't think I've ever heard you cuss that much," Amber finally said.

I began to fiddle with my belt buckle. "Sorry," I mumbled, not meaning it.

"When did you begin feeling like this?" Elizabeth asked.

I grew self-conscious and shrugged. "A little bit before winter break."

"You still act like you're best friends." Amber glared at me, her sparkling necklace blinding beneath the kitchen lights.

I sat on the countertop, the bangles on my wrists jangling against one another. "Yeah, well, it's not in my nature to be a complete and utter bitch, even if someone doesn't deserve my kindness." Taking a deep breath, I attempted to ease the overwhelming sickness hurting my stomach. "How much can I actually tell you guys? Because I'm having difficulty trusting people lately and I don't need this to bite me in the ass later."

They exchanged glances, hands on hips, ankles wobbling slightly. "What have you been keeping from us?" Shannon asked.

I fiddled with the skinny straps resting on my shoulders. "I thought me and her were best friends until I realized she's been using me for alcohol, attention and safe rides home."

Amber laughed—it sounded so mean, I flinched as if she'd slapped me in the face. "That should be no surprise. She does whatever she can to get whatever she wants. Sorry I'm not sorry, but once you came into the picture, I lost my best friend."

Although hurt and angry, I managed to keep my mouth shut. *You can keep thinking that, bitch, but your failed friendship isn't my fault. You're just mad because Claire chose me over you. Fuck—you can have Claire back.*

"She's always been like that," Elizabeth added tenderly. "How did you just realize it?"

I wished I had another drink. *Why am I even bothering? I can hide in my room until May.* "If you'd really like to know, there were a few things that stood out to me." I threw up my hand to count off the list on my fingers. "She drinks my alcohol without asking. She tells me I'm fat when she's drunk in an attempt to make herself feel prettier. She never has time to listen to my problems but has plenty of time to make me listen to hers. She flirts with any boy I might even consider talking to—Lamont and my boyfriend included. She's a bitch." I grabbed a handful of chips and shoved one into my mouth. "She takes my friendship for granted. She's manipulative. The backstabbing and the drama are

189

things I can't handle anymore. We're not only roommates—all of us are supposed to be friends." The words were out of my mouth before I could stop them, the salty potatoes burning my chapped lips. *I've definitely said too much.*

I was ready to excuse myself from the kitchen so I could cry in the privacy of my own room but froze when Amber cleared her throat. "I get that. The thing is, I want to trust you guys—I *really* do. I just think it's too late. You shouldn't feel uncomfortable at *home*." She sighed. "This is the last place I want to call home. I don't even want to come back to Sonoma next year."

Elizabeth and Shannon gasped as my heart plummeted into my toes. "Amber," I breathed. "You can't be serious."

"How are we supposed to know how you're feeling when you hide in your room and don't tell us anything?" Shannon asked, her voice rising one octave.

Amber began to cry harder, her sobs interfering with her speech. "Every—everything here—is—is—so fake. I—I can't take it—any—anymore."

Elizabeth swatted at her tears. "Amber, don't say those things. You need to talk to me about how you're feeling—you're not allowed to leave."

"I don't want you to go!" Shannon wailed.

My body grew numb as I remained glued to the granite countertop, my drunk eyes transfixed on the scene unfolding before me. Three girls—three young, wild and free girls—were sharing their true feelings with one another shamelessly, and for some reason, they'd decided to include me. Even though we'd been trying to avoid it in order to keep peace within the house, the truth finally exposed itself and decided to join the party.

*What am I doing? I can't hide—these are my friends. My real friends.*

I slid off the countertop, the wooden bottoms of my flats clanking against the wooden floor and wrapped my arms around Amber. Her tears crawled down my bare shoulders, her body shaking against my chest. "I'm so sorry I wasn't there for you. I've been so involved with my own insecurities that I didn't notice yours. I know we haven't had the chance to get to open up, but from here on out, I'm here for you. No matter what. Amber—" I held her shoulders and forced her to look at me. "I want to be your friend—and I want you to believe that."

She wept harder. Elizabeth and Shannon moved in to join our hug and I found myself surrounded by tears, apologies and future promises of *real friendships*. In that intoxicated moment, I realized I had more in common with these girls than I originally thought. *Why did I let Claire tear me apart from them? Why did I push away? Why didn't I notice their pain?*

190

"I don't want us to keep secrets from each other anymore. This is our *home*," I whispered. "We should all be comfortable here. Why don't we put all of this behind us?"

Everybody nodded, snot and tears mixing with our newfound laughter.

"This is gonna be the beginning of a beautiful friendship," Elizabeth added happily.

"I love you guys. Thank you. Really," Amber sighed.

This was proof that alcohol held great power over basic human emotions. It had the ability to bring together four *very* different girls who were too scared to step on one another's toes—who weren't giving each other much of a chance to be themselves. It connected four hearts that had been hardened by jealousy, loneliness and fear.

As we cried in one another's arms, a silent pact was made. A true friendship was formed. This was a life-changing moment for me. This is what would get me through my final semester at Sonoma State University.

# Chapter Ten

VALENTINE'S DAY WAS not something I usually celebrated—the notion that there was an assigned day for a man to make a woman feel special often sickened the hopeless romantic in me. But now that I was playing for the "I'm in a relationship" team, I was excited to partake in the obnoxious activities the holiday was known for. I'd purchased a large box of overly priced chocolates, a stuffed dog that sang a sappy song while flopping its red ears, and white boxers with cartoon hearts, and sent them in a pre-priced box that was scheduled to arrive on Zachary's doorstep the morning of Valentine's Day. New to the game of hinting at what I might want, I didn't tell him to get me anything in particular—maybe I was secretly testing him to see what he would do—but when I received a thin red envelope in the mail on Thursday, my disappointment made me feel guilty.

Not wanting to spend the evening alone, I invited Andrew over to join me for pizza and romantic comedies. He smiled when I opened the door and extended his arms wide, two bottles of champagne in one hand, and a bouquet of yellow roses in the other. "Happy Valentine's Day, you bitch," he yelled happily, wrapping me in a painfully strong embrace. "What did the stud muffin give you? Other than up-close and personal picture messages of his dick?"

I closed the door and shushed him. "Can you not say things like that so loudly? I don't need people thinking I'm a hooker."

"You're in a relationship. Nude selfies are expected." He placed the bottles on the counter top, shoved the flowers into my chest and helped himself to the cabinet filled with plastic cups. "Did he get you a necklace? Red roses? A stuffed bear the size of your bedroom? Also, you need a vase for those so they won't die. Do any of you even know what a vase is in this house?"

I half-smiled and shrugged. "He gave me a card."

"I know those roses aren't red," he continued not hearing me. "But I'm not looking for sex. I didn't want to give you the wrong impression." Andrew turned abruptly. "I mean *other* than the card. That's just a mandatory nicety."

I tossed the red envelope that had been sitting on the bar top at him and watched as it bounced off his chest before it slapped against the ground. "Andrew, stop talking for just one minute and listen. He gave me a card. That's it. But he wrote a really sweet poem."

He bent down to retrieve the envelope. "You've got to be shittin' me."

I reached for one of the champagne bottles and listened to the pop of air being released from the glass. The cork shot against the ceiling and ricocheted into the sink. "I wasn't expecting to drink today. We can't get too wasted, okay? I have homework to do."

He was still staring at the card with the teddy bear holding a heart on the front. "I'm your gay best friend and I brought you flowers."

"You weren't even listening to me."

"You don't want to get too wasted—I heard you. I ignored you because I'm still in awe."

I shrugged again. "Maybe he couldn't afford anything more."

He threw the envelope back at me. "I don't care if him buying you roses means he can't afford to eat for three fucking weeks. It's Valentine's Day. A good boyfriend buys you fucking flowers."

"Hand me those cups and let's not talk about it anymore. I don't want to feel ungrateful. He really put a lot of effort into that poem."

"Ungrateful? He didn't give you anything. You have nothing to be grateful for."

Pouring the champagne much too quickly, I cursed when the bubbles overflowed onto my fingers. "He wrote me words from the heart. Why isn't that enough?"

Andrew took the bottle from me, his shaggy black hair falling in front of his eyes. "I don't fucking care if he gave you his social security number. As a boyfriend, you have an obligation to give your girlfriend the world—*especially* on Valentine's Day. It's the day of love and what better way to pronounce your love than by spending your money on material possessions?"

"Can we please drop it?"

"At least you know I love you. I brought you roses *and* alcohol."

I smiled. "Don't you have some hot jock waiting for you to play with his balls?"

He handed me the glass of champagne and held his own in the air. "I gave that up just to be with you." We clinked glasses. "Besides, he already made it to third base this morning."

Nearly spitting the bubbly liquid all over the kitchen, I wiped my forearm across my lips. "A little discretion, please."

"At least I got something to brag about."

194

I held up my hand. "Again, we aren't going to speak of that."

"I'm just saying, you deserve the world. You're an amazing person."

I blushed. "Thank you—but no more."

And nothing else was said, until the two bottles of champagne were gone, one movie watched, and a box of Oreos devoured, the roses sitting on my desk in a large glass because, as Andrew pointed out, no one in the house owned a vase.

"You should call him."

I hiccupped and giggled. "And say what? That he needs to take gift lessons from gays?"

"Yes ma'am. Because if he keeps this up, ain't no woman gonna suck on that."

"Life isn't only about dicks, you know."

He chuckled. "Speak for yourself. I'm young and beautiful. I've got plenty of good dick ahead of me."

I knew it was a bad idea to call Zachary because the alcohol had gone straight to my head, but I wanted to prove to Andrew that Zachary was a good boyfriend. "You'll see. I'm sure there's something else in the mail."

Andrew scoffed, preparing another snide remark, only restraining himself because Zachary answered the phone. We exchanged pleasantries before he thanked me for the wonderful gifts I gave him. It was my turn to talk—to ask him if there was a bouquet of flowers still on its way—but I just couldn't do it. *He went out of his way to write you a poem. He knows what poetry means to you. That means more than expensive chocolates.* I sighed, too ashamed to make eye contact with my sassy best friend. And because I didn't feel it appropriate to voice my disappointment, I said something I would've been too scared to admit in any sober state of mind.

"I love you, Zachary Cameron."

Andrew's eyes widened like a deer that spotted a snarling lion, Zachary's voice grew teary like rain forming inside a cloud, and my heart expanded to the size of the stuffed animal Zach didn't get me for Valentine's Day.

"I do. I love you, Zach."

Andrew placed his palm over his face and shook his head. "That was not a part of the plan. You're not allowed to drink anymore, you slut."

I smiled and rested my head on Andrew's shoulder, Zachary's voice mumbling excitedly in my ear. *It's the truth. I'm in love with Zachary Cameron.*

#

I SHOULD'VE KNOWN better than to drink so recklessly, but I was still so elated from my confession to Zachary a few days prior, I didn't think anything could bring me down—not even a drinking challenge that I wouldn't have been caught dead participating in only a couple months ago.

It all began when Adam and his housemates knocked on our back door. Claire informed them we'd be attending the annual Valentine's Day dance, which was hosted by one of the larger fraternities on campus, and she wanted Adam to join her. Essentially, the dance was a lingerie party of epic proportions—one that I hadn't planned on attending until Andrew dragged me across campus when we'd been way too drunk off of champagne and forced me to buy a ticket with him. I'd tried arguing that I shouldn't go because I was in a committed relationship, but his intoxicated logic of "I don't care bitch, you're going" had won out in the end.

Maybe people are onto something when they say that falling in love makes one do stupid things. Because when Adam walked into the living room and asked me if I was ready to go "shot for shot" with him, I agreed without hesitation, eliciting screams of disbelief and delight from my roommates.

"I was only kidding." He crossed the room in five quick strides before hugging me so tightly, we both swayed side to side. "I didn't think you'd have the balls to do it."

I gulped. "Well, I mean if you're kidding…"

He patted my back. "No way! We have to do it now."

"Well, okay?" I didn't want to let anyone down, my peers smiling at me as if I'd just found the cure for cancer. I silently prayed that Adam would forget this exchange in ten minutes time, the rum on his breath proving he'd already pre-gamed with his friends.

This was my first mistake.

Claire, Amber, Elizabeth and Shannon giggled, their cheeks already glowing from the vodka slowly warming their bloodstreams. Each of us was dressed to impress, eager to show off the fourteen days we'd consecutively gone to the gym together despite the fact that I hadn't initially planned on going to the dance. Amber and Shannon matched one another wearing sheer, black teddies, white lace around their breasts, spandex shorts underneath. Claire wore a red slip complete with built-in push-up bra and black furry material stitched along the bust. Elizabeth decided it would be funny to wear a tight white-shirt with plaid boxers, knee high socks and brown moccasins, her petite frame still managing to look sexy against the soft cotton. And I'd loosely followed my sister's advice: "So what if you look like a ho? It's a lingerie dance. Wear a cute slip that shows off some tit and a little bit of leg. There's nothing wrong with letting the boys imagine your goodies. Just don't let them touch you." I'd purchased a lavender slip that hung down to the middle of my thighs, had a plunging V-neck and black velvet skirting the hem.

That was my second mistake.

I hadn't anticipated that, as the night wore on, my slip would do just that— slip. Slip so far down, in fact, that my lacy black bra became the focal point of my ensemble. No matter how many times I pulled it up, it would fall back down, and Adam had showed up before I'd had the chance to change.

It was too late now.

"C'mon girl. Let's get this night started," Adam said bringing me back to my worst nightmare.

In a last-ditch effort to not make a raging fool out of myself, I lifted my chin and pushed my shoulders back, doing my best to appear confident and intimidating. "You sure you wanna do this, Adam? It will end badly for you."

My plan backfired immediately. When he snapped his fingers at his roommates, they produced a handle of rum out of thin air. "We'll just see about that. Choose your poison, turn up the music and let's do this already!"

A bead of sweat fell between my shoulder blades. I pleaded for help from my friends, but instead, they shoved me into the kitchen, handed me some girly flavored vodka and wished me luck.

Adam lined up three shot glasses, took them one after the other, chugged some soda and wiped any liquid remnants from his chin. "You're up, little Miss Sassy."

*You can do this, Roxanne. Don't let him smell your fear.* "Oh, it's on." I followed suit, the vodka burning places in my stomach I didn't know existed, my only sense of relief coming from the orange juice Amber had been holding for me on the sidelines. *Don't disappoint everyone. Just keep playing. You got it.*

Thankfully, I was able to get away with pouring myself half-shots, Adam too drunk to pay attention to such petty details. I reasoned that I would still get drunk, just hopefully not to the point of throwing up.

That was my third mistake.

"Where has this Roxy been all year?" Shannon asked a little too enthusiastically.

197

The music coursed through my blood, mixed instantaneously with the alcohol and began to pump overconfidence into my brain. "I don't like this Roxanne," I said, the kitchen beginning to sway just slightly.

Shannon grabbed my cheeks and pinched them. "I love this Roxanne. She's fun!"

"Don't let Adam always drink first," Amber warned, pulling me toward her even though she was doing everything except whispering. "That's a sure-fire way to black out. Make sure you take control and show him who's the boss."

I didn't have the heart to tell her that the outcome of this game was going to end poorly for me no matter who drank first. *Don't be stupid. Find a way to throw it over your shoulder or something.* But every time I even looked at a shot glass, it felt like seven hundred sets of eyes were all counting on me to keep the party going. I didn't want to let anyone down.

I continued to drink.

Alcohol seeped through our organs, leaked from our pours and stuck in sweaty molecules against the wall.

I swallowed the seventh shot of the night when Adam tapped my shoulder. "Girl, we gotta get to the dance soon. They're gonna close the doors when they hit capacity. You have a ride, right?"

"Do we have a ride," I scoffed. "When am I not prepared?"

Adam shook his head, a crooked grin on his face. "Oh, I'm sorry. I totally forgot who I was talking to."

"Just gotta call him really quick." I crept away from the chaos and called the man I knew I could always count on.

"Roxaaaaaaaay! What is up, ho bag?" Andrew slurred into the receiver.

"Andy? What are you doing?"

"I'm in line at the dance with a group of men in neon colored marble bags. What're you doing? Are you here, yet?"

My throat constricted, mouth suddenly dry. "No. I'm waiting for you to come pick me and my roommates up."

After a quick moment of silence—I noticed my ears were ringing slightly—Andrew cursed. "Fuck. Fuckityfuckfrack. Roxy, I'm *so sorry.* I totally spaced. Some guys invited me over to pregame and they promised me liquor and long—"

"No," I snapped. "Do not even say you chose a stranger's penis over your best friend."

"Hey," he argued, clearly hurt. "Don't say things like that. I'm really sorry. I totes fucked up."

My eyes began to water. "What am I supposed to do? I promised the girls a guaranteed ride."

He must've heard my voice waiver because he told all of his friends to shut up. "Don't cry. How much have you been drinking?"

I shrugged. "A lot."

"Okay, no wonder you're freaking out." He paused, whispering something I couldn't quite make out. "You always have a plan B. Isn't there someone else you can call?"

"No there—" I glanced down at my naked wrist. "I might have someone."

"Good. Now get your cute ass over here so we can dance."

I hung up the phone and dialed the person who was always residing in the forefront of my mind, like a bad headache after being in the sun all day.

That was my fourth mistake.

"Hello?" His voice sounded surprised.

Probably because the last time we'd spoken to one another, I'd cussed like a sailor and insulted his manhood. If I hadn't been so drunk, I would've probably assumed he only answered because he'd deleted my number from his phone and didn't know who was calling him. Instead, I talked to him as if we were best friends who spoke on the phone daily.

"Lamont! What're you doing right now?" I looked into my bathroom mirror, wiping the smudged lipstick away from the corners of my mouth.

"Why are you calling me?" He paused. "Are you drunk right now?" He asked in his sexy monotone voice.

My heart flopped into my throat, inhibiting my ability to breathe regularly. I grasped onto the bathroom counter suddenly feeling lightheaded. "Maybe I'm a little drunk. But what does that matter? You're drunk all of the time. Don't judge me for being drunk. You're drunk!'"

He chuckled. "Well, you've changed since I first met you."

"Is that a bad thing?" I snapped.

"Nope," he nearly whispered. "Not a bad thing at all."

I couldn't respond, my hands beginning to tremble.

He cleared his throat. "So, what's going on? I thought you never wanted to talk to me ever again."

"I always want to talk to you," I slurred, opening up my medicine cabinet to find my hairspray.

199

"Oh, do you?" he asked, coyly.

I flipped my hair and sprayed the bottom with hairspray before flipping it back up and spraying the top. I closed my eyes and placed my hands on the counter again, feeling dizzy. "Don't play dumb," I spat. "You know I always want to talk to you and that's the problem."

He chuckled again. "Aren't you going to the dance tonight?"

I remembered why I called him. "Can I ask you a huge favor?"

When he didn't answer immediately, I grew irrationally anxious.

"Please?" I continued. "I need your help."

"Do you need a ride to the dance?"

I smiled. "How did you know? It's like you're in my head or something." All adrenaline flooding through my body pushed the alcohol further into my bloodstream. "Would you mind helping me? My other ride bailed, and I promised the girls I'd find one for us. It's just me, Lizzy, Claire, Amber and Shannon."

"Sound like lots of titties." He paused, the silence again making me nervous. I wondered if he was with Tiffany and had to make up some excuse to leave. I then wondered if he would actually leave her for me. I hated myself for wanting that. "Sure, I can help you," he finally said. "What time should I head over?"

"Now?" I asked a little too eagerly. "I mean—you know—we all haven't seen you in awhile. I'm sure everyone would like to hang out for a few minutes before you have to drive."

He laughed. "Everyone, huh?"

I sat down on my bed, the comforter feeling cool against the back of my thighs. "Yes, everyone. But especially me."

Although I couldn't see him, I could've sworn his was smiling. "I'll be there in five."

When he hung up, I ran downstairs, carefully eyeing my blue pumps as they hit each stair, holding tightly onto the railing to prevent myself from falling flat on my face. "Alright girls," I shouted. "Andy bailed but I was able to nail us another ride!"

They all squealed, poured me a follow-up shot and pulled me into a dance circle. I was relieved they didn't ask who was driving us, too consumed by intoxication to care that I called the one guy I wasn't supposed to contact ever again—*especially* when consuming overly grandiose amounts of hard liquor.

# CHAPTER TEN

My fifth mistake occurred after ten half shots of vodka and too little food in my stomach. My heels clicked against the sidewalk, the chilly air reddening my skin, my vision teetering from side to side. I scanned the parking lot for his big, white truck, my heart rate thumping in the frontal lobe of my brain. When I spotted my tall, dark and handsome man walking toward me, the grin on my face numbed my cheeks.

He covered my body in a hug that made up for all the time we'd lost. I pressed my cheek into his chest and rocked back and forth slowly. *I hate that this feels so damn right.* I closed my eyes. *I wonder if he feels the same way.* "I've missed you," I whispered.

He let go and stepped back. "No, you haven't. You have a boyfriend."

I propped my fists on my hips. "That doesn't matter. I'm still allowed to have my feelings. You don't have to say it back. I'm fully aware you don't need me to fuck you anymore." I was slurring—bordering on sloppy—but at that point, I didn't care.

He smirked. "You're the one with the boyfriend. There's nothing in the rules of being single that says I'm not allowed to sleep with other girls."

It felt as if he'd just punched me, knocking the wind out of my lungs. The world tilted in different directions and I worried I might be sick. *You're fine. Just breathe. He's one hundred percent correct, and you have no reason to be upset with him. Even if he looks flawless in his stupid black sweatshirt and those stupid dark jeans.*

"I shouldn't have said anything. Forget we even had this conversation. It's freezing out here—let's—let's just go inside." I grabbed his hand only to have him yank it away from me.

"You're really drunk, and I don't think your boyfriend would approve of your behavior."

I turned sharply, ignoring the fact that my ankle almost twisted painfully in my too-high-high-heels. "Why do you keep saying that? Lamont, you're my *friend* and there's nothing wrong with that. Just because Zach is my boyfriend—"

"I would prefer if you didn't say his name around me."

"Excuse me?"

He stood silently, stuck his hands in his pockets and kicked at a pebble on the ground.

I sighed. "Let's just get inside. Thank you for helping in such short notice. We all really appreciate it." *Especially me. You being here means everything to me. I've missed you.*

"When are we leaving?"

I grabbed onto his wrist and tugged, pulling his hand out of his jeans, refusing to release my hold on him. Eventually, he quit resisting and followed. "You'll have to ask the girls. I'm guessing relatively soon. You might have to force them into your truck. They're all, what one might consider, 'white girl wasted.'"

"And you're not?" he chuckled.

"I didn't say I wasn't."

I opened the dorm's backdoor, thankful to escape the cold—but in the ten minutes I'd been gone, chaos had taken control of the party. Claire stood dancing on top of the coffee table, Amber was straddling Adam's roommate on the stairs, Elizabeth was intently studying a blank TV screen, Shannon and Adam were searching frantically for snacks in the pantry and the rest of the boys were in the kitchen pouring alcohol into one another's mouths.

"I see what you mean," Lamont mumbled.

"Lamont!" Elizabeth shouted leaping off the couch. "I haven't seen you in forever! What're you doing here?"

I dropped his wrist when she approached him, clearly looking for a hug. "I'm your DD for the night."

Of course, Claire obnoxiously descended from her self-made pedestal and rushed Lamont as if she were a linebacker. "Oh my God! You're the best DD in the whole entire world!"

*Stop being jealous*, I ordered myself. *He doesn't like her like that. He's told you that a million times. Besides, you have a wonderfully loving boyfriend who is behaving himself at home—there's no reason to be swooning over this guy who chose sleeping with your best friend over being in any sort of relationship with you.* I wandered into the kitchen, ignoring Claire's flirtatious squeaks and squeals to the best of my envious ability. I poured another shot and gulped back the burning liquid. *Stop being jealous right fucking now. You have an amazing boyfriend.* Claire kissed him, wrapped her leg around his thighs, and clung onto him like a sock fresh out of the dryer. *Stop being jealous.* I poured another shot. *You have a boyfriend.*

"Does Zach know Lamont's here?" Adam asked, elbow resting on my shoulder, breath smelling of gold fish—probably the bag of gold fish I'd intended on eating upon returning from the dance.

202

I swallowed the vodka. "Nope," I managed before chugging the remaining Sprite. "Ignorance is bliss and all that." I paused, watching as Lamont politely tried to get Claire off of him. "You know how much Claire's had to drink tonight?"

He swallowed a shot. "Nope," he coughed. "Ignorance is bliss and all that, right?"

"I'm sorry she does this shit to you."

He nodded. "I'm sorry he does this shit to you."

I nodded. "It hurts to love someone who will never love you back."

We watched as Lamont's cheeks turned red, frustration blazing in his eyes. Claire squeezed her thighs tighter, Elizabeth now trying to pull her off from behind.

Adam sighed. "You wanna take another one?"

I smiled at Lamont. When he returned the gesture, paying no attention to Claire's advances, my heart cried out for his affection. "If you take one, I have to, right?"

He chuckled. "Where have you been the entire semester?"

#

THE NEXT THIRTY minutes resembled trees rushing by when one is sitting in the back of a speeding vehicle in the middle of a dark forest. Not only did my good judgment leave the party early because I'd taken far too many shots, but my eyes refused to cooperate with me—whenever I was able to keep them open, they remained fixated on Lamont. His black hair was freshly cut, dark brown eyes lingering on me, no facial hair littering his handsome face. Whenever our skin accidentally touched, the emotions I'd locked away in the recesses of my heart would awaken.

I stood beside him at the bar top and leaned against his arm, half in a daze. *I've already made a million mistakes tonight. Why stop now?* I toyed with the black and white "I Love Boobies" bracelet on his wrist and smiled coyly at him. "I do believe this is mine."

He raised an eyebrow. "I didn't think we were still playing that game."

I pouted. "You just don't want me to have it."

He pulled it off his hand and snapped it onto mine. "It looks better on you anyway. You can keep it."

"Well, aren't you just the sweetest boy in the whole wide world. I think you deserve a kiss."

"Roxy, you're really drunk," he mumbled, a shit-eating grin plastered on his face.

I shifted my neck so that my chin was resting on his shoulder. "Well, thank you for pointing that out, Captain Obvious." I kissed his cheek and lazily squeezed his thigh. "You shaved. It looks nice."

He absent-mindedly rubbed his chin. "I'm gonna grow it back. Just trying something different."

I nodded, not really listening. "Come to the dance with me, Lamont."

He shook his head, pulling away ever so slightly. "I don't have a ticket."

"They're selling them at the door."

"I don't have any money."

"I'll pay for you."

"I'm not in costume."

"I'll help you take your pants off."

Looking at the clock on the microwave, he announced it was time to leave. "No. I'm here to drive you. End of story." He pushed me back softly and stood to rally the girls.

I rested my feverish forehead on the cool, granite counter and took a few deep breaths. *What am I doing? I have a fucking boyfriend.* Keeping my shoulders back, I followed the girls to Lamont's truck and sat silently in the front seat. My eyes remained glued to the window, the black tunnel of too much alcohol threatening to consume my consciousness. The next thing I knew, Lamont's truck was idling beside the curb in front of the dance venue's doors. As the girls struggled to escape the confines of the backseat without collapsing onto the asphalt, Lamont patted my thigh.

I stared at his hand briefly before blinking at him.

"Be safe, please. If you need a ride back to campus, call me. I'll text you tomorrow if I don't hear anything from you. You know—to make sure you're alive."

I climbed out of the truck. "I wish I could believe you, but I've heard that line from you one too many times. Thanks again for the ride. Like you said, end of story."

"Roxy," he began before I closed the door, doing my best to close off my emotions, to ignore the hollow sensation spreading through my chest.

Swishing my hips from side to side, I followed the girls over to the frat boys collecting tickets and stamping wrists. I forced myself not to look over my shoulder, fighting the urge to see whether or not Lamont was watching.

#

THINGS WENT TO from bad to worse the instant my roommates and I stepped foot inside the building. Not only was our group separated due to the immense number of people in the crowd, but Claire had managed to remain glued to my side, which meant I was stuck babysitting her. I was in no condition to care for another human being—I was struggling to take care of myself. My stomach hurt, my vision was growing dangerously blurry, I was conscious of how much of my skin was exposed, my feet felt like lead in my pumps, and I couldn't stop thinking about the boy who wasn't my boyfriend.

Claire latched onto my elbow and aggressively dragged me from one side of the dark room to the next. "I need to find the hottest guy here."

"What about Adam?" I shouted over the music.

She shook her head vigorously. "No. I don't want to dance with him."

Having reached a state of inebriation where I no longer cared about hurting feelings, I rolled my eyes. "Why not? You talk to him every day. Clearly, he adores you and it would appear that you adore him. Shouldn't you be *begging* to dance with him?"

She frowned. "Do you see me tonight? I look hot—*really* fucking hot. Besides, he's a horrible dancer. I need some hot frat boy who can *actually* keep up with me."

"Claire, I know you're drunk but—"

"And he's not that cute," she interrupted. "I've been starving myself all week and I'm not wasting how good I look on Adam."

"Wait, what?" I glanced down at her stomach.

She moved her hands from the top of her ribcage to her hips. "I need someone who's on my level."

The alcohol was beginning to flood my brain. "No. No, not that." I yanked her off the dance floor and pushed her into a dark corner. "What the fuck do you mean you've been starving yourself?"

Her nonchalant shrug took me by surprise. "It's not a big deal. I don't throw up or anything. I just didn't eat much the last few weeks so I would look like I do tonight. I probably lost more than ten pounds, easy."

"Claire, I used to study the body. That kind of behavior can—"

She shoved me slightly. "Don't lecture me. You dropped out of pre-med so what do you know?"

The threat of tears hit me like a hurricane off the coast of Florida. "I'm just trying to help. You're gonna fucking kill yourself doing that."

"I don't need you," she spat. "You don't know anything."

"Fine. Leave me alone. Try not to be stupid, if that's possible for you."

"Who's being stupid?"

When I turned around, Adam smiled at me. He'd finally found us. Claire scowled, forehead wrinkled, cheeks flushed with frustration and anger.

I glared at Claire, crossing my arms over my chest. "Yeah, Claire. Who's being stupid?"

Adam beamed at Claire and wrapped his arm around her waist—a deep frown from Claire was thrown in my direction. "Nobody," she mumbled.

"That settles that." I fiddled with my fingers. *I don't feel good. I want to go home.* "Why don't we look for the girls?"

As we began to mill through the crowd, Claire connected her elbow sharply with my ribs. "I don't want to be seen with him in public," she whispered angrily.

I smiled maliciously at her, patience wavering rapidly. "Maybe you should've thought that through before you invited him over."

She glared. "I need to ditch him. Help me."

"I thought you didn't want my help," I hissed. "What do I know, remember?"

Adam was bouncing beside Claire completely oblivious to her disdain. He was happy—the girl he loved was radiating beautifully in his arms—and she was trying to pull away from him. *All he wants to do is make her happy and she'd rather find some shallow asshole that only wants her for her body. Will she ever realize how lucky she really is? To be loved by such a great guy?* I swallowed the acid beginning to rise up my throat. *Will I ever realize how lucky I am? To be loved by such a great guy?* Unable to handle Claire's immaturity and Adam's puppy eyes, I excused myself to use the bathroom before I yelled at both of them in front of everybody. However, I never made it to the safety of the florescent lighting and plastic stalls—I stopped and sat on one of the tables located behind the dance floor, put my face in my hands and cried.

Maybe it was because I was drunk. Maybe it was because my body was exhausted. Maybe it was because I didn't know who I was anymore. Maybe it was because I was alone and both of the boys I loved were nowhere to be found.

Or maybe it was because I wanted Lamont to be here dancing with me when I should've been at home, looking forward to a video chat with Zachary.

"I should've never come," I moaned. "I'm so fucking stupid."

Lucy's words rang loudly against the headache beginning to take form. *As long as you don't have a ring on your finger, you have nothing to feel bad about.*

"Your sister is a horrible influence. Imagine how you'd feel if Zach was thinking about some other girl right now." I sobbed harder. "I wasn't cut out to be a doctor. Maybe I don't have what it takes to be a girlfriend, either." Taking a deep breath, I opened my eyes and swiped away my tears. *I miss Lamont. I miss Zach.* I burped. "Somebody help me. I want to go home."

And just at that moment, I noticed a figure emerging from the smoke and lights of the dance floor. He was moving toward me quickly. When my eyes adjusted to the movement, I smiled and stood. "Hey, Ad—"

He pushed past my shoulder roughly, soon trailed by a concerned Elizabeth, an angry Amber and a confused Shannon. I reached out just in time to grasp Amber's arm. "Hey, what's going on? Are you okay?"

Rivers of mascara streamed down her cheeks. I assumed my face looked the same. "Why don't you ask Claire?" she snapped before yanking her arm away.

I stood there, dumbfounded. *What did I miss?*

#

NOW THAT THE adrenaline in my body was flying like a free-falling man through my bloodstream, the effects of the alcohol I'd consumed earlier subsided to a heavy buzz. If Claire had not been a total brat and left the dance with the rest of us, I could've been sound asleep, my drunken dreams allowing me a blacked-out slumber. However, it was already two in the morning and Claire had yet to return home, throwing cow-sized quantities of crap into an already crappy fan.

According to what little information my friends would offer, Claire had ditched Adam shortly after I went in search of a restroom because she wanted to "dance with Amber, Lizzy and Shannon." Ten minutes later, Adam so happened to find the three girls in question dancing with one another, Claire nowhere to be seen. Adam then spotted Claire pinned against a very tall, very muscular, very dark basketball player, their faces only distinguishable from one another because of the difference in skin tone. Instead of taking his anger out on the boy—who easily had a solid ten inches on him—Adam proceeded to march off the dance floor, where his hand made direct contact with the nearest concrete wall. To stop him from doing it again, Amber, who had originally spotted Adam storming away from the giant orgy, grabbed his bloodied hand and asked what the problem was.

When he pointed at Claire, Amber crumpled into Adam's chest, the dark boy with Claire being the latest object of Amber's affection. Somewhere amidst the sheer tragedy of it all, Elizabeth and Shannon comforted Amber briefly before hightailing it after Adam, hoping he wasn't on the verge of doing anything more idiotic than punching an inanimate object.

Luckily, my brain was still capable of some level of reasoning, so I was able to ask a security guard if he could call us a cab and safely got the five of us back to campus. The night grew worse. Adam, Elizabeth, Amber, Shannon and myself were impatiently waiting in the living room for Claire's unlikely return.

"I don't understand why she's doing this to me. I give her everything she asks for. I love her with every ounce of my being, and she doesn't care. I don't deserve any of this bullshit," Adam whined cradling his black and blue hand.

"Yes, you do," Amber snapped. "If you had a backbone and grew some balls, you would tell her to go fuck herself."

Adam glared. "Don't you take out your jealous bullshit on me. She's the one dry humping your dark chocolate."

Shannon held up her hand as soon as Amber opened her mouth. "Stop it. Both of you just stop it. This isn't helping anything. We abandoned Claire at the dance. How's she gonna get home?"

I stood, walked to the kitchen and grabbed a bag of peas out of the freezer. "She's gonna be fine. I doubt she'll come home anyway. Here—" I tossed the bag at Adam, bouncing it off his chest. "Put this on your hand. By the looks of it, I'd say you probably broke it."

Adam's eyebrows crumpled together as he propped the bag onto his injury. "You *really* think she's the type of girl who would spend the night with some random guy?"

*Dear God Adam. Get your fucking head out of your ass.* "As a matter of fact, yes, I do believe she's that kind of girl because she does it every fucking weekend. You two talk every goddamn day. Why don't you ask her to tell you the truth? Because you are devouring her lies. Amber's right—you let her treat you like a beaten dog and you keep running back to her. You're being a fucking idiot."

Silence ensued.

"Man," Amber whistled. "How much did you drink, Roxy?"

I flushed. "That's as much of a mystery to you as it is to me."

208

"What do you mean *every weekend*?" Adam asked, a high-pitched panic breaking through his voice.

My cell phone rang, preventing me from replying with some rude remark. I sighed angrily and walked up the stairs in a huff. "Figure that one out yourself, Romeo."

I collapsed onto my bed not bothering to change out of my lingerie. "Hey Sis! What're you doing up so late?"

"Roger is outta town and I'm not used to sleeping without him next to me."

"That's why you should get a dog. With the baby on the way and Roger needing to go to conferences all of the time, a dog might make you feel more comfortable—safer, even."

She chuckled. "I don't feel unsafe. I just miss my hubby. Dogs are gross anyway. I'm not about to sleep in a pile of fur all over my sheets."

I rolled my eyes. "How goes the pregnancy thing?"

"As well as expected. I'm beginning to feel a little off balance—like my equilibrium is off. I've never weighed this much my entire life."

"Now, you have an excuse to eat and Mom won't get on your ass about it."

"God, pregnancy is a beautiful thing. My ass looks so good in sweats. Don't think I'm off the hook with Mom, though. She still nags me about what I eat and now she nags me about taking prenatal vitamins. Why are you up so late?"

"Tonight was the lingerie dance thing, remember? My friends fucked up."

"Was your lingerie slutty enough?"

"Too slutty, in my opinion."

Lucy laughed. "Did you drink?"

"More like, what didn't I drink?"

She laughed again. "Good for you! This is exactly what you should be doing. You'll hate yourself in the morning, but that's all part of growing up."

I sighed, my mouth dry, my ears ringing. "Lucy, something is wrong with me. I had Lamont give me and the girls a ride to the dance—"

"Sweetie, this might be a tough question for you to answer, but why the fuck are you dating Zach?"

"Because I love him."

Her hesitation sent a sickening feeling straight through my gut. "How can you love him and love Lamont at the same time?"

"I need your help."

"I'm sorry Roxy. You're on your own with this one. My only advice? If you're serious about either of those guys, stop thinking with your vagina and start using your brain."

My running mascara began to stain my pillow. "What if I'm thinking with my heart?"

"Then you're bound to make a mistake. You're a *relatively* smart girl. You'll figure it out. How about you get some sleep? This might be the vodka talking."

"Lucy, I don't know what I'm doing."

"Promise me you'll get some sleep. And drink a glass of water before you go to bed—try to avoid that gnarly hangover. Love you!"

When she ended the call, I noticed a text message awaiting my attention. Despite my uncertainty and dread, I smiled, my heart and brain completely at odds with one another. Rather than call Zachary to let him know I arrived home in one piece, I fell asleep, Lucy's words infiltrating the deepest layers of my dreams and Lamont's text message tattooed on the back of my eyelids.

*Hope you're home safe. Glad you called. I want to see you again. Soon.*

# Chapter Eleven

I WAS FUMING. On the *one* day Zachary was off work, wasn't scheduled to attend class and had no homework to complete, he managed to ignore *all* of my attempts at contact. I wanted to reach my hand through the computer screen and strangle him because I knew that's where I'd find him. After two phone calls, three Facebook messages, four hours and five texts, my temper exploded like an active volcano, hot lava tears erupting from my eyes. In an attempt to steady my unstable emotions, I stripped out of my sweats and slid into the bathtub. The water was verging on too hot, the bubbles smelled of soothing lavender and the silence made it possible for me to think clearly. *Zach better have a legitimate excuse as to why he's been ignoring me all day. If it's because he's been playing that stupid video game all day, I'm going to lose it.* I took a deep, shaky breath. *Video games. I'm losing to video games. At least Lamont left me for a flesh and blood human being. Not a stupid digital whore.*

Whenever Zachary and I spoke briefly on the phone, he whined about the lack of time we had to converse, insisting that he loved me more than anyone—or *anything*—in the world, and reminded me how much he missed me. However, those words didn't prevent him from putting our relationship, putting *me*, on the backburner because he was too engrossed in some idiotic computer game. In my attempt to be "cool" and "understanding," I'd convinced myself that his obsession with video games wasn't a real problem, even if it did distract him from the important aspects of life: school, work, chores, family, responsibilities. Me. I would bite my cheek when he admitted to pulling an all-nighter in an attempt to finish a paper because he'd lost track of time "in the game." I tried not to cringe when he rambled on for hours about *leveling up* and *smashing noobs* that would talk trash to him through the speakers. After consulting my roommates about the issue, they suggested I join Zachary and his friends every once in a while to steal away some of his gaming time. I hadn't foreseen the hours I would wind up wasting on the computer as I leveled up my character, mountains of homework building up on my desk right beside the lack of sleep I was acquiring. I'd done my research and tried to comprehend the magnetic pull of the computer world on the male brain. Nothing made sense to me. I couldn't understand how someone would put a *game* before an *actual* human being.

211

*Enough is enough*, I thought as I dipped my head beneath the bath water. *I'm not gonna play second fiddle to a video game. I'm tired of being second best.* Emerging to take in another deep breath, I shook my head. *What if we aren't doing such a great job at this long-distance thing? What if we're not as compatible together far away as we are close together. Maybe I should've listened when he told me to really thing this thing through before I jumped head first into the deep end.* I flattened my hand, spread my fingers and watched the bubbles fall back into the bath water. *A video game. I don't even know if Lamont plays video games. He's been texting me so much, I don't think he'd have time to play a video game.* After taking another deep breath, I submerged my head under the water again, trying to drown any inappropriate thoughts that plagued my head involving Lamont. My long-distance relationship was on the fritz, but I didn't want to admit it.

It also wasn't only the fault of Zachary's inability to separate himself from his video games like an adult.

It was my fault for letting Lamont back into my life.

When I brought my head back above water, I wiped the droplets away from my eyes and stared at the bathroom ceiling.

Earlier in the day, Lamont sent me a text that threw my sanity straight into a vortex. He decided now was an appropriate time to inform me that if I didn't have a boyfriend, we would be together. *In a real relationship. Boyfriend and girlfriend.*

I'd questioned him and this sudden change in desire. *Not too long ago, you wanted nothing serious with me.*

His reply left me staring blankly at the screen of my phone. *I can't stop thinking about you. I know I like you and I've liked you for a while. I just wasn't ready for a relationship then. I am now. And I can't think of anyone else I'd rather be with.*

I dunked my head back beneath the water wondering if drowning would be more pleasant than being emotionally torn between two different boys. *Maybe I'm not meant to be in a relationship with anybody. Ever.* When I resurfaced, my ringtone was blaring through the bathroom doorway.

"Of course," I spat. "You finish your game and decide to call me back. Well, screw you. Now is not a convenient time for me." I turned on the faucet again to drown out the incessant ringing. The urge to yell at him—to scream until the air was snatched from my lungs—was bubbling from my pinky toe to the tips of my thumbs.

I pulled on the drain, watching the popping bubbles disappear around me. *You and Zach aren't logically supposed to be together. It makes no sense. He has school and work to worry about. You have school and writing to worry about. You both are on two opposite sides of the state. He wants video games. You want a boyfriend who wants you.* I wrapped a towel around my soaking hair and another around my body.

The phone continued to ring.

Although not one who enjoyed engaging in any type of confrontation, I couldn't remain quiet any longer. I'd finally learned how to stand up for myself and I wasn't going to back down now. My feet left soapy prints on the carpet, water dripping from my arm onto my desk. "So. You *finally* decided to call me back, huh?"

"Are you okay? You're worrying me. I'm sorry I missed your calls. For some reason, I didn't hear my phone ring."

*I know you're lying—unless you turned your phone off because my calls were distracting you from that freaking game. I'm not an idiot.*

"No. I am *not* okay. What were you doing?"

He hesitated, which made me even angrier. This wasn't the first time this conversation had taken place.

"Zach? Did you not hear me?"

"I heard you," he croaked. "I'm really sorry."

"What do you have to be sorry for, Zach?"

Another hesitation. "Are you mad at me?"

I bit the inside of my cheek. "Just tell me what was so important that you've been ignoring me."

"I wasn't ignoring you."

My head shook as I sat on the bed. "Stop avoiding the question. Don't you think neglecting to respond to me qualifies as ignoring?"

"I can't respond to you all the time."

"No?" I countered. "But you have all the time in the world to play that stupid fucking computer game?"

His silence was beyond infuriating.

"How fucking hard is it to answer your phone for one fucking second?"

"You need to calm down. You don't need to cuss at me." He snorted. "I didn't realize I had to tell you what I was doing every second of the day."

*Don't you tell me to calm down.* "You damn well know that's not what I mean. We've had this conversation *countless* times before and you don't take me

213

seriously. I'm sick of it. We don't get to see each other like people do in *normal* relationships. We only talk on the phone for a few minutes before bed. Then, when one of my classes gets cancelled—finally giving us the opportunity to actually talk at a normal hour—I try to be a good girlfriend and want to dedicate that time to you, and yet, you spend the *entire* day playing a fucking *video game*. I don't get why you always put that game before me—before *everything*." I took a deep breath, curling my knees up to my chest. "I'm not putting up with it anymore."

"Roxanne, what are you trying to say? You're not even gonna give me a chance to talk?"

The crack of his voice brought tears to my eyes. *Don't let him turn this around on you.* "I did give you a chance to talk. This isn't the first time we've been through this."

"But, Roxy—"

"Zach, stop." My anger was fading into fear. *He loves me and wants me to be happy, but I don't think I can take the distance.* "I really don't know—if I—" *Am I overreacting? Would Lamont really give a relationship a chance? I don't want to be alone anymore.*

"Roxanne," Zachary said before taking a shaky breath. "Are you suggesting we break up?"

*Will that finally make me happy?* My voice hitched in my throat as my body began to shudder. I crumpled into a ball on my bed, the strength I needed to argue faltering. "To be honest, I don't know what I want. I'm hurting—you keep doing this to me and you don't care that it kills me."

"Please, Roxanne, my little woman," he whispered, his voice hoarse. "Don't say those things. You're breaking my heart."

"Yeah, well, you've already broken mine. If you don't care, why should I?"

"Stop saying that I don't care because that's not true."

I sighed. "If you *actually* cared about what I think or feel, you wouldn't put those stupid games before me over and over again."

"I told you I was sorry."

"This isn't the first time! Sorry doesn't mean anything anymore," I snapped.

He was quiet. "Do you *really* want to end this?"

I held back a sob, my face already moistened by snot and tears. "I'm just wondering if it might help our relationship if we take a break." My heart smacked against my chest as a painful silence lingered through the speaker. "Zach? Are you still there?"

"Is that what you want?"

"I—I don't—"

"Because if you end this, that's it," he continued. "There won't be any 'getting back together' once you've gotten whatever this is out of your system. I can't handle these games. My heart can't be tossed around. If you broke up with me, nothing would be the same between us. How could I still see you as the sweetest woman in the world if you hurt me like that?"

*Oh, now you don't want to play games?* My body grew cold from the damp towel sticking to my skin. "What if I'd said that same thing to you when you talked to me again?"

"I'm lucky—and so, so grateful—you gave me a second chance. You're the sweetest thing in the world and I love you more than anyone else I've ever loved before, but it wouldn't be that way if you broke up with me. I wouldn't be able to pretend that our relationship is perfect like it is now because you don't think what we have is worth working on."

"You think what we have is perfect?"

He grew quiet. "In my mind, yes, it is."

"Zach, I don't—" I paused, my mind reeling. *What would my life be without him? He's made me happy. Should I take a chance with Lamont? Or should I suck it up and try to make this work with Zach?* I took a steadying breath. "I don't want to break up with you."

"Are you positive? Because I don't want you to be unhappy—and you sound pretty unsure about us right now."

I reflected on a potential relationship with Lamont. While he was capable of making me feel like a princess, he more often than not succeeded in making me feel like an unwanted hooker. "I'm sure. I just—no—you need to start caring about me. And more importantly, you need to show it to me. Right now, I *really* feel like trash."

"I wish you understood how much I love and care about you. I'm sorry I messed up. Fuck. I'm sorry I've been messing up. I won't do it again—I promise."

Although my heart wanted to believe him, my brain told me to be weary. "I love you, Zach. I won't give up on us."

#

MY DOOR WAS closed, a bottle of Aspirin on the nightstand, two empty jugs of water littering the floor, my eyes beginning to squint from the immense amount of reading I'd been forcing myself to finish throughout the day. The school week

215

had been a difficult one filled with surprise quizzes, seemingly endless chapters read and analyzed, poetry workshops that I was so impressed with, I'd begun to question my own writing talent, and flashcards imprinted with artwork from indigenous people. Mix in the fact that Zachary and I tried unsuccessful phone sex for the first time, and I'd enjoyed a night at Baskin Robbins with Lamont, there was nothing more I wanted to do than climb under my sheets and sleep the entire weekend away.

Just as I pushed my books and papers on the floor to lay my head on my pillow, the Molly plush wrapped tightly in my arms, the door handle shook vigorously. Needing peace and quiet, I'd locked it, going against the dorm's open-door policy. Groaning, I closed my eyes as tight as they would go, hoping that the incessant pounding and knob jiggling would stop.

"Roxanne Vaughn! Get your ass out of that bed right now!" Amber shouted.

"No," I moaned. "I need a nap."

"Why the hell is your door locked?" Shannon asked.

"Because," I said slowly. "I. Need. A. Nap."

"Let us in and then we'll leave you alone," Elizabeth added.

Sighing, I zombied my way across the floor, unlocked the door without opening it and fell back onto my bed. "What do you want?"

Amber turned the knob again, shoved open the cheap wooden door and spooned me, giggling when I tried to pull away from her. "You've been locked up in here all week. We've missed you."

Elizabeth sat in the computer chair. "We never heard how ice cream with Lamont went."

Shannon nodded, her back leaning against the closet. "Have you eaten this week? I honestly feel like I saw you once, maybe twice, in the past seven days."

"I've missed you all too. Ice cream was fine—nothing special. We enjoyed pleasant conversation while managing to avoid anything having to do with Zach. And yes, I've been eating macaroni and cheese at midnight and coffee in the afternoon. I also have my little mini-fridge over there filled to the brim with fruits. What've all you been doing?"

"We're all tired of seeing Claire and Adam sucking face. Now that they're 'Facebook official' they're being disgustingly cute. In short, nothing important," Amber whined. "But we did get an invitation to a party tonight. Can you come?"

I shrugged. "Sweetie, I need sleep before I can even think about needing to get dolled up for some party."

"What if I told you that Lamont's roommates are hosting?" Shannon smiled.

216

My heart rate picked up immediately. "And why would that make it any more appealing?"

"Your face is red," Elizabeth teased. "I'd say it is *rather* appealing."

"Come wake me up in two hours and then I'll let you know."

"See you in two hours!" Amber shouted before planting a wet kiss on my cheek. "We know you're gonna say yes, so don't pretend you're not."

The girls scampered into the hall, neglecting to close the door behind them, their laughter making me smile. "If I can convince myself I'm only going because they want me to, then maybe everyone else will believe I don't want to go because of Lamont." I sighed and put my cheek on my pillow. "She's right though. I'm definitely going."

#

AFTER MULTIPLE SHOTS of silver tequila were poured down my throat, the girls—already sweating profusely and talking at an outrageously loud volume— decided it was time to get a move on. Danielle, who'd been kind enough to offer her services as designated driver, herded us out the door like a group of patients awaiting their results from the latest anxiety medication test group.

Although buzzed, my anxiety didn't waver. Sure, I'd seen Lamont on Tuesday, but I was of sober mind and body, covered head to toe in an unflattering sweat suit. Now, I was exposed. Amber had lent me a denim mini-skirt and I'd paired it with a sparkly black long-sleeve shirt, strappy, black high-heels on my feet. In the dorm, with the girls clapping and howling at me, I'd felt sexy. Standing in front of Lamont's house, my uncertainties about him flooded straight to the forefront of my brain. One moment, he acted as if I carried a flesh-eating disease, and the next, he'd tend to me as if I was a precious flower worth millions of dollars. *Now is not the time to analyze how he feels. Go into this expecting him to ignore you—in fact, go into this planning on ignoring him first.* My knees wobbled. *Stop being nervous.*

"I don't want to hold your hand all night tonight," Claire said, scowling. "Do you think you can manage *not* running off and disappearing with Lamont?"

"Do you think you can manage *not* being a bitch for just one night?"

"Claire, leave Roxy alone," Elizabeth blurted before Claire was able to cause a scene. "To be honest, you're driving all of us crazy with this weird obsession you have with their relationship. Roxy is the smartest one in the house—give her some credit and stop treating her like a child."

"Seriously," Amber agreed. "You need to let Roxy live her life without butting in all the time. Just because your relationship with Adam is a ticking time bomb doesn't mean Roxy and Zach have to be in a shitty relationship."

Shannon nodded. "Let it go, Claire. We all love Roxy and think she deserves to have some fun tonight."

I smiled at the girls, my heart swelling full of love. I wanted to hug them, but Claire stood in my way.

Not surprisingly, she ignored the other girls and zeroed-in on me. "Do you think this is some kind of joke?"

"Well—yeah. I don't know why you care so much. Do you want Lamont to like you?"

"Can everyone please stop?" Elizabeth begged. "We haven't even gotten into the party yet and you're already starting unnecessary drama."

I shrugged. "Claire started it."

Shannon shook her head. "You're all arguing over a hypothetical situation that might or might not happen. Can we get along? Please?"

"Why do you care about Roxy's personal life anyway?" Danielle asked.

"You're all impossible," Elizabeth sighed.

"Because I'm her friend. She has a boyfriend and forgets that when she's with Lamont."

Danielle snorted. "Who dubbed you the boyfriend police?"

"Look, you're not there comforting her every time Lamont breaks—"

"Who cares? As a friend, you shouldn't be a bitch about that. If Roxy wants to have sex with—"

"Lamont!" I shouted, silencing Danielle immediately. "Hey! How are you?"

The six of us were standing on the front porch before an open door where Lamont ignored the others' presences and focused on me. Claire puffed out her chest and flashed a fake smile in his direction, oblivious to Amber's disdain. I was more than delighted when his eyes didn't budge, still glued to my body, slowly working his way down from my thick hair to my painted toes. *Now this is what I've been waiting for.*

"I wish somebody would look at me like that," Danielle said loudly. "Jesus. You both can fuck me."

"Shut up," I growled, cheeks hot with embarrassment.

"Hi Lamont!" Claire bounced up and down, nearly banging her chin against her push-up bra. "I feel like I haven't seen you in forever."

He didn't seem to hear her, his eyes melting straight into my curves, his hands hanging lamely at his sides. Keeping cool, I pushed past him without a word, leading the girls through the music and into the kitchen where plastic cups and throw-away shot glasses were lining the counter available for use. *That's right, Roxy. Make him wish he'd never even looked at Tiffany.* I didn't bother glancing over my shoulder, knowing without a shadow of a doubt that Lamont would be unable to resist the long legs I'd chosen to expose beneath the denim skirt. For the first time since Lamont and I had met one another, I was the one controlling the game.

Unfortunately, my assuredness wavered when the girls and I bumped into him playing Beer Pong in the garage later that night. His teammate was a short brunette in a tight black tank top that exposed her big breasts and olive colored skin. *Why is it always a tiny brunette with big boobs?* I thought back to Zachary and the busty brunette from the party in San Diego, took another gulp of my cocktail and tried not to submit to the doubts gnawing at my brain. *Don't you feel bad about yourself. You're kind of brunette—albeit a redheaded brunette—and you have boobs, too.* I watched their interactions from afar, sipping my margarita, hating the giddy sensation that tickled my insides whenever Lamont smiled, even though it wasn't at me. Based on my short analysis, I assumed that Lamont and his Pong partner were most definitely having sex—or at least close to it: her arm around his back, his lips brushing the top of her head, fluttering eyelashes, and frequent hugs. The jealousy was poking incessantly at my heart, my mind urging me to consume my drink at a quicker rate.

And yet, when Lamont spotted me staring at him, I didn't shy away—didn't blush or divert my attention like I would have a few months back. The cougar inside kneaded my stomach affectionately, a deep, rumbling purr vibrating through my limbs. *Time to make a move.*

Without a word, the girls trailed me around the two Beer Pong tables, nearly knocking me over when I abruptly halted next to Lamont.

"What are you doing?" Claire hissed.

"I'm gonna say hi to Lamont."

Danielle laughed. "You mean he didn't get a good enough look at you earlier?"

"Let her have her fun," Amber said, patting my shoulder.

"I don't think it's a good idea," Claire argued.

I put my lips around my water bottle and sucked down more margarita. "I'm not gonna jump on his dick if that's your concern."

Danielle, Shannon, Amber and Elizabeth laughed, their boisterous voices easily capturing Lamont's attention.

"It would, however, be rude to ignore our very gorgeous host who so kindly allowed us into this soiree." I smiled at him and cuddled up to his side, ignoring the penetrating glares of both Claire and Lamont's big-breasted partner.

"Are you winning?" I asked, tilting my head back.

He smiled down at me. "Right now I am, but not if you keep distracting me like this."

Claire coughed, Shannon and Elizabeth pulling at her elbows to get her out of earshot.

"Who's got next game?"

"You've got a long line ahead—"

"Lamont," his partner interrupted. "It's your turn."

He dismissed her with a quick wave of the hand. "Amber can play for me or something. I'm busy."

I tried not to look smug. "We'll talk later. I don't want to ruin your game."

He shook his head and handed Amber the little white ball. She scooted past him, winking at me while simultaneously shoving the brunette to the side. "What're you drinking? Can I get you a beer?" Lamont asked.

"No thank you. I'm drinking a margarita." I shoved the bottle into his face. "Wanna try it?"

He winced. "I don't do tequila. We've never been very good friends."

I forced him to take the drink. "Well, now's the night to make amends. Create a blank slate."

The way he stared at me made me nervous—like he was holding onto every word and hoping for a sign of my feelings for him. He put the bottle to his plump, tan lips, gulped and raised his eyebrows at me. "Why does it taste like chocolate?"

I giggled. "Oops. I do believe that was my lip-gloss. Totally forgot I was wearing it."

He leaned in and whispered, "I'd love to taste more of it later," his hand spinning the rubber bracelet sensually around my wrist.

I shivered and turned away quickly, asking the girls to migrate with me to a different room, reminding myself not to act on impulse. *Distance. All I need is a little distance.*

#

AS AMBER, SHANNON, Elizabeth and I were mingling with fellow partygoers in the dining room area, a set of arms wrapped around my stomach and pulled me into a strong body.

"Can I talk to you?" a deep voice breathed into my ear.

Goose bumps prickled my skin, my lungs struggling for breath. "Can we talk here?" *Where we're surrounded by people.* "I don't want to leave the girls." *I don't want us to be alone.*

He pulled me tighter. "They're fine. They won't even notice. They're talking to those guys and they're super drunk. You'll be back before they ask you to join the conversation."

"What about your Beer Pong partner? She's probably looking for you."

"What about her? The game is over."

"She seemed to be latching onto your arms a little tighter than your average partner should. Unless, of course, you're partners elsewhere."

He huffed. "Can you just stop talking and listen to me for one second?"

"I'm really sorry Lamont, but—" I sighed, allowing my back to relax against his chest.

"Please?" I could note the desperation in his voice, and it made me selfishly yearn for *all* of his attention.

"Okay, fine. But for ten minutes. Tops."

He took hold of my hand and guided me through floods of people, not giving me the chance to tell Amber, Shannon and Elizabeth where I was going. When we made it to his room, I assumed he would kick out the partiers spilling beer on his comforter or snorting cocaine off Chris's desk, but instead, he dragged me through the closet's doorframe, turned on the eerily dull, overhang light bulb and slid the splintered, wooden door closed.

"I can't believe you still wear that thing," he said, eyes smiling at me.

I nodded, my hand instinctively reaching for the bracelet. "It's a part of me now. I feel like I'm missing a limb when I don't wear it."

"I'm glad I gave it to you that night. You know, instead of Shannon."

My chest constricted, my pulse raced, the temperature of the small space rose to an uncomfortable level and I briefly wondered if I might faint in front of him once again. Turning my back on Lamont, I studied the shirts and pants hanging around me, my hands grasping opposite elbows, the sense of claustrophobia sickening me. *I shouldn't be here. I have a boyfriend.* Whistles and catcalls sounded from those milling around the bedroom, the taunting slowly suffocating me. I needed to escape the close confines of the dark little box before

221

panic fried my nerves. *Zach trusts me. I'm in a closet with Lamont. I'd kill him if I found out he was in a closet with some other girl.* My hand had just grabbed the edge of the door, my body slowly beginning to shut down, when I noticed Lamont's body shift in my peripherals. He leaned against the low dresser, his face pale, eyes moistening.

I took a deep breath, the guilt and compassion in my heart keeping me from thrusting the door open. "Lamont?" I asked, placing my hand gently on his shoulder. "Are you alright? What's going on?"

"I need to talk to you," he mumbled.

I gave him a reassuring squeeze. "I know that. Here I am. Talk."

He remained silent, his lips forming words without sound. I studied his face, scanned his chest and followed the path down to his white Nikes before returning to the hands he clasped over his thighs. *He's the one who broke your heart.* I ran my hands through the different colored shirts trying to distract my heart from falling straight into his lap. *He's the one who didn't want a real relationship. He's the one who said Tiffany was more beautiful.* Sighing, I turned my back. *This has gone too far. I need to get out of here.* I faced away from the hanging jeans and tried to smile. "Honey, you're really drunk right now. Why don't I grab you a glass of water?"

As I turned to push through the door to freedom, Lamont grabbed a hold of my hand. "Are you—still—fuck—are you still with him?" He toyed with my fingers. "Zach. Are you still with Zach?"

My hands twitched, uncomfortably close to the zipper of Lamont's jeans. "Yes, Lamont. Zach and I are still in a relationship. Why would you think we'd have broken up my now?" Our eyes interlocked like Romeo and Juliette's during their first exchange of love. *Patience. He's drunk and you know how he is when he's drunk. Just need to be patient.* "Can you tell me what's going on?"

He allowed himself to lose his focus in the coats behind my shoulders. "Are you happy?"

I closed my eyes and inhaled deeply, the familiar scent of Copenhagen swirling around me as if in a dream. I took a step closer, hypnotized. "Why do you care?"

His drunken gaze hovered over my face briefly. "Are you happy with him or not?"

"Yes," I growled. "I'm *very* happy with him." *Are you happy that you ruined everything?*

222

Lamont dropped my hand and slouched his shoulders, his face suddenly alive with frustration and jealousy. "How is that possible? You don't get to see him! He's five hundred fucking miles away."

"Clearly, Sailor Jerry is talking—"

He placed his sweaty palm on my cheek, the sheer shock of the caring gesture stunting my ability to speak. "Don't you think you'd be happier with me? I'm five minutes from you—*I'm right here.* I know how to treat a girlfriend right. Or at least, I did before I met you."

I cringed. "What's that supposed to mean?"

"With Melanie, with Tiffany, with anyone—it doesn't matter—I only thought of you. I still *only* think of *you* and it drives me crazy. Please, Roxanne, I miss you."

In that moment, the dark closet grew darker. My breathing slowed and I stumbled backwards, my shoulder blades colliding with the clothes behind me. *Oh my God.* I drew a hand over my heart. *Does he love me?* I wiped the sudden heat from my forehead. *Is he telling the truth?* My eyes burned—I couldn't stare into his sincerity. *I can't do this.* It didn't help that my body was buzzing from the tequila and I still hadn't moved beyond the fight Zachary and I had the previous week. *Am I happy with someone who's consistently putting video games before me? Am I happy being in a relationship where I'm lucky if I see him once a month? Am I happy with Lamont?* I shook my head, rubbed my arms and took a deep breath. "If you were playing a video game, and I called you, would you ignore my phone call?"

The question caught him off guard. "What?"

I slowed the sentence. "If you were playing a video game, and I called—or texted—or whatever—would you ignore me?"

He grinned lopsidedly. "A video game? Over a girl? No. If you called, I'd answer. If you texted, I'd respond when I died and was waiting to respawn. Why?"

His answer forced my arms tighter around my chest. *Don't let him do this. Don't let him break you. Remember what he did with Tiffany. He had his chance.* I straightened my back, chin lifting. "I'm sorry, Lamont. I believe you know how to treat your girlfriends right—but you chose Tiffany. And initially, you chose Melanie. If you weren't willing to break up with her for me, why should I break things off with Zach for you?"

He winced. "I was stupid. I want to be with you."

"You're too late." Despite my desire to climb into his arms and nuzzle my face under his chin, I held strong. "You were too busy *fucking* Tiffany to even give me the time of day."

"Stop bringing her up."

I shrugged. "You made your choice—the *beautiful* one."

"This fucking sucks. I want to kiss you. I really want to kiss you. I miss you, Roxanne. I fucking miss you." He placed his hands on my waist and pulled me closer. "Me and Tiffany didn't have anything. Not like what you and me have. It's special." He stared into my eyes. "I didn't mean it when I said that. You're the most beautiful girl I've ever met. I can't just let you get away."

*It's a trap. He only wants sex and you know it.* I turned my cheek, squeezing my eyelids shut when his lips moistened the skin below my bottom lashes. "Lamont—please—please don't do this. I can't."

"Nobody has to know."

I grew angry. "That's the thing," I spat. "You *always* want to keep me a secret. From day one, you made me pretend that *nothing* happened between us. That was the first time you hurt me. And I gave you another chance—we have sex. Oh, but *nobody* can know about that either because Melanie can't find out the *truth*. That was the *second* time you hurt me. And then Tiffany—you have no problem flaunting her around like a fucking trophy. Was that because she's the most beautiful woman you've ever met? And I'm some troll you can't admit to having any feelings for?"

The louder my voice grew, the more Lamont's shoulders slumped. "Roxanne, stop it. You're taking this all out of proportion."

"Am I? Because everything seems pretty fucking clear. I don't know why I keep forgiving you. I'm tired of—"

It was something I should've anticipated, but when he smashed his mouth against mine, I froze. The neurons in my brain fired left and right, one half telling me to push him away, the other half urging me to pull him closer. I didn't fight it—the foggy mist of tequila hovering around me prevented me from keeping an emotional wall between us. I kissed him for longer than I should have and allowed myself to get lost in the ecstasy of the moment before I placed my hand on his chest, reluctantly pushing him away. The closet was too small. This was all too real.

We breathed in sync with one another, the silence creating an environment that was too intimate for me to walk away from.

"Roxanne." Lamont grabbed hold of my trembling hands. "Please, stay. Spend the night with me," he pleaded.

I couldn't meet his gaze. "Lamont—please, stop it. I can't do anything with you. I have a boyfriend," I squeaked.

"I don't want to have sex. I want to lay next to you."

"Lamont—"

He held up his hand, pausing the doubt inching up my vocal chords. "I'm being serious. I only want to talk. No sex."

"Why do you do this to me? Why can't you just let me go?" The tears began their ascent to my eyelashes. "You only want me because you can't have me. You just want the chase."

"That's not true. If you would let me talk, I could make you understand."

Through the closet door, I could hear the girls calling my name.

"Where the fuck is she?" Claire huffed angrily.

"Probably fucking Lamont in the bushes somewhere."

"Danny, that's not funny."

"Have you been drinking?" Elizabeth asked.

Danielle laughed. "Sorry I'm not sorry."

"How the hell are we getting home?"

"I'm calling you a cab. I wouldn't drive you guys home in this state. Besides, you should find Roxy before you get ready to leave."

"Lamont, I'm sorry but I need to go." I turned to run away, but he grabbed my arm and pulled me against his body.

He kissed me again, this time with a desperate urgency I'd never tasted. I yanked my lips away from his and stared into his dreamy, dark eyes—blood shot and droopy, the alcohol was obviously commandeering his senses. *Stop. You need to be strong enough to stop this from happening. Stop before he breaks your heart all over again.*

"Lamont, I need to go." I patted his thigh, walked beyond the sliding door and refused to look back. He had yelled after me, but I did my best to pretend I hadn't heard a thing.

I found Elizabeth and gripped onto her forearm, my fingers leaving red prints on her skin. "Get me out of here," I whispered urgently. "I want to go home."

#

MY BODY REFUSED to sleep, my brain repeating the conversation with Lamont over and over again, my heart teetering between Lamont and Zachary, my fingers

225

itching for pen and paper so I could spill my uncertainties without any restraint. Poetic verse came easily, black drops of mascara falling from my jaw before staining the pages of my notebook. *I went from hermit to socialite, and that has done nothing but blur my sight. Once alone and now in love.* I paused, tapping the end of my pen against the paper. Maybe *there's a reason why nothing good rhymes with love. It's too fucking complicated. Even for paper.*

My writing was interrupted by a loud knocking; a knocking that was coming from the backdoor, which was located directly beneath my bedroom window. I wiped at my tears, not believing who I saw when I peeked through the blinds. I ran down the stairs on the balls of my feet, terrified that even the slightest noise would wake my slumbering roommates. It was three in the morning, and there, standing at the door, was Lamont in a sweatshirt and basketball shorts, his body swaying from side to side.

"What the hell are you doing? How are you here?" I whispered furiously.

"I drove my truck."

"You *drove* here? There are cops out everywhere!"

He nodded. "I know. I can't really remember driving."

"You're not making it any better, you know that, don't you?"

"I'm just telling you the truth." He burped loudly before I slapped a hand over his mouth.

"Just tell me what the fuck you're doing here."

"You don't need to cuss," he mumbled into my palm.

"I know I don't *need* to. I swear, people think I'm not allowed to be mad or something."

When I lowered my hand, he shrugged. "It's you. You're too good of a person to be like the rest of us."

I tried not to feel insulted, as if being called a good person was a bad thing. "Lamont, *why* are you here?"

"I already told you—I want to talk. You didn't give me a chance earlier."

I sighed and ushered him through the doorframe. *Yes I did. You just didn't utilize the time given.* "Go straight to my room and be quiet. If you wake the girls, I'll fucking kill you." When he looked over his shoulder, I nodded. "Yes, I fucking cussed. That's how fucking serious I am."

No longer so far beneath the influence of way too much low-quality tequila, I was capable of somewhat organizing my thoughts without falling prey to uncontrollable emotions. The problem was, I couldn't let him leave and still have a clean conscious. He was far too inebriated to drive, and I didn't need anything bad happening on my watch. I also couldn't drive him myself because I knew if I got pulled over, I'd blow over the legal limit. Although not drunk, I knew time was the only thing that could get alcohol out of the body. I sighed, turned off the light, relocked the door and tiptoed up the stairs. *Hear him out. Maybe he'll leave you alone once he gets whatever he has to say off his chest.*

When I closed the bedroom door, I leaned my back against it and inhaled sharply. "Lamont, what are you doing here?"

He sat on my bed and kicked off his shoes.

"Whoa, whoa, whoa," I said walking across the room. "Don't get too comfortable buddy boy. You'll be going home soon."

He sneered. "You're gonna let me drive home like this?"

"No, no, no," I hissed. "Don't you dare turn this around on me. I wasn't the one who asked you to be here. Besides, you shouldn't be here. I have a—"

"I know," he snapped. "A boyfriend. You don't have to keep reminding me. I get it."

"Zach would *murder* me if he knew you were here. So, you better start talking because I'm already regretting opening that door."

He sat in silence, focusing on the seams of my comforter. "I think you and me have something special. We could be happy together. I haven't stopped thinking about you since day one. I miss you, Roxanne—please believe me. I really, *really* miss you."

"Yeah, right. You miss having sex. You miss Tiffany because she was available whenever you needed her. Let's be real."

He cringed, head shaking. "No, Roxy. No. That's not it."

"Then what do you mean?"

"I just—I want—to—to hold you."

My heart latched onto every word despite the red flags waving inside my brain. *He's not thinking straight. You know how much he adored Tiffany. He's just upset she's gone and he's running back to you because he thinks you're easy. He wants you because he can't have you.* "Lamont, you're obviously trashed. This is a conversation we should have when sober."

He held my hand, head still shaking. "I won't be able to talk about it then."

I took my hand away and shoved both beneath my armpits. "Why can't you talk to me when you're sober?" I was shouting, no longer concerned about waking my sleeping roommates.

"I'm sorry. I know you hate it, but I can't share my feelings easily. That's why I want to talk to you now. I've had a lot on my mind."

227

My shoulders fell forward. *I don't want to hear this.* I closed my eyes and told myself to remain strong. *This is what I get for ignoring Zach's goodnight call.* I took a deep breath, stifling my anger. "Then you better start talking because I would like to get some sleep tonight."

His intoxicated eyes took in my rosy cheeks, post-party hair and mascara-smudged eyes. While I grew self-conscious, his smile grew to the size of the fifth of Sailor Jerry he drank earlier. "I want you to give me a chance. I know it's not the best timing because you're happy with Zach, but I honestly believe you'd be happier with me." He paused, rubbing his hands on his thighs. "There's something about you—something different. No matter how hard I try to ignore the feeling, I can't stop thinking about you—I always come back to you. I'm stuck on you."

"Lamont, please. I need you to stop right there."

"No. You need to hear me out. You told me to talk and I'm not gonna stop. I can't stop thinking about you. Not Melanie. Not Tiffany. *Only you.* You're the girl I miss. I want to be with you."

A tear snuck through my eyelid and silently wove a path down my cheek. I allowed it to fall onto the comforter, hoping it would remain unnoticed. "Why? Why me?"

Lamont stared at my dampened eyes. The room was dark, but I feared he could see the raw emotion ripping right through the resentment I held toward him.

"You have a killer personality. You're so much fun. You're sweet and friendly. You're obviously gorgeous. We always have great sex. Why wouldn't I like you?" He placed his palm on my cheek, rubbed his thumb across my skin. "I know you know how much I care about you, Roxanne. You know me better than anyone else does—you do. And you make me fucking happy."

I sighed and slowly pulled away from his touch. *What am I doing? It's four in the morning. Zach is asleep. This isn't fair to me. To Zach. To Lamont. How is it possible to be in love with two boys at the same time?* I began to hate myself. My strength shattered beneath my feet. *Can I be with Lamont and Zach without either of them knowing? I want both of them—I want it all.*

"You know my feelings, but Lamont, I can't keep doing this with you. You refused to break up with Melanie when I wanted to give you *everything*. I'm not going to break up with Zach and jump into whatever *this* is with you. And, you seem to keep forgetting that when we were both single, you chose to be with Tiffany—fling or not, sorry or not, you hurt me, and I can't just let you do this to me over and over again. Bad timing is a thing between me and you, but the truth is, you had your chance and you blew it."

"Tiffany was a rebound, I swear. I didn't want to rebound with you. Roxy, please trust me. I'm ready for a relationship."

My tears came out from hiding, making themselves visible to the boy who rejected me so readily. "I don't think I can trust you."

Lamont grabbed my hands and held them to his chest. "Why don't you? How can I prove to you that I'm ready?"

"You can't do anything. It's too late for us."

His eyes collapsed to his lap, sadness penetrating the usually calm demeanor of his voice. "Can I kiss you one last time?"

*This is a bad idea. Kick him out. Say no. Don't be an idiot.* I shrugged. "Okay, but only one. I mean it."

When our lips connected in a tangle of fireworks and sad love songs, I wished I wasn't in a relationship with Zach. I wished for another time, another place, where our pasts didn't exist and I could kiss Lamont Carwyn forever.

#

THE NEXT MORNING, I awoke to the sound of chatter in the living room. The girls were already awake, laughing with one another, the TV volume even louder. I groaned and closed my eyes, wanting to sleep because I hadn't gotten more than two hours of shut eye, but it was too late. My body wanted coffee, and my stomach was grumbling for something to soak up my hangover. My brain was still having a difficult time comprehending how I'd succeeded in sending Lamont home relatively sober and completely unnoticed, when I found Danielle, Claire, Elizabeth, Amber and Shannon convened on the couches, bright eyed and refreshed. *It's only nine-thirty. Why is nobody else feeling miserable?* Without bringing unnecessary attention to myself, I remained quiet, searching through the pantry for a packet of oatmeal and a filter for the coffee pot.

"He's such an asshole. I told him not to leave—I even asked him for the fucking keys. I knew he was blacked out, mumbling and stumbling through the remainder of the party like a prick. Next thing I know, I go outside because I needed to find Nathan, and the fucker's truck was gone."

I grabbed a bowl from the cupboard. "Nathan's truck was gone?"

"No. Who else drives piss drunk at three in the morning?"

My hand absently fiddled with the blue rope necklace touching the collar of my nightshirt. I quickly moved my hand down to the coffee machine, lifting the lid so I could add the coffee grounds. "Let's be real. We were at a party full of idiots last night. I need a better hint."

"Danny?" Elizabeth interrupted. "What were you doing looking for Nathan?"

She shrugged, her dirty blonde hair pulled into a messy bun on top of her head. "We'll get to that part later." Turning to me, Danielle frowned. "Lamont. After you left, he wouldn't fucking shut up. I told him a million times to just let it go, but he wouldn't listen. At one point, I *literally* pushed him back inside the front door. Do you know how hard it is for someone as short as me to overpower someone as tall as him?"

Forcing a laugh, I pressed the brew button on the machine, moving over to my bowl to add water to the dry oats. "I can imagine that was a difficult task."

"No, you don't understand. He ruined a pleasant night. I take my eyes off of him for five minutes to have sex with Nathan and poof—he vanishes."

"Wait one fucking second," Amber interjected. "You had sex with Nathan? I thought you said you were just looking for him?"

The microwave beeped, my oatmeal steaming, the bowl hot against my hands. I walked over to the couch ready to join in on the drama.

Danielle shrugged. "I was getting to that, but yes, we fucked. It was just what I needed. I went looking for him because I wanted another round. Since Lamont took off, I decided to just let it go and let myself have a good time. I haven't even showered yet and I wreak of—"

I held up a palm. "Okay, okay, we get it."

"No need to make a big deal out of it. It was sex. Great, no-strings-attached, drunk sex."

"You don't think it's a big deal?" Elizabeth asked. "He cheated on you! With two different girls in one week's time. You walked in on it happening. Danny, he broke your heart."

"Calm down. Let's not get dramatic here," Danielle argued. "We were drunk. We had sex. Baddabing, baddaboom. No feelings were acquired during the exchange of fluids."

"If you're gonna continue sleeping with him and cry because he doesn't love you the way you love him, I'm ignoring your phone calls. You do this to yourself," Amber replied.

"Thanks for the support, Bitch," Danielle snapped.

"I'm not gonna support your idiotic behavior."

"So much for always being there for your friends no matter what."

Amber snorted. "You're the one who said that last night, not me."

"Roxy," Claire began curiously. "What's that around your neck?"

I froze and held the spoon in my mouth as four heads snapped in my direction. *Are you serious, Claire?* My body started to sweat under the pressure. I slowly removed the spoon, swallowing a small scoop of my breakfast. "A necklace."

"Oh my God!" Danielle gasped. "That's not your necklace—I've seen him wearing it for almost two years now. You're telling me that you just listened to me talk about Lamont and you didn't say a damn thing?"

"Roxy, what's going on?" Shannon asked.

"That's Lamont's necklace! He fucking drove here!"

"What the hell was he doing here?" Claire demanded.

I gulped. *What was he doing here?* I wondered. "Now, before all of you assume the worst, let me begin by informing you nothing happened. Besides, we talk enough about Lamont. Why don't we continue talking about Nathan?"

"No, no, no. Forget about Nathan. If *nothing happened*, why are you wearing his necklace?"

I shrugged, imagining how good it would feel to lodge my spoon straight through Claire's eye socket. "I fell asleep with it on."

"First the bracelet, now the necklace," Elizabeth teased.

Amber grinned. "How did I not hear you guys?"

"Because there was nothing to hear. We talked."

Everyone wrinkled their foreheads skeptically.

"You're all being ridiculous," I nearly shouted, spoon flailing in hand, oatmeal bits landing on my pajama pants. "I wasn't expecting him to come over. He showed up at the back door and said he needed to talk. I wanted to send him home but, obviously, he was drunk as a skunk. I'm honestly upset he came over—the last thing I want is for someone to get hurt in a drunk driving accident."

"You're not telling us everything," Shannon pried.

I blushed slightly, shoved some oatmeal into my mouth and wished I hadn't come downstairs. "I haven't had my coffee yet. I'm not mentally ready for this."

"You guys totally kissed," Elizabeth giggled.

"God—puke. Don't be so cute about it," Danielle joked.

I smiled shyly.

"Roxanne!" Claire screamed. "How could you? What about Zach? That's cheating! I fucking told you you'd do this!"

I cringed at the sound of the word—the way it rolled off her tongue, through my brain and over my heart—but calmly finished chewing before swallowing. *Cheating. I'm a cheater.* The oatmeal landed with a thud in the hollows of my stomach. "Before you start throwing those kinds of judgments at me, you need to take a step back and chill out. Do you see this?" I held up my left hand and pointed to my bare ring finger, my sister's advice pouring out from my mouth. "I'm not married. I'm only twenty years old. I didn't bang him. I thought the kiss would bring some much-needed closure to our relationship."

"Well, did it?" Amber asked.

I dropped my oatmeal bowl on the coffee table, the spoon falling to the floor. "No—of course it didn't. I'm more confused than ever."

Danielle laughed, stood and stretched. "Would you like me to bring the necklace back to him? I figured while I still smell like Nathan, I might as well go back for thirds."

"Don't think we're done talking about that," Elizabeth added sternly.

"Yeah, whatever. It's just sex. If Roxy can fool around with Lamont while she's in a relationship with someone else, then you shouldn't give me shit about Nathan."

"Don't throw me under the bus, like that," I mumbled, the oatmeal not settling well with the way the word *cheater* sounded.

She laughed. "Am I bringing the necklace to him or not?"

I fingered the blue and black rope gingerly. "No. I'm gonna hold onto it for a little while. See if he can face me when he hasn't been drinking. Be a man and what-not."

She shook her head. "Why are you dating Zach again?"

"Because I love him."

"Oh really?" she challenged. "Who was on your mind when you went to sleep last night and woke up this morning?"

I frowned. "Just go have sex already."

"Hey—no judgment. But maybe you should sit down and really think about why you're in a relationship."

"When I come to a solid conclusion, you'll be the first to know."

# Chapter Twelve

"ZACH'S VISITING THIS weekend, so please, *please* keep Lamont's name off of your tongues when he's around," I requested, frantically picking up the trash littering the living room.

"Will you be able to keep your tongue off of Lamont?"

I glared. "Amber, that's not funny."

She smiled. "In all seriousness, if you don't want to think about Lamont, you should probably return that *thing* you wear around your neck all the time."

Instinctively, I grabbed the black and blue rope I'd refused to remove since Lamont had put it on me the night of his party.

Elizabeth and Danielle laughed.

"You're pathetic, you know that?" Shannon asked.

I sat on the ground, covering my face with the notebooks in my hands. "Yes, I'm fully aware of that."

"Then give it back before you let that necklace get to your head," Danielle ordered. "He was drunk."

"Stop rubbing it in. He's already asked for it. I just keep lying—saying I'm too busy. I'm too afraid he's gonna take back everything he said to me. Blacking out is usually his excuse for not remembering admitting his feelings to me."

"Well, you need to get your head out of your ass," Claire added. "You have a boyfriend. Why are you still talking to Lamont? You shouldn't have taken that necklace in the first place."

"I know that but I can't take back what already happened." I shoved the notebooks into the magazine bin and stood, beginning to collect articles of clothing that made the living room resemble a closet. "FYI, you all suck. I'm giving it back to him today so you can stop giving me guff about it." I paused and threw the clothes into a pile by the stairs. "Promise me—no Lamont this weekend. Even if you go to a party at his house, don't say a word. The last thing I need is for Zach to pester me with questions. Or wonder why we wouldn't be attending the party with you guys. Or insist we attend the party." *If you were a good girlfriend, there would be no reason to hide anything from him.* I shook my head, took a deep breath and put my hand on the staircase's railing. *I am a good girlfriend.*

233

"Roxy," Claire snapped. "Stop cleaning and go return the necklace. We can finish up here." Her hand on my shoulder was anything but comforting and I squeezed the railing to refrain from pushing away from her. "I'll go with you if that'll help," she continued.

I shook my head and marched up the stairs. "No thanks. It's just Lamont. I'll go over there once my room is done. I don't want Zach to think I live like a pig." *And I 'm not ready to take this off. I don't want to face reality, yet.*

#

MY PALMS WERE sweating despite the cool breeze blowing through the open window. I'd stalled as long as possible and now, I was in a panic. I rubbed the necklace between my thumb and forefinger. It may not seem like anything special to a random person crossing my path, but the thin blue and black rope was the only way Lamont had admitted his possible feelings for me—a token of his love despite the fact that he had been incredibly drunk and probably regretted giving it to me.

The black and white rubber on my wrist pulled against the hairs on my skin. "What is wrong with me? Why do I obsess over every little thing Lamont does? Why is it so hard for me to let these trinkets go? He only wants me when he drinks. It's obvious he doesn't care about me. Why is that so hard to accept?"

I pulled my car in front of the driveway, the front end kissing the bumper of Lamont's truck, and left my emergency flashers blinking. If the situation escalated, I needed a reason to leave.

Opening the driver's side visor to check my makeup in the little mirror proved to be more difficult than anticipated. My hands were trembling, and I couldn't seem to get a grasp on my distress. Even taking slow, deep breaths wasn't helping. Grabbing a hold of the rope, I stared into my reflection. "You're just giving him the necklace, which, I may remind you, belongs to him." I shook out my hands, cracked my knuckles, pulled my curls into a ponytail, picked the lint off my jeans and closed my eyes. *Don't cry. It's a stupid piece of rope. So what if Lamont said he hasn't taken it off in two years? So what if it made me feel special?* Then, before I lost my nerve, I glared at the big white truck, opened the car door and marched my way up the driveway. *There's no reason to be afraid. He's just a boy. Just a really stupid boy.* My knuckles rapped against the wood before my finger pressed the little white bell.

My heart dropped when Dylan, Lamont's housemate, answered the door. His shaved head was covered by a backwards neon pink baseball cap, his chin

234

covered in a blonde beard. His smile was warm and welcoming but unfortunately, he wasn't the boy I was looking for. He eyed me curiously.

"Hey Dylan. How are you?" I asked.

"Hi Roxanne. Lamont isn't here. You just missed him."

I looked over my shoulder and gestured at his truck. "You know, if he doesn't want to see me, he doesn't need to make his roommates accomplices."

Dylan laughed. "We're boys. We don't work that hard to avoid people. Even girls. Him and Chris went to get food."

I nodded and wiggled my toes. *There's no way he's not home. He's too scared to see me.* "You really expect me to believe he's not here?"

He smiled crookedly. "You wanna come in and scope out the house?"

*You're sounding crazy.* "No, that's fine. But can I have you give him something for me?"

"If it's a kiss, you're shit out of luck."

I smiled earnestly. "Even though that'd be hilarious, I wouldn't make you do anything that extreme." My fingers tingled as I unlocked the necklace and held it out. "Could you please return this to him? He let me borrow it the other day and I feel bad about keeping it for so long."

Dylan nodded, grabbed the rope and grinned. "I've never seen him take this thing off and I've known him for a helluva long time. How'd you convince him to give it to you?"

*I just pretended I didn't love him anymore. He'd probably give me a ring if I pretended like he didn't exist.* "He was drunk. I was drunk. Something like that."

Another laugh. "I'll make sure he gets it back. He'll be bummed he missed you. He talks about you too much. Maybe seeing you would've shut him up for a few days."

I shrugged. *He talks about me?* "It was nice seeing you, Dylan."

When I descended the small pathway back to my car, I tried not to fall prey to the bitter disappointment beginning to crawl into my stomach. After days of wondering what Lamont would say upon my return, I didn't even get the satisfaction of receiving an answer. I closed the door, rammed the key into the ignition, pulled hard on the gearshift and turned around in the col-de-sac. *It's better this way. No muss, no fuss. Dylan just saved you from another awkward encounter.*

Yet, I couldn't rid myself of the sadness poking at my heart. I wanted to see Lamont.

To see if the love was still there.

To see if it was just a figment of my imagination.

To see if he wanted one last kiss.

#

MY PHONE RANG loudly, the music breaking through my dream sequence and nearly startling me off the edge of the bed. I jerked into sitting position, one of my hands slapping against Zachary's bare chest.

"Crap. Sorry babe," I mumbled, completely forgetting that I wasn't the only one chasing sweet dreams. "Instant reaction."

He groaned and turned away from me. *Who's calling at two in the morning?* The ringing silenced, leaving me with the sound of crickets chirping outside the window and Zach's heavy breathing inviting me to fall back asleep. I smiled down at my boyfriend, eager to snuggle against his warm skin.

Except as soon as I shifted to meld my body into his, the phone cried out again.

"Who is it?" Zachary asked, grumpy.

I yawned, propped myself on my elbow and grabbed the phone, taking a sideways glance at the screen. My lungs fell out of my mouth and smacked against the pillows. *You know I don't answer your booty-calls.*

"Hello?" I whispered hoarsely, slyly maneuvering my legs away from Zachary's and out from beneath the covers.

"Roxanne?" Lamont asked, his voice deep.

I walked to the bathroom, closed the door, flipped the light switch and sat on the toilet seat. "Yes. What's up?"

"Hey!" I could almost hear his smile. "I'm at a party. Where're you?"

"At home. Trying to sleep. It's two in the morning."

"Come out and drink with me."

"No. I'm—"

"Wait!" He shouted over a burst of loud music. "I can't hear you."

I put my face in my palm hoping that Zachary was sound asleep. "I'm gonna go."

"No, Roxanne, wait." The music disappeared as a door slammed. "Alright, what're you—ow—shit—son of a fuck." Scuffles and thuds sounded behind Lamont's curses.

"Is everything okay?"

"I think I just broke my ankle."

"You—what?"

236

He burped. "I'm gonna walk home. It's a cockfest around here."

I knew I should've just hung up, but I couldn't stop myself from worrying. "Where are you?"

"In the middle of a street somewhere."

"Get out of the street and walk on the sidewalk. Don't be stupid."

"God you're bossy." He burped. "My ankle hurts. I need another beer."

When I heard the hiss and snap of a beer can, I began to rifle through my drawer for a hair tie. "That would qualify as being stupid. You can't drink in public."

"I'm a man. I can do whatever I want."

"There are police everywhere. You know they have nothing better to do than patrol around for drunk idiots. You're gonna get arrested."

"Fuck the Po-lice."

I sighed. "Just stop. Tell me exactly where you are."

His shoes crunched over gravel, a pause between each step. "My ankle is fucked up. It hurts to walk. The beer isn't helping."

"Then stop being dumb and sit down. Text me the nearest address you can see. I'll come get you."

After I clicked off the phone, I pulled my curls into a sloppy ponytail, brushed the grime off my teeth, grabbed a sweatshirt off of the floor and turned off the light. Not bothering to find shoes, I crept out of the bathroom and tried to pry open the bedroom door unnoticed.

"Where are you going?"

I froze, my skin crawling off my bones. "I'll be right back. My friend Danny just called and she needs a ride home."

Zachary began to rise. "I'll get up and go with you."

"No," I spat too quickly. Coughing, I smiled. "Thank you, but I'm alright. I'm just driving Danny home—maybe to get her a burger—and I'll be right back."

He yawned and nodded. "Hurry back. It's cold here without you. I love you, Little Woman."

I cringed, the guilt pinching my arm. "I love you too, Zach."

Not wanting to risk waking any of the girls, I snuck out the back door, running barefoot atop the chilly cement, my keys jingling in my hands. My cellphone beeped, an address flashing across the screen.

I opened the car door and smiled. "I'm on my way, Lamont. I can't wait to see you."

#

I FOUND LAMONT two streets sooner than anticipated. Having not taken any of my advice, he was still limping down the middle of the street, a tall can of Coors Light in hand.

When he spotted me, that drunken grin I couldn't resist spread across his face and he waved.

I unlocked the passenger side door and gestured for him to get in. "Thanks for listening to me and not drinking in public."

"Your car is way too fucking small." He compressed his long legs into his chest, his head nearly hitting the roof.

"Maybe you're just too big."

"Yeah, well, my ankle really fucking hurts."

I smirked. "Stop your complaining. I'm sure you're overreacting."

"No. I think I broke it."

"You wouldn't be walking on it if you broke it."

He frowned. "Maybe me drinking isn't making it feel as bad as it really is."

I patted his forearm. "How'd you do it in the first place?"

"It was your fault."

I snorted. "What did I do?"

"You were talking too quietly on the phone and I had to leave the house to talk to you."

"What happened when you left the house?"

He reached down and rubbed his ankle. "I tripped down the stairs and landed funny on my ankle. The ground was super uneven."

I laughed, not caring that Lamont was glaring at me. "Not my fault you're an idiot."

"It's not funny. I'm seriously injured."

"Put some ice on it when you get home and quit being a baby. Learn how to walk like a civilized human being."

"You should learn to talk on the phone." He paused, burped and cracked his neck. "Don't take me home. I need my truck. It's on campus."

"Lamont, it's almost three. I'm not going to shout on the phone in the middle of the night. It's called an inside voice." I made a turn. "Why is your truck on campus?"

"We pregamed at Robert's dorm before we went to the party."

"Well, too bad. I'm not letting you drive home drunk."

"I need my truck tomorrow morning."

"Someone can take you in the morning, then."

238

"They won't be up early enough." He shook his head and reached for the door handle. "Drop me off here. I can walk the rest of the way."

"Are you nuts?" I hit the break. "Your ankle is hurt. You'll make it worse."

"I need my truck and if you won't take me there, I'll walk."

I tightened my grip on the steering wheel. "Fine. I'll take you to your truck. But please wait to drive home—please."

He released the handle, leaned back and crossed his arms over his chest. "I've done worse."

I turned on the radio and tapped my thumb against the steering wheel. *I need to go home. I can't just leave Zach there by himself while I'm frolicking around town with Lamont. He's a grown man. I shouldn't have to babysit him.* And then my nervous system short-circuited. I glanced down at my thigh.

At his hand resting on my thigh.

"Thank you."

My eyes trailed up his arm, passed the rope on his neck and stopped at the sincere smile spread across his face. *Tell him to move his hand. It's not appropriate.* The light turned green, removing my attention from the giddy feelings swelling through my stomach.

"No problem. You're a friend of mine. I don't want you to get hurt."

He squeezed gently. "I've missed you."

I ignored him, pulling into the campus parking lot. "Lamont, where's your truck?"

Turning right quickly, I wove my way through parked cars, potted plants and streetlights. I spotted his truck and glanced at the clock. It was already nearing three-thirty. *I need to go home. It's time to drop him off and call it a night. If he drives home, he drives home. Lamont is not my responsibility.* I stopped my car beside his, engine still running.

"Please, get home safe."

"Why didn't you call me when you gave Dylan my necklace?"

Surprised, I jerked my head back. "Excuse me?"

"You should've called me instead of giving it to Dylan." He touched the blue and black rope with the hand that had been on my thigh. "Why didn't you tell me?"

*Because my boyfriend was only a few minutes away and I was too afraid I'd crawl into your bed if I saw you. Because I was too afraid you'd take more than just the necklace back.* I shrugged. "You weren't home. You asked for it earlier in the week and I stopped by when I had a free moment."

"You should've texted me. I wanted to see you."

Glancing down at the Boobies bracelet, I tried to hide my smile. "Honestly, I'm surprised you remembered who you gave it to."

He frowned. "Don't say that. I haven't taken it off in two years—I wouldn't give it to someone I didn't care about. Melanie asked me for it all the time and I never gave it to her."

I hated that my body rejoiced with his admission. *That means he has feelings for me.* I looked to my left, through the window, beyond the cars and upward toward the dorms. *It doesn't matter how he feels. Zach loves me. It's too late.* "You should go. None of that—it just doesn't matter anymore."

"It does matter. I care about you."

*Yeah. You care about me whenever you've had too much alcohol.* "Lamont, go home. Text me in the morning and let me know how your ankle feels. Ice it before you go to bed and maybe take some Advil."

He didn't move to leave. His hands remained shaking between his knees. "Do you still care about me?"

I rested my forehead on the steering wheel, turned off the ignition and listened to the bass of the music synced to the beat of my heart. "Obviously, I still care about you. I wouldn't be here and you'd be limping around town trying to find your way home."

"Then why are you with Zach?"

"Please," I begged, turning to face him. "I don't want to have this conversation again. Me and you are *friends.* That's how it has to be."

"But Roxy, I—"

*He's gonna say it. He's gonna admit he loves me.* The silence was too long. *Say it, Lamont. If you say it and you mean it, I'll leave Zach. I love you. Tell me you love me too.*

And then the moment broke like a twig when Lamont reached for his ankle and cursed. "I need to go home. Thanks for the ride. Wanna give me a hug?"

*I want to give you the world.* "Of course," I croaked.

He walked around the front of the car and met me by the door. "I'm glad I got to see you. I'll text you in the morning."

And before I could stop myself, I fell into Lamont's embrace, sharing a kiss that made me forget my boyfriend was sleeping in my bed. I was sober, which meant I didn't have a way to write off my actions. *I love him.*

When we split ways, I didn't bother to watch Lamont's truck. I rushed across the parking lot, pulled into the nearest available spot and ran into the dorm, careful not to make a sound once I stepped foot inside. I tread lightly up the stairs, pushed open my bedroom door and rolled into bed beside Zachary. Still half asleep, he smiled at me.

"Welcome back, Little Woman. You're such a good friend. Everyone is so lucky to have you. I love you."

I sniffled and nodded, silent tears falling onto my pillow as I stared up into the darkness, wishing that Lamont had been the one to say those words, and wondering why I couldn't be happy with a man who loved me more than Lamont ever could.

#

I SCRIBBLED FRANTICALLY on a copy of my latest poem, my fellow students commenting on and critiquing the piece I'd turned in for workshop. The class had shifted the desks into a giant circle so we could talk to one another about our work. I was the last to be workshopped, my anxiety building as four others had their poetry dissected like the frogs I'd been forced to tear apart in Anatomy class. When I'd read their poetry, I'd been impressed by their multiple uses of imagery, rhythm, rhyme, and repetition.

Apparently, the rest of the class thought their poems resembled the fresh pile of manure that had just been dumped on the giant grass field in the middle of campus.

My work wasn't receiving much better praise.

"It's too cliché. Everyone has read love poems before. You need to come up with metaphors that have never been heard of."

"The narrator in the poem seems a little clingy. Your stereotypical girl in love with a guy she can't have. The idea is old. Make it fresh."

"The narrator is so whiny. There has to be some way to make her problems stand out without the underlying complaints."

I could feel my cheeks turning red beneath the thick layer of foundation I'd applied. My eyes struggled to blink back tears. The poem had been about the feelings I'd been experiencing as of late, my heart split between two boys who were located on completely different sides of the personality spectrum. The students' comments were digging a hole deep into my heart, their judgments attacking me on a personal level.

"Your word choice isn't strong enough. The emotion is there but it would be more palpable if you had words with intense meanings behind them."

241

"The imagery is there. Just amp it up a notch."

I sat silently and listened intently, my hand beginning to cramp, my pen quickly running out of ink. When the class ended, my ego having been thrown into the middle of the freeway and run over by multiple semi-trucks, I packed up my notebook without making eye-contact with anybody. The class cleared out quickly, leaving me alone with my gray haired, glasses wearing, wrinkly skinned, professor.

"Roxanne, I'd like to have a quick word."

I slung my backpack over my shoulder and nodded timidly. "Yes, Professor? Is everything alright?"

"I know this is your first creative writing workshop and I noticed your shoulders slumping forward with every additional comment. I don't want you to get discouraged."

I shrugged. "I used to be a scientist. Poetry is something I'm passionate about, but I know I have a lot to learn."

"Ms. Vaughn, you have natural talent. For someone who hasn't been in a creative writing class, your work is superb. Read over my notes when you're rewriting these pieces, but try not to let the words of your classmates overwhelm you."

"Thank you, Professor. I look forward to your commentary."

She smiled, her straight teeth yellow, gums a light pink. "Unlike the Sciences, writing is subjective. Keep writing. Every chance you get—just write."

I nodded, thanked her again and left the classroom wondering if I'd made a mistake switching majors, and worrying that my family had been right. Despite my professor's encouragement, each student's critique had felt like a bee sting, permanently scarring my skin.

#

"I AM SO done dealing with your fucking boyfriend. He's a stupid piece of shit and needs to control himself when he drinks."

I turned down the music and sat on my bed, half dressed. "Whoa, whoa, whoa. Luke, a little context, please."

It was Saint Patrick's Day—an excuse for college students everywhere to drink until well past belligerent—and I was in the middle of getting dressed for a little get together. The girls were in the kitchen pregaming and I was running late. The last thing I needed was an angry phone call from my best friend in San Diego regarding some undesirable behavior from my uncontrollable boyfriend, whom I'd already refused to speak to because he ignored me the previous night.

"He drank way too much last night and turned into a fucking asshole."

I sighed. "He was out partying?"

"Yes. He came over to my apartment with his group of friends. I didn't invite him to the party, but my roommate did, apparently."

I thought back to the busty brunette from the party in San Diego and tried not to scream.

"It was clear they'd already been drinking," Luke continued. "But that didn't stop him from drinking my alcohol."

"Luke, I didn't even know where he was last night. He didn't call or text—nothing. He disappeared into thin air after eight. Clearly, he'd been too drunk to even think about me."

"He was out of control."

"I get that but I'm five-hundred miles away. How am I supposed to do anything?"

"Have you talked to him today?"

I bit at a hangnail. "Nope. I refuse to answer him. He needs to learn that he can't fall off the face of the planet just because he can't handle his liquor."

"I'm not the only one pissed at him. My roommate has banned him from the apartment."

My cheeks began to burn, embarrassment grasping at my heart. "I'm really sorry, Luke. Tell your roommate I'm sorry too. I don't know what else to say. He's an idiot. He's not my responsibility."

He sighed. "I know that. I don't mean to yell at you, but he won't pick up my phone calls. I tried to be a good friend—I told him to stop drinking—but he wouldn't listen to me."

Glancing at the clock, I stood and put Luke on speakerphone so I could apply my makeup. "Can you tell me what exactly happened?"

"That fucker pissed all over my bed. I had a bag of clothes sitting next to it and when I reached in to try on one of my new shirts, it was soaking wet—and it fucking smelled like piss."

I applied some foundation to my cheeks before searching through my makeup bag for eyeliner. "I mean, you had a ton of people there. How do you know it was him?"

"My roommate saw it happen."

I paused and stared at the phone sitting on the bathroom counter. "What do you mean your roommate *saw it happen?*"

"She walked into my bedroom, asked Zach what he was doing, and he turned around—dick completely out—and started laughing, spraying it all over the place. It stained my fucking wallpaper."

My hand flew over my mouth. *She saw his penis. He showed the busty brunette his penis. Oh my God.* "Luke, I'm so sorry. I don't understand why—how—what he—crap." I shook my head, trying to gather my thoughts. "This is *not* okay. Is there anything I can do?"

"Tell him that nobody wants to see him again until he learns how to drink without acting like a complete jackass."

"I hope your holiday gets better."

Although upset, I could hear his smile. "Thanks Roxy. I love you, and I miss you like crazy."

"I miss you too, Luke. I'll see you in, like, a week during spring break. Go drink. I'll see what I can do about Zach."

Once I hung up the phone, I stormed into my room and pulled a dark green t-shirt over my head. *Who the heck does Zach think he is? How could he do such a thing? And to our friends! I'm going to kill him.*

"Roxy!" Amber shouted through the door. "Are you ready yet?"

I grabbed my black converse off the rack in my closet. "Almost. I need—like—ten more minutes."

When I slid my right foot in the shoe, I dialed Zachary's number. He answered on the second ring. "Little Woman! I've been worried—"

"What the hell were you doing last night, Zachary Cameron?"

He hesitated—just one moment too long—making my temper jump ten levels higher.

"You are *such* an ass! I just received a phone call informing me how much of a raging idiot you were last night."

"I—Roxy—you don't—who called?"

I resisted the urge to chuck my phone out the window. "Why does that matter? Zach, you urinated on Luke's bed! On his brand-new clothes! On his wallpaper! You're twenty-three years old! Will you ever learn to control your liquor?"

"You know I always celebrate Saint Patrick's Day!"

"Yeah, but did you have to drink so recklessly?" I screamed. "I celebrate plenty of holidays without losing control of my actions. Why are you *such an idiot*? Luke's roommate saw your penis! You just whipped it out for everybody to see! That is *not* okay. Do you have an excuse for that?"

244

He remained silent.

"Zach, answer me. You need to understand that your behavior is unacceptable." *Hypocrite. You haven't exactly been acting like an angel lately. Look what you're doing with Lamont.* "I'm not dating the same jerk you were when you were a freshman."

"Roxy, I'm sorry."

I huffed. "You don't sound sorry."

"Look, it was an accident. I was just having fun with my friends and I lost count of how many drinks I had."

"I hope it was worth it. You've now been banned from that apartment and your girlfriend doesn't want to speak to you ever again. I'm so embarrassed. You embarrassed me from five hundred miles away! Do you know how difficult it is to do that?"

"I told you I was sorry," he whispered.

"Yeah, well, I'm sorry too. Sorry that you turn into a huge jerk every time you drink. You *always* have. You should know your limits by now. I'm going out with my friends tonight. Maybe I should drink like you and see how it makes you feel."

"Roxy, please—"

I finished tying my shoelace. "You won't be hearing from me for the rest of the night. See how you like being ignored. I'll be too busy making a fool out of myself and—how did you phrase it? That's right. I'll be *having fun*."

When I stood, I pressed the end button and stared at myself in the mirror. My bust pushed against the tight material of my t-shirt, my butt barely covered by the plaid miniskirt I purchased earlier at the mall, four-leaf clovers dangled from my ears, green socks rose up to my knees and black Converse adorned my feet. I barely recognized myself.

However, as usual when I looked at this stranger in the mirror lately, I liked what I saw.

When I walked into the bathroom to finish up my makeup, Elizabeth entered the room, Amber and Shannon trailing close behind. "Is everything alright?"

"We heard yelling," Shannon added.

I nodded, careful not to smudge my mascara. "Zach makes such an ass out of himself whenever he drinks. I can't handle it."

"It's Saint Patrick's Day! Forget about him and let's have some fun." Amber puckered her lips in the mirror. "I mean, Claire isn't here this weekend.

That's enough reason to celebrate, don'tcha think?" She studied my outfit and smiled. "Is that a kilt you're wearing?"

I grinned, smearing red lipstick on my lips. "Well, it is an Irish holiday."

"You are blossoming into a beautiful butterfly," Amber said, full of pride. "What would you do without us?"

I shook my head. "Probably be really freaking miserable."

"Is Danielle on the way?" Shannon asked.

Elizabeth nodded. "Maybe this time, she'll *actually* be a responsible DD."

"Honestly, we should all bring a little cash," I suggested, finishing up with my blush brush. At the beginning of the semester, I didn't even know what a blush brush was. "You know, in case something happens and we have to hail a cab."

"While we still have the chance, why don't we get in some last-minute Pong practice?" Elizabeth asked.

After turning off the lights and closing the bedroom door, I followed the girls downstairs, my auburn curls bouncing around my shoulders. "We've been practicing all week. There's no way we'll lose."

In preparation for the Beer Pong match I'd convinced Elizabeth to join, we'd decided to work on our technique throughout the week. Pushing the wooden dining table against the wall, we measured eight feet from the edge and stuck a strip of duct tape on the floor. From there, we placed ten red cups on the surface nearest the wall, four rows carefully aligned from four cups to one. Every night, amidst homework assignments and studying for midterms, we would stand on the tape and throw Ping-Pong balls across the table, analyzing the exact arc necessary and at which speed to toss.

"We never practiced drunk, though. Think it'll matter?"

I handed her a ball from the table while I rolled a second between my fingers. "Myth has it that you get better as you drink. All we need to do is make sure we sink that last cup." I tossed the ball effortlessly and watched as it sank into the cup at the front of the pyramid. Elizabeth followed suit. "We'll be fine. Just keep the game face on."

"What're you playing for anyway?" Amber asked.

"The boys have to cook us dinner if they lose. We have to cook them dinner if they win."

"Good thing you both have an advantage." Shannon smirked.

"What're you talking about?"

246

"Isn't it obvious?" She gestured to my chest and my legs. "Lamont always has a tough time keeping his eyes off you. Distract him with some skin and you're guaranteed to win."

#

UPON ENTERING THE garage with a bottle of iced tea flavored vodka mixed with lemonade, and a six-pack of Shock Top beer, I felt my confidence soaring through the clouds. Although the girls had taken a couple of shots prior to Danielle arriving at the house, I'd denied any of their offers in anticipation of a long night, but my body buzzed as if I were five shots deep. I'd been attending the gym every day and limiting my food intake in preparation for the holiday. I wanted Lamont to want me and seeing his jaw drop—just slightly behind his beer can—reinforced my incredibly vain, and completely out of character, thoughts. *I look good. I look really freaking good.*

"You boys ready to lose?" I swished my hips as I descended the four concrete steps, my tennis shoes echoing through the silence.

"I hope you're prepared to cook us dinner," Chris said, his giant smile forming dimples on his cheeks. "We're looking forward to a fuckload of homemade spaghetti."

"Yeah, whatever. You won't know what hit you when we're done here," Elizabeth added, walking down the stairs behind me, another six pack in hand.

Lamont didn't join in on the witty banter, his eyes locked shamelessly with mine. I hated that those brown beauties made me blush so easily. He wore a green t-shirt with a white clover on the front, dark blue jeans and white sneakers. A black hat rested backwards atop his head and the rope necklace we'd shared hung just above his collarbone. I wanted nothing more than to kiss his jaw and work my way up to his lips.

I kept my composure, placed my alcohol on the Beer Pong table and sauntered over to the boy who had my heart wound tightly around his little finger. "How's it going, Handsome?"

The surprise etched on his face was more than gratifying, but he managed to maintain his nonchalant attitude. "You're crazy if you think you stand a chance. Me and Chris—we're undefeated."

I stood on the tips of my toes and threw my arms over his shoulders, careful not to touch my makeup-covered face to his shirt. "Me and Lizzy are about to change that."

His hands pulled my lower half closer to his. "Why don't we just skip the game and call it a tie?"

Giggling, I pushed him away. "You're afraid you're gonna lose. Admit it."

"Can you two stop being so disgusting?" Danielle asked obnoxiously as she entered through the doorway. "If I'm gonna see you two fuck all night, I'm gonna need to start drinking immediately."

Chris and Lamont were the only ones at the Della household celebrating the holiday. The other three roommates were lounging on the living room couches, a twelve-pack of green beer on the coffee table, video games exploding on the television.

"Surprise, surprise. You offer to be our DD and end up drinking anyway," Amber huffed.

I laughed. "That's why I made sure we all brought cash. We had a feeling this would happen, did we not?"

Danielle shrugged. "I'm trying to get laid tonight."

"Nathan is waiting for you," Chris said.

Amber and Elizabeth glared.

"C'mon Lizzy," I urged, pulling on the crook of her elbow. "Let them be stupid together. Don't get distracted. We have a game to win."

#

THE RULES OF the tournament were simple: best two out of three. The first round was a warm-up to get the four of us amped up—and drunk. We also had to get used to the length of the table, which was relatively easy considering the wall-to-duct tape measurement was close to perfect. Every game was close, lasting until both of our teams only had one cup each. Finally, on round three, last cups standing, the game was becoming increasingly difficult. My Arnold Palmer-vodka mixture was gone and the last beer of my six-pack was located in the red cup in my hand. My vision may have been blurring, but my Pong game had never been better.

"Looks like someone's been practicing," Lamont taunted. "I was expecting you to play like you did at Robert's."

"That was ages ago," I replied. "Beer Pong isn't the only thing I've gotten better at."

Amber and Shannon snickered, clinking their drinks in the air, Lamont's handsome smile nearly knocking me to the ground.

"We can do this, Lizzy. Only one more cup."

She nodded, golden eyes half-closed, a lazy grin hanging from her chin. "This is what we practiced for. How many times have we sunk that last cup?"

248

I caught the ball Lamont tossed too far. "At least a million." My tongue felt fuzzy—slippery against my teeth. I was slurring. *I need to stop drinking. I don't want to completely lose control.* I looked at the cups on the table, empty beer bottles scattered around the garage floor. *Why did I offer to drink so many of Lizzy's beers?* Then the image of Zachary exposing himself flashed throughout my mind. Him not caring about the fact that there would be repercussions the next morning. *Oh, right. That's why.* I took a sip of my beer. *Fuck it.?* "You need to focus, Lizzy."

She held the ball between her eyes and threw it across the table. It bounced to the right of the cup. "Ah, shit," she moaned frowning at me.

I patted her back and placed my red cup on a corner of the table. "It's okay, Buttercup. I got this." Stumbling sideways, I closed my left eye, curled my tongue over my lip and tossed the ball. It hit the rim of the cup before bouncing straight into Chris's palm. I stomped my feet angrily. "Son of a bitch. Lizzy, did you see that?"

She nodded slowly. "You were robbed, man."

I sighed, leaned over and rested my cheek on her shoulder. "I think I can hear that cup laughing at me."

Elizabeth hiccupped. "That probably means it's time for you to stop drinking."

That's when I heard the familiar sound of a clink and a splash followed by deep-throated cheers. When I glanced down at the table, I noticed the white ball floating in my beer—not the final cup, but the one I'd set on the table when I threw the ball.

"You didn't make it. Why are you cheering?" Elizabeth asked.

"Death Cup," Chris stated, arms crossed over his chest.

"Death—what? I—I don't get it," I stammered.

The boys laughed, high-fived and bumped chests.

Shannon and Amber approached the Pong table, drunk concern hidden beneath their lifted eyebrows. "You boys didn't make the last cup. Why are you celebrating?"

Lamont pointed to the cup with my unfinished beer. "It's called Death Cup. When you're a pussy and can't drink all your beer right away, you create the Death Cup. If the other team makes Death Cup, game ends. No rebuttal."

"In layman's terms, *you lose*," Chris added, slurring his words so the single "o" sounded like ten of them.

Elizabeth and I exchanged frowns. "We've never heard of that before."

249

Amber and Shannon nodded. "Besides, you guys never mentioned that when you were explaining the rules."

"Everyone who plays Pong knows what it is. Guess you two should've studied the game a little harder," Lamont teased. "You're playing two undefeated champs. If you were serious about the game, you would know the ins and outs of it." He wagged his pointed finger at me. "And you'd learn how to finish a beer."

I narrowed my already squinted eyes and placed my fists on my hips. "You cheated! That's not fair!"

The boys shrugged. "Bring out the chef hats and aprons, ladies."

"And don't forget to finish the rest of the beer."

I frowned. "This isn't fucking fair."

"We can help you," Shannon offered.

"Free beer is free beer," Amber said grabbing the final cup off the boys' side of the table.

I nodded, snatched the Ping-Pong ball out of my cup and swallowed the beer that lost me the game.

Lamont came over and wrapped his arms around my body. "Sorry I'm not sorry."

I laughed and pushed him away. My skin was too warm, cheeks too pink, brain too muddled and heart pumping blood too quickly. All I wanted to do was cuddle into Lamont's arms and fall deeper into the pit of infatuation that was devouring my self-control.

"Do any of you wanna go to a party? Travis just texted me and said he's throwing something at his place," Shannon mentioned, wiping the foam from her upper lip.

"You still talk to Travis?" Elizabeth asked. "He really hurt you. I thought you never wanted to see him ever again."

Shannon dismissed her with a wave. "We don't talk like *that*. We're just friends. He informs me of parties, mostly."

Amber and Elizabeth looked skeptical. "Now, define 'friends.' Roxy changed that term a long time ago."

I frowned. "Hey—not cool."

The girls snickered.

"I'm being serious," Shannon whined. "Do you guys want to go or not?"

"Let's take some shots first," Lamont suggested, slamming a handle of rum on the table.

"Do you have shot glasses?" Shannon asked.

He shook his head. "Straight from the bottle."

Although I told myself it was time to stop drinking, I grabbed the handle and held it toward the girls. "What do you guys think?"

All of them nodded, gesturing eagerly for me to gulp it down.

Not even questioning their advice, I chugged quickly, the rum tasting like water on my tongue. Wiping off my chin, I realized the problem: the liquor didn't burn my throat. It didn't make me cringe. And the instant I felt the liquid slosh against the beer and vodka already present in my stomach, I knew I'd made a mistake.

The girls each took a sip before Amber grabbed my arm. "Let's get outta here. The party'll be fun."

"How're we gonna get there? Our DD is drunk," Elizabeth complained.

"I'm sure her mouth is around something other than beer," I said, laughing when Amber shook her head.

"I can drive," Shannon said confidently. "I haven't had as much as all of you and his house is, like, down the street. No big deal."

"We can take the truck," Lamont offered. "Think you can handle it?"

Shannon shrugged. "A car is a car. How hard can it be?"

Once the rum was capped, Chris excused himself to play video games with the other boys and Lamont went in search of his keys. I placed my palm on my forehead and took a deep breath. "Guys, I'm *really* drunk."

Amber giggled. "I can't believe you drank the Sailor Jerry like that. Not gonna lie, I'm impressed. We used to have to pressure you to drink a beer. Look at you now."

Even though I thought I smiled, I couldn't have been too sure—my cheeks were numb. "I think that was a mistake."

"You seem to have a problem keeping your eyes open," Shannon joked.

"C'mon girls. Let's get going," Lamont said from the top of the stairs. "Truck's outside."

Struggling to make my way up the steps and into the living room, I almost told the girls I didn't want to join them. I wanted to go home, lay down and fall asleep. It felt like gravity was weighing my body down, my limbs no longer attached to their joints. Lamont grabbed my hand and pulled me behind him, the shoes on my feet dragging against the ground.

"I don't know if I should go," I mumbled.

But the next thing I knew, I was sitting in the back seat of the truck between Lamont and Amber. Laughter was spilling from my mouth, but I couldn't remember why. Lamont's hand was on my thigh and the girls were talking excitedly to one another.

"I don't want to go," I whispered to nobody in particular.

Lamont kissed the side of my head. "Me neither."

My neck crumbled beneath my jaw, my eyes too heavy to keep open. "But we should go. Be polite."

"Once we park, let's get out of here. Walk back home. Just you and me."

I shivered despite his hot breath. "We need to stay with the girls."

Shannon took a sharp turn, my face now resting comfortably on Lamont's shoulder. "We can't leave them."

"Fuck girl," Amber said, laughing. "I thought you said it was down the street!"

"They'll be fine. I want to spend alone time with you."

"Everything's fine," Shannon said, the wheels of the truck screeching to a stop. "We're almost there."

"Then maybe you shouldn't stop in the middle of the street," Elizabeth cautioned, her face resting against the truck's cool window.

*Oh my God*, I panicked. *No. Nonono. Don't freak out. I'm okay. I'm fine. I'm in control. I can keep my shit together.* Another turn nearly threw me onto Lamont's lap. My head was spinning, the street came in and out of view, my vision blurring to the point of blindness. My brain tried to fight it, tried to keep me in control, but the alcohol was moving too quickly into my liver, and before I knew it, the world around me turned black.

#

"YOU NEED TO stop moving. Let me take care of it," Lamont murmured.

I rested my hands on his shoulders and looked down at his face. *What is going on?* Nodding, I felt my body relax, my knees bent next to Lamont's hips. "I'm sorry."

He bit his lip, shifted slightly and grasped onto my sides. "Don't worry about it."

*How am I doing this?* "I don't want you to think I'm terrible."

He smirked, his hands moving me up and down—I noticed I couldn't even feel anything. My entire body seemed to have gone numb to the usually sweet sensations associated with such intimacy. "It's not like we haven't done this before. You're drunk. It's fine."

*No no no no no. I shouldn't be doing this.* I closed my eyes, felt the rum slowly taking away my consciousness again. I tried to fight it, willing myself to

252

unstraddle Lamont and go home hoping that it was all a bad dream. *Get off of him. Get off of him. Why can't I move my legs?* I leaned my head back, Lamont's hands resting on my breasts. I opened my mouth to tell him to stop, but he covered it with his lips, stealing away whatever strength I attempted to muster. *I love you, Lamont. Why don't you love me?*

"God, you're so sexy," he groaned.

I smiled, loving how focused his eyes were on me. I was the center of his world and that was as close to love as I could hope for. *Stop it! He's going to break your heart. He's obviously using you for sex, he—!*

#

WHEN I AWOKE, my eyes remained closed. I could hear male and female voices coming from somewhere close, laughter filling my ears. I listened intently, trying to understand why the girls had company over so late.

But then I recognized Danielle's high-pitched giggle and felt my stomach clench.

I opened my eyes and found myself alone in Lamont's dimly lit room beneath his beige sheets and black comforter. My heart began to race, shocks of anxiety shooting straight to my fingertips. *What am I doing here?*

Glancing to the side, four red numbers blinked at me. *04:00.*

*No. This can't be happening.*

The pillows smelled of laundry detergent and Copenhagen. I frantically felt around my body. Fully clothed, panties in tact, socks still on. I thought I was in the clear until images of me riding Lamont and him rolling on top of me began to fall into place.

"No," I whispered. "There's no way."

Fumbling around the sheets, I finally found my phone, panic threatening to suffocate me. As I dialed Shannon's number, I wasn't sure what made me feel worse: the fact that I had sex with Lamont or the fact that I woke up in his bed alone.

#

WHILE THE TOASTER ticked, warming the piece of bread I desperately needed to absorb the alcohol in my stomach, the girls told me about the party. Travis and Shannon made out. Elizabeth fell asleep on the kitchen table in the middle of a King's Cup game. Amber drank too much green beer and wound up dancing alone in the middle of the living room.

"Did I even make it into the party?" I pulled my peanut butter out of the fridge. "The last thing I remember is realizing I was blacking out in the truck and trying not to."

Amber shook her head. "You got out of the truck with us but when we turned around to talk to you, you and Lamont were gone."

"Literally vanished," Elizabeth said.

"It must've been that Sailor Jerry you drank. You took it like a champ but it obviously pushed you over the edge," Shannon laughed.

The timer buzzed. I grabbed a knife and began spreading the topping on my toast. Even though I knew I needed to eat, my stomach churned at the smell of the peanut butter. "Guys, I messed up. I'm almost positive I had sex with Lamont."

"*Almost* positive?" Elizabeth asked.

"Not gonna lie—it's a bit fuzzy. I'm having a difficult time wrapping my head around it. I remember him telling me not to move. That he'd take care of it. And then I woke up alone in his bed."

"Oh, Sweetie," Amber cooed sympathetically. "Are you alright? How did that happen?"

I took a bite of my toast and shrugged. "I wish I could give you answers but I'm at a loss. I'm kind of numb. We'll see how I feel in the morning."

"What're you gonna do?" Shannon asked.

"What else can I do? Don't tell Zach. Deny whatever Lamont says. Pretend I was at the party with you. As far as I'm concerned, if I can't remember it, and if Lamont doesn't remember it, and nobody was there to witness it, it didn't actually happen. Kinda like if a tree falls in the woods. If nobody is there to hear it, does it really make a sound?"

# Chapter Thirteen

THE PLANE RIDE was agonizing; it gave me way too much time to think about all of the stress I was going to deal with once I landed in San Diego. Zachary and I were fighting more than ever, our phone calls morphing into screaming matches and our text messages over analyzed. It was because of his behavior the night before Saint Patrick's Day, but it was also because I'd finally surrendered to the feelings I had for Lamont. I was a pot calling the kettle black—blaming him for cheating on me and for being a terrible boyfriend, when in reality, it was me doing everything wrong. I didn't want to be in a relationship anymore, but I didn't know how to tell Zachary the truth without seeming like a horrible person. So, when my dad picked me up from the airport, I told myself to act as if nothing had changed since the last time we were in San Diego. Zachary and I were supposed to be in love. And I was determined to remind myself of that fact every single day.

#

ZACHARY AND I walked along the sidewalk, hand-in-hand, his light-yellow polo shirt and khaki pants clashing against my flashy, black and white party dress. His brown shoes remained in step with my zebra print high heels, our difference in style mimicking the different feelings we had for one another. I smiled at him when he kissed my cheek, but it didn't reflect the embarrassment I was already experiencing being seen with a man who wore such ridiculous outfits to parties. At another time in my life, I found this to be one of his more endearing quirks, but now, I wanted the strength to ask him to change into something a little more appropriate.

"Please don't overdue it tonight. You're supposed to drive me home and I will refuse to get in the car if I see your eyes so much as glaze over even in the slightest," I said harshly, still having not forgiven Zachary for his Saint Patrick's Day nonsense.

His grip around my hand loosened slightly. "Roxy, I promised your father I would bring you home safely. I would never put you in danger. I know I fucked up but that had nothing to do with you. That was just me thinking I could handle more liquor than I could."

255

"I'm sorry if I sound like a jerk, but I'm just having a difficult time trusting you lately." *I can't even trust myself.*

His shoulders slumped before he dropped my hand completely and stepped in front of me. "I don't know what's going on in your head right now but there's something you're not telling me. What's wrong?"

*I can't stop thinking about Lamont. I want to be with him. I want him to love me like you love me. I slept with Lamont. I cheated on you. And I want it to happen again. And again. And again.* My breaths came quickly, my head feeling as light as notebook paper, my balance beginning to tip heavily to one side. I reached out for Zachary's forearms and closed my eyes. "I need to sit down," I whispered.

He helped lower me to a cinderblock wall, my heart nearly ripping itself away from my other organs. "What's going on?"

My skin turned red, the chilly breeze fighting against the sudden sweat. "I don't know. I'm freaking out."

He crouched before me and patted my thighs. "It's okay, Little Woman. Just breathe. I know things have been tough lately, but we're okay. Take deep breaths. Do you want to go home?"

*I want to go back to Rohnert Park.* I shook my head and inhaled through my nose, fearful that my tears would leave black stains on my cheeks. "No. I promised Luke I'd see him at this party. I'm sorry. I'm just stressed out about me and you."

"Then talk to me. Let's figure it out."

*I don't think you and me should be together.* "I don't feel like we're on the same page anymore."

"Well, what's changed?"

*I've been talking to Lamont. I've been seeing him more often. I had sex with him. I've fallen so deep in love with him that even a team of naked firemen would be unable to pull me out of this hole.* "We fight all of the time. We barely talk anymore. And I'm having a difficult time trusting you whenever you go out. I worry all night long."

He frowned. "Other than St. Patrick's Day, what have I done to make you feel this way?"

I shrugged. "I wish I had an answer for you, but I don't. I just keep thinking you're gonna hook up with some other girl." *Hypocrite. You're the one who shouldn't be trusted.*

256

He squeezed my thighs and stood. "Let's get into this party and forget about the drama. Let's see some old friends and enjoy ourselves. I love you, Roxanne. I will *never ever* hurt you. You are *my* Little Woman and nobody else matters to me. I can *promise* you that."

*I'm the one hurting you. Hurting me. It's not you.* When he kissed me, I placed my hands on his cheeks and smiled into his eyes. "I love you, Zachary Cameron. I'm sorry. I think I'm just freaking out because of the distance. It's getting really hard."

"Don't they say that time apart makes the heart grow fonder?"

We began our ascent up the stairs to the party house, the music and loud voices emitting from the windows finally reaching our ears.

"Like I said," he continued. "Let's forget about it for tonight. I will only drink enough to get me a little buzzed and I'll sober up before I drive you home. I just want to be here with *you*."

*I wish I could say the same.* "Okay. Sounds like a plan."

#

I SCREAMED WHEN a familiar voice yelled my name from across the living room. Her newly dark brown hair—she was blonde last we spoke—was spaghetti straight, her pale white skin colored with blush and bronzer, her strong soccer player legs flexing beneath a dark blue dress as she ran toward me. My best friend from high school, our bond severed by the attendance of different colleges and opposite social groups, flung her arms around my shoulders. No matter our differences, alcohol—being the miracle it is—made it seem as if two years hadn't gone by without us so much as liking one another's photos on Facebook.

"Lacie! Is it actually you?" I asked, stumbling slightly to the side.

She kissed my cheek. "Roxy Vaughn! What the fuck are you doing in San Diego?"

I smiled. "Getting drunk, clearly. How've you been?"

"Sleeping with guys who apparently have girlfriends and attempting to do classwork when I'd much rather be partying. Pretty usual stuff these days," she said running a hand through her hair. Her hazel eyes shimmered beneath her gray eye shadow. "Whaddabout you? How's Nor Cal?"

I pulled on the back of Zachary's shirt until he stood beside me and kissed him. "I have a boyfriend who lives in San Diego and I'm taking sixteen units. I don't have to deal with my parents on a daily basis and I have a gay best friend who's destined to be a doctor. Pretty usual stuff, too, I guess."

257

Lacie laughed. "At least you're not living with your parents." She smiled at Zachary. "You go to SDSU, right?"

He nodded and smiled back, showing off his crooked and yellow teeth. "Two grades ahead. How do you know Roxanne?"

Lacie threw her arm around my waist and pulled me close. "High school best friends! Dumb bitch decided to leave San Diego, and I haven't seen her since.""

"How do you know Zach?" I wondered.

She sneered. "This guy walks around the pool half naked *all of the time*. Everyone knows who he is. That speedo can be seen for miles."

I tried not to glare at my boyfriend, who was blushing. Patting Zachary's chest, I tried to let my previous drunken infatuation with his quirks overwhelm the underlying anger attempting to break through my good mood. Before I was given the opportunity to make a comment I was sure to regret later, a tall, somewhat darker skinned girl with dark brown hair and fire engine red lipstick on her large lips invaded our intimate circle.

"Lacie, there's no more booze. Unless someone plans on making a liquor run, let's get the fuck out of here."

My old friend laughed. "Jasmine, I need to introduce you to this girl. Roxy, this is my best friend, Jasmine. Jasmine, this is one of my friends from forever ago, Roxy."

I shook hands with this Spanish girl, her dark brown eyes large like a baby cow's, and unintentionally pushed Zachary out of the conversation. I asked Jasmine questions about school and work, inquired as to what Lacie had been doing since she graduated from high school, and then moved the conversation to boys, observing all of the good looking party-goers who had matured quite well since the last time I saw them. They asked me about Northern California, the party scene in Sonoma, and we exchanged numbers so that we could get together during break. I drank and drank throughout the conversation, not realizing just how hard the booze was hitting me until I'd forgotten why I was mad at my boyfriend. He was acting strange, which made me believe something bad had happened, but I found myself wanting to throw myself at him. He winked at me and brushed his hand against the back of my arm, shivers rushing through my spine.

"We've gotta get going, but it was so good to see you, Roxy. Don't be a stranger!" Lacie said, squeezing me in a tight hug before she and Jasmine left the house.

"They seem nice," Zachary mumbled into my ear before placing a soft kiss against my temple.

I nodded and cuddled against his chest. "I'm really glad we came here. I haven't seen Lacie in forever. Maybe we can actually become friends again."

"Another long-distance relationship, huh?"

Even though I chuckled, my stomach squirmed. *At least this is a relationship I can't cheat on.* "How about we go home? Luke already left and you heard the girls—no more booze." I sloppily leaned against his body hoping to feel my insides light up. "Why don't you take me home and take advantage of me?"

He grinned. "Let's hope your parents are asleep. I would love to make love to you without worrying about your father reconstructing my face."

I pressed my lips hard against his. "The only instrument I'm interested in right now is yours."

"You are not the quiet wallflower you once were, Roxanne."

"Is that a bad thing?" I asked.

He shook his head. "I just love watching you grow up." As he grabbed my hand, I felt the familiar warming sensation spread between my legs.

I took a deep breath, relief surging through my heart. *I still want to have sex with him. I still have feelings for him. That's a good thing, right?* We left the party and made love on the couch, but as I listened to his soft snores, there was only one man on my mind.

And he was snoring five hundred miles away.

#

I KNOCKED ON the door, rolling from my heels to my toes, anxiously awaiting his answer. My heart thumped with excitement and a little flame began working its way down my belly.

We didn't exchange a single word when he opened the door, my needs consumed by his tall, dark and handsome allure. I wrapped my arms around his shoulders and hungrily devoured his lips, our feet clumsily making their way through the hallway and into his bedroom. He lifted my shirt over my head before he lowered me onto the comforter.

This had become our routine.

It began the day I returned to Rohnert Park, the overwhelming desire to convince Lamont to admit his feelings to me overriding any self-control left in my reserves. Initially, the act of cheating on Zachary when sober sent me over the edge. I'd returned home and locked myself in the bedroom, my mind, body and soul consumed by a world-shattering panic attack that left me shaking as if I had a fever.

A quick conversation with my horny, very pregnant, and emotionally charged sister put everything back into perspective, allowing me to rendezvous with Lamont without collapsing into a nervous breakdown afterwards. "I'm not saying that what you're doing is just and moral, but you don't have a diamond on your finger. You're twenty. Have fun. There are a lot of boys out there and you'll have plenty of time to limit yourself to one when you get older."

And because I wanted an excuse to not feel guilty for my undesirable behavior, I told myself if Lucy said it was okay, then it was okay. The thing that left me rattled was my inability to break up with Zachary even though I wanted to be with Lamont. This feeling of being wanted by two boys boosted my confidence in ways I'd never experienced, while simultaneously proving just how afraid I was of being alone, unloved and unwanted.

"I have class in an hour," I whispered, my fingers yanking at the button of his jeans.

"Chris'll be home soon anyway. Promise me you'll come back tonight? To cuddle?" The sincerity in his voice made me pause briefly enough to look into his eyes. "Please?"

My body arched toward his, wanting nothing more than for him to be inside of me. "Yes. I'll come over. Anything to see you." When I reached for the rubber on the table to our right, Lamont grasped onto my wrist. Startled, I sat back. "Is everything alright?"

"Let's not use one of those today." He nibbled on my neck, his hands unhooking the bra behind my back. "I think it's time we do it the right way."

Although hesitant, his sensual touch and rushed whispers encouraged me to agree, my heart hurting from beating too hard. *Does this mean he loves me?* I ran my palms across his skin, the pads of my fingers tingling as if I'd been electrocuted. The unopened condom remained dormant on the nightstand, my phone vibrating beside it. While I climbed on top of Lamont, my lips moistening the sweet spot by his jawbone, my boyfriend was calling to remind me that he would be arriving in Sonoma in a few hours. Just in time to get home from class and shower away the smell of sex and disloyalty.

"I think you can be a little late to class," Lamont whispered.

Giggling, I moved my hips back and forth, slowly at first, our rhythm beginning to mesh. "You already made me late to two classes this week."

He grasped my hips, closed his eyes and bit his lower lip. "Let's make it three. "

I arched my back, pushed my body harder against him, and rocked my pelvis until Lamont gasped. It felt good, no rubber blocking his skin from mine. I rolled over to his side and cuddled beneath his collarbone, his heart beating beneath my ear.

"Maybe I can be a *little* late to class."

He nodded. "Just miss class completely."

The phone rang again, the vibrating nuisance unable to interrupt my bliss. His arms wrapped around my torso and his lips kissed the top of my head.

"Shouldn't you get that?" Lamont mumbled.

Caught in the moment, I let my guard down and forgot where I was, forgot that I was in bed with a boy who was scared of the truth. "I love you, Lamont."

His body stiffened. It wasn't a drastic move, but it was abrupt enough for me to notice. He didn't respond, but his pulse quickened. In a futile attempt to recover, I kissed him and crawled out of bed. "I gotta get to class. Text me later about that cuddle session."

He nodded briefly. "Yeah, I will."

We both knew it was a lie, but I left the house hoping that maybe—this once—he was telling me the truth.

#

CLASS HAD BEEN a struggle to sit through. My stomach hopped up and down, my eyes darting to the phone sitting in the open pouch of my backpack. I was anxious, my pen resting on a blank notebook page, my brain unable to listen to what the professor had to say. We'd just read the first five or so chapters of *Moby Dick*, and for the first time in my educational life, I'd refused to read something assigned to me.

I'd opened the book five times only to drift off to sleep, to begin day dreaming and having to read all over again, or to get angry because this book was said to be an American classic and I couldn't find any of the deeper meanings my fellow classmates were able to lob back and forth so easily. Now, I couldn't even pretend that I was engaged with the themes in the novel because I was so focused on my black-screened phone, willing Lamont to text me about getting together later. Zachary would be in town, but I could devise a lie to sneak out for a few hours if Lamont wanted me to.

But even after class, as I frantically threw clean and dirty clothes off my floor into the laundry hamper, my phone didn't light up. Zachary was running late, Lamont wanted nothing to do with me and I sat alone in my room, realizing what my life would be like if I lost both of these boys who had become the suns of my solar system. I would return to being that socially awkward and lonely girl who didn't have friends and who cried every night because she didn't have that full feeling of happiness that was associated with accomplishments and memories one could share with real friends.

Most importantly, she wouldn't have the affection of a boy who made her feel wanted and beautiful—who made her feel human and deserving of a decent life.

The phone rang, my feet springing across the room, my heart dropping straight to my knees. It wasn't Lamont. It was Zachary. He was outside finding a parking spot. He was so excited to see me. I placed the phone upside down on my desk and hugged my elbows. The black and white bracelet mocked me, laughing at my feelings for Lamont, shaking its disappointed letters at me because I still hadn't learned my lesson.

My fingers nearly ripped the rubber from my wrist, but I couldn't do it. The bracelet had a string linked to my heart and removing the small trinket would rip half of that beating organ straight through the center of my chest. I took a deep breath and promised myself I wouldn't cry.

Zach loved me. And that should've been more than enough.

#

I OPENED MY eyes and smiled at the handsome face lying on the pillow beside me. He kissed the bridge of my nose, both of my eyelids and my forehead. I giggled, my body totally consumed by love.

"I'm so lucky," I whispered.

"Good morning to you too," he replied huskily.

I kissed his lips. "Really, Zach. I'm so lucky to be here. With you."

He smiled, eyes crinkling. "You are so gorgeous. Inside and out. I'm the lucky one."

"I couldn't imagine a better way to start Cinco de Mayo than to cuddle next to you."

When he scooted closer, pressing his naked body against mine, I wrapped my leg over his thighs and nibbled on his lip. His eyebrows arched. "Is that an invitation?"

I nodded. "How about a wake-up call?"

Zachary lifted the sheet and smiled. "Looks like I'm already up for it."

I moved my hands down his muscular, flat stomach and into his grey boxer briefs. He shivered, sucking in a quick breath. The up and down motion beneath the blanket matched my jogging heart, the need to *really feel* Zachary overshadowing the need to be a responsible adult. When he shifted on top of me, his arm reaching for the golden wrapper shining brightly on the nightstand, I grabbed his wrist and shook my head.

"I want you," I breathed. "I want all of you."

Shock penetrated his curious green eyes, a nervous grin questioning my words. "Really?"

I rubbed the pads of my fingers over his chest and sighed. "Yes. What better way to celebrate the holiday than to fully share ourselves with one another?"

"Why the sudden spontaneity?"

*Because I'm determined to love you more than Lamont and I'm hoping this'll help.* "I love you. And I trust you." I blinked, trying to focus on my arousal. *I need you to trust me.* "I just—I want to feel what it's like."

His smile was so bright that it made my darkened heart hiss. "I love you, Roxanne. And I trust you, more than anything."

When our bodies connected, I gasped, pressing my lips into Zachary's shoulders. *You shouldn't trust me. Don't trust me. I don't trust me.* However, as guilty as I felt, the sweet sensation pouring from between my legs to every nerve ending shocking every layer of my skin caused me to slice my nails across the tense muscles in his back. *Stop thinking about Lamont. Stop wishing you were with Lamont. You love Zach.* I gasped, biting my cheek shortly after to prevent myself from shouting, afraid my true guilty pleasure would roll off my tongue.

#

WHISTLES, CAT CALLS and clapping followed me as I strutted along the outskirts of the pool, gorgeous, yet obnoxious, fraternity boys hogging all of the lounge chairs, their tan skin shining from banana scented tanning lotion.

"Damn girl. You look like the spitting image of Mexican independence."

"Ay dios mio! Come over here Mamacita."

"Mex-ico! Mex-ico! Mex-ico!"

"You just made red, white and green my new favorite colors."

"Why don't I steal you away to Mexico and we get married?"

"Want some Tequila? Because 'dat ass is about Tequilme."

Although flattered, I held my breath as I walked past them, my cheeks flaring red behind my overly large sunglasses. I was already self-conscious as it

263

was, sucking in my stomach as far as it could go without physically hurting myself.

Typically, I wasn't the type to dress up for the holiday, but the girls had convinced me to go to the mall with them earlier in the week, where I came across a kiosk displaying an array of festive bathing suits. Initially, I was uninterested, my small collection of swimsuits perfectly suitable for the pool party the girls wanted me to attend with them. But then, just as I was about to give up and go home, a sexy monokini captured the attention of my peripherals. I approached it, transfixed, much like a mosquito flying toward a bright light. With cash meant for groceries lingering in my wallet, I pointed to the bathing suit, smiling as the Asian woman put my new merchandise into a bag.

Before we went to the pool, I put the suit on and looked in the mirror shaking my head. I didn't want to wear it, thought I looked ridiculous in it, but the girls had walked in just as I was about to take it off and insisted that I looked "sexy." The only reason I even kept it on was because they whispered that we might run into Lamont, and if he saw me looking like this, he'd regret not telling me he loved me.

At this point, though, I thought nothing would convince him of that. Still, that didn't stop me from wanting to try.

Luckily, I already had quickly consumed two extremely strong margaritas in the dorm, the thought of being seen in such a risqué outfit in public making me beyond anxious.

Red and green material covered my breasts, a deep-V reaching my belly button, a white string keeping my boobs perky and contained. It was backless, aside from four white strings dangling down my spine, the bottom of the suit rising right below my back and curving nicely around my cheeks. The crest of an eagle was printed on the right side of the white butt.

It was something my sister would've bought for me—possibly something she wore when she was in college.

I found the girls in a corner of the shallow end of the pool. "Are you guys sure this isn't totally ridiculous?" I asked as I lowered myself into the water. "I have another bathing suit I could put on—one that isn't so...I don't know. 'Look at me?'"

Claire, Amber, Elizabeth and Shannon held plastic cups with twisty straws sticking out just above the rim. They giggled, each scooting around another in order to wrap me in multiple hugs.

"Keep it on," Amber said. "You look great. I wish I could pull off something like that."

Shannon shook her head. "Your tits would be everywhere."

Elizabeth nodded. "Roxy, just embrace the compliments. It's not everyday you have an excuse to wear something like that."

"That's because I'm not a hooker," I mumbled.

Claire laughed. "No, but you are a girl in college. You're just acting like the rest of us."

When I frowned, Shannon nudged me. "Maybe not like her," she whispered.

"Hey," Claire said. "I heard that."

I gestured to Amber's cup and took a generous sip from her straw when she nodded at me. "Ohhh, that's yummy. I can't wait 'til Zach gets out here."

"Where is he anyway?" Elizabeth asked.

Amber smiled. "You keeping him leashed up like a good boy?"

"Oh, stop it."

"Yeah," Claire added. "If I were him, and my girlfriend was in *that* suit, I wouldn't let her out of my sight."

I laughed. "That's because you don't trust Adam. Zach trusts me." *Even though he shouldn't.* "He's making margaritas. He told me to find you guys and he'll meet us when the drinks are done."

Claire scowled. "Oh, *really*? Why don't you go say hi to Lamont and see if Zach trusts you then?"

My breathing quickened. *He's here already?* I shook my head. "He doesn't want to see me."

Amber shrugged. "Then that's all the more reason to go say hi. You look *amazing*. Make him suffer."

Claire sighed. "I was only kidding."

"I'm not," Amber said. "It's your turn to knock him down. Make him feel like an idiot."

"Where is he?" I whispered, scared he'd hear me if I spoke too loudly.

The four girls stared behind me, silent. Turning around slowly to follow their gazes, I spotted Lamont entering the black, metal gate with the rest of his housemates. I inhaled, grinned, readjusted my boobs and lifted my glasses onto my head.

"I hope I don't throw up."

265

Elizabeth chuckled. "Look at the bright side. That will give you more room for alcohol."

"Wait, where are you going?"

Ignoring Claire, I made my way over to the pool stairs, praying to God that my green eye-makeup was still intact. As I rounded the corner, ready to pounce, someone stopped me by touching my shoulder.

"Hey Little Woman! It's crazy out here. I started to think I wouldn't find you."

I made eye contact with Lamont briefly before whirling around to face my boyfriend, lowering my sunglasses as the sun nearly blinded me. Immediately, I felt uncomfortable, nervous about how Lamont would react to Zachary, and afraid that Zachary would see how I reacted in the presence of Lamont. He handed me a red, plastic cup filled to the brim with a blended margarita before placing his free hand on my hip. Similar to the feeling I'd experienced when Zachary displayed public affection in front of Luke, I had to resist the urge to step away from him.

And then I reminded myself about how Lamont reacted when I admitted my love, and remembered he never texted me that night. How he hadn't texted me since. And in reality, I wondered if he even cared about me anymore beyond our secret sexual escapades. Hurt and angry, I decided it was time to shun my awkwardness and prove to Lamont that I was happy without him. I smirked, pulled Zachary's pelvis into mine and kissed him. *Eat it up, Lamont. Eat. It. Up.*

Zachary smiled, his goofy teeth exposed for the rest of the world to see. I tried not to feel embarrassed. "Wow. I should offer to make you drinks more often."

The tequila made me shiver with pleasure. "Extra strong—you trying to get me drunk or something?"

"You caught me," he whispered, kissing the tender spot beneath my earlobe. "Where are the girls?"

Clasping onto his hand, I pulled him through the crowd of college students to the pool corner where my roommates were gathered. Lamont stood on the opposite side, hat backwards, wearing a white t-shirt and blue board shorts. Black sunglasses covered his line of vision, but the Cheshire-esque grin and slight head nod proved that he saw me.

And approved of what he was looking at.

*I hate you for looking so good. For not loving me.*

266

"Cannon ball!" an un-athletic boy on top of the bathroom roof yelled, gathering the attention of all the pool attendees. He jumped, ignoring the screams and protests of the girls in the water—including myself.

"My hair!"

"My makeup!"

"My phone!"

"You prick!"

"You ruined my drink!"

The moans and groans of others echoed my own, laughter from the boys—and Zachary, in particular—heightening my frustration.

I slapped my boyfriend's arm. "It's not funny, Zach."

"Yes it is," Zachary said, clutching his ribs. "That guy is fat. Anything with a fat kid is hilarious."

"No, Zach. Don't be mean."

"That guy is such a prick," Claire snapped, wiping the water droplets off her face without smudging her mascara.

"Wow. Did you see how close he was to the wall?"

Amber scoffed, pulling her dampened hair into a ponytail. "Too bad he missed."

The girls and I laughed, Zachary letting out a whistle. "Damn. That's brutal. You think *I'm* the mean one?"

I elbowed him. "It's true. That guy's an idiot."

He frowned. "I've done that before. Am I an idiot?"

Making eye contact with Amber who bit her lip to avoid laughing, I nearly threw back all of the remaining contents of my drink. I knew drinking that quickly wasn't a good idea, but I needed as much courage as possible. "Sweetie, my drink is almost empty. Would you be a doll and make me another? It's super delicious."

Shaking his head, he grabbed my cup. "Of course," he said unenthusiastically. "Do any of you ladies need anything?"

I frowned, hating that I felt bad for hurting his feelings.

They each denied his offer politely, thanked him and watched him go.

"Nice save," Amber snickered.

"I'm sorry he's so obnoxious."

Elizabeth shrugged. "It's Zach. We know how he is."

"I do believe you sent him off for another reason," Shannon accused.

267

I blushed. "Not intentionally, but now that you mention it, I should go say hi." I licked my lips. "This sucks. Why am I so nervous to see him? I hate that he gets me all riled up like this."

Amber winked. "Don't even stress. You look fucking hot."

"Try not to have sex in the bathroom. It's unsanitary."

Claire elbowed Shannon, spilling part of her drink. "Roxy's boyfriend is here. Stop encouraging her bad behavior."

"Have a little faith. Just a hug. No nudity, I promise."

Claire sighed. "If Zach gets mad, don't come crying to me."

I grabbed her drink and took a generous gulp. "Again, thanks for the vote of confidence." My lungs reached for a taste of air, butterflies clogging up the pathway to my mouth. "We're just friends."

"Maybe if you keep saying that out loud, it'll actually become the truth."

I stuck my tongue out at Amber, turned away and waded through half-naked bodies toward my target. I ignored the hands that pinched my butt, the frat boys shoving drinks beneath my nose and the pick-up lines dancing through my ears. Although that sort of attention would usually make me uncomfortable, something about the approval of my peers helped me move forward despite the fact that Lamont wanted nothing to do with me.

When I reached him, it became clearer than crystal that he was intent on believing I didn't exist. He didn't get up to give me a hug, he didn't smile—he didn't even look at me. The girl sitting on the lounge beside him had wholly captured his attention. *It's the girl from his party. His Beer Pong partner. I knew it. The lying bastard!* I took off my sunglasses and glared at him.

"Lamont?"

He touched the girl's chin with his index finger, still avoiding my eyes. "What?"

My stomach didn't settle well against his tone. "Did I do something to offend you?"

He shrugged. "Where's your boyfriend?"

*What did I do to make you hate me?* "What's that matter?"

"Because you shouldn't be talking to me."

*Why do you push me away?* "You were fine with it the other day."

Another shrug. A giggle from the girl.

"I can't believe you're doing this to me again."

268

Then he finally turned toward me, his sunglasses slipping to the bridge of his nose. "You have a boyfriend. I don't want to play these games anymore. Do your thing and I'll do mine."

The girl touched Lamont's arm and smiled greedily. Unable to speak, my vocal chords twisting like broken guitar strings, I nodded mutely. The world turned to a dull grey, the music dimming, the happiness of others making my skin itch. *I wonder if this is what it feels like to get shot through the heart.* I spotted Zachary just outside the gate, his head cocked to the side. *I'm the one playing games?* I walked to him, asking if we could sit in the grass, alone. I wasn't in the mood to be in a crowd any longer. *I should've known it was too good to be true. When you want everything, you get nothing.*

#

THE DAY BEFORE Zachary was scheduled to go home, we thought hanging out by the pool, eating junk food and drinking margaritas would be the perfect way to say goodbye to one another. It had been nice, just the two of us, talking, tanning and flirting like we did back when I was in high school, the summer before he started college. We decided to call it a day, take a shower and make dinner once we were both sunburned and sufficiently buzzed. I stood in the shower scrubbing soap all over my body when I first noticed something rather unusual.

A bump.

A large, almost red—no, *really* red—bump located on the most sensitive skin between my thighs. An area I considered sacred—I always made sure to keep it clean and manicured—was tainted. My hands froze, foamy suds streaming down my arms and legs. I studied the bump, my wet hair sticking to my chest, and soon found a second one. A third. They weren't the typical bumps one acquired when using a razor. They were bigger. Scarier. Threatening.

The first wave of panic hit me.

*Zach cheated on me.*

A second wave took me under.

*I cheated on Zach.*

The third left me choking for air.

*I didn't use protection.* I stepped out of the shower, water dripping beyond the curtain, solidifying into a puddle on the bathroom floor.

*I trusted Lamont. Zach trusted me.* My head fell into the toilet, margarita and Doritos leaving my mouth in acidic chunks. *Lamont gave me something. He's been lying to me. He's sleeping with that other girl.* The bathroom door opened, Zachary rushing to my naked side, worry radiating off the fingertips that touched my shoulder. *Zach trusted me.* I turned my body to the side hoping that Zachary wouldn't see proof of my infidelity. *Go away, Zach. Please, go away. Don't look at me.* I couldn't speak to him. I continued to purge, guilt and fear of being found out destroying the inner linings of my digestive tract. *Lamont gave me herpes. And I gave them to Zach. They'll both leave me. I'll never find anyone to love me again. Not with something like this.*

#

"STAY WITH US," Shannon urged from the front seat of the car. "We've already found some great three-bedroom places. Amber and me can share a room and you and Lizzy can have your own."

Elizabeth and Amber clapped. "Oh my God, yes! We could throw the best parties and won't have to worry about campus police shutting us down and putting us on probation."

I smiled. "The world isn't ready for the four of us."

"No Claire," Amber swooned. "No Claire! No drama! Just girls' night after girls' night. It would be so much fun."

The four of us were sitting in Shannon's car, searching frantically for "For Rent" signs so the girls would have a place to live off campus the following year. They dragged me along to pull me out of my dungeon, afraid that I'd died from too many paper cuts or lack of natural lighting. Having Zachary visit set me back on my studies and I'd been spending all of my free time attempting to catch up. Despite the massive amount of reading and writing I had yet to complete, I eagerly accepted their invitation, asking if we could make a stop at Starbucks first.

I sipped my latte. "That place was *really* nice. How much would it be if we lived there?"

Elizabeth turned around in her seat. "Are you *actually* considering it?"

A giddy sensation filled my lungs. "I haven't heard from San Diego State yet. Maybe I didn't get in." For once, that thought didn't depress me. The potential of staying in Rohnert Park actually sounded appealing.

Amber shrugged. "Is it bad that I hope you didn't get in? You're one of my best friends. I want you to stay here. With us."

"Not that you didn't get in," Shannon added. "You're super smart and they'd be stupid not to accept you."

"I'm worried if I stay here, I won't graduate on time."

"Sure you will. You take, like, a million units every semester. It would be amazing for you to stay here," Elizabeth said. "You complete us. What're we gonna do without you?"

270

The thought of potentially living with these girls for the rest of my college career excited me—the thought that these girls wanted to live with me filled me with emotions I hadn't experienced in a long time. Acceptance. Approval. Love. These were emotions I'd wanted to find from my family but knew better than to expect. And finally, *finally*, I'd found a family away from home.

"Why do you want to move back to San Diego, anyway?" Amber asked. "Your family is hot and cold, your relationship with Zach is on the rocks and your friends—*us*—are sitting right here. In front of you."

"That's because of Lamont. When Zach and me are together, everything is fine. It's when we're apart that everything falls apart."

Shannon raised an eyebrow through the rearview mirror. "Then is that why you want to go back? To mend your relationship with him?"

I shrugged, guilt flooding over me once more. "Maybe that's part of it. I do love him. But I want to graduate in four years. Meet professors so that I can get my foot in the door for grad school."

"Just be careful. Make sure your heart and mind are on the same page. Because once you make your choice, there's no going back," Elizabeth warned.

"How about we just focus on house hunting? I'd rather not think about what I'm gonna be doing in a few months from now."

Unfortunately, once I returned home, I checked my mailbox and found a white envelope that contained SDSU's logo on the corner. I ripped it open with trembling hands and stared at the letterhead, uncertain tears forming in my eyes.

I was accepted into San Diego State as an English and Comparative Literature major.

And I wasn't sure if that's where I wanted to go anymore.

#

"I'M SURPRISED HE invited me, honestly. He's made it pretty freaking clear these past few days that he wants nothing to do with me," I mentioned to Elizabeth and Shannon as I studied my clothing options.

Claire and Amber were both out of town, Claire for dance and Amber for cheer, which left me and the other two girls with the time to bond. I thought it might give me a chance to disappear for the weekend, but Elizabeth and Shannon refused to let that happen.

"Well, technically, he invited the entire dorm. It'd be pretty messed up if he singled you out and said you couldn't go. He may be an asshole, but I couldn't see him doing that to you," Elizabeth said.

"Can I invite Andy?"

Shannon nodded. "I don't see why not. Are you sure he's not already planning on going? Everyone else in the vicinity of Rohnert Park is."

"Great. I get to watch him make out with that whore by the pool."

"She's in one of my classes." Shannon frowned. "I overheard her talking the other day and she said her and Lamont have been hooking up for a while now."

My Cinco de Mayo breakdown raised to the surface, turning my rosy cheeks a pale shade of white. "That's not what I want to hear."

"Maybe she was trying to impress her friends," Elizabeth said reassuringly. "You might not even see him."

"Oh, please. We all know that I'm gonna see him. It's his birthday party. I can't just avoid him." I rubbed my eyes, exhausted. "I knew they were together at his last party. I could sense it. I was just hoping he wanted me more."

The girls exchanged curious looks.

I sat on the bed and sighed. "What?"

"Roxy, he did choose you. But you didn't choose him. You had Zach. Here. In his territory. You've rejected him as much as he's rejected you."

"You may not want to hear it, but you might've hurt him—people can only take so much, you know?"

I rubbed my palms along my thighs. "No, that's not it. The other day, when me and Lamont were together, I told him I loved him. Everything changed. I messed up."

They shrugged. "He's pushed you away before. It's obvious to everyone but you that he loves you."

"His behavior is a defense mechanism," Shannon agreed.

*Yeah, right. I know he doesn't love me.* "I'm probably leaving Rohnert Park. What's the point of creating something real with Lamont when it's likely I'll be returning home—to Zach—in San Diego?" I asked.

"Then maybe you should stop playing with Lamont and finally let him go. You're gonna end up hurting everyone involved—including yourself."

#

DANIELLE, SHANNON, ELIZABETH and I pushed through the front door shortly after throwing back three shots of vodka in the car. The party was already in full swing, strobe lights blinding those entering from the dark, loud music overwhelming the serenity of crickets chirping in the wet grass, the unmistakable scent of cheap alcohol replacing the perfume I'd spritzed on my neck before we left the house.

272

Andrew was standing with his hip against the wall, white suspenders standing bright against a purple shirt and grey pants. His black hair was now long enough to put into a man bun and his trimmed beard framed his jaw nicely. When he spotted us, relief brought his commercial smile to his face. "Fucking finally!" he shouted. "There are so many basic bitches in this place. It's about time some beautiful girls made an appearance."

Danielle swooned. "I know we've been through this before, but you're sure you're gay?"

Andrew nodded. "You gotta V where I want the D."

"I'd gladly grow a D for you."

Elizabeth shook her head. "I'm sorry. We usually don't bring her out in public."

"You hobags need to lay off my best friend." I threw my arms over his shoulders and hopped so that my thighs rested comfortably above his bony waist. "I missed you! We brought vodka."

He patted my back. "If you wrinkle my shirt, I will be forced to end our friendship."

"Oh, hush." I climbed down before planting a red lipstick print on his cheek. "The only way that shirt would be wrinkled is if you were straight and it were crumpled in a ball on my bedroom floor."

The girls laughed while Andrew snatched the vodka bottle from my hand. "Holy shit. Share the goods. I need to be on your level."

"When she drinks, she's unreachable," Shannon joked.

"We gotta drink it in private," I whispered loudly. "We don't want any of these basic bitches to cramp our style."

Andrew grinned. "My little girl is growing up."

Shannon grabbed my arm. "Let's get this show on the road. I need to keep my buzz going."

Elizabeth motioned for all of us to follow her down the hallway toward Lamont and Chris's room. "Danielle basically lives here. She can get access into their room."

"Can we find another room?" I asked, the sight of the white door making it difficult for me to swallow.

Danielle snorted. "It's too early in the night for him to be having sex."

Andrew placed his arm around me, the vodka bottle resting against my hip. "I don't think that's what the problem is."

273

"Then there is no problem." She turned the knob and pushed open the door, finding the room totally deserted. "You wanted private? I gotcha private."

Andrew placed the vodka atop Chris's desk and gestured to the purse hanging from my shoulder. "I'm guessing that's where you're keeping the chasers?"

I reached into the bag and produced a packet of plastic shot glasses. "I've also got shit to drink from. It's party time! Let's get *fucked up*."

"Who is this girl?" Andrew asked my roommates. "What did you do with Roxanne?"

Shannon smiled. "Out with the old and in with the new."

"You guys are totally bad influences."

Danielle cozied up next to Andrew and nodded. "That may be true, but look how much happier she is!"

"Are you gonna stop talking or am I gonna have to drink by myself?" I asked.

The girls and Andrew hollered and cheered, each filling a small glass with the apple flavored liquor.

"Hey, no one's allowed—"

We turned around to find Lamont observing us from the doorway.

"Shut the fuck up. It's just us," Danielle snapped. "This is basically my second home."

Lamont didn't argue. He continued to eye me curiously, seemingly oblivious to the others. To fit the "neon" theme, prepared to be surrounded by black lights, I adorned myself in a bright pink tank top, a tight white pencil skirt and silver heels—it wasn't risqué per say, but the clothes hugged me in just the right places, my long legs exposed enough to make any intoxicated boy look twice. I blushed beneath Lamont's gaze feeling naked, vulnerable and inadequate.

Andrew leaned in toward my ear. "You alright? Should I kill him?"

I shook my head. "I'm okay. It's his birthday."

"You just give me the sign. I'll pounce on a bitch."

"Let's take a shot with the birthday boy!" Shannon shouted. "C'mon Lamont!"

He nodded mutely, closed the distance between us, wrapped his arms around my body and nuzzled my neck, his goatee tickling my skin. "I didn't think you were gonna come."

274

After a quick surprised glance at my friends, who had been urging me to let loose and live life one night at a time, I returned the embrace and smiled into his shoulder. "Happy birthday, Handsome. How about that shot?"

That was the forth—and fifth—shot I'd taken in two hours and my body was definitely reacting. "Let's go dance or play Beer Pong or flip-cup or something," I suggested to the group. "We should probably give the birthday boy back to the party. They are here to see him, after all." *And this is probably the last time I'll be out with all of you guys. Two more weeks, and there's a chance I'll never come back.* I took a deep breath and forced a smile. *Don't think like that. These are your best friends. Even Lamont is happy to see you. Enjoy whatever time you're gonna get with everyone.*

Lamont waited for Andrew to pass him before closing the door behind all of us. "You are allowed in my room but *nobody* else is. Last time, someone threw up in the sink and I'm not dealing with having to clean that up again."

We nodded and walked ahead of him, greeting each of his roommates, the girls engaging in eye-sex with attractive boys and me laughing whenever some pathetic girl attempted to make the move on Andrew. We entered the garage where a Beer Pong tournament was in full swing, black lights the only form of illumination provided. My skirt and teeth glowed in the dark. Lamont laughed when I smiled at him and planted an abrupt—and unexpected—kiss on my lips.

"What was that—?"

"Lamont!" a mousy voice interrupted me. "Where the hell have you been? You disappeared right in the middle of our game."

I slowly lowered my fingers away from my mouth, the electricity disappearing once the brunette girl from the pool came into focus. In the black light, her orange shirt glowed white, white stripes in her plaid shorts grabbing my attention, white hooker heels adorning her small feet. I cringed when Lamont pushed past me, his focus now on the Ping Pong ball in the girl's hand.

"Is that the slut you were telling me about?" Andrew asked.

I nodded once. "I hate her. And it's irrational."

He kissed my temple. "Remember, give me a sign, and I'll pounce."

"How about a drink?" Shannon asked.

Turning away from Lamont and the brunette hugging one another, I nodded. "Now *that* sounds like a brilliant idea."

\#

"TEN, NINE, EIGHT!"

275

The entire party stood in the kitchen and living room counting down to midnight.

"She's gonna kiss him. I just know it."

"SIX, FIVE, FOUR!"

Andrew shrugged. "I'm drunk enough to kiss you if that makes you feel any better."

Lamont smiled at the crowd from his post atop the fireplace mantle. He was turning twenty when the clock struck twelve and you could see the sheer excitement radiating off his extremely drunk—likely blacked out—face. Marsha had conveniently placed herself in front of him, while I hid in the crowd amongst my friends, mixed drink in hand.

"The last thing I need is to fall in love with someone who prefers penis. No offense."

"TWO, ONE!"

As the crowd shouted *happy birthday* and threw confetti and splashes of beer into the air, the unthinkable happened. There, in the middle of the living room where the Sonoma State student population was watching, Lamont stepped off his pedestal, ignored Marsha's outstretched arms, pushed through the mayhem and kissed me. His forearms squeezed around my lower back, my feet lifted from the ground, and his mouth melded with mine as if a flame ignited between us, our bodies burning with passion. Desire. Love.

The music silenced while Lamont twirled me in a circle, our hearts coming together in a waltz of betrayal, honesty, hate and necessity. *Me. He chose me.*

The screams, the cheers, the applause—none of it mattered. Because there, in front of *everyone*, Lamont swept me off my feet. *He loves me.* I kept my eyes closed, afraid reality would set in and I would wake up from a beautiful, drunk dream. *I want to stay here, in this moment, with Lamont, forever.*

#

"WHERE ARE YOU going?" Kevin, one of Lamont's roommates, placed his hand on the wall in front of me, and stopped me in my stumbling tracks.

I blinked at him, the black lights beginning to exhaust my pupils. "Are you a gatekeeper or something?"

He stood in front of me. "No one is allowed back here."

We were standing in the hallway that led to the house's bedrooms. "I have VIP status. Lamont told me I could be over here."

"Well, he's fucking some chick in his room right now, so I can't confirm that information."

CHAPTER THIRTEEN

I swallowed, the hallway spinning behind Kevin's buzzed, blonde hair. "What are you talking about?"

He smiled. "She promised him birthday sex. The two of them have been locked in there for a while now."

"You're lying," I whispered.

He stepped to the side and pointed at the door. "Go ahead and see for yourself if you don't believe me."

When Kevin walked away, I continued my journey through the hallway, my hands plastered against the wall in an attempt to maintain my balance. Although trembling, I wrapped my fingers around the silver doorknob and turned.

It was locked.

Tears crashed down my cheeks. I stumbled back away from the door, from my remaining emotional stability, from the boy I was willing to give up everything for, until my back made contact with a wall. My breath was knocked from my lungs. I slid to the carpet, my knees touching my chin—I didn't care if the world saw everything exposed beneath my skirt. I already felt naked. *This isn't happening. Lamont loves me. I love him.*

A pair of boat shoes invaded my train of thought, a comforting hand patting my shoulder. "Roxanne, are you alright? What are you doing?"

I followed the bare legs up to light blue shorts and a white polo shirt, my makeup smeared and my nose resembling Niagara Falls. "He's fucking that girl. He kissed me in front of everyone and now he's having sex with that bitch."

"Pretty sure Lamont told me you're the one who never cusses."

I shrugged. "Guess he's fucking wrong."

Dylan frowned and crouched to meet me at eye-level. "He's really drunk. He doesn't know what he's doing. He adores you. He's being an idiot."

"He doesn't love me. He's fucking *her*."

"I think you're really drunk." He paused and chuckled. "Maybe they're just—talking. She likes him but I swear to you, you're the one he wants."

I cried harder. "I'm not an idiot. The door's locked." Breathing grew difficult. "I hate him. He always does this." I paused, wiping snot on my wrist, on the rubber bracelet. "Am I not pretty enough or something?"

Dylan frowned. "Roxanne, you're beautiful. He's really lucky to have you." After a beat, he stood. "I'll grab a tissue. You need to stop crying. Right now."

I coughed and rested my forehead on my knees. *He's right. Lamont isn't worth crying over. He's not relationship material. He never will be.*

277

Dylan returned with a handful of Kleenex and smiled half-heartedly. "Maybe you should drink some water and go out on the patio. Get some air."

"You're such a *good guy*. Why are you even friends with him?" I blew my nose and bit my lip. "I hate him."

"You don't hate him." He bent down and hugged me. "We're all stupid in some way or another. Lamont loves you. He just doesn't show it."

Even after Dylan walked away, I remained perched pathetically against the wall across from Lamont's closed door. The tears may have been dry but my body still trembled from devastation. *Why is he doing this to me? And why can't I let him go?* And then his bedroom door creaked open, Marsha escaping into the party before I could analyze her appearance, but I could see Lamont making his way through the darkness of the bedroom. I heard the uncapping of a bottle, the running of a faucet, an elongated gargle and an abrupt spit. My hands tightened around the tissues. *Mouthwash? He's using mouthwash? He fucking went down on her. They had sex. He had sex with her. I know they had sex. I know it.*

Just as I was debating how to grab my purse out of his room without bringing any attention to myself, Lamont stood over me and smiled. "Come with me. You owe me a birthday present."

*I owe you a castration. That would have been an anatomy lesson worthwhile.* I hesitated.

He cocked his head to the side. "Are you alright?"

*That's why I'm sitting on the floor looking like a fucking raccoon.* Instead of slapping his hand away, calling him select names and storming out of the party, I allowed him to lead me into his bedroom.

"My presence here is present enough," I responded hoarsely.

"I want to tell you something." He sat on the edge of his unmade bed and invited me to sit beside him.

I didn't move. "What?"

He placed his hands in his lap. "You know, I've noticed lately that you're dressing a lot like your roommates."

I glanced down at my outfit. "Is that a bad thing?"

"Not *bad*, no. But I think you should know that you're much more beautiful just being you. You don't have to be like everyone else."

*He's buttering you up. Don't listen.* But I felt myself melting, my legs wobbling beneath me. "I thought you liked girls like this."

He shook his head and patted the bed again. "You gonna join me or just stand there?"

I took a deep breath and moved to sit beside him. "Did you want to talk or something?"

"I've always wanted to have birthday sex. I want to do it with you."

*I'm sitting on their sex sheets. The room reeks of sex.* At that point, I should've stood up and left, but something about the way he said it made my mouth go dry. "What makes you think I want to do that with you?"

Lamont pouted. "It's my birthday. C'mon Roxy. You'd be my first birthday sex ever."

I inhaled and exhaled, trying to stop the room from spinning. *Don't let him in. Don't let him talk you into this. He's lying. Stop letting him do this.* "You already had sex. I think it's a little late for you to be making that statement."

"What are you talking about?"

Lamont had always been difficult for me to read, but now, after the amount of alcohol I consumed, I couldn't tell if he was being serious or trying to lie straight to my face. "Kevin told me. And I saw her leave the room." *You washed your mouth out.* "I'm not stupid, Lamont."

He reached out his hands. "Kevin doesn't know what he's talking about. I didn't have sex with her."

*Oh, so, you just ate her out?* I slowly traced my fingers over his palms. "Was she not good enough? Did you not finish?"

He dropped his hands to his thighs and snapped, "Roxy, I didn't sleep with her."

Part of me worried that I was pushing him away, but the other part of me told me to remain strong. "Then what were you two doing?"

He pulled me atop his chest, a giggle brushing the inside of my lips. "We were talking." *Like all those times we "talked?"*

"With the door locked?"

He gently placed me on the bed and looked down at me. "She wanted some privacy."

We kissed. My eyes were drunk and tired, my mind insisting that I run away, my body aching for his touch, my heart hoping that maybe this would finally seal the deal—prove that he truly did love me. *He's blacked out*, my logical side screamed. *This is a mistake. He's going to hurt you.* But my emotional side grew more absorbed by each kiss. *I want to make him happy. I want him to love me. He could be telling me the truth. He told me he was waiting for me.*

279

I clambered over him and slid my panties past my heels. "Happy birthday, Lamont."

He breathed heavily into my neck. "I'm so glad I get to spend it with you."

#

I SAT CROSS-LEGGED on the floor, post-coitus, looking through my purse for my phone. Four missed text messages from Zachary hoping that I was having fun with the girls, to text him when I got home, and to remind me that he loves me and misses me more and more every single day. Still on the high from engaging in some drunken lovemaking, I ignored my boyfriend's messages and was about to call out Lamont's name when his hushed voice stopped me.

I shifted to my hands and knees and stealthily crawled forward, cocking my head to the side so I could decipher what he was saying.

Lamont was in the closet with the wooden sliding door closed, but his drunken voice moved easily through the cracks. It sounded as if he were having a conversation with someone, but he and I were the only ones in the room together.

I scooted closer and leaned against the wall, my stomach beginning to flip over itself. He was on the phone, talking about the birthday party and how much he'd had to drink. I smiled to myself, eagerly waiting for him to bring up my name and tell whoever it was that he and I shared a magical moment together.

"It happened. It was so much easier than I thought. I had sex with the first and was too drunk to finish. And then Roxy was just waiting for me outside. She was basically begging for it. Thanks man. I know. I told you I could pull it off. One right after the other and neither of them has a clue." And then he laughed, the rest of the conversation drowned in my confusion, the need to throw up overwhelming my body. "Happy birthday to me."

The phone in my hand vibrated. Andrew was wondering when I wanted to leave and reminded me to use protection—Lamont and I had been missing for quite some time and people were beginning to talk. Spread rumors. Paralyzed by my desperation and stupidity, I couldn't feel my feet, my fingers tingling from the anxiety tightening the passageways to my lungs. I texted him two words. *Help me.*

In less than sixty seconds, the bedroom door opened, Andrew, Shannon and Elizabeth rushing to my aid. Tears were pouring down my face at a rate that threatened to dehydrate me to the point of fainting, and the ability to keep my eyes open suddenly became impossible.

"Take me home," I sobbed, Lamont's voice seeping through the closet like a noxious gas.

Andrew held my face with his freshly manicured hands. "Sweetie, talk to me. What happened? Did he hurt you?"

I nodded, snot now dripping into my mouth. "Take me home." I ripped the bracelet off my wrist and threw it on the floor beside me. Get me out of here, now."

"I'll fucking kill him," Andrew said to the girls. He scooped me into his arms, ordered Shannon to grab my purse and told Elizabeth to call a taxi immediately. "I'm here, Roxy. You're okay."

My body quivered like a baby bird fresh out of the egg, Andrew's arms a protective nest saving me from whatever other harm Lamont could cause me. "Please don't leave me," I croaked.

Andrew kissed my head. "I'm not going anywhere."

"He slept with her. He slept with that dumb bitch," I wheezed. "And then he tricked me into sleeping with him. I hate him."

The girls followed Andrew outside of the bedroom door and closed it behind him. "How are we gonna get out of here without making a scene?" Shannon asked.

Andrew continued walking through the hallway, not caring about the people whispering around us. "You're worried about making a scene? Lamont just broke Roxanne's heart."

And when those words crashed over my head, I stuffed my face into Andrew's chest and screamed.

#

"YOU'LL BE OKAY, Roxanne. Keep that stubborn chin of yours up and don't let him bring you down. You're leaving. He's lucky you're even saying good-bye."

Andrew and I sat together in my room, our last finals taking place the next day, my flight home the one after that. Having been preoccupied with an outrageous amount of reading and writing, my mind hadn't been given the time to focus on the black hole growing in place of my heart. The bracelet was gone, but my feelings for Lamont persisted. Clothes were packed, but the need to unpack it all lingered. Letters had been written and sealed, but it seemed as if so much would remain unsaid. This was my final opportunity to say good-bye to Andrew, and despite technological advances that would allow us to speak to one another through a screen, the thought of being in San Diego without him terrified me.

"Me and Lamont have been through too much for me to take off without letting him know I'm not returning," I replied before taking a generous gulp of the

Frappuccino Andrew had bought me. "Even though he treated me like crap at his birthday."

"No. After everything he's done to you, he deserves to be alone forever." He scoffed. "He doesn't deserve your time."

"I've been trying to tell myself that from the night we first kissed."

"Forget about him. This is about you and me." Andrew lay down on the bed and threw his arms behind his head. "I can't believe you're actually leaving. You were nothing but a scared little mouse when I first found you shaking beneath your lab coat."

I placed my drink on the note-cluttered desk and joined my best friend, my head resting on his chest. "I know. So much has changed in so little time. It's hard to believe this semester was real."

He kissed my head. "Oh, Honey, it's been real. I've had sex with so many beautiful men, I think I've lost count."

I sighed and patted his chest. "You know, when it's just me and you, you don't have to talk like that. I promise I won't tell anybody you have a heart."

"You are sadly mistaken. Somebody took that away from me two years ago and never gave it back. You're the only person I've loved since then, and you're a woman."

I rolled over, looked him straight in his beautiful eyes, kissed my fingertips and planted them directly over his heart. "Well, technically, you've trusted me with it, so—that person you thought stole it forever? They handed it to me in the beginning of the year and asked me to mend it for you."

For the first time since Andrew initially introduced himself to me when I was hiding in the back of the classroom, I watched as a few tears broke through his carefree façade. "And now you're leaving."

I sniffled, wiped his tears away with my thumb and smashed my cheek against his collarbone. "You saved me, Andy. Saved me from myself. Saved me from Anatomy. Saved me from being unhappy. I'll never be able to show you how thankful I am."

He took a deep breath and ran his hand over my hair. "When you become a famous writer, put me in one of your books. Then we'll call it even."

#

BEFORE I TALKED myself out of it, I grabbed the tear stained and ink smudged envelope off my desk, told my roommates I would be back in time for our farewell dinner, and sprinted to my car. I struggled to fit the key in the ignition, my heart matching the arrow jumping up and down on the speedometer.

"Lamont, I know you and me haven't had the best history—" I shook my head and cursed. "No. No, that's awful." The light turned green and the car behind me honked. My grip tightened on the steering wheel and my foot pounded on the accelerator. "I'm sorry!" I screamed as the driver of a blue Prius gave me the middle finger. "I'm in the middle of a crisis! The boy I love doesn't know I'm leaving this place forever." I inhaled and exhaled, the air conditioner doing nothing to cool my warm blood. "Roxanne, you can do this. You've talked to him a million times. It's just another conversation between two adults. All I need to do is say good-bye."

After puffing out my chest and somewhat convincing myself this conversation wouldn't be different from any other casual chitchat, Lamont's truck came into view, parked where it always was in front of his house. "Do not turn this car around. Park, text him and get this over with."

Lamont and I hadn't spoken face to face since his birthday party. We had one heated text message argument the following day, Lamont denying sleeping with Marsha, me accusing him of being a lying bastard. He told me I was overreacting. I called him an asshole. He reminded me that I was the bad person because I was the one with a boyfriend. I refused to respond, crying into Amber's arms while Shannon and Elizabeth rubbed my back, Claire shaking her head from the doorway. Because he was right—he was a free man, and I was the one who was a cheating piece of crap.

I attempted to ward off my anxiety, staring at myself in the rear-view mirror. *This is it. This is the end. This is for the best. No need to cry. Do not cry in front of him. No matter what.*

I stepped out of the car just as the front door opened. There he was. Once upon a time, I thought he was the one—my Tall, Dark and Handsome, even though we never really belonged to one another. Now, as I approached him, I wondered how I could've ever believed we could be anything other than just friends. The image of him screwing Marsha, throwing her aside and screwing me, had haunted me for two weeks, and that image solidified in my brain when he smiled at me.

"Hey!" I said with faux happiness. "Aren't you relieved the semester is finally over?" *Aren't you glad you'll never see me ever again?*

He nodded before giving me a hug. It was stiff. Lacking emotion. Lamont was just as uncomfortable as I was. "Yeah. I'm ready to be home for a little while."

283

"Any fun plans for the summer?" *Gonna get back together with you ex? Gonna visit Tiffany? Gonna break more hearts?*

He shook his head. "I might have to quit dipping. I went to the dentist and they told me I could get mouth cancer."

I blinked back my surprise. "That's awfully responsible of you."

He chuckled, grabbed a Copenhagen container from his pocket and packed it behind his bottom lip. I couldn't help but notice his wrist was naked. *I wonder if he found it.* "Don't be too proud of me just yet. It's easier said than done." *He probably threw it away.*

"Lamont, the reason I came over is because I need to tell you something."

"You're not pregnant, are you?"

His accusation made me angry. Then I thought about those red bumps, which were becoming more noticeable each day, and grew even angrier. "No, dick. I'm not pregnant. But I'm glad you have so much faith in me." *But you did give me something that I'll probably have to live with for the rest of my life.*

He smirked. "Then what else do you need to tell me?"

"I'm leaving."

"Well, no shit—"

I held my hand up. "Shut up and listen for once in your fucking life."

His eyes narrowed. "You need to stop cussing. It's not very becoming of you."

"Like I care what you think."

There was an awkward silence between us.

"Look," I began. "I'm leaving and I'm not coming back."

I didn't know what to expect, but his lack of reaction wrenched a knife straight through my stomach. "Where're you going?"

"San Diego State. I received an acceptance letter a few weeks ago. I want to graduate on time and that's not going to happen here."

He shrugged. "Congrats, I guess?"

I frowned. "Do you even care?"

Another shrug. "You've obviously made up your mind."

"Well," I prodded. "Is there any reason I should stay?" *If you tell me you love me right here, right now, I'll stay.*

One final shrug. "Nope. Nothing I can think of."

I pursed my lips together, rubbed at my naked wrist and nodded once. "On that note then, it was nice knowing you and I should get back to packing."

284

He gave me another hug void of intimacy. It felt like I was hugging a stuffed animal that no longer provided comfort for a frightened child. He even patted my back as if we didn't know one another. As if we hadn't seen one another naked on multiple occasions. As if I hadn't confessed my love to him. "Get home safe."

I walked back to my car and drove down one block before completely breaking down, my sadness steaming up the windows. "Why do I keep hoping he'll care? It's over. Get it through your stupid head, Roxanne."

#

A BOX OF Kleenex remained empty on the coffee table, damp tissues crumpled beside me, Shannon, Elizabeth and Amber. Claire and I had said our final good-byes earlier that afternoon, our friendship non-existent, the tension between the two of us unpleasant and strained. She'd left the house to hang out with Adam, probably doing whatever she could to make sure she wouldn't be present for my final night in Rohnert Park.

I knew saying farewell to my three best girlfriends was going to be difficult, but I had no idea it would feel as if the world was falling apart.

"You're not dying. This isn't the last time we'll see one another," Amber said, her big blue eyes surrounded by pink puffiness. "You're only a plane ride away."

I blew my nose. "Yeah, but what am I gonna do without all of you?"

"We'll always be your best friends," Shannon added. "We'll be here for you, no matter what."

"It's just not the same," I whined. "I wouldn't have survived the year without you guys. Between Lamont and Zach, changing majors, getting out of the house—I wouldn't have been able to get through it all without you."

Elizabeth dabbed her eyes with a tissue. "We'll Skype. Call. Text. Nothing will change. We just won't be living together anymore."

"It sucks," Amber said. "But you need to do this. School is the most important thing. You deserve to graduate on time. Pursue whatever makes you most happy."

I closed my eyes and took a deep breath. "Promise me nothing will change. Promise me you'll visit. Promise me I'm not making a huge mistake."

The girls all looked at one another before smiling earnestly at me. "We promise, Roxy." I was hopeful they were right, but a small, nagging voice in my head kept telling me everything was about to change. For better or for worse, I was afraid to find out.

# Chapter Fourteen

AS ZACHARY AND I sat on the overly stuffed couch in my parents' TV room, I struggled to keep composure. I should've been comforted by Zachary's warm hand on my thigh, one of my favorite romantic comedies playing on the screen, but my chest felt hollow. I'd returned to San Diego three nights before and I hadn't stopped shedding tears since. Try as I might, I couldn't focus. The nonexistent bracelet around my wrist still adorned my heart, making my stomach clench and my jaw cringe. Lamont's text messages from earlier that day burned the back of my eyelids, my responses unable to express how broken he'd made me feel.

*How could you do this? What we had was special.* His texts rolled through quickly, one right after the other. *Why didn't you tell me sooner that you were leaving? You didn't even give me the chance to say good-bye. Why did you tell me you were leaving at all? Just to be a bitch?* I closed my eyes tight, willing the words to go away. *Not only did you ditch me, but you left the girls. They're devastated you're gone. They were ready to move in with you and you don't give two shits. You'll never find what you had up here down there.*

"I'll be right back," I croaked to Zach, rushing to the bathroom for a tissue. *I can't believe you chose him over me. You know how I feel about you. And I know you want me. Why did you leave? For him? It won't last. What did I do to deserve this?*

At the time, I'd crumbled to the ground. I'd begged him to stop. I'd attempted to explain myself again—about graduation and actually getting classes. But he hadn't listened. He continued to pummel my feelings straight into the ground.

*You don't belong in San Diego. You belong here. With me. With the girls.*

I hadn't responded, Molly licking the warm tears from my cheeks, the phone continuing to vibrate against my fingertips. *If you stay in San Diego, I don't want you to text me. No Facebook. No calls. Nothing. Not a word. You've hurt me for the last time.*

I'd wanted to scream at him—remind him about Melanie, Marsha and his birthday and Tiffany. About how he broke my heart over and over again. Instead,

I told him I was sorry, as if I was wrong in choosing to get away from his toxic behavior in an attempt to find my own happiness.

And as I blew my nose one last time, I dropped to my knees, afraid I was going to vomit, Lamont's final text still glowing in my mind, a flu-like shiver shooting through my body. *I didn't get into a relationship with Tiffany because I didn't want to ruin any chance of something happening between me and you. I should've dated her. I missed the chance to be with the most beautiful girl I've ever met because I thought you wanted to be with me. Biggest mistake I've ever made.*

I cried out for Zachary, dry heaving, stomach muscles clenching until I thought they might bleed. I wanted to convince myself that he was drunk, that he didn't mean what he was saying. But I knew this was the real Lamont. He wanted to hurt me because I broke his heart.

That meant one thing.

*I messed up. He loves me. He was just too scared to admit it.*

Zachary rested his hand on my shoulder, his palm radiating guilt straight through my heart.

*What have I done?*

#

"MAKE TWO BOXES. I don't know how hungry you are, but I know I can eat an entire box by myself."

Lucy sat on the dark brown couch in the living room, shouting her orders through the door that connected to the kitchen. Her stomach protruded from her hot pink t-shirt and blue sweatpants, her straight blonde hair pulled into a messy bun atop her head, her face completely naked and glowing. It still baffled me how incredibly beautiful Lucy was without even having to try.

"Good Lord. Are you eating for two or something?" I teased.

"Ha ha. Haven't heard that one before."

I poured the noodles into the boiling water, grabbed two mineral waters from the fridge and collapsed onto the cushion beside my thirty-two week pregnant sister. "Where's your loving husband at? You shouldn't be eating mac and cheese. Who's buying the groceries around here?"

She unscrewed the water bottle lid and sighed. "On another business trip. He's trying to make his practice well known. Meet the right people, pass out his business cards, try to gather clients. I think he's trying to impress Dad. Especially with the baby coming and all."

I nodded and crossed my legs beneath me. "Are you okay with it?"

288

Lucy shook her head. "I hate it. I really miss Roger. Every night I crawl into bed without him, I don't get much sleep. I want him to be successful, but I also want him to be home. I'm worried he won't be around when the baby is born."

"Don't think like that." I patted her thigh, surprised at how big it was. Lucy always went to the gym and kept her thighs toned—something was wrong. "Roger loves you. He's trying to do everything he can to make your life easier. But sweetie, have you been keeping up with your normal routine?"

Another shake of the head. "I haven't had the motivation. I get home from work and watch TV. I can barely get out of bed in the morning. This kid is sucking up all of my energy."

"Lucy, you've always loved to work out. I'm not saying you're fat, and I'm not saying you need to lose weight. You look absolutely stunning, as always, but are you happy?"

She looked at the water bottle and swiped at her moistened eyes. "You don't know how badly I wish this was wine."

"That bad, huh?"

"Talk about something else. Tell me about your life. How are things with Zach?"

It was my turn to wish I had the power to turn water into wine. "They're alright. He's my best friend in the whole world. I love him. I always want to spend time with him. But—I don't know. I still cry all the time. I just feel—"

"You miss Lamont, don't you?"

I looked over my shoulder and noticed the water spilling over the sides of the pot. "Uh-oh. Don't want to burn the house down."

Lucy laughed when I ran into the kitchen to stir the noodles. "Glad to see you still like to avoid your problems. I was beginning to think you weren't my sister anymore."

"What's that supposed to mean?"

She sipped her water. "You've changed so much this year. You've developed an attitude. You have a boyfriend. You drink. I didn't think my little sister existed anymore. It's like you're growing up or something."

I stirred the noodles until the bubbles faded. "But isn't that what you told me to do?"

Lucy chuckled. "I'm not saying it's a bad thing. I'm just glad you're still you. I don't want you turning into me."

I furrowed my brows. "I think your hormones are messing with your brain."

289

She laughed. "Still cracking jokes, huh? Glad to see someone in this family is getting laid regularly."

"Can you not?" I strained the noodles and took the dairy ingredients out of the refrigerator. "Maybe I'm just funny. Has that ever crossed your mind?"

"Nope. Definitely not."

I mixed in the fat free milk and unsalted butter. "I'm the one making you food. You should be nice to me."

She smiled. "Then you might think I like you. And we can't have that, can we?"

#

JASMINE OPENED THE front door and welcomed me in with open arms. "Roxy! I'm so glad you could make it. Zach, it's nice to see you again. Welcome to my happy home—parents are out for the weekend, which means we get to drink!"

We stepped through the doorframe and gave Jasmine a hug—me first, then Zachary. "I'm glad you invited us! I'm excited to see everyone. It feels like forever."

"Beers are in the fridge. Help yourself to Jell-O shots, chasers and vodka. And there's chips in the pantry."

I smiled and gestured at Zachary's hands. "We brought goodies too!"

"Beer and vodka. Hope you're thirsty," Zachary attempted in his own awkward, sweet way.

Jasmine grabbed the box of beer and led us into the kitchen. "There's no such thing as too much alcohol. We're always thirsty around here."

"Roxy!"

I glanced over Jasmine's shoulder and saw Lacie running toward me. "Lacie, hi!"

We threw our bodies against one another and giggled as we swayed back and forth. "You're home! You're finally home," she slurred happily. "And you're staying here, right?'

Despite the nausea that still followed me around whenever I thought about not returning to Sonoma, I did find myself smiling. I wasn't even forcing it. Knowing that I had friends who cared about me made the transition back to San Diego a little easier to fathom. "Yes ma'am. I'm here to stay."

Jasmine and Lacie squealed. "You're gonna be an Aztec!"

"We're gonna see you on campus! I can't believe it."

I nodded mutely, the vodka reaching out to me from the countertop. *They aren't Lizzy, Shannon and Amber, but they care. They're here because they're your friends. It's not fair to compare—there's no reason to compare.* "I'm mainly excited for the sun. I can't even begin to explain how much I hate clouds. And the rain. I look like a ghost."

"I didn't want to say anything, but you do look like you haven't seen the sun in a few years," Lacie teased.

I nudged her shoulder and smiled. "You mean sunshine is a thing? I don't know if my skin is gonna be able to handle it."

Jasmine poured three shots of vodka and unscrewed the top of the orange juice bottle. "How about we cheers to Roxy joining our sweet little crew?"

After we clanked our glasses together, the night raced by in a blur. As the front door opened and closed, the house grew more and more crowded. It nowhere neared the ragers I'd attended in Rohnert Park, but there was something pleasant about this smaller group of people. These were the people I'd known in high school and catching up with them had slightly mended the break in my heart. Then Luke made his appearance, bringing happy tears to my eyes. By that point, touching my nose with my forefinger had proven difficult, my emotional instability approaching the point of no return. To my inebriated state of mind, the feelings I experienced when I saw Luke were so similar to my feelings for Andrew that I almost cried out the wrong name.

Completely ignorant to the fact that I was in the general vicinity of my boyfriend, I smacked a kiss right onto Luke's lips. "Thank God you're here, And—uh—Luke! I was afraid you wouldn't show up."

He laughed, handsome head tossed back, white teeth glistening against the lighting on the ceiling. "Sounds like someone's been drinking."

"Who, me?" I grabbed his arm and pulled him into the kitchen. "Just a smidge. You need to catch up so me and you can catch up."

"I'm having trouble deciding if you're coming onto me or simply offering me a drink."

"A little bit of both." I opened the refrigerator, gave him a Jell-O shot and then handed him some cranberry juice. "I do believe you're capable of pouring your own shots. Meet me at the Beer Pong table when you're ready."

He nearly choked on the Jell-O. "You sure you wanna play?"

"I've been practicing. You won't even recognize me."

Lacie wrapped her arms around my stomach and rested her chin on my shoulder. "I think we should all take a shot together."

Jasmine nuzzled against Luke. "Did somebody say shot?"

Luke lifted the vodka off the counter and held it in the air. "Let's cheers to Roxanne being home! For good!"

It felt great to be surrounded by the familiar faces of my past. Buzzing from the mixture of cheap vodka and even cheaper beer, I was able to pretend that the last two years of my life in Sonoma had never happened. I'd been sucked into a time warp—into a world void of Lamont, Andrew and the three girls I regarded as sisters. Sonoma was nothing but a figment of my cruel imagination.

Sometime later, I sat on Zachary's lap, gazed into his bloodshot eyes and experienced that burning love we shared before the beginning of the second semester. Everything was back to normal, and for the first time since I pulled my car into my parents' driveway, I didn't feel like I was on the verge of an emotional breakdown.

That was until Jasmine ran to her room crying, Lacie rolling her eyes, reluctantly following, and a vibration tickling the insides of my jean pocket.

It was a text message from Luke. *Please come into the kitchen. I need to talk to you.*

I kissed Zachary hard on the lips. He was in the middle of a Beer Pong game with Lacie and they were losing pathetically. So pathetically, in fact, that Zach was sitting down in order to regain composure. And now that Lacie had disappeared to comfort Jasmine, Zachary was gonna have to find himself a new partner. "I'll be right back. Start picking up your game, Lovebug. Maybe find someone who actually knows how to play." When he chuckled, I touched his cheek. "I love you."

He flashed a lopsided grin. "I love you, too."

As I rounded the corner to discover what had happened to Jasmine and to ask Luke if everything was okay, a large hand gripped my shoulder and yanked me into the laundry room. It was dark, the only visible light shining through the door's slats.

Drunk and confused, I slapped Luke's hand. "What the fuck are you doing?"

He leaned against the doorframe with a red cup in hand. "I need to talk to you."

*Why do boys always want to talk to me in closets?* I crossed my arms over my chest. "Are you gonna explain why Jasmine is crying? Lacie said she thought she saw you guys hooking up in here. Is that true?"

Concern lined his forehead. "We didn't hook up."

292

I snorted. "You can tell me if you kissed. I won't be mad at you."

He took a large gulp of his drink and shook his head. "No, I swear Roxy. Nothing happened. We were just talking and I think she got the wrong idea."

I began tapping my foot. "What's going on? I don't need Zach to think I'm macking with you in here. We gotta speed this up."

Luke scoffed, stumbled to the side and spilled whatever was in his cup on top of my shoe. "Like he even fucking cares."

I placed my hand on his chest to prop him up straight. "When did you get so drunk?"

He shrugged. "It's your fault. You gave me hundred proof vodka. I think it's in my DNA now."

We stood in silence for a few moments staring at one another.

"Luke, my love," I began gently. "You look nervous. What happened with Jasmine? Are you okay?"

He chuckled, another large gulp of alcohol sliding down his throat. "Jasmine wanted to talk. She confessed her feelings for me and I told her they weren't mutual. I was just being honest."

"Okay," I drawled. "That is rather unfortunate, but she'll be okay. She's drunk. She probably won't even remember in the morning. There's nothing to feel bad about."

He held his hand out. "I'm not done. I didn't tell her the whole truth."

I waited for him to continue.

"Me and you—we're best friends, right?"

For a minute, I saw Andrew, his vulnerability only exposed when under the influence. I blinked, reached out and squeezed Luke's forearm. "Of course we are. I love you, Luke."

"Where's Roxy?" Lacie shouted from beyond the door.

"She's in the closet with Luke," an undecipherable voice replied.

I cringed when whistles and claps seeped through the door's slats. A flashback to Lamont's party smacked me in the chest when Lacie began banging on the door, telling us to wrap it up. The sudden need for fresh air consumed me. *Stop freaking out. This isn't Lamont. You're just talking with Luke. It's just like talking to Andy.* I took a deep breath and urged Luke to continue. *Except you never kissed Andy.*

"I'm afraid you're gonna hate me."

"Unless you murdered someone I care about, I see no reason for me to ever hate you."

He tilted his head back, emptying the remaining contents of his drink. "That'd be easier to admit than this." After dropping the cup to the floor, he fiddled with the hem of his designer shirt. "I've ben having these thoughts lately. I mean, I've had them from time to time before, but now they happen more frequently—"

A knock at the door startled us. "You better be using a condom in there."

"It's a shame your parents didn't use one the night you were conceived. Fuck off!"

Luke stared at me, surprised. "When did you get so sassy?"

I bashfully fiddled with my fingers behind my back. "I swear it only happens when I'm drunk."

"Roxy, I'm gay."

I blinked. *What?*

Then breathed. *That's it?*

Then blinked. *Oh my God.*

Then smiled. *Lose a gay, gain a gay.*

I threw my arms around him and giggled. "Oh, Luke! This is great news!"

He placed his hands on my hips and looked down at me. "You're not mad?"

"Mad?" I shook my head. "Why would I be mad?"

"Well, last time you were in town—"

I held up a hand. "You're not the only gay man I've been attracted to."

When my words truly sank into his brain, Luke lifted me into the air and twirled me around once, crashing ungracefully into the side of the washing machine. "I'm so glad you're not mad! I was so afraid you'd hate me."

"My best friend up North is gay. I needed one down here, too."

He kissed me on the forehead. "Don't tell anybody, though. You're the first person I've told."

I gasped and held my hands up to my heart. "Lil' ol' me?"

"It feels so good to finally tell you."

"Well, if we're going to be honest with one another, you should probably know that I've been cheating on Zach."

His smile flipped. "What?"

My eyes watered. "In Sonoma. I loved the guy."

"Oh, Roxy," he cooed, pulling me into my body, rubbing his hands up and down my back. "I'm sorry. I had no idea you and Zach were having problems."

"We're not. It's all me. I'm the fucked up one."

"You're here now. You chose Zach."

I nodded and wiped my nose across my forearm. "It still hurts though, you know?"

"It'll pass. I don't like Zach much anymore, but I can see how much he cares about you."

I nodded again. "Nothing leaves this closet."

He smiled. "Well, nothing except for me."

I laughed and settled my cheek against his chest. "Thank you for trusting me. I love you, Luke."

"You've got a big heart, Roxanne. Stop putting yourself down for it and embrace it. You're a beautiful person. Inside and out. Don't forget it."

#

I SLID THE purple bathing suit bottoms past my thighs and arranged the material so that the bumps on my skin weren't visible. It was more than embarrassing. The single bump I'd found on Cinco de Mayo had multiplied into a colony spread unevenly across my skin—pink with a white dot in the middle. Since they resembled pimples, I'd tried popping a few, the resulting swelling and blood proving that I had something bad growing on my skin. Shaving only seemed to make it worse, and as the bumps settled their city happily on the most sensitive patch of skin on my body, the desire to be intimate with Zachary crumbled to pieces as if in an earthquake.

After checking the mirror, making sure—yet again—that no bumps were visible to the human eye, I slid the black cotton dress over my head and lathered my arms with tanning oil. *Roxy, you have to tell him. You can't hide this from him forever. If he finds them on himself—he'll kill you.* I took a deep breath, walked up the stairs and greeted Zachary at the front door. Both of my parents were at work, which gave Zachary and I some alone time. I should've been excited, but I was exactly the opposite. I'd been running out of excuses as to why I couldn't have sex, and having my parents home always saved me from spreading the bumps to Zachary.

Now, I was shit out of luck.

And because we didn't use condoms that one time, Zachary never wanted to use them anymore.

And whenever I pulled one out, he thought it was because I didn't like his penis the way it was.

It was becoming a headache.

"It's beautiful out today," I said once I gave him a peck on the lips. "I thought we could sit on the deck and soak up the Vitamin D."

As I opened the screen door leading to the back patio, Zachary snatched my elbow and twirled me into his body. "I can think of another D you might want more."

I cringed. "Look, Zach—"

"You gonna give me another excuse?" He dropped my arm and lowered his gaze to the floor. "I give up. Did I do something wrong? Like, are you not attracted to me anymore?"

Molly nosed my hand when she opened the remainder of the screen and studied me. Her tongue was lolling to the side, concern showing through her large brown eyes. *Oh, shut up, Molly. I'm gonna tell him. Don't rush me.* "No, that's not it at all."

He crouched and rubbed Molly's ears, avoiding my guilty gaze. "Then what the hell is going on? Ever since you've been home, you've done nothing but mope around and avoid all of my sexual advances. I know you're sad, Roxanne, and I'm trying to be understanding, but I want you. And you're making me feel rejected." Molly licked his nose. "How long is this going to last?"

"What? You tired of me having emotions?" I glared at my dog. *You traitor.* "You don't have to be a dick about it," I snapped, stomping onto the deck. "You know, sex isn't everything, Zach."

"You know that's not what I meant." Zachary stood and followed me. "Talk to me. What the hell is going on?"

Molly's tail thumped against the screen, banging against the innermost crevices of my brain. *Just tell him the truth. He deserves to know. Maybe he'll still love you. Maybe he'll walk away and you can return guilt free to Sonoma.* I looked at Molly, who barked at me. *Okay, fine. I'll tell him.* "I found something—something—weird."

Zachary frowned. "What's that mean?"

I gestured below my waist. "Here. Around Cinco de Mayo, I found—a—a bump."

He sat down on the chaise lounge and took off his sunglasses. "What does it look like?"

I slowly rubbed Molly's fur, wondering if the fall from the deck to the dirt backyard was enough to kill me. "Well, there are more now. Some are bigger than—"

"Do they have white centers? Are they red?"

My stomach churned. "I—yes. And I need to tell you—"

296

He rubbed his eyes with his thumb and index finger. "Would you mind if I looked at them?"

Molly and I made eye contact again. *What did he just ask me?* "Uh—I—don't—I—"

"Roxy, please," he snapped. "It's not like I haven't seen your vagina before."

"This is different."

He stood and steered me into the house. "No, it's not. I need to see them. Just trust me."

I swallowed the knot in my throat and closed the door before Molly walked inside. *This is all your fault. You're staying outside until my embarrassment subsides.* Zachary led me down to my bedroom and into the bathroom. "If my parents come home, I'm gonna be in a lot of trouble and you'll be banned from the house."

"Then drop your bottoms, pronto."

I sighed, trying not to succumb to the panic slowly making it's way through my nervous system. *He's going to find out the truth about Lamont. He's gonna tell me I have herpes. That I'm a lying, cheating whore.* "Zach, I really don't—"

He pulled the bikini bottoms down to my thighs. "Stop complaining and just hold your dress up."

*Take deep breaths. You can do this.* I closed my eyes and held the dress fabric between my sides and my elbows. I tried to pretend I was at the doctor's office when in reality, Zachary's face was inches away from my infidelity. I felt his hand touch the inside of my thigh and his breath warmed my skin.

"Yeah, that's what I thought. I need to tell you something," he said, moving my clothes back to their proper positions. "You may want to sit."

I didn't know what I was expecting, but the guilty tone now present made my heart heavy. "Uh—what?"

He sighed. "You have this thing called Molluscum."

I raised an eyebrow. "Excuse me?"

"Roxy, sit," he said, gesturing towards my bed. "I didn't mention it because I thought it went away."

My butt hit the mattress hard, confusion making my legs weak. "You're not making sense."

He sat beside me. "It's technically an STD, but it's totally curable."

Anger rammed my heart against my ribcage. "You wanna run that by me one more time?'

His fingers began picking at one another. "A few months ago, when I still lived in the frat house, we shared a shower. I was hungover from a party. I'd forgotten my towel, so I just grabbed the one that was on the rack."

I forced back the acid burning in my throat. "You—you—"

"A few days later, I noticed some bumps around my penis. I didn't think much of it until I shaved and found more appear. After a few weeks, I finally went to med services and they told me I had Molluscum. I asked how I got it, they told me it was from the towel and—"

I stood abruptly and walked into the bathroom to get away from him. *All of this time, I thought Lamont gave me—and I gave Zach—I thought this was my punishment—it was all Zach.* "You fucking liar."

His face contorted, his handsome features caving in on themselves. "Little Woman, no, please listen. I didn't know I could give them to you. I thought they were completely gone."

"Then why didn't you tell me?"

"Honestly, I thought it was a non-issue. I did the treatment."

"I trusted you! You—you did this to me!"

He began biting his nails. "Roxy, I'm sorry, but there's no need to freak out. It's one hundred percent curable. Just think of it as a bad rash."

"All this time, I thought—and you—how could you have kept this from me? We talk every single day! How could you hide this?"

"You need to listen to—"

"No!" I screamed, smacking my hand against the doorframe. "Get out! I can't look at you. Go home. Get out of my fucking house right now!"

He didn't argue. When I heard the front door shut, I released a breath I didn't realize I was holding and wiped hot tears from my cheeks. *I don't have herpes. It wasn't Lamont's fault. It was Zach. He lied to me. He fucking lied to me.* I fell facedown on the bed, silently thanking God for not giving me an incurable disease. For not punishing me for my lack of loyalty. *Lamont didn't do this to me. Lamont didn't lie to me. Zach did.* I wheezed, the reality of the situation setting in. *I chose the wrong guy. I made a huge mistake. And I can't go back and change it.*

# 

EVEN THOUGH I'D transitioned back to life in San Diego—got a job as a busser at a restaurant, went on regular dates with Zachary, somewhat mended the relationship with my parents, proceeded with treatment back to sexual health, attended multiple girls' nights with Jasmine and Lacie, scoped out men for Luke while enjoying frequent lunches—the loneliness that had held my heart hostage for the past two months had yet to release any prisoners of war. Molly's companionship helped to ease the pain, but she had begun to struggle making her way down the stairs that led to my bedroom, her hips falling prey to old age. I'd also begun to feel guilty about crying into her fur every single night, my sorrow a dark cloud burdening an innocent civilian.

I needed something that could fill the void left by my own selfish decision to leave my best friends and the potential love of my life.

And that something presented itself when Lucy and I were shopping at the mall for maternity clothing on one sunny Saturday morning.

"Hello ladies. Would either of you be interested in adoption?" The woman was nice. Her voice wasn't pushy and her kind demeanor lured me in.

The small location was once a puppy mill that had been closed down due to protestors and improper treatment of animals. The Humane Society had taken refuge there for their adoption event: rambunctious puppies wrestled one another in small cages behind glass, bunnies rested beneath hay and pellets, hamsters ran around on wheels and old dogs looked up at me with hopeful eyes. My sister cooed and rested her hands on the glass, a baby Golden Doodle capturing her attention. I, on the other hand, turned a corner and felt myself stumble.

In a giant playpen stocked with toys and carpeted towers, I found the answer to my prayers. Kittens. All shapes and sizes, different fur lengths, big ears and bushy tails. They ran around in circles ceaselessly, some pouncing on stuffed mice and others trimming their claws on scratching posts. I squealed with childish delight.

"Where do I start?" I asked the friendly woman who now resembled an angel.

"What're you doing?" Lucy hissed.

The woman maneuvered around the individuals gathered at a half-moon table, each talking to a different Humane Society representative, and handed me a pen with a clipboard stacked full of paperwork. "Fill these out here. We just need to make sure whichever animal you decide to take home will be safe and treated well. How many people in the household?"

"This isn't a good idea," Lucy whispered.

"Two," I replied, ignoring her. "Just me and my sister."

"And are you both ready for a new family member?"

When the woman smiled at Lucy, my sister snorted. "Oh, yeah, because my big ass belly doesn't give that answer away."

299

I elbowed her. "Don't mind my sister. Pregnancy has made her extremely sarcastic."

The woman nodded. "I was the same way. So, I totally understand. Any animal allergies?"

"Nope, none," I lied, purposefully ignoring my mom's allergy to cat dander.

Lucy shook her head. "Roxanne, *really* think about this."

The woman patted my sister's arm. "Kittens are great for new borns. I had a kitten when I had my first baby. Cuddling with her was the only way I could sleep peacefully."

I thanked the woman and pulled my sister away before she could call me out on my lies. While she lectured me about being an impulsive idiot, I quickly wrote down all of my personal information on . I then yanked Lucy over to the kittens' playpen and stared at the mewing balls of fur pawing at one another.

Lucy's eyes glistened. "They are pretty fucking cute."

Someone tapped my shoulder, gestured to a seating area in a separate playpen, and asked which kitten I would like to see first. At random, I said "the black one," and watched as the Humane Society volunteer reached into the pile of kittens, grasping his hands around the belly of an itty-bitty black kitty.

"Oh my," Lucy cooed. "Look at that little face!"

The bundle of fur curled into a ball on my lap instantly, small vibrations tickling my legs. I leaned my face toward the cuddly creature and giggled when his whiskers twitched, our noses touching. "You're coming home with me, little guy."

"He is awfully cute."

The volunteer smiled, took the kitten and placed the critter into a cardboard carrier. He ushered me to a back room where I pulled out my credit card and learned a plethora of information regarding the kitten's basic needs. They didn't question Lucy and me any further, handed me a complimentary bag of cat food and showed me out the door, my new little friend mewing in his carrier.

When Lucy and I buckled our seatbelts, I pulled the kitty out of his confinement and cuddled him against my chest. He kissed my nose again, reassuring me that adding him to the family was the right decision.

As was returning to San Diego.

And leaving Lamont behind.

"You're going to love Molly. She's old, but she's a sweetheart."

The kitten meowed once more before settling quietly on my lap.

"Mom's gonna kill you," Lucy said, changing lanes. "You know how much she hates cats. Almost as much as she hates you. Almost."

"Very funny." I scratched the kitten's back with my pinky finger. "Tell Mom and Dad it was your idea. They won't kick me out if they think you suggested it."

"Why do I have to be involved?"

"Please?" I begged. "You know they think your ideas are always good ideas. As long as your name is mentioned, I should be safe from murder."

Lucy sighed. "What're you gonna name the kitty?"

I smiled at the tiny little face, big ears twitching side to side. "Sherlock. The kitty that's gonna solve all of my problems."

"You know that's a lot of pressure to put on an innocent little animal."

*Yeah, but I haven't felt this happy since before I left Rohnert Park.* "You just wait and see. He's going to be my savior."

"Think he'll get you to return to the sciences?"

I snorted. "I didn't say he could work miracles."

My sister shrugged. "Hey, you're actually smiling. It was worth a try."

"Have you given any more thought into having me edit your journal?"

Lucy laughed, her belly bouncing up and down. "How about we focus on how to get mom to not kill you first."

#

LUCY AND ROGER had been sleeping in the guest bedroom for three days and nights, the new prodigy child due any time now. I was at work, ignoring my mother's and father's phone calls and text messages, divulging myself in busy work to pretend that I wasn't being the world's worst sister. Even when the healthy baby girl was brought back to the house—Hannah Lovelace, six and a half pounds, green eyes, blonde wisps of hair and light pink skin—I did everything in my power to avoid long periods of interaction with my niece. Sometimes, I'd sneak into the room when she was sleeping and gaze down at the perfect little creature, jealous of her carefree life. Other times, I'd pour myself a glass of champagne when my parents weren't home, tease my sister about being unable to join me, and watch as the small child judged me for being imperfect—my auburn curls with dark brown streaks, my hazel eyes, my rosy cheeks. Even though I loved the small child for being a part of my family, for being born healthy, and for making my sister happier than I'd seen her in months, there was something that didn't quite sit right with me. Daisy Buchannan once said that all a girl could be was a pretty little fool. But being born into the Vaughn family made life much

301

more difficult than that. I prayed every night for the small child—prayed she wouldn't be a huge disappointment like me. That she would be just like her mother and father, her grandma and grandpa. I decided to spend as little time with the baby as possible to prevent her from learning any bad habits from me.

Even when Lucy and Roger returned to Los Angeles to proceed with a daily routine that included Hannah, I remained invisible in my household. My parents were glued to their phones and computers, eagerly seeking updates regarding their grandchild. I didn't mind too much. My dad was so preoccupied, he didn't even mind when I asked him if Zachary could study in my bedroom, with the door closed. Life had returned to normal.

I was ignored.

And that's just the way my family liked it.

#

I CAN'T BELIEVE you're *actually* here," Shannon squealed as the cab pulled up to the dance venue.

"School only started a little over a month ago, but it's not the same without all of you," I replied. "I told you I'd be back as soon as possible."

It was the weekend before Halloween and the annual dance event, *Freaky Tales*, was taking place at a large paintballing venue only ten minutes away from campus. After purchasing a plane ticket and asking the girls to purchase me an extra ticket for the dance, I'd been way too excited for my short, four-day trip to Rohnert Park. Three weeks hadn't passed by quickly enough.

The summer had been difficult to get through. My mom nearly threw me out of the house when I returned home with a new pet. After one week of convincing them that a kitten was no big deal, I came home to my mom screaming at the poor little creature because his black fur already coated every visible surface and claw marks had been raked into the side of her favorite chair. If it weren't for Lucy lying to my mom and saying the kitten was her idea—an attempt to help me with my attitude problem—I probably would've been homeless, eating cat food with my new pet. Everyone eventually warmed up to Sherlock because it was impossible to resist his light green eyes and charming meow, but he and I often remained hidden in my room, only to interact with my parents when dinner was served at seven o'clock sharp. Having the baby born also helped keep some of the peace between all of us.

Jasmine, Lacie and I had become fast friends, watching movies and underage drinking whenever the opportunity presented itself. My bussing job made me enough money to go out with Zachary and my friends, but I hated my coworkers. The greatest thing about having a job was the ability to leave my house whenever my parents and I fought, chatting with customers providing the perfect escape from whatever drama my mom usually tried to start with me. The "rash" that had nearly ended my relationship with Zachary was treated and completely healed. And even though he and I were doing better than ever, in a moment of vulnerability, I admitted to him it would take some time before I could give him my entire heart because the feelings I had for an old love still somewhat remained. I may have left out Lamont's name, but the tears rolling down my cheeks surely gave away the truth. The greatest part was that Zachary never held it against me. Not even when we bickered. He always promised his endless love to me and kissed me until the tears would subside.

Then school started. I hated that I didn't recognize any of the faces in the ocean of the 45,000 students flooding the massive campus. I did everything in my power to avoid the sadness haunting me whenever I had time to think and immerged myself in eighteen units of literature classes that fried every neuron in my brain.

This escape to my past was exactly what I needed to get away from the pressures of too much homework, parents that couldn't stop talking about how proud they were of their infant grandchild even though she'd done nothing of merit, and a needy boyfriend that complained whenever a day went by where I couldn't make the time to see him. Being treated like a slave at work, rather than a capable human being, had also begun to take its toll on my temper. I understood that clearing people's plates made me a peasant of sorts, but seeing people snap their fingers at me to get my attention made me nearly slam my tray atop their tables. Rohnert Park was a place where my sad reality didn't exist. I hadn't felt this free—and happy—in months.

"Here, keep the change," Amber slurred, handing the taxi driver folded up cash. "We have a dance to attend."

As soon as the yellow door closed behind me, I knew I'd taken a few too many shots of tequila. Elizabeth, Shannon, Amber and I linked elbows in an attempt to steady ourselves in front of the security guards checking in students at the entrance.

"How're they gonna turn a paintball arena into a place to dance?" I asked.

Amber shrugged. "I'm sure they're just gonna clear out one of the big ass rooms and hold it there. I don't think it would be safe to have paint balling obstacles available for a bunch of drunk college kids to fuck around with."

Shannon laughed. "Let's hope they cleaned up the paint. I'd hate to ruin my new shoes."

"Guys, make sure we stick together. This place is gonna be packed," Elizabeth said pulling me closer to her side. "It's gonna be impossible to find one another if we split up."

"At least we don't have to worry about Claire and Adam this time around."

I snorted, resting my head on Shannon's shoulder. "Are they even together anymore?"

Amber chuckled. "Were they even together when they were together?"

The four of us laughed as we made our way to the back of the line. In honor of the Halloween themed dance, we'd decided to wear costumes that were simple and sexy.

And disgustingly cliché.

Exotic animals.

Amber was a giraffe. Her shirt was yellow with brown patches all over her back and stomach, brown booty-shorts hugged her big butt, and knee-high brown socks and black ankle-high boots completed the ensemble. She had a brown headband with ears and horns, she straightened her long, brown hair and applied dark brown makeup around her sapphire eyes.

Elizabeth was a tiger. She found an orange camisole and painted black stripes along the sides and back. She rocked a short, form-fitting black skirt, attached an orange and black tail, and wore high black heels to show off the muscular legs she'd developed from coaching little kids' soccer over the summer. She put tiger ears on her head, exaggerated black eyeliner around her golden eyes and curled the ends of her dirty blonde hair.

Shannon was a cheetah. She put her shoulder length brown hair into low pigtails and tied cheetah-print bows around the hair ties. She sported a cheetah print corset that had black lace around the bust and two black bows lined up with each of her hipbones. She paired it with black spandex and cheetah-print wedges, brown and black makeup around her hazel eyes and big, black hoop earrings.

I tried to be a little more original with my costume, spending a small—and irrational—fortune with no regrets. I found the perfect wolf costume while perusing different Halloween websites. It included a grey corset with brown fur wrapped around my breasts, a grey miniskirt lined with brown fur along the hem, furry gloves, and fur legwarmers that covered my four-inch high, silver heels. The best part of the costume was the hood. It had fur along the edge and big, hairy, grey ears on top. I finished it off with long, fake eye-lashes and silver diamond hoops dangling from my ears.

Boys whistled, their heads turning 180 degrees, throwing compliments at us as we walked by. While the girls smiled in every direction, I kept my eyes on the lookout for a tall, dark and handsome gentlemen I wondered might make an appearance, the big, fluffy wolf tail swishing against the backs of my knees.

Once we reached the front of the line, we were patted down and pushed through the crowd, our hands struggling to remain locked together. I was swarmed by old classmates, exchanging hugs and other pleasantries, the loud music making it difficult to think straight, let alone attempt to engage in a normal conversation. And somewhere between all of the chaos, I found myself detached from my posse and completely alone in the entryway.

The only lights in the building could be found near the restrooms in the back and those emitted from the obnoxious lighting machine flashing on and off in front of the DJ booth. Spotting the girls was going to be a hopeless task. Most of the girls on the dance floor had ears on their heads, resembling some sort of wild animal, my drunken eyes unable to differentiate the silhouettes from one another. The dancing mob was covered in a haze of fog from machines located in each corner of the room, making the search for my fellow forest dwellers futile. *Why did we have to wear such skimpy costumes? Why did no one think to wear something with pockets so we could at least have our phones?*

"You can't hide that curly hair from me, Miss Thang!"

There, emerging from the crowd, was an extremely good-looking boy dressed in nothing but cheetah print boxer briefs and ears resting on top of his black hair, which was pulled back into a flawless bun.

"Oh my God, Andy!"

We threw our arms around one another, my heart exploding through my chest.

"Go figure. You're dressed like a wild animal, too. I thought I was being original."

He kissed my nose. "I'm not a *wild* animal. I'm a *party* animal. Get it?"

I laughed. "Very clever. That black eyeliner does wonders for your eyes. You should wear it more often."

He slapped my shoulder. "You bitch. I look this fabulous all of the time. You must've just forgotten that down in the land of beautiful people."

The truth was, I didn't think I'd be seeing my once-upon-a-time best friend because he'd never returned any of my calls. And remembering that made my happiness dissipate slightly.

"Roxanne Vaughn, tell me what the fuck you're doing in Rohnert Park."

I slapped his oiled chest. "Maybe if you answered your phone every once in a while, you would know."

"Well, I've actually been a little preoccupied."

"What the hell has taken up so much of your time that you've been such a crappy f—"

Another good-looking boy with blonde hair and soft facial features rested his hand on Andrew's back and planted a kiss on his cheek. Andrew smiled and winked at me.

I raised an eyebrow. "Oh, I know that look," I cooed. "Andrew, my dear, are you in love?"

Although dark, I swore I could see him blushing. "Roxy, this is my *boyfriend*, Allen. Allen, this is my best friend, Roxy."

"Thank God," Allen teased in a high-pitched voice. "I was beginning to think you were cheating on me with a woman. I can't be dating a lesbian."

I giggled. *Allen and Andy. How adorable is that?* "Boyfriends, huh? Allen, you must be something very special. That is a word I *never* thought I'd hear come out of this one's mouth."

He shrugged. "Initially, we both just wanted to be fuck buddies. But then we developed feels. Who would've thought?"

"I'm happy for you, Andy. Even if hell must've officially frozen over."

Andrew laughed. "You whore. It was great seeing your beautiful face. Let's have lunch this weekend and catch up when we're not completely shitfaced."

*I can't believe it. I'm gone for one summer and Andrew falls in love. What else am I gonna miss? Why didn't he text me? Has he already found a new best friend?* I sighed as the two lovers made their way back to the dance floor, and wobbled my way back to the short wall that separated the dancing area from the entryway. My vision was beginning to tilt sideways as the music throbbed against my eardrums. Unfortunately, the alcohol hadn't been strong enough to smother the dread that was replacing the lack of dinner in my stomach. *Don't panic. There's no reason to panic. If Andy could spot you without even knowing you were here, then you can find the girls.* I stared at the entrance, hoping to recognize someone that walked through the threshold. I glanced over my shoulder wondering how I should begin the hunt for my crew. *I could probably find them easier in the strobe lights, but I'd wind up dancing with some creep.*

I leaned my elbows atop the small wall and tapped my toes to the beat of the music. *What if they're not even looking for me? What if they're like Andy? What if they don't care about me anymore? They're just doing this to be nice because I'm the one who asked if I could come visit. I'm the one who asked if I could stay at the house we were supposed to live in together. I'm the one who moved away.* Closing my eyes, I swayed a little, allowing the tequila to eat away any remaining panic streaming through my blood. *Don't think like that. These girls are your best friends. I'm sure they're just as worried as you are.* When I opened my eyes, however, I spotted one of the last people I wanted to see in Rohnert Park. She was dressed in a Ninja Turtle costume and appeared obnoxiously wasted.

"Hey Claire!" I shouted over the music.

She appeared confused at first—as if she was staring at a walking corpse—finally registering the familiarity of my hair and face. "Oh my God, Roxy!" We awkwardly hugged over the top of the small wall, the concrete pushing against my hipbones. "What're you doing here?"

"Shannon, Lizzy and Amber invited me up for the dance. My birthday's tomorrow, so they thought this would be a fun way to celebrate. I can't believe I'm already gonna be twenty-one." I kept the smile on my face even though the lie suddenly saddened me. *I doubt they would've even remembered to ask.*

Claire nodded, a small frown tugging at her dimples. "That sounds fun! How are the girls? I haven't heard from them since—"

"Roxanne? Is that you?"

My heart short-circuited when that all-too-familiar, deep, sexy voice touched my ears. Lamont hurdled over the wall in one long stride, ignored Claire's greetings and lifted me into a hug. I wrapped my legs around him, squeezing my thighs tight, my miniskirt riding up my butt. His lips easily found mine, reigniting the chemistry I tried so hard to stifle over summer. The tantalizing mixture of Copenhagen and beer mingled with my taste buds. *Why did I leave this? Why did I think I'd find something better with Zach?*

"I missed you," he whispered into my lips. "What the fuck are you doing here? Is it really you?"

"I'm here with the girls, but I lost them." My blood rushed straight to my head. "I've missed you, too. I can't believe you found me."

"Me neither. Just walked in. It's so fucking good to see you. To feel you."

I smiled, too drunk and far too happy. "How did you see me? My curls are hidden, for once."

"I still saw them sticking out of that hood." He chuckled against my cheek. "I heard someone yell your name. I didn't believe it at first. But here you fucking are." He placed me back on the ground, but his hands remained firm on my waist. "Why didn't you tell me you were gonna be here?"

My insides melted around my dancing heart. "I didn't think you wanted anything to do with me."

"Is that a joke?"

*Considering we don't talk anymore? No.* "Well, it's been months—"

He silenced me with his lips. "How about we forget all of that? You're here now. Right fucking in front of me."

"I missed you. So much," I whispered, the heat from his mouth lighting the fire inside of me once again.

Lamont spun me around and pushed me through the crowd of students bumping and grinding on the massive dance floor. "You gonna be with me all night?"

Shivers tingled my bones. *I would stay with you forever if I could. If you'd let me.* "I don't see why not. Think you can keep up with me?"

He smacked my bottom and kissed my cheek. "Push our way to the front."

"Follow my lead. I'll get us to the center." I latched my hand around his wrist and fought my way through drunk and sweaty individuals trying to elbow me away from them. Had I been sober, I probably would've had a panic attack, the lack of oxygen usually strangling me with claustrophobia. "No bracelet, huh?" I shouted behind me.

"It didn't match my costume."

I tried not to feel bitter. *I know you don't have it anymore. There's no point hiding the truth.* "Yeah, right. Because black doesn't match your camouflage bandana and your black face paint."

He laughed, clearly not catching my sarcasm. *It doesn't matter. It's just a stupid piece of rubber anyway.*

When we made it close enough to the DJ to potentially make me deaf, I lost complete control of my emotions. I pressed my butt against Lamont, relishing in the rhythm of our bodies meshing perfectly together. Before I began drinking at the girls' house, I'd told them I was one hundred percent over his games and proclaimed my hate for him. He'd hurt me too badly on his birthday and followed that up with spiteful text messages when I returned home. I promised myself I wouldn't be an idiot all over again. And yet, here I was.

I blinked. *What're you doing? This can't happen. You're happy with Zach. Don't ruin your relationship all over again. There's nothing special between you and Lamont anymore.* Lamont, however, was making that very difficult to believe. He spun me around to face him, shifting our bodies so that my pelvis made direct contact with his, and connected his face to mine, daring my tongue to engage in a romantic cha cha amidst all of the lust swirling around us. I wanted to blame the feelings rushing through my soul on the tequila, but something about our bodies moving together felt right. I wrapped my arms behind his neck, used my hips to put pressure on his lower half, parted my lips and welcomed the kiss I'd missed for the last five months. I felt him grow hard against my leg, a sensual sensation spreading through my lower stomach. *Don't do this. Don't let him do this. You know he doesn't care. He didn't contact you all summer. He's looking for the easy lay.* As my knees shook, I realized I needed to take control of the situation. I was digging myself into a hole and I was struggling to put the shovel down. Being beside him was too comfortable; it felt as if the summer had never happened and we were in love once again.

"You know, you'd be my girlfriend if you lived here," he whispered.

The dance floor swirled. "Wh—what did you just say to me?"

He smirked. "Oh, nothing."

"Oh, no no no," I said, grabbing his chin. I forced him to look at me—to *really* look at me. I needed to know if he was telling the truth. "I do believe I heard the words 'you' and 'girlfriend' in the same sentence. Did my ears deceive me?"

He pulled me into his arms, my legs dangling uselessly beneath me. "You know how I feel about you. That hasn't changed."

Instead of waiting for a response, he gave me one sweet kiss, placed me on the ground and started dancing again. *Girlfriend. I'd be his girlfriend.* The small flame of hope burned brightly as it soaked up the alcohol in my system. *Don't overanalyze. Be reasonable. You live in San Diego now. You're both drunk.*

"Are you happy?"

I stopped dancing and hugged myself, flashbacks to the night he gave me the necklace plaguing my brain. *Lamont, we can't go over this again. It doesn't matter anymore. It's too late.*

He embraced me from behind, intertwined his fingers with mine and nibbled on my earlobe. "Roxy, are you happy without me?"

The alcohol smashed all logic straight into a brick wall. I didn't want to talk anymore. I didn't want to shed any more tears. So, instead of answering, I rested my cheek against his and swayed to a slower beat, ignoring the music and the people around us. *This is where I belong. Here, with you, I'm happy.*

#

HIS HEADBOARD TAPPED against the wall like a hammer ramming a dull nail through the deepest layer of my heart. My skirt was around my stomach, my leg warmers now adorning my ankles. The camouflage face paint Lamont had smeared on his face now covered my arms, chest, cheeks, lips and thighs—evidence that I'd succumbed to temptation.

As his moans pierced my ringing ears, my body began to tremble, my head beginning to feel heavy, my fingers going numb. I wasn't as drunk as I was at the dance, and the severity of the situation hit me like a wrecking ball. "Lamont, I need to stop."

He froze mid-thrust. "What?"

I pushed at his shoulders until he reluctantly moved off of me. "I can't."

My skin felt charred, my stomach grumbled unpleasantly, and I was having difficult breathing. *I can't do this anymore. I love Zach. I don't want to hurt him.* I stood up, straightened my skirt and steadied myself against his dresser, fumbling through the darkness for my wolf hood.

"What're you doing? You're supposed to spend the night."

I swallowed back the urge to stroke his cheek and apologize. "Lamont, I can't do this. You and me? We just end up hurting everyone in the end. You have nothing to lose, but I do. We've never been given the chance to be together. Don't you think there's a reason for that?"

He glared through the moonlight. "That's not fair. You've never given me that chance."

"Even if I did, it wouldn't matter."

That time, I saw straight through those beautiful brown eyes that were usually the barriers for his soul. "Why's that?"

"Because I love you." I walked to the door and put my hand on the knob. *Stay strong. Don't let him know you're hurting. Don't let him see you cry.* "But you don't love me. And even if you did, you'd never admit it. And I need to be with someone who has the capacity to love. I'm more than just sex."

He turned away, fiddling with the sheet beneath him. "Why do you always do this? You know I have a hard time talking about this kind of stuff, but that doesn't mean I don't care about you."

I turned the knob, knowing if I didn't walk away now, I'd completely break down in front of him. "You only want me when you can't have me. I'm more than just a mouse for you to chase when you're lonely. I'm sorry, Lamont. But you and me? We're done. I've said this to myself a million times, and every time I've come running back to you with open arms. I can't do this anymore. I love you, but I can't."

I left before he could say anything, closing the door on our relationship with a soft click.

CAT AND MOUSE

# Chapter Fifteen

"DON'T FORGET THAT your final poetry pieces are due next week. Please sign up on Web Portal for your conference time. We will discuss all the work you've done this semester and see where your grade stands. Don't be late! Each meeting is only fifteen minutes."

Jocelyn Palmer had quickly become my favorite professor despite the tremendous workload she assigned and the unreachable standards she set for her essays. I'd spend many a night crying because of the unforgiving red marks branded into my papers, but spent many more absorbing her critiques in an attempt to prove that I was, in fact, a poet.

The students began packing up their bags, dropping off the pop quiz Professor Palmer had given at the end of class on her desk. I took my time, shoving each notebook into my backpack, a loose-leaf falling out of my hand and onto the floor. Before I could reach out and grab it, five perfectly manicured fingers snatched it up.

I swallowed, suddenly unable to moisten the inside of my mouth. "H—hi— Prof—Professor Palmer."

Her eyes scanned the paper left to right before she held it out to me, her silver acrylics sparkling. "Ms. Vaughn, have you considered joining the MFA program here?"

I flushed. "Yes, Ma'am. I hope to apply next fall."

"The deadline every year is December 31ˢᵗ. Start writing. The guidelines are listed online."

Smashing the paper into my backpack, I nodded mutely.

She smiled. "That—on that paper—didn't look like poetry to me."

I couldn't believe how anxious this woman made me feel. "It's a short story."

She tapped her toe on the ground three times, her thumb and forefinger resting on her chin. "I want you to do something different for me. Instead of writing four poems for the final, I want you finish that short story of yours and turn it into me."

"But, Professor, I don't write fiction. I'm a poet."

She nodded, her blonde curls bouncing off her shoulders. "And yet, only two semesters ago, you were a doctor."

My lips formed a straight line, the stubborn half of me wanting to argue, the logical half of me understanding what she was getting at.

"Just do me a favor and do what I say, otherwise, I'll give you a failing grade."

"What?" My heart plummeted. "Can you do that?"

Professor Palmer laughed. It was loud. It was sincere. It made me feel like an idiot. "I'm the professor. I make the rules in this classroom."

I nodded, defeated. "So, one short story."

She smiled, her big, white teeth beautiful, yet oddly scary. She was an amazing educator, but she made me feel like a child all over again. "I'll see you in my office next week."

#

"I DON'T KNOW if I should hold her. What if I drop her? What if she cries? What if she poops? What if she throws up? I'm not equipped to handle this kind of stuff."

Lucy laughed. "Since when did you become such a pussy?"

"Are you allowed to talk like that in front of the baby?"

Another laugh, the gorgeous, pink child bouncing happily in my sister's arms. "I'll have to start watching my language very soon. Their little brains turn into sponges."

I was at Roger and Lucy's house for the weekend. Roger out of town—another conference with some outrageous pharmaceutical company trying to sell him their latest Botox product—and Lucy requested that I keep her company for a few days so she could get some sleep.

"I'm being serious. Babies make me nervous. So much could go wrong."

"If Roger and I can keep this baby alive and healthy for two and a half months, you can handle her for a few hours right now. This'll be good practice for the rest of the weekend."

I fiddled with Hannah's rattle. "Can't I do something else for you? Cook your food? Grocery shopping? Buy you new clothes? Anything?"

Lucy held her arms out, Hannah's little legs chubby beneath her diaper. "I. Need. Sleep. I'm only asking you for three hours. There are bottles of breast milk in the fridge. She should nap for at least an hour. Change her if she needs it. You owe me."

"I don't know how to change a baby. Can you show me?"

314

"It's not that hard. Just wipe front to back. Haven't you seen the movies?"

I sighed. "Lucy, I'm being serious."

She placed one hand on her hips, the baby resting comfortably on her forearm. "So am I. No better way to learn than through trial and error."

I hesitantly grabbed the baby, treating her like a fragile glass statue. "This is just ridiculous. What on earth do I owe you for?"

"If it weren't for me, you and Sherlock would be in a cardboard box eating cockroaches in some dirty alleyway."

Hannah smiled toothlessly, her blue eyes friendly. I returned the gesture despite my uncertainty. "That's a low blow, bitch."

Lucy produced a fake gasp. "How dare you cuss in front of my innocent angel?"

I cradled Hannah in my arms and poked her nose, which resulted in a giggle. "If she cries, I'm waking you up."

"You're a natural. If anything, this'll teach you to always wear a condom."

"Can we not have the condom conversation again?"

She shrugged. "Just saying. Have fun! I'll have my alarm go off in three hours. Four, tops. I promise."

I sat on the couch and held up the soft Eeyore blanket-stuffed animal combination I gave Hannah the last time I visited. She snuggled it beneath her chin and promptly closed her eyes, her chest rising up and down rhythmically. My back muscles finally relaxed. "You really are a pretty little thing," I cooed. "Don't tell my parents I said anything, but I hope you've got some of those rebel genes in you, just like me."

#

THE DAY REMINDED me why I'd decided to date Zach in the first place—more than that, it helped me remember why we initially fell in love. Maybe it was the enchanting environment that had me mesmerized, maybe it was the fact that we'd officially been together for one year, but it was the happiest I'd felt in a long time. Zach and I held hands while walking down Main Street, screamed on roller coasters, stood in line to take pictures with costumed characters and consumed too many snack foods with high sugar contents. Zach looked handsome bathed in the Anaheim sunlight and his kisses oozed the love I'd craved since my return to San Diego. Whenever I gazed at him, my heart swelled to a point where it made my chest hurt. *This is what love should feel like. No games. No back and forth. No chasing.*

As the day wound down and the moon lifted into the sky, Zach and I made our way to the front of Sleeping Beauty's castle. The park was decorated for Christmas with snowflake silhouettes moving across the castle's exterior, pink, blue and white lights swirling together as more people filed onto the street to catch the firework extravaganza.

A stuffed Winnie the Pooh was squeezed between my ribs and bicep, a princess crown atop my head, and my cheek rested against Zach's shoulder as "oohs" and "awws" erupted from the crowd. Fireworks brightened up the sky, music blaring from surrounding speakers, lights dangling from tree branches to resemble a winter wonderland.

"This is beautiful," I whispered, my eyes reflecting the hearts exploding above me.

Zach kissed my temple. "You're beautiful."

I smiled up at him and softly touched my lips to his. "Happy Anniversary, Zach. Thank you for a wonderful day."

We regarded the fireworks together, fake snow beginning to fall from the sky around us. I held my arms wide to relish in the moment, Winnie the Pooh slipping from my side. As it hit the ground, Zach grabbed a hold of my right hand and pulled me around to face him.

"Roxanne," he began seriously. "This last year has been the highlight of my life. We've been through some crazy shit—good and bad—but I've never once doubted my feelings for you. The day I pulled away from you all those years ago was the day I realized my true love for you. I was young and terrified. Not one day passed without me thinking about the mistake I'd made by pushing you away. I'm so happy you gave me a second chance to prove my love to you—to show you how much I really do adore you." He reached into the backpack he'd been sporting all day. "Roxanne, Little Woman," he cooed before dropping to one knee beside the plush Winnie the Pooh.

Every muscle and nerve ending in my body tensed. "Zach? What're you doing?"

"I want to spend the rest of my life by your side. I don't want to risk losing you again. You're the best thing that's ever happened to me. I will never love anybody as much as I love you. You're the one. You're who I want to spend my life with." He opened the small black box. "Will you marry me?"

I stared at the itty-bitty diamond, mouth agape. The snowflakes stuck to my hair, my sweatshirt, Zach's ball cap and his flushed cheeks. *A proposal?* The diamond sparkled beneath the white lights hanging from the branches above us.

*Stop standing there like an idiot. Say yes. Prove to him that you love him—prove to yourself that you're not in love with Lamont. You owe this to him. You love him. He loves you. Take a chance. Say yes.*

"Okay," I croaked, tears beginning to fall with the snowflakes now piling around my shoes. "Yes, Zachary Cameron. Yes."

He smiled, his big green eyes making my heart float straight into the clouds.

"I knew you were the one from the day I met you," he said earnestly, sliding the ring over my knuckle. "I'll never stop loving you."

We embraced while people around us whistled and clapped. I cried into Zach's neck, the ring suddenly weighing my hand down. *Be happy. You're in love. What could be better?* My dimples crinkled when Zach kissed my forehead. *You're gonna marry a guy that will do anything for you—that makes you feel like a princess. He loves you for who you. He doesn't play games. He's graduating from college with two degrees. He applied to get into the credential program. He has a job. He's trying to make something of himself. He has aspirations. You won't have to worry about being alone anymore. He'll always love you.* I looked at the ring over Zach's shoulder and sobbed, Zach mistaking my tears of uncertainty for tears of joy. *I hope I'm not making the biggest mistake of my life.*

\#

STILL TWIRLING AMIDST cloud nine after announcing my engagement to my friends and family, I believed nothing could bring me down. Initially, I'd been scared to tell everyone, but upon waking up the morning after Zach put the ring on my finger, I cuddled my pillows happily. I was engaged to my best friend, and despite my fears that I didn't love Zach enough to accept a proposal, I knew that Zach would make a very doting husband.

I was amazed someone found me loveable enough to be their future wife.

Even my parents' disappointment and constant passive aggressiveness didn't crush my spirit. Lucy was against marrying Zach until I asked her to be my Maid of Honor—her scream scaring the baby and Roger, who were both napping at the time. Jasmine and Lacie agreed to be my bridesmaids, the idea of dressing up and day drinking more appealing than the idea of two people vowing to be together through better or worse. The wedding wouldn't happen until after graduation, leaving me plenty of time to focus on work, school and caring for my furry little babies. I was finally happy.

I'd mistakenly put my guard down.

On a beautiful, January afternoon where birds were chirping outside my window, I locked Sherlock in my bedroom and walked into the garage. Molly, who had begun to grow grey hairs around her muzzle and who now slept for a vast majority of the day, looked up at me with her big brown eyes, her tail weakly moving up and down. My parents were in the garage on their hands and knees, petting Molly's fur. Panicked, I threw Molly's leash to the ground and collapsed next to my dog—my best friend. She grunted as she tried to shift toward me.

"What happened?" I managed to ask, my hands rubbing Molly's velvety ears.

"She can't stand." Big goopy tears streamed down my mother's cheekbones smearing her usually flawless makeup. "Your dad found her in the backyard. He kept calling her name, coaxing her to eat dinner—you know how much she loves food—but she wouldn't move."

I looked at my dad and noticed the tears present in his big, blue eyes that rested beneath brown eyebrows peppered with grey. I'd never seen him cry.

"How did she get here, then?"

My dad sniffled. "I carried her."

"So—so—she—" My body hurt. My heart fell into my stomach. My eyes leaked with despair.

My mom and dad glanced at one another before nodding, heads hanging low. "She's immobile."

I buried my face into Molly's side and allowed the sadness to rack my body. "How is this happening? Why is this happening? She was *fine* this morning! She can get up. She's just tired. Right Molly? You're just tired."

My mom touched my back. "Sweetie, she's old. She's spent her whole life walking up and down the stairs to go to bed. And then those big hills in the backyard that she loved so much. Her hips are old. These things happen."

My tears rolled into Molly's coarse fur. "No. She's not old enough, yet. This isn't fair. She's fine. She has to be fine."

My dad kissed the top of my head. "She's old and her hips are bad," he repeated after my mother. "This was bound to happen sooner or later. We're just glad you were home for it and not away at school."

I lay down fully on the dirty garage floor while my parents called the Humane Society to make arrangements. "I'm so sorry, Molly," I whispered. Her tail thumped at the sound of her name. "I'm so, so, so, so sorry. I don't know how to help you. I don't know how to make you better." She licked my nose when I kissed her. "You're my best friend in the whole wide world. I don't know what I would've done without you. I wish there was something I could do." She was scared—I could see it in her eyes—but she remained calm. I knew then, the best thing I could do was let her know just how loved she was and how she always would be loved no matter where she was. "Who's my pretty girl? The best puppy a girl could've asked for." She whined and rested her chin on the ground. "I love you, Molly. I'm not ready for you to leave me yet. Who's gonna stay up listening to me cry at night? Who's gonna wake me up with sloppy kisses? Who's gonna lay at my feet when I'm watching TV? Who's gonna keep Sherlock company? Who's gonna save me from all of the tough stuff I'm supposed to go through? You're my best friend. You're not allowed to leave yet." She breathed heavily through her nostrils, my tears landing atop her furry nose. "Oh, Molly," I sobbed. "I'm gonna miss you."

When my parents drove off with her in the backseat of the car, I sat on the couch in the living room, Sherlock wrapped in my arms, and continued to cry. Seeking the comfort and love of my peers, Sherlock scratching at my arms from impatience, I posted the news alongside a picture of Molly when she was just a puppy on Facebook. The night passed slowly, my heart broken, my soul bruised. I waited for five people to text me—to contact me in any way, shape or form—to tell me they were sorry for my loss. That they wished they could be here to give me a hug and wipe away my tears.

But no comforting words came. Not for a day. Not for a week. Not for a month. Never.

Zach, Lacie, Luke and Jasmine held me as I cried.

Amber, Shannon, Elizabeth, Andrew and Lamont did nothing.

They didn't say one single word. Didn't comment on the picture. Didn't text. Didn't call. Didn't care.

And that was all I needed to realize that such an important chapter in my life was over.

#

WHEN WE LANDED in Las Vegas early Friday morning, Lacie, Jasmine and I lugged our suitcases into a cab and stared out the window, dazed, as all of the hotels on the strip crawled by. The traffic was bad, bumper to bumper for most of the drive, but none of us minded. We still couldn't believe we were here.

It was time to celebrate Lacie's twenty-first birthday, and time to find out if these two girls had accepted me as one of their best friends.

"Let's get dressed and start drinking. The pool parties are already raging," Lacie said, throwing her stuff on the bed closest to the window.

I jumped onto the other bed and threw my hands behind my head, legs stretched out wide. "Well, I claim this one, ladies. All for myself. Sorry I'm not sorry."

Jasmine playfully slapped my shin. "You can have it. Lacie and I will cuddle."

Lacie pulled off her tank top and began rummaging through her suitcase for a bathing suit. "No, we will not cuddle. Keep your shit on your side of the bed. I'll elbow the shit out of you."

Jasmine snorted. "Does being twenty-one entitle you to be a bitch?"

Lacie's hair was promptly tossed up into a messy bun. "No, but it's my birthday and I can be a bitch if I want to. Roxy, if I have the chance for birthday sex, Jazz is sleeping with you."

I shook my head. "Wrong. I'll in the bathtub. Less audible in there."

"Hurry the fuck up and get dressed," Lacie ordered. "We're missing precious tanning time."

"We're in the middle of Satan's scrotum," I replied, fluffing my pillow. "I wouldn't worry about the lack of sun. Enjoy the air conditioning while you can."

The girls laughed, Lacie already in her pool attire, Jasmine sifting through her luggage. "Should we pregame?" She produced a pink bottle of champagne and held it up to her bronzed cheek. "Drinks are expensive around here."

"That's why you find boys to buy that shit for you."

My diamond ring stuck to the hem of my comforter, reminding me of the anchor weighing me down back in San Diego. "Nobody'll buy me drinks as long as this thing is on my finger."

"Right. Like anybody can see it."

I glanced down at my lap quietly as Lacie slapped Jasmine's shoulder. "Invest in a filter. You can't just say shit like that."

"What?" Jasmine argued. "That thing's fucking tiny. He could definitely afford something more with that load of grant money he got for school."

That hit a soft spot. Zach had been stingy with his *free* money while I worked hard and never received anything from the government, only to be sitting on a pile of loans the size of Texas—especially because my parents refused to help me with anything.

At my false attempt to chuckle, Lacie sat down and placed her hand on my thigh. "Sweetie, you have to remember, we're in Vegas."

"I know that. But I can't mess around. There's a ring on my finger."

"If you can even call that a ring," Jasmine mumbled.

320

Lacie sighed, grabbed my hand and slipped the small, silver band off my finger. "And now there's not. As easy as that."

"I can't—I don't know—" I bit my lip, guilt already consuming me.

Lacie gave me the ring and patted my forearm. "You're forgetting the golden rule."

I stared blankly.

"What happens in Vegas, *stays* in Vegas."

#

WHEN I FIRST purchased the twenty-one-dollar Margarita at the busy pool bar, I'd complained. Although incredibly potent, I couldn't help but feel the drink was incredibly overpriced. The girls laughed when we clicked the pink cups together, celebrating our first of, hopefully, many trips to Sin City.

"These better get us plastered, or I'ma be upset. I had to work hard for this money," I said, puckering when the sourness of the lime touched my tongue.

"Just enjoy it. You're on vacation. We promise you'll get drunk, so stop doubting us," Jasmine said, sipping her own pina colada.

Lacie nodded. "We'll just drink these and then go talk to some boys. Get some courage."

Although skeptical at first, due to the desert heat and my extreme thirst, I finished my drink quicker than what would be considered responsible.

And I happily entered the land of total inebriation.

Jasmine, Lacie and I eagerly waded into the cool, germ infested water. The two girls exposed their bodies beneath skimpy bikinis while I half hid behind a black one-piece. I may have changed while up in Sonoma, but some of my old self-consciousness had begun to plague me once again. I returned to wearing my plain clothes, only bringing out my revealing clothes when I'd already consumed alcohol. I even noticed that I was the only girl at the pool with my hair in a ponytail. My curls would frizz into a jumbled mess if I let them play freely in the water, every other female letting their straight blonde, brown and red hair mock me as if I wasn't good enough to join some exclusive beautiful hair club.

Jasmine and Lacie had actually given me crap about it in the hotel room wondering if I even owned a bikini. After confirming that I didn't live under a rock so yes, I did have normal twenty-year-old girl clothes, I admitted I felt more comfortable in a one-piece.

They, on the other hand, had no problem using their bodies to trick boys into buying them shots of vodka, rum and tequila. They flirted left and right, laughing at things I didn't find funny and smiling coyly whenever someone new caught their attention. They were good friends though—they didn't leave me out, making sure the boys brought back three shots instead of two. I appreciated the gesture and took the shots happily, feeling as if they'd accepted me into their two-woman wolfpack.

As the day wore on, I forgot about the diamond ring sitting on the bed-side table and instead focused on the freedom I hadn't experienced in a long time. I didn't have to worry about impressing anybody. I was able to just be me with my two best girlfriends. I bought myself a margarita refill and watched the spectacle unravel before me: men chasing women, women chasing men. I knew the games they were playing, and I was thankful I didn't have to partake in the madness anymore.

It was sad, yet, extremely beautiful.

I told myself to write about it later. *Why is it that people are so obsessed with playing cat and mouse? What happened to love and stability?*

"You alright?" Lacie slurred, resting her arms behind her on the cement.

I sipped from my drink and smiled, the familiar buzz of confidence I often had in Rohnert Park overwhelming me. I stared at the pool around me, smiling at boys who made eye-contact with me, and closed my eyes, soaking in the warmth of the sun. Freedom had never felt so good. "I'm fucking fantastic. In fact, why don't we find some more boys? I think it's time for another birthday shot."

The girls cheered, shimmying their breasts from left to right, a bachelor party to our left whistling at us. I held my drink up in the direction of the boys and nodded my head, making sure to flash them my naked left hand in the process.

#

I NEARLY DROPPED the frozen margarita in my hand all over my brand-new lime green high-heels. Luckily, my brain reacted faster than my heart. My fingers tightened around the plastic cup, my shoulders rose beside my chin, and my hips swished from one side to the next, nearly dislocating my lower spine.

"Lacie, Jazz," I said, my voice barely loud enough to hear over the traffic.

They tightened to my sides, their high-heels clacking on the cement in tune with mine.

"What's wrong?" Lacie asked.

"Straight ahead."

Their eyes followed my shaking, pointed finger. Jasmine squinted. "Is that—"

"Dude," Lacie laughed. "There's no fucking way."

"That's him," I whispered."

When recognition lit up his face, the city slowed—the cars stopped honking, their lights leaving red trails midair; the sloppy drunks stumbled, their drinks spilling and hovering just above the ground; promoters' fliers left their hands and flew through the wind at a snail's pace.

*Why is he here of all places?*

"Should we turn around?" Jasmine asked.

I shook my head. "We already made eye contact. I have to say hi."

"What happens in Vegas," Lacie taunted, her elbow digging into my ribs.

Swiftly, before either Lacie or Jasmine could notice, I slipped the ring off my finger and held it between my palm and margarita. I'd put it back on my finger after having a complete melt down the night prior. A combination of too much mixed liquor and sun-exposure at the pool that day left me crying in the bathroom while the girls rallied in the hotel bar that night. Although I hadn't kissed any of the bachelor party boys like Jasmine and Lacie had, I'd let one of them hold me behind the pool waterfall, his body warm against mine. And it had been the groom. The man who was to be married in two days' time.

The guilt was too much for me, and after waking up the following morning, I'd almost told the girls I would just stay in the hotel while they continued their drinking escapades. And then I remembered it was selfish to worry about my own issues when we were in Las Vegas for Lacie's birthday. This was my chance to connect with these girls, and I didn't want to blow it because my conscience reminded me what a terrible person I could be, especially when drinking.

So, here I was, on the way to a club where Lacie was guaranteed a free birthday drink instead of watching cable television in the hotel room.

I took a deep breath. "Be nice to him, please."

"Don't mention his penis," Lacie hissed to Jasmine, the two of them laughing hysterically.

My tall, dark and handsome was here. In Las Vegas. Standing in front of me. "Lamont!" I squealed, arms out wide. "What brings you to Sin City?"

He swept me into a hug, his hands wandering over my skin-tight, off the shoulder, quarter-sleeve, silver dress. "There's no fucking way you're real. I must be hallucinating."

I stepped back to admire the handsome boy I'd convinced myself I didn't love anymore. My unsteady hands, rapid heartbeat and perspiration beneath my bra proved otherwise. "You look great." And in his dark blue button-up, black pants and white Nike's, I wasn't lying. Even the small amount of scruff on his upper lip and chin was endearing. "Oh—uh—these are my best friends, Lacie and Jasmine."

They exchanged uncomfortable hugs before Lamont gestured to his entourage. "Roxanne, you remember Chris and Michael."

I nodded and awkwardly hugged the two boys who were considered Lamont's most reliable wingmen. I believed they both hated me because I was the relationship type and that was poisonous for their single best friend. Besides, I didn't like them much either. Michael was greasy looking. Black hair, black eyes, pale skin and a constant sneer stamped on his face. Chris was still cute, but the way he'd wanted to use Claire solely for sex had made him less attractive to me, even if I didn't particularly like her. He glared at me. *Look, bud, I didn't plan on running into you guys. Don't give me that look.*

"We're here for Chris's birthday. Fucker's finally twenty-one," Lamont said. "We're doing it right."

I chuckled. "You say that as if you've been twenty-one for years. You just turned legal drinking age a month ago."

"It's Lacie's birthday too!" Jasmine announced.

"We're birthday twins!" Lacie added.

The boys stared.

"Why don't we go somewhere and grab some drinks?" I asked, hoping to ease the tension.

Lamont nodded at me. "Where at?"

"We're going to the Cosmo," Jasmine said. "If you want to come, that's fine."

The ring was burning a circular brand into my palm. Shoving the straw into my mouth, I somehow managed to grab the ring and store it in the side of my bra without anyone being the wiser.

On the walk across the strip, Lamont wouldn't leave my side. Our hands brushed together more than once, and I prayed my makeup would conceal my obvious delight. His boys were scouting their potential hookups while my girls became engrossed in planning how to score free drinks from unsuspecting boys at the club. I secretly hoped that Lamont would offer to buy me a drink as soon as we stepped through the club doors. I didn't go out much, and when I did, I was standoffish. I'd never had someone buy me a drink, and the thought of Lamont being the first was weirdly exhilarating.

Being around him was dangerous, however. I knew he was toxic, and I knew I couldn't control my emotions around him. The smart thing to do would've been to run away. Instead, I let my heart do the talking. When he turned toward me, not hesitating to plant one of the most delicious kisses I've ever tasted on my lips, I grew giddy, believing more than anything that he and I running into one another on the strip was fate.

Someone somewhere was trying to tell me something.

I kissed Lamont back, wondering if maybe this was a test—was I supposed to be with Zach? Or Lamont? At that point, it seemed as if Lamont was the one for me.

Yet, as the night progressed, my mood plummeted fifty thousand leagues under the concrete.

We arrived at the Cosmopolitan hotel with the intention of going into Marquee nightclub, only to be distracted by a live band and fancy bar one floor beneath the club's entrance. I'd purchased each of the boys a glass of bourbon in an attempt to ease any remaining tension between the group, and in the hope that Lamont might offer to buy me a drink as well. Jasmine and Lacie didn't help the situation. They sat away from the boys with their arms crossed and scowls plastered on their faces. I'd tried to usher them over to the group but was promptly rejected.

I walked toward them and asked if everything was all right.

"What the fuck, Roxy? We're meeting up with a group of people in the club. They have a table and bottle service. What's the hold up?" Jasmine snapped.

"Lamont says they're waiting for a friend."

"Then they can meet us inside," Lacie said, her tone pissy.

I groaned. "We can't leave them. It'd be rude. Can't we wait, like, ten more minutes?"

"It's my birthday. What do they matter? You're here for me."

*She has a point. Who cares about Lamont?* "Let me just tell—"

"We'll meet you in the club," Jasmine decided. "Text us when you get in."

And with that, the girls left me with three drunk boys and a very heavy heart.

"What's up with them?" Lamont asked when I returned to their small circle.

I shrugged. "They're waiting for us in the club."

"Well, Travis isn't coming. He got caught up gambling or something. He's meeting us back at the hotel."

I tried to hide my frustration. "Then hurry up and drink. We have a club to get into. Bottle service and everything."

"We don't really want to dance," Michael said.

I began to lose my patience, all polite habits flying out the window. "Well, I do. So, it was nice seeing you boys. Happy birthday, Chris."

As I turned to leave, Lamont set his drink down heavily on the wooden table beside his chair and frowned. "You're leaving? Now?"

I glared at him, upset. "You're here with your boys. I'm here with my girls. They don't wanna do the same thing. And I'm not gonna sit here and do nothing."

"Yeah, but—" He stood and grabbed my hands. "We met here. In Vegas. A place where there are millions of people all of the fucking time. You can't just leave me."

*I want to believe it's fate too, but I can't keep doing this to myself. And I care about my friends.* I stared into his big brown eyes. "Yeah, but—"

He silenced me with a kiss, those little sparks I read about in romance novels warming my core. It was strange, though. My body was shaking at his very touch, but my brain was fighting with me—it was telling me to leave. To let him go. To say good-bye. Usually, I would want to make love with him. For the first time since we saw one another outside of that house party at the beginning of sophomore year, I didn't want to bring him to my bed. I wanted to see if he had the capacity to show affection for me outside of the bedroom, in front of his friends, in front of everyone.

I thought of Zach and sighed. *Maybe Lucy was right. Maybe a ring really does make you a different person.* I knew being with Lamont was wrong, and I was tired of making excuses. I didn't want to be the cheating, lying girlfriend again. "Lamont, I'd love to spend more time with you, but I need to be with the girls. It's Lacie's birthday. I wouldn't even be here if it weren't for them."

He looked beyond each of my shoulders. "You mean the girls who ditched you?"

"They didn't ditch me," I said defensively, even though his words stung. "It's your stupid fault they left me in the first place. They're waiting for me in the club. So, if you want to be with me, we have a line to wait in."

We walked up the stairs. I called the girls. No answer.

We waited in line. I called the girls. No answer.

"I can't let you in with white tennis shoes," the bouncer told Lamont. "Black shoes only."

We walked back down the stairs. I called the girls. They answered. "The club was dull. These super cute boys invited us on their party bus and now we're on our way to another club. In Encore."

"You didn't think to tell me that?" I asked.

A short silence. "You're with Lamont."

"I told you guys I was gonna meet up with you in the club. I'm not here to be with him. I'm here to be with you girls."

There were a lot of jumbled noises—music, laughter, traffic—that covered whatever excuses Lacie and Jasmine were making. It was my own fault for believing they would wait for me. When it came to alcohol, those two girls did almost anything to make sure they would get drunk for free. It was my own fault for choosing Lamont over my friends.

I hung up the phone. The Encore hotel was on the opposite side of the strip. I took a deep breath, trying to control my anger and frustration. If I had a hotel key, if I had been smart enough to ask the girls for an extra one, I would've returned to the hotel room and called it a night. "The girls left. So, whatever you guys wanna do, we'll do." I didn't want to be in Las Vegas alone, so I was stuck with them. At least until I found the Flamingo hotel and could wait in the lobby for the girls to return.

Somewhere between Chris and Michael rolling their eyes and Lamont ordering another drink at the bar, I found myself tired and sober. We all wound up taking a long walk—Lamont was obviously blacked out because he wouldn't stop pulling at my dress and wandering off on his own—to gamble away all of the boys' money at Cesar's Palace.

Despite my annoyance at the miscommunication between the girls and myself, walking into the casino put me into better spirits. I had forty dollars in my bra stored beside my ID and my ring, just waiting to be used in a slot machine. Lamont, however, decided this was the opportune moment to glue himself to my side. Initially, it didn't bother me. At least having a guy beside me would deter creeps from approaching me. But when he started questioning the way I was playing virtual poker, my patience began to wear thin.

"Lamont, shut the fuck up."

"Sheesh. As an English major, I thought maybe your vocabulary would've gotten better. Not worse."

"I know what I'm doing," I mumbled.

"Yeah, sure." He was sitting on the stool at the machine beside me, beer in hand, a sneer on his inebriated face. "If you know what you're doing, why do you keep losing?"

"It's because I have bad luck. This isn't a game of skill."

He laughed. "You're betting way too much at one time."

I slammed my hand on the machine. "If you're so good, then why don't you play?"

"Jesus. It's about fucking time." He grabbed my hand, pulled me off the chair and led me to the nearest Blackjack table. "Let me show you how it's done."

"This isn't what I meant. I wasn't done—"

"Will you just relax for one fucking minute?"

I pursed my lips and crossed my arms before sitting on a stool, Lamont taking the seat next to mine. He pulled out a twenty-dollar bill and placed it on the table, joining a game that two other men with large stacks of chips were already playing.

A waitress approached me and asked if I would like a drink. Although hesitant, I decided to order a beer, hoping it would help ease the tension building around my shoulders. I watched as Lamont won hand after infuriating hand. Unless he knew how to count cards—he swore he did, but there was no way in hell he was telling the truth—then I'd come across one lucky man.

"How are you doing that?" I asked, sipping the cool beer.

"Honestly, I was just talking shit earlier." He leaned over and kissed me. "This doesn't usually happen. You must be my Lady Luck."

I snorted, leaning closer to him. "You don't know how wrong you are. I'm like a walking superstition. Incredibly unlucky."

He kissed me again. "Whatever, Lady Luck. You're not allowed to leave my side tonight." He placed his hand on my bare knee. It was warm. It made me melt slightly into the stool. I shook my head. "You're all mine," he added.

After he'd lied to me so many times before, I knew his words really didn't mean anything. His actions always spoke so much louder.

We remained seated at that table until Lamont was up one hundred dollars. He handed me a twenty for helping him win and I walked away in search of a place to find another drink. I tried contacting Jasmine and Lacie, only to discover they were back on the party bus en route to another club. No longer in the mood to do anything but mope, I collapsed onto a stool and stared at the bright screen of the Sex and the City slot machine. Even my favorite television characters couldn't pull me out of my negative mood. I don't know how long I'd been sitting there before Lamont wrapped his arms around my stomach and nibbled on my earlobe.

Try as logic might to fight against emotion, that flame of love rose up through the ashes of cynicism. *I don't fucking get it. How do I still have these feelings for him?*

"What're you doing over here? You made me lose my money."

"Oh, it's my fault?" I laughed, leaned back and allowed myself to enjoy the feel of my head on his chest. "I was looking for a bar but got sidetracked."

"Good idea. Let's get you something to drink."

I smiled. *This is it. He's finally gonna buy me a drink.* We made our way into the Lobby Bar, which was a small dark square with too little seating and too loud of music. As I placed my elbows on the black countertop, Lamont wrapped an arm around my waist and signaled to the bartender with the other.

"What do you want?" Lamont spoke close to my ear.

I smiled shyly at the bartender. "I'll have a margarita."

Lamont nodded. "Make that two."

I glanced up at him, surprised. "I thought you didn't like tequila."

He shrugged. "It reminds me of you. So, I don't mind it so much."

"When did you become so sweet?" I asked, wondering if he was being sincere, or just trying to put the moves on me to get me in bed tonight.

Lamont was so close to my ear, his chin hairs tickled me. "If it'll convince you to come back to Sonoma, I'll buy you a drink every single night."

I hated myself for swooning.

After the bartender provided the requested beverages, he wiped his hands on the towel hanging from his back pocket and nodded. "That'll be twenty-six dollars."

Lamont tensed, all romance and sweet gestures vanishing with two overly priced margaritas. "Are you serious?"

The bartender nodded. "Thirteen bucks each."

Lamont placed a ten-dollar bill on the counter. I waited for him to produce more—he had just won a bunch of money at the Blackjack table—but he simply stared at the bartender as if challenging him to argue. I looked at Lamont, the money, and the bartender before shaking my head. *You've got to be fucking kidding me.* I bit the inside of my cheek, trying to mask my disappointment. I pulled the twenty Lamont gave me out of my boob stash and told the bartender to keep the change. Now, the ring burned against my skin, urging me to walk away. *He doesn't even like you enough to buy you a fucking drink. When are you going to just accept that he doesn't love you and never will?*

329

I attempted to make conversation with Lamont while I sipped my drink, his quickly emptying into his already slumped over body. He answered my questions with as little words as possible, usually trying to silence me with hard kisses, and wandering hands. His frequent concern as to whether or not I was drunk began to get on my last nerve. His request to have me spend the night at his hotel pushed me over the edge.

"I'm not going to Excalibur," I said.

"We can stay in your room, then."

I sipped my drink. "No. We can't."

"Why not?"

"Because we're not sleeping together."

He was baffled. "What?"

"You heard me."

He pointed to my glass. "Then drink more. I want to have sex."

"Lamont, stop. Now. I'm not having sex with you."

"Then why the hell have we been hanging out all night?"

It took an enormous amount of restraint to not throw my margarita at him. To not scream at him. To not cry. To not walk away and pretend I never knew him. My naive little heart felt bruised and battered. *I can't do this anymore.* That was all he still cared about—all he would ever care about when it came to me. "If that's all you want from me, then you're talking to the wrong person. I'm not that kind of girl. I've changed. I'm not an idiot anymore."

"You never gave me the chance to be your boyfriend. It's not like I can ask you to break up with Zach and move to Rohnert Park. Even if I said I loved you, you'd never believe me."

The ring in my bra was now engraving a circular brand into my ribs, my fingers turning white against the glass, my eyes zeroed in on Lamont's, my ears buzzing with the way his admission rolled off his tongue. "Wh—wha—wait. I'm sorry. What did you just say?"

"I love you, Roxanne."

In that instant, I was taken back to Rohnert Park—to the nights when I laid awake dreaming of the day he would finally tell me that he loved me. I never imagined it would take place in Las Vegas. And I never imagined it would be when Lamont was blacked out, eyes rolling back into his head.

But it made sense. He never spoke the truth to me when he was sober.

"I've loved you for a long time," he admitted. "I was too scared to tell you."

I should've thrown my drink at him and told him to back off. My brain screamed at me. This was part of his strategy—his last-ditch effort to get me to have sex with him. He knew my feelings. He knew what it would take to break down my barriers. But my heart urged me to lean forward. To fall into his arms. To break off my engagement. To move back to Rohnert Park and give us a chance. "I love you, too, Lamont," I whispered.

My emotions tumbled one after the other. I fell into his embrace, wishing we were in a different place and a different time. Because even though I still yearned for his love, I'd changed. I was smarter. More mature. I'd learned from my mistakes. *But he loves me. All of this time. He's loved me.*

"Please stay with me tonight."

"I'd love to," I breathed against his lips.

He sighed into me. "Thank God."

I smiled. "You miss me that much, huh?"

"I just can't wait to have sex."

I pushed away from him. He was the only man I could love and hate at the same time. I calmly finished the remains of my drink and wiped my lips on my forearm. *He only wants you because he can't have you. Things will never change. He doesn't love you. And you shouldn't love him.* "Do me a favor and go fuck yourself, Lamont."

I turned on my heel and walked away. I hoped I'd feel empowered from the whole thing. Instead, I felt defeated. For a split second, my heart believed him. And that moment of weakness made me wonder how much I'd actually changed. I hugged my elbows and shivered when I heard Lamont's footsteps following me. I wiped at my tears, sniveling like the silly little fool I was.

No words left his mouth. No apologies. No romance. No nothing.

I watched a tear roll off my nose and drop onto the cement in front of me.

\#

I SAT WITH my back propped against the wall outside my hotel room, Lamont sleeping soundly in my lap. Lacie and Jasmine were on their way back from the club to let me into the room before they continued their drinking escapades. Therefore, I wound up sitting, half asleep, leaning against a wall and pissed off in the hotel hallway, my feet blistered and bleeding, and my stomach grumbling with hunger.

"Lamont?"

Not so much as a twitch.

His phone, however, buzzed on the floor beside his arm. I carefully reached over his shoulder, picked it up off the ground and felt my stomach rise in my throat.

"Lamont? Can you hear me?"

Still nothing. Out cold. *You shouldn't read his text messages. You have no business looking at who he's talking to.* I slid my finger across the screen and clicked on the messages icon. *So what if her name has a heart next to it? You know he doesn't love you.* My thumbs scrolled through the conversation that was taking place between Lamont and some girl named Tiffany. *It was all a ploy to get you into bed.*

And then the light bulb flashed above my head.

Tiffany—with a heart next to her name.

Tiffany—my best friend from Sonoma State.

Tiffany—the one Lamont called the most beautiful girl in the world.

My brain pounded against my temples, hands shaking.

*I wish you were here.* Sent at nine-thirty. About twenty minutes after Lamont first kissed me on the walk to the Cosmopolitan.

*I hope I get to see you sometime this summer.* Sent at nine forty-five. Around the time my girlfriends left me because I didn't want to hurt Lamont's feelings. Because he claimed he wanted to spend time with me. He missed me.

*I can't stop thinking about you.* Sent at eleven-thirty. When we were making our way to Cesar's Palace to gamble together. We held hands for half the walk. He called me his Lady Luck. He wouldn't leave my side.

*I miss you.* Sent only about forty minutes ago. While his head was on my thighs, shortly before he fell into a blacked-out slumber.

I closed the messages, my heart aching all over again. It hurt—it *really* hurt. He only told me he loved me in a final attempt to get me naked. The sincerity in his voice had been faked. The emotion in his eyes was nothing but a figment of my imagination. My stupid false hope that our love existed somewhere in our once connected, now totally separated, universe left me feeling lower than I did when I left Rohnert Park.

I scrolled through the contacts in search of Chris's phone number. I pounded the screen before shaking Lamont's head off my legs. "I hope this carpet gives you face herpes, you lying son of a bitch," I spat, fighting the temptation to rake my nails across his handsome cheeks.

Standing, I placed the phone next to my ear, tapping my heal right next to Lamont's nose. Chris answered with an audible slur, and we fought until Jasmine and Lacie turned down the hallway toward me.

"Just have sex with him," Chris shouted angrily. "You ruined his chance of getting laid by someone who won't fuck with his emotions."

"No. He ruined his chance because he's a fucking idiot. He's blacked-out and passed out on the fucking floor right now. Come pick his lying ass up. I'm not dealing with his bullshit anymore."

"Oh shit," Lacie said. "I don't think I've ever heard some many expletives in one sentence from her."

Jasmine saw Lamont on the ground and raised an eyebrow. "What the fuck is the village idiot doing here?"

I hung up the phone and shrugged. "He wouldn't leave me alone. I'm too fucking nice to leave him dead in a ditch. Although, now, I wish I had."

Lacie unlocked the door and pushed it open. "Throw his ass in the fucking bathtub."

"I'd rather leave him outside. He fucking deserves it."

Jasmine laughed. "Well, he's waking up, so, we have to do something." She grabbed his shoes and threw them in the bathroom. "Alright, Village Idiot. Get in the fucking bathtub. Your friend is on his way."

Lamont pushed past Lacie and Jasmine in a zombie-like manner.

"No—" Jasmine grabbed Lamont's arm in an attempt to guide him through the bathroom doorway. "Your bed's in here."

He aggressively yanked his arm away. "No."

I sat on my comforter and watched as Lamont undid his belt and dropped his pants to his ankles.

Jasmine's eyes widened. "Is he serious right now? Is this really happening?"

I couldn't help it—I laughed.

"Roxy, control your man. Get him in the fucking bath tub."

"Dude, what the fuck?" Lacie shouted as he unbuttoned his shirt and let it fall to the ground.

"Firstly, he's not my man. Secondly, he's dangerously drunk. And thirdly, I can't even control him when he's sober."

"I'm tired," Lamont grumbled. He crawled into Lacie's and Jasmine's bed despite their protests. "Sleep."

"We're leaving. He better be out of here by the time we get back or we're switching beds."

"Chris should be on his way to get him."

Lacie shrugged. "Wanna come with us?"

Although tempted, I declined. "I would, but I gotta wait for Chris. I don't want to be stuck in the same bed as him. I'd much sooner die."

Jasmine patted my thigh. "Good for you, Boo. You've finally learned your lesson."

Lacie laughed. "Maybe one of these days, you'll learn to wear your ring, even when around members of the opposite sex."

I half smiled. "Go drink for me."

When the door slammed behind them, I pulled my ring out of my bra and tucked it into the top pocket of my suitcase. I watched Lamont's chest rise and fall beneath the sheet, happy that I'd refused to have sex with him, but devastated with the way the night had down spiraled. *Tiffany. Beautiful fucking Tiffany. Why does it have to be her?*

#

I FOUND MYSELF sitting cross-legged in the white Chevy truck I told myself over a year ago I'd never see again. My stomach reeled when the truck turned, the silence stretching around my neck like a hangman's noose. The airport terminals were growing closer, no longer a desert mirage playing tricks on my eyes. *Should I say anything? Should I even try?* I looked down at my fingernails and began to pick at my lime green nail polish. *Is it worth it anymore?*

More than ready to escape from the bad choices I'd made in the last two days, I glanced out the window and waved goodbye to beautiful Sin City. Even at the early hour, the city was raging with life. People walked along sidewalks gawking at massive buildings, lines snaked outside hotel doors and cars honked at one another. Weekenders departed making room for the next round of sinners.

Despite last night's fiasco, Lamont kept his promise and met me in front of the hotel first thing after checkout. My girlfriends and I had discussed sharing a cab to the airport, but after he'd left the hotel room with a scowl glued to his slightly sobered up face the night before, I knew he and I needed to talk.

A lot was said—how much was truth and how much was liquor? I didn't know. I needed to find out. I wanted to confront him about Tiffany and about him loving me, but I was too scared he'd say he didn't remember any of it happening. I was even more afraid he'd tell me he never wanted to talk to me ever again. I hated myself for being so weak—in Sonoma, I'd slept with him

334

because I thought that would make him love me. Now, I figured because I stood up for myself, he would want nothing to do with me. I cleared my throat, but still didn't say anything.

When he finally turned in my direction, he smirked, so I pressed my lips together even tighter, watching as McCarran International Airport grew closer.

Glancing at the hand resting on his thigh, I stifled the cry burning in my throat. *You were strong last night. You did the right thing.*

The terminals were right next to me.

It was too late to turn the truck around.

*He doesn't deserve an apology. Don't forgive him. Not this time.*

As Lamont slowed the truck next to the curb, my head began to spin. I wasn't sure if it was the lack of sleep, the lack of water or the lack of a clear conscience, but I suddenly needed to lie down. Turning away from him, I opened the door and placed my black Converse on the sidewalk, bracing myself against the handle. The dry heat felt like a cool mist compared to the stifling silence inside the truck.

To my surprise, the ignition clicked off and the driver's door opened. I smiled, dropped my carry-on backpack to the ground, hauled my overly packed suitcase off the backseat and proceeded to stare at the crack beside it. Even though his white Nike's came into view, I was too afraid to look at his eyes. *Why did I think he would change? Why did I think things would be different? Why did I think he meant it when he said he loved me?*

"You probably shouldn't forget this."

A quick gulp. A dry swallow. A lifted gaze.

"It would be a real tragedy if you couldn't do you hair in the morning."

I chuckled, embarrassed. "Thank you. That would have been a disaster," I replied as I grabbed my toiletry bag from his grasp—a bag filled with too many cosmetic products, too many hair supplies, and too many scented sprays to count. "Guess that means I should get going then, huh?"

He silently shifted his weight from one foot to another, his eyes darting from my face to his truck.

"Thank you for driving me," I said softly. "You didn't have to."

Though brief, he flashed a smile.

A smile that made it difficult to breathe.

"I promised."

I nodded. "Yeah, but you—"

He jingled the change in his pockets. "Stop. Don't be weird. It's no big deal."

His deep, monotone voice sent a whirlwind through my chest. *Remember how he treated you last night. Remember how he's treated you this entire time.* I began to wish he hadn't stepped out of the truck. *He's in love with Tiffany. Not you. Never you.*

"Well, thank you. Get back to your boys. I've kept you long enough."

He shook his head. "I could use my Lady Luck at the tables tonight."

My heart hiccupped. *Was that an invite to stay?* "Not my fault you kept playing cards after I left you." *He wants someone to screw. You're nothing more than a whore to him.*

"You shouldn't have left me in the first place."

"Yeah, well, worse stuff has happened." I hoped for a chuckle, but instead, I spotted pity. Big, brown, beautiful pools of pity. There was something else lurking—nostalgia, maybe? "Look, Lamont—"

He stretched out his arms and embraced me. While I should have pushed him away, I pulled him tighter, my cheek pressed firmly against his chest. *Let him go. It's time you finally let him go.*

"I'm going to miss you," I croaked.

"I'll miss you too, Roxanne." He ran his eyes down my face, focusing on my lips. "I'll *really* miss you." The tone of his voice matched my own—he was telling the truth.

He leaned forward, eyes closed. I couldn't rationalize my behavior. Nothing about it was logical. But my heart pushed me to meet Lamont halfway.

When our lips touched, I experienced the same dizzying sensation felt when we exchanged our first kiss two years ago. A missing puzzle piece pressed perfectly into the void Lamont had left in my heart. *He's going to hurt you all over again. Stop it. Push him away!* I grew lightheaded. Afraid I'd fall, I wrapped my arms around him even tighter. I kissed him as hard as I could, memorizing the feel of his mouth, his tongue, his scruffy chin. *Maybe last night was just a misunderstanding. Maybe he really does love me.*

He stopped kissing me, placed a moist peck on my forehead and pushed my hips away from him. "You're going to miss your flight."

*And maybe I should stop pretending he'll ever change.* I sighed, pushing my auburn curls behind my ears. "Vegas wouldn't be such a bad place to remain stranded."

He didn't respond, his hands returning straight to the depths of his pockets. His eyes lit up and that charming smile shot through my chest like a stray bullet. "I almost forgot," he said pulling out a black, rubber bracelet with BOOBIES inscribed in white, block letters. "I know you won't believe me, but I've kept it this whole time. I still wear it. It reminds me of you." He paused, smiling. "Thought I'd give it to you—you know—for old time's sake."

"Why weren't you wearing it last night?"

He shrugged. "It doesn't look good with dress clothes."

As I reached for it, unbelieving, Lamont closed his fingers around the small circle and placed his hands behind his back. "What hand is it in?"

That small gesture nearly killed me. "Are you serious?"

"Oh, c'mon. But this time, I'm not switching which hand it's in, just so you get it. You gotta guess right this time."

I guessed his left hand, the same hand it was in before, and was given an adorable smile as a reward—a smile that told me he, too, remembered the moment we fell for one another. Lamont placed the bracelet on my palm and gently closed my fingers over our memories. "I should've given it back a long time ago. I should've never let you take it off. I was an idiot, Roxanne. I just—I hope whenever you wear this, you'll think of me."

"You're not an idiot," I said, sadly. "Bad timing." I paused. "Always bad timing." I couldn't say anything more. Couldn't admit I didn't need a bracelet to think about him. Couldn't admit I doubted I'd ever love anybody like I loved him—that all-consuming love that made you do stupid things you never thought you were capable of doing.

Like running back to the person who hurt you over and over and over again.

After a small lull, Lamont shuffled his shoes and cleared his throat. "Have a good flight. Let me know when you land."

He didn't wait for a response.

The truck roared to life as the airport and its patrons faded away. I looked through his back window, straight at the rear-view mirror, hoping he'd take one last look at me. *Just one last look. Prove you meant what you said last night. Give me a sign that I didn't waste my time with you.*

But his focus remained on the road ahead of him—the road without me.

It was my turn to move forward.

Sighing, I slung my toiletry bag over my shoulder, followed suit with my carry-on backpack, and grabbed the handle of my suitcase. I couldn't help but wonder if meeting Lamont in Las Vegas was the sign I'd been searching for all along. A sign that, maybe, I wasn't ready to let go of my past just yet. Or, perhaps, a sign that we were never meant to be together in the first place.

I wiped away two tears, sniffled and licked my lips. The sliding doors opened and welcomed me into the air-conditioned lobby. I wandered toward the departure and arrival screens, stretching the bracelet around my wrist. *Am I really doing the right thing?*

"Sweetie! Over here!"

My head jerked up, a grin forming across my face.

"Hurry up and check your bags! We have a plane to catch," Jasmine shouted across the airport.

"Don't listen to her. Take your time. We could use another few days here," Lacie replied.

Jasmine elbowed her and shook her head adamantly. "I have work tomorrow. Hustle your little ass up."

"Little ass?" Lacie questioned. "Have you seen that thing, lately?"

Blushing, I tried to ignore the giggles from the women behind the counter. "Give me one second!" I shouted, their hands holding coffees, their hungover eyes masked by obnoxious sunglasses.

I looked at my bare left hand and my newly adorned wrist, choking back a sob. *Why does this hurt so much? I'm with Zach. I don't need Lamont to love me anymore.* I took a deep breath and smiled at the airline's associate behind the desk, handing over two of my three bags.

They barely made the weight limit, but the associate strapped a white tag around both handles and clumsily threw the bags onto the conveyor belt. The girls were already in line to get on the plane, but I needed a few more minutes to myself. To think about my behavior over the weekend. To wonder why I ran into Lamont after all this time. To question if I was making the right decision by marrying Zach.

I sat down in a comfortable grey chair, flipping the tiny diamond ring from one palm to the other, squeezing the silver between my thumb and forefinger. "What am I doing?"

Lamont's bracelet still rested on my wrist. I closed my eyes and allowed my body to be consumed by the past. Pure and innocent love was dirtied the instant we had to hide our first kiss—the girlfriend, the secrets, the cheating. Yet, somehow, it was all worth it. As long as Lamont truly loved me, or at least pretended to love me, everything else might fall into place.

I believed he would complete my jigsaw puzzle of a life.

I believed he would be the one to make me happy. "Maybe I didn't fall in love with him. Maybe I fell in love with the game."

I slipped the ring back on my finger and held it out. The bracelet and the ring—two circles that stood for two different things: my infinite love for Lamont and my infinite love for Zach. Those two things didn't belong together. They never belonged together. The faded and cracked rubber clashed with the diamond's sparkly shine.

It was time to make a choice once and for all.

Holding my breath, I stretched the bracelet out until it snapped against my skin and split in half. I walked up to the gate and quickly looked back before the flight attendant took my boarding pass and told me to keep moving forward.

I'd thrown the bracelet into the trash where it belonged.

Jasmine and Lacie were waiting for me in the plane, the middle seat available between them. "Saved the worst seat for me, huh?"

Jasmine winked. "You said you needed time to think. We were beginning to think you were gonna miss the flight."

I sat down and nodded. "Definitely considered it."

"Glad you still joined us. I'd be devastated if you left me on this flight with Jasmine."

She reached over me and slapped Lacie's arm. "You whore."

"Can we not start this already?"

The girls giggled. "Just trying to get your mind off all the bullshit."

"Yeah, we should be the one's complaining. We're hungover. You're not."

"I'm emotionally hungover. It's worse."

They laughed, each plugging a set of headphones into their ears.

"I'm proud of you for walking away," Lacie said loudly, talking over her music.

I nodded, resting my head on my seat's headrest. *She's right. I finally stood up to him. That has to mean something.* I glanced at my ring. *Now what?* I sighed happily, wondering how so much could change in such little time.

The mouse had retired.

The cat had grown tired of chasing.

The game was finally over.

Turn the page for a sneak preview of the second book in *The Games We Play* series:


# Little Bird, Big Sky

# Chapter One

"MISS VAUGHN," THE Indian man wearing a blue button-up in need of ironing said. "It appears you were born and raised here in San Diego but left for a couple years to attend college at—" He paused, readjusted his rectangular bifocals, and squinted at my application. "Sonoma State University."

I nodded, doing my best to hide how nervous I was. "That's correct, Sir. I wanted to see if Northern California was a good fit for me." My hands were folded in my lap, my engagement ring swimming in the depths of my purse alongside Chapstick, loose change and food crumbs. I didn't believe my relationship status would determine whether or not I was accepted for this position, but I found myself feeling more confident when I wasn't wearing the small, gold band with the small, white diamond.

His eyes lingered on my chest just long enough for me to wonder how this gentleman got a job in human resources in the first place. "Why did you come back?"

*Because I needed to stop drinking so recklessly,* I thought. *Because my anxiety was controlling me. Because I had to run away from the boy I loved to be with the boy who loves me.* "Well, I want to graduate in four years and with all of the staffing cuts, it wasn't gonna happen in a small school like that," I said instead, trying to analyze his reaction. When he stared at me silently, I wiped my hands on my thighs and forced myself to continue. "And—well—and I want to get in to the Master of Fine Arts at San Diego State and—I—I thought—well—that meeting the professors may—you know—help."

He raised an eyebrow. "So, you're an artist."

I blushed. "I *want* to be a writer. A poet."

After he leaned back in his chair, he rubbed his fingers over his beardless chin. "That's not something you hear every day." He studied me intently. "That's rather ambitious of you."

I clamped my jaw to fight the urge to tap my heel up and down. *Yeah, right,* I silently scoffed. *Why don't you tell my parents that?* Knowing that first impressions were important during interviews, I dressed to impress—not to my mother's standards, but I did my best. I owned one white button-up, which my mother mentioned was too tight around my chest and stomach. To overcompensate, I wore the comfortable, black slacks I currently had for my bussing job—the only pair of black slacks I've ever owned in my life. I thought that they were flattering, but my mom felt otherwise, letting me know that if I walked the twelve miles it took to get to Sea World, I might lose enough weight to make my clothes fit.

At least, get them to fit, sub-par.

*Not that it matters how you look,* she'd said as I was applying mascara to my lashes. *You're interviewing to be a waitress. I'm sure if you look homeless, they'll hire you.*

I had ignored her to the best of my ability, spraying my auburn curls with product, applying one more layer of lip-gloss and leaving the house without saying good-bye for fear that my parents would make another comment that would make me even more nervous than I already was. Maybe I wasn't following my family's footsteps—Mom's a Gynecologist, Dad's a Plastic Surgeon, and sister's a Gastroenterologist—but a serving job would guarantee me more tips than bussing at a buffet gave me.

"Ambition is a great attribute to have," the Indian man added, fingering the corner of my one-page resume. "Why don't you tell me why you'd like to work for Sea World?"

*Because my boyfriend told me you were hiring. Because I'm tired of people treating me like a piece of trash. Because I'd like to make some money so I can move away from my parents.* "I have friends who work in the park," I answered, lying slightly. *Well, I have one friend who works in the park. One boyfriend. Okay, a fiancé.* "And they mentioned this is an amazing company to work for. So, I wanted to experience firsthand what they were talking about." *I mean, he also talks about how much it sucks, but anything has to be better than what I'm doing now.* "And I love killer whales," I added for good measure.

He smiled, his right front tooth slightly overlapping the left one. He asked me a few more questions regarding *what if* scenarios and how I would handle them. I answered each question with a false confidence—as if I wasn't the kind of person who avoided eye contact with strangers, went into the bathroom and cried if a guest yelled at her, or the person who didn't complain about working in the food industry because she felt like a servant. *I'm great with customer service. Don't believe otherwise. Let him know just how good you are, Roxanne.* I took a deep breath without letting the Indian man figure out just how nervous I was getting as the interview continued. "I think that a friendly smile can go a long way, especially if someone has been dealing with children and crowds all day long." *There you go. Don't crumble beneath the pressure. Keep it cool and confident.* I made eye contact and flashed what I felt was my best movie star smile, awaiting his response.

"You're exactly what we're looking for at Dine with Shamu," the Indian man said pleasantly, folding his hands together on top of his desk. "You have a wonderful personality and obvious knowledge of the restaurant industry. Your answers today exceeded all expectations." He itched a stiff patch of gelled hair. "Let me file your paperwork so we can prepare your employee profile. Do you have any questions?"

*Could you let my parents know that I exceeded your expectations?* My cheeks began to hurt, I was smiling so wide. "So—I—I got the job?"

The man chuckled. "Yes. Yes, you did." He held out his hand, which I eagerly shook. "Welcome to the Sea World team, Miss Vaughn."

"Thank you so much," I replied. "I can't wait to start."

He nodded. "Good luck with your poetic endeavors. Maybe you'll find some inspiration here."

I blushed and shrugged. "Thank you," I said again. When I left the HR building, out into the fresh air, I inhaled the scent of salt and palm trees, Sea World being located on the backside of Mission Bay. I looked to the left, beyond a black gate next to the security office, and saw employees laughing with one another.

My smile widened.

After the Las Vegas trip that had gone from entertaining to embarrassing in sixty seconds flat only one month prior, this was exactly what I needed to break me out of my zombie-like trance. Lacie and Jasmine, my two best friends, promised to keep my secret safe—what happens in Vegas, stays in Vegas and what not—and didn't pass judgement, or make me feel like a terrible person, even though I made bad decision after horribly bad decision while in the Nevada heat. Nobody was to find out that I'd kissed my ex-lover, Lamont Carwyn. Nobody was to find out I admitted my love to him in a moment of weakness. Nobody was to find out he broke my heart all over again because he was in a relationship with one of my ex-best friends from Sonoma State.

We may not have engaged in coitus, but I had emotionally and physically cheated on my *fiancé*. Before the engagement, when Zachary Cameron and I were long-distance boyfriend and girlfriend, I *had* engaged in that horrendous sexual behavior. Too many times. Far too many times. The entire sophomore year, actually, without my boyfriend ever discovering the truth.

Lamont had been my tall, dark and handsome—a boy I loved for too long, that cliché game of *Cat and Mouse* defining our unofficial relationship. Since I'd ran into him while in Las Vegas, my seemingly never-faltering feelings waivered, my brain finally convincing my heart that Lamont just *wasn't good for me*.

Somehow, I'd even gathered up enough courage to tell Zachary the half-truth. I mentioned that the girls and I bumped into Lamont on The Strip, and parted ways after grabbing one quick drink as a group. Zachary had nodded, hugged me and thanked me for my honesty, and I never brought up the Las Vegas trip around him ever again. I also hadn't been tempted to look at Lamont's Facebook profile, miraculously not caring about his relationship with the woman he once called the most beautiful girl in the world—or at least, I refused to let myself look at it, not wanting to fall into a black hole of heartbreak all over again.

Now, as I made my way toward the employee parking lot, I slid my engagement ring back on my finger, ecstatic to tell my fiancé the good news. He was, after all, the one who discovered the job opening for me. He actually already worked at Sea World, at a barbeque restaurant called Calypso Bay Smokehouse, and had heard from one of his coworkers that the fine dining restaurant, Dine with Shamu, was hiring. Although Zachary didn't always talk highly about his job and had intended to only be there for one summer, he wound up staying because he didn't want to move back into his father's house, for some reason preferring to live in the small, illegally built, room located behind a furniture shop off of University Avenue.

In a not-too-nice side of town.

The ARCO across the street was always packed because they boasted the cheapest gas prices in San Diego, but there had also been a shooting at the night club only a black away six months prior. The last thing I needed was my parents chewing me out for even *thinking* about crossing the street light into that side of town, so they didn't know that Zachary moved out of his dad's house four months ago.

I found Zachary leaning against the front door of his dinged up and dented Honda Civic, Aviator glasses framing his sharply angled face. His white t-shirt hugged his body nicely, his softer physique replacing his once muscular one due to poor eating habits and lack of exercise. I sucked in and flexed my own stomach muscles, hating how my belly pushed against the button of my pants. *I really need to start making time to work out.* I brushed my bangs behind my ear and lifted my gaze to see my own rosy cheeks reflected back at me in Zachary's sunglasses.

"My, oh, my," he said before emitting a low whistle. "My fiancé is *gorgeous*."

"Oh, hush," I hissed, glancing around to make sure nobody was near enough to overhear us. "You're gonna make me blush and it took me forever to cover up these cheeks."

"Well, I love your rosy cheeks."

This time, I really did blush, flattered. "Thank you, Handsome."

When he smiled his coffee-stained, in-desperate-need-of-braces teeth at me, simultaneously lifting his Aviators so I was exposed to his meadow-frolicking eyes—the ones with golden rays as warm as a San Diego Spring day—the heel of my wedges caught on a rock, causing me to stumble. I fell against my fiancé's chest.

He wrapped his arms around me and chuckled. "Did you just fall for me again or are you just clumsy?"

I shrugged into him. "Maybe a little bit of both?"

He leaned forward and kissed me, hesitantly at first, intensifying the passion when I played with his tongue, pulling his body closer to mine. Maybe it was because of my newfound elation from getting a new job, but something inside of me awoke—something that had laid dormant since Zachary's proposal in December.

The feeling reminded me of the giddy sensation I had the first time Zachary had visited me in Rohnert Park. I actually *desired* my fiancé, which was strange because I had become used to being intimate with Zachary out of guilt and obligation. *I've missed this more than anything. Why can't I feel like this all of the time?* When I pulled away, I slowly opened my eyes, wanting nothing more than to savor the sensation curling my toes.

"I take it the interview went well?" he breathed, his forehead resting against mine.

I smiled. "I got the job."

He lifted me into the air, twirling me in a circle, again reminding me of our first night together in Rohnert Park. "I knew you'd get it—you're the sweetest little woman in the entire world. They'd be *crazy* not to hire you."

"Thanks for believing in me."

"You know what this means?" He grabbed my hands. "I get to see you outside *and* inside of work."

My smile widened. "You mean we can eat lunch together?"

He nodded. "If we plan it right, we can find a way."

*If I didn't love him, I wouldn't feel this excited, right?* "That sounds like the best part of the job," I whispered, my emotions beginning to overwhelm me.

"Oh, my Little Woman," he cooed, kissing my cheeks—the right, then the left. "You've made my day."

Although we hadn't been intimate with one another in over a month—I'd already overused the "I'm sorry baby, I'm tired" excuse that shouldn't be a problem until *after* marriage—I now found myself eager to climb all over my fiancé.

"I can think of something that might make your day even better."

His eyebrows climbed up his forehead. "Are you saying what I think you're saying?"

I nuzzled against his collarbone. "Well, my car *is* at your place." I feigned a yawn and kissed his neck. "I might need a nap before I drive home—or, you know—something like that."

He smirked and smacked my bottom. "You should have job interviews more often."

It was an innocent joke, but I felt my walls rise up around me. *Don't take it personally—he didn't mean it like that.* I pulled away and frowned. *But every joke has a little bit of truth to it, doesn't it?* "Is that all I am to you?" I snapped. "Is that all that *really* matters?"

Zachary frowned. "Don't be like that."

I shrugged. "You started it."

He placed his hand on my butt and squeezed. "Stop being such a brat and get that cute booty in the car."

Even though my intense desire had faded, I smiled and kissed my fiancé on the lips, doing my best to fight the nagging annoyance settling in the pit of my stomach. "You know I love you, right?"

"I love you, more, Little Woman," he replied.

*And that,* I confessed to myself. *Is why I chose you instead of Lamont.*

#

"ROXY, JUST TAKE the damn prescription," my sister demanded. "Mom takes it. I take it. This world would be a better place if *everyone* took it. It's *no big deal.*"

I sat in Lucy's office, sandaled feet dangling off the side of the light blue plastic chair. The white paper crinkled beneath my jean shorts, my pale thighs glowing against the florescent lighting. "You're a stomach doctor. I don't think this is *really* under your jurisdiction."

It was noontime and I'd brought my older sister some lunch. I'd driven up to Los Angeles after my final shift the day before so that I could see my niece. It was my last weekend off before the beginning of the school semester, and my sister had invited me to stay with her in order to spend time with Hannah before I "disappeared from the human world" and "became a hermit" even though English majors had "nothing worthwhile to study." Although I didn't care much for my brother-in-law, I accepted the invitation because my sister was blood, and I one-hundred-percent adored my niece.

I thought I'd be a nice sister and bring Lucy lunch, but my nice gesture had somehow morphed into a doctor's appointment that I wasn't at all prepared for.

"Thanks for assuming I don't know what I'm doing, little Miss Know It All," my sister replied. "But anxiety in our family runs through the stomach."

I shrugged, pretending she wasn't correct even though she hit the nail on the head. "I know my own body better than you do. I don't need to take the strong stuff—five milligrams of Lexapro is just fine."

"Obviously, it's not." She shook her head, her straight, blonde hair brushing against her shoulders. "I know you hate listening to me, but this is your *health*. I take my profession very seriously."

"I think a vast majority of my problems have come about *because* I've listened to you."

Her forest green eyes narrowed. "Mom is worried about you."

I snorted. "If she was *really* worried, wouldn't she *do* something about it instead of *gossiping* to you about it?"

"You *always* take what I say the wrong way. Why don't you just accept that your mother cares about you?"

*Because she doesn't care. I've had to take out student loans for following my own dreams instead of hers. How is that care?* When I remained quiet, studying the cartoon diagram of a stomach on the wall, Lucy threw up her hands in defeat.

"Do you *want* to suffer through life alone?"

I began playing with a curl. "Why do you think there's a problem? I already told you, *I'm fine*."

"Oh *really*?" she sneered, crossing her arms over her chest. "Then why do you cry all o the time? And why do you always have panic attacks?"

*Because I don't want to get married yet, but I don't know how to tell Zach that without hurting his feelings.* I began swinging my legs, now focusing on the white tile beneath my feet. *She doesn't need to know. She'll just tell Mom and then she'll rub it in my face that she was right.* "School is just stressing me out. I graduate in May. I'm applying for grad school and really—"

Lucy, who had reached into her purse producing a brown baggy filled with mini chocolate chip cookies, began mocking me with her free hand as if it were a puppet. "Cry me a river. You're an *English* major. Boo hoo." She popped a cookie into her mouth. "You write *poetry*. Like that's *so difficult*."

I ripped a piece of white paper out from beneath my leg and began to roll it between my palms. "Can you not—"

"Feel free to complain to me when you're in your final year of med school."

"That's not gonna happen."

She smirked. "Then you should probably stop complaining."

I glared at the crumbs sticking to her crimson lipstick. "Since when do you eat cookies?"

"Since when did you become the food police?"

I shrugged. "You know what they say—a moment on the lips..."

Lucy's eyes widened, a few crumbs falling to her light purple scrubs. "Why are you being such a bitch? I'm trying to *help* you."

"*Help me*?" I rolled my eyes. "I'm so tired of you and Mom guilting me about being a writer instead of becoming doctors like you. You both like to butt into my business and *usually*, you guys made my situation worse. *You* guys make my anxiety ten times worse any time you try to *help*."

"Stop blaming other people for your problems and man up—anxiety is an inner battle." Another bite of cookie, crumbs gathering for a party on her chest. "Just take the Lorazepam when you're having a panic attack. It's not for everyday use anyway."

I stood and began pacing the miniscule square space. "Why do you have such a hard time listening to me? I don't need it."

"I think I know what's best."

I turned and faced her like a bull with its eyes on a matador. "*You* know what's best? My entire life, you've been giving me advice that's come back to bite me in the butt."

"Oh *really*?" She snapped. "Like what?"

"Hmm, let me think," I said, sarcastically. "Like when you told me it's fine for someone to *cheat* on their boyfriend as long as a ring isn't in the picture."

"That's *not* what I said!"

"Yes it is!" My mind wandered back to Sonoma State—when Lamont had a girlfriend and kissed me, and when my boyfriend, now fiancé, Zachary had no idea I was engaging in intercourse with Lamont frequently because I was in love with him. "You said as long as neither me or Lamont were married, what we were doing was *fine*."

She chuckled. "You just *love* to play the blame game." Lucy turned around and began rifling through her cabinets. "I think I have a sample in here—"

"I don't *want* a sample of anything!" I sat down heavily, the paper crinkling beneath my thighs. "This is what I'm talking about. You just do whatever you want to do without listening to me."

"I *am* listening—for the eight hundredth time, I'm trying to help."

*Then maybe find some Viagra for women. Getting it up will save my relationship.* "Well, stop. I don't need help."

Lucy continued fiddling through the cabinet, looking at each small box before tossing it back in. "So, you're going to take one pill when you're having a full-blown panic attack. Half of one if you have to drive and function at some normal capacity." She nodded, taking out a small box before shaking it next to her ear. "Just don't drink any alcohol when you take it. May seem like a fun idea—but believe me, it's not."

I crossed my arms over my stomach and held my elbows. "If you were *actually* listening to me, you'd stop trying to push these pills on me. I'm done," I whispered, eyeing the small engagement ring that refused to sparkle in the florescent lighting. "Lucy, I should get going."

For the first time since I entered her office, she *really* looked at me. "Why don't you tell me what's *actually* bothering you?"

"I—I—just—"

My sister placed her hand on her chin. "I think some sun would do you wonders."

I rolled my eyes.

"No, I'm being serious. You live in San Diego. Aside from the fact that you look like you're from Nebraska, Vitamin D will help your anxiety."

"Okay—I'm done trying."

Lucy washed her hands. "Oh, c'mon. Don't be so sensitive." She dried her hands on three paper towels. "Is this about your upcoming nuptials?"

"They aren't *upcoming*," I said a little too quickly.

Lucy raised an eyebrow. "I think we've found the problem here Quickdraw McGraw."

The chilling sensation began at my fingertips. *I'm okay. I'm okay. I'm okay,* I told myself. The churning in my stomach rose to an uncomfortable pain. *I'm okay. I'm okay. I'm okay.* The ringing in my ears was nearly deafening.

I hated that my panic attacks worked like clockwork—the symptoms were always the same, and my two-word mantra had become the only way to slow them down. Unfortunately, one the latter symptoms began, it was almost impossible to stop the train wreck. The worst was when my skin would itch as if I were wearing a Christmas sweater knit by my aunt. And as if that sweater was glued to my skin, unable to rip off how uncomfortable I felt.

Lucy took note of my suddenly pale face. "Yup. I knew it." She rifled through her diaper bag sized purse. "None of that school bull crap made sense." She pulled out a water bottle and shoved it into my hands. "Sip this and breathe. Deep breaths in and out. I'm being serious. *Breathe.*"

I nodded, trying to hold back my tears, the water slowly bringing life back into my fingers. *I'm okay, I'm okay, I'm okay.* "It's complicated," I croaked.

Lucy leaned back against the counter. "Try me."

I breathed in and out, my stomach feeling tight, as if I had just finished a round of sit-ups. "I'm not looking for advice."

She shrugged. "You may not want to accept it because you don't like to think your family loves you, but I'm here for you."

"Don't you have other patients you need to help?"

She glanced at the clock on the wall. "You're not leaving until we talk."

*I could just lie again, or I could tell her the truth and get this suffocating feeling off of my chest.* "I don't want to be intimate with Zach anymore," I blurted.

"Did that start when he bought you *that* ring? Because I totally understand."

My shoulders slouched. "*This* is what I'm talking about."

When I stared at my shoes, she cleared her throat. "You know I'm only joking." She paused. "Ish." Another pause. "Well, you should know that's a possible side effect of Lexapro."

"Not wanting to get it on with your fiancé?"

"Not wanting to get it on with anybody," she answered matter-of-factly. "Low libido is definitely a real thing."

I looked at her, surprised. "Really?"

"Well, do you find yourself wanting to do the nasty nasty with anyone else?"

I thought back to Las Vegas when I didn't want to have sex with Lamont. *And here I thought I didn't want to sleep with him because I learned my lesson.* I sighed. *Nope. Just Western Medicine controlling my body.* "I want to have sex sometimes—but that excited feeling doesn't last very long."

She nodded. "I'm not saying *that's* the problem—maybe you're not attracted to your fiancé anymore—but the pill causing problems may be a possibility."

"Crap," I whispered. "What if I'm not ready for marriage yet?"

"Then why did you say yes?"

Tears began to flood my eyes. "Because I love him. When the man you love asks you to marry him in the middle of a huge crowd beneath fireworks and fake snow, you say yes."

"Maybe try *not* to think about it." She reached into her diaper bag again, producing a bottle of sparkling water. "You aren't getting married *yet*. Sometimes, engagements last a while. Just pretend you're not wearing the ring and it'll be as if nothing's changed." She smirked. "It's not like it weighs anything anyway."

"Welp," I said, slapping my hands on my thighs. "I think that is my cue to leave."

Lucy laughed. "Take the medicine when you're having a bad day. I swear you won't worry about Zach or school or anything."

I rolled my eyes. "How about you recommend a physician in San Diego, so I don't have to deal with you when I'm having health issues?" I stood and began making my way toward the door. "I'll see you later."

"Wait," Lucy said. "Think you could babysit Hannah tonight?"

I stared at her. "I have to go home to get ready for school."

She frowned. "Oh, c'mon! I know you. You were ready for school a month ago."

*I hate that she knows me so well.* "But with traffic—"

"Roger and I don't wanna stay out too late," she interrupted. "Besides, you'll hit more traffic now than you will tonight."

I wanted to argue, but she gave me her well-practiced puppy eyes.

"*Please*," she begged. "Roger and I need a night away from the little one. We're forgetting what it's like to be adults."

"Fine," I sighed. "Can you bring me back something for dinner?"

She clapped her hands. "Deal! We'll bring you back cheesecake." She wrapped me in a hug. "Thank you for doing this. Roger and I caught ourselves watching Sesame Street without Hannah, and we *really* need a break."

"You know you could *hire* someone to watch her—there's this thing called a *babysitter*."

"I may be carefree about a lot of things, but I'm not about to leave my flesh and blood with a complete stranger." When she let go, she reached into the pocket of her lab coat and scribbled something onto a small notepad. "And I'm not kidding about the prescription. Take it when you're having a panic attack." She paused. "Or get rid of the thing that is making you feel anxious all of the time."

Even though Zachary came to mind, I refused to let Lucy believe my upcoming nuptials weren't the only problem in my relationship. In fact, I refused to let myself believe that. "But you're my sister. I can't get rid of you."

"Maybe find some time to get laid," she said handing me the prescription. "You're not as funny as you were when you were getting the D regularly."

My cheeks flushed pink. "I hate you. Do you know that?"

She beamed. "The feeling is mutual, Baby Sis."

#

"HOW'S SEA WORLD?" Luke asked, picking up his menu. "You happier than you were before?"

"*Much* happier," I replied. "I still bus tables, but I'm serving drinks, too. So, I actually make tips!" I paused. "And I'm trying to make friends, which, you know—is strange."

One of my best friends and I sat in a small booth at BJ, a restaurant located at one of the local malls, Grossmont Center. It was way too hot outside, the early September weather reaching record highs, so each of us suggested an activity that required air-conditioning; I said lunch, he said a movie. We decided to make a full date out of it since we hadn't been able to hang out much during the summer. Although school had already begun for me, I didn't mind having a reason not to study, especially when I had the day off of work.

Luke began his first commission-based job as a women's shoe salesman at Bloomingdales—one of those upscale, overly priced retail stores in the heart of Fashion Valley, a mall I could only visit when my mother selected an outfit for me that made others believe I knew the difference between Fendi and Prada. The job was *perfect* for him. He had the fashion sense of an editor at Vogue, while I, on the other hand, was happy wearing sweatpants and t-shirts that I found—and smell checked—on my floor.

The two of us made quite a pair: Luke sporting his Lucky Brand jeans and red button-up that was ironed first thing in the morning, and me in my Target brand sweatpants and my baggy Batman t-shirt that I found crumpled beneath my bed. Although my closet was filled with expensive clothing my mother had approved and purchased, insisting that I wear them so I would look like a Vaughn, I refused to wear any of them. I told her the clothes were beautiful but didn't look right on me.

She said with a little makeup and the right shoes, the clothes would look fine. I had told her that would be like her buying off-brand cereal and trying to convince me it was the real thing.

Luke smiled. "Oh, my bad—you *love* your job. Is the world coming to an end? Did I miss the memo?"

"I know, *right*?" I replied. "It's like having a good job has turned me into a whole new person."

"Well, that makes one of us."

I frowned. "Not diggin' the shoe biz?"

He shrugged. "Maybe it's because we haven't been *super* busy, but I thought I'd be swimming in commission by now."

"You got this job like three months ago. Give it some time."

"I like to think I'm handsome and charming enough to have quickly developed a reliable clientele."

I chuckled. "You're *gay* and sell *women's* shoes. It's only a matter of time until you're the guy every woman is asking for."

He snorted into his water. "I'm in this business to make money—I don't have *time*."

I giggled, unrolled the black, cloth napkin in front of me and placed it on my lap. "You gays have *zero* patience."

"So, Roxanne, why don't you tell me about the boys from Dine with Shamu?"

'Why? You interested?" I asked, playfully.

"No, not me. But *you* should be."

I glanced at my thighs, avoiding eye-contact, fiddling with the fork and knife on the table. *He's just joking.* I breathed, my face feeling feverish. *There's no reason to panic. No reason to feel guilty about anything.* I sipped my water, the ice burning my teeth. *I've done nothing wrong. I'm okay, I'm okay, I'm okay.* "There's a bunch of cute guys, but I'm *not* interested. I have a fiancé, and if you remember, he works—like—three feet away from me."

The waitress interrupted us, asking if we wanted anything other than water. My initial response was no thank you—it was too early for any alcoholic beverage—but then the tingling in my fingers intensified. "Actually," I said, interrupting Luke's response. "Could I get a margarita please?"

The waitress smiled and nodded. "Blended or on the rocks?"

"Blended. No salt."

She asked for my ID while Luke breathed a sigh of relief. "Thank God! I thought I'd be drinking by myself."

"Never stopped you before," I joked.

Luke smiled at the waitress, who batted her lashes and flushed just slightly. "I'll have a dirty martini with three olives, please."

"Anything else?" she asked, flirtatiously.

He shook his head. "We'll probably get an app, but we need drinks first."

She nodded, being sure to soak in Luke's light mocha skin, five o'clock shadow, dark brown eyes and high cheek bones.

"That girl is gonna ask you for your number before—or give you her number—by the end of lunch."

Luke ignored me, crossing his hands in front of him calmly. "You do know it's completely harmless to look at beautiful men. You just can't touch."

I sighed, fingering the corner of the napkin on my lap. "There's such a thing as emotional infidelity."

"Let's be real. Looking is the most harmless thing you can do moving forward."

"Can you *not*?" I asked, slapping his hand. "I'm a different person, believe it or not. I'm a good fiancé. Doing all of the things I should've been doing since day one."

"Oh, *right*," he snorted. "Is that why you texted me the other day about running into that good-looking guy from your English class?"

The waitress returned with a pitcher of water, filling Luke's glass to the top while ignoring mine. "Your drinks will be out shortly. Did you think about that appetizer?"

"How about the avocado rolls?" I suggested.

She ignored me, still focusing on my best friend.

"How about the avocado rolls?" Luke said, repeating my order.

She nodded and scampered off.

"I would've liked a water refill," I mumbled, my anxiety still simmering in my blood.

"Did he look cute?" Luke asked, handing me his water glass.

I drank generously. "Can we talk about *anything* else?" I frowned. "How about politics?"

Luke laughed and studied the menu again. "I thought Zach worked at the BBQ place across the park?"

I rolled my eyes. "You don't understand what *changing topics* means, do you?"

He smirked at me over the menu.

A droplet of water cascaded down the glass. "It's my fault he doesn't anymore. I encouraged him to apply for this Zoological Assistant position that opened up."

The waitress dropped off our drinks and avocado rolls, Luke again ignoring her advances.

"He has *zero* animal experience," I continued. "So, I didn't think he'd have a chance. But—of course—God hates me, and Zach *somehow* got it." After taking a sip of the margarita, I grabbed a roll and took a bite. "He guides people in wetsuits from Dolphin Stadium to the back of Dolphin Point, which is *literally* across the Shamu pool from Dine. He's seen me laughing with a male coworker before and he questioned me about it."

"He is *literally* the most insecure person I know."

I shrugged. "With how bad of a girlfriend I've been, he has every right to be."

"Not really—he doesn't *know* about any of that." Luke sighed, grabbing an avocado roll for himself. "Sweetie, have you put any more thought into *not* marrying him?"

*Too much, too often.* I stayed silent.

"I only ask because whenever you talk about him lately, you seem a little freaked out."

*That's because I am freaked out. But I made him a promise—I said yes—I can't back out.* "I know you care about me, but I *really* don't want to talk about him anymore. I feel like he's taken over my entire life and I would just like to spend a couple hours thinking about *anything* but him."

"Well then," he said, before sipping his margarita. "What are you gonna get for lunch?"

"I haven't even looked at the menu yet."

Luke smiled. "How about another cocktail?"

"*One* more. I don't want to fall asleep during the movie."

The waitress returned, flirted with Luke again, and asked if we wanted to order entrees yet.

When she walked off, Luke rolled his eyes. "Maybe we should just get snacks at the theatre. I'm tired of this girl eye-fucking me."

"Must be *so hard* to be *so handsome*," I teased.

He finished off his martini. "It's annoying when straight girls treat you like a piece of meat—I'd rather have a cute guy treat me *that* way."

I sipped my fruity beverage. "So, have you engaged in any homosexual coitus lately?"

#

"HOW CAN I help you, Miss Vaughn?" Jocelyn Palmer, the professor of my short fiction class, smiled her professionally whitened teeth at me, hear dark purple lipstick making me rethinking having purple as my favorite color.

I cleared my throat, uncomfortable, nervous and feeling as tall as a mouse. "Do you think I could ask you some questions about the MFA program?"

We were still in the small classroom located in Hepner Hall—an old building in the center of campus that was similar to a maze because of the confusing room numbers—the shades lowered, the only lighting coming from the florescent bulbs on the ceiling.

I felt like I was back in my sister's doctor's office all over again.

My professor nodded curtly, her blonde curls slightly falling in front of her right eye. "Have you given any more thought about pursuing fiction instead of poetry?"

The previous year, in Professor Palmer's poetry class, she had accidently found one of my "not meant for anyone to ever read" short stories and forced me to turn in one for my final—threatening to fail me if I did otherwise.

"Yes, I have, ma'am," I said, still bitter about her not liking my poetry. "I think I have some pages of a potential novel written."

"That's great and all, but I have some bad news for you." She paused, taking note of my fidgeting hands. "And despite what you and my failing students may think, I really *hate* being the bearer of bad news." She paused again, placing her bronzed cheek on her palm. "That's not what you should be focusing on."

My heart deflated, my hands falling to my sides. "But—but—you—the website—I thought—but—a writing sample?"

"For starters, learning how to complete a sentence may help." She glanced at her hot pink watch before gathering together the pens and papers that littered the wooden desk at the front of the classroom. "I have another class to get to. I really don't—"

I nodded, knowing what she was going to say next. "That's okay. I'll just email—"

She shook a pen in my face. "The last thing I need is another email spamming my inbox. How about you sit those sweats down and put your note taking to good use?"

I promptly sat in the desk to my left and whipped out a glittery notebook. "Do you think—"

"I think," she said, interrupting me. "You should start writing and stop talking. Yes, the MFA website wants a thirty-page writing sample. No, they *do not* want an excerpt of a novel. You need *two very different* short stories that *really* showcase your writing." She checked her watch again, brushing a strand of curls behind her ear. "The program is on the experimental side of the spectrum—the focus tends to be on socio-political issues."

I scribbled frantically, my handwriting getting worse and worse the quicker she spoke.

"You need *three* glowing—like absolutely radiant—letters of recommendation from your professors. Be persistent. Professors are always busy and usually don't have time to help—but don't be annoying because then they won't want to help. Take the GRE. Just don't concern yourself with the math—"

"But don't you *dare* fuck up the writing portion," a deep, male voice concluded from the hallway.

Professor Palmer and I looked towards the classroom door. "Very PC of you, Ezra."

The brown skinned, black haired man strolled into the room and sat on the corner of the professor's table. "Make sure you write that down," he said, pointing to my notebook.

"Don't f—um—*mess*—around," I mumbled, the pink ink barely legible beneath my shaking hand. "So, how do I study for it?"

"There's a purple book you need to buy from Barnes and Noble," Professor Palmer said.

"Aren't you running late for a class?" the man asked. "Or are you hoping they'll just give up and leave before you get there?"

Professor Palmer flushed. "If you hadn't so rudely barged in, I'd be on my way already."

"Giving this young woman an unfair advantage, I see."

Professor Palmer scoffed. "The program could use some diversity."

"She looks pretty white to me."

"I meant her different writing style—Ezra, do you ever think before you speak?"

I flinched, unsure if she was complimenting or insulting me.

"Now," my professor continued. "Are you done being you? Because I'd rather not miss my next class entirely."

The man chuckled. "I'll get out of that beautiful curly hair of yours. I just heard your voice and wanted to see if we're still on for coffee tonight."

"Ezra," Professor Palmer said sternly. "There's this thing in your pocket called a cell phone. Next time, please refrain from this inappropriate behavior and make use of modern technology."

The man smiled, pulling his wavy, shoulder-length hair into a beanie he produced from his back-jean pocket. He reminded me of a prince from a Disney movie, his hair so feathery, I wanted to stuff my pillowcase full of it. "If you'll excuse me, I have students taking a test down the hall. I should probably get back to them and make sure they're not cheating." He paused, hand on his chin, light hazel eyes glancing at the ceiling. "Oh—wait—they can't. They all have different essays."

Professor Palmer shooed him away with her black tipped, glitter topped, acrylic fingernails. "Go easy on the poor critters. They're only freshman."

He winked. "They gotta learn early." And then he disappeared, his tennis shoes squeaking against the hallway tile.

"He sounds—uh—nice?" I managed, trying not to blush.

Professor Palmer grinned, her hazel eyes gleaming a shade of gold. "That's Ezra Castillo. Mainly teaches graduate classes, but the English Department stupidly gave him an undergraduate Classical Literature class this semester." She twirled a loose curl. "He's nice, but he's a hard ass—especially on his students."

The lingering tension made me smirk. *Oh my goodness. Are they—a thing? Professor Palmer has human emotions?* "Is there anything else I should know?"

She placed the pens and papers into a camouflage patterned satchel and sighed. "Last thing—but the *single* most important thing—is the personal statement. Avoid clichés. Stand out. Use your failed pre-med experience to your advantage." She glanced at her watch one final time and sore under her breath. "Don't be afraid to brown nose. Jim Harvey is the granddaddy of the program. I *highly* recommend mentioning how much you'd like to take one of his classes."

"I have a class with him now," I said, feigning excitement. "Film and Literature." *And I hate everything about him and the graphic films he's made us watch so far.* "He's—" I paused, carefully trying out the words in my mind before allowing them to take shape. "He's an interesting character."

Even though she chortled, Professor Palmer said nothing further on the topic. "I'll email you the letter I wrote so you have something to refer to—and there's Google. Now, I have to go. If there are any other questions, make sure you ask me at a time that won't put me behind schedule."

"Um—wait—Professor," I nearly whispered.

Jocelyn Palmer turned around, waiting for me to continue.

I bit my lip. "Is fiction the right path for me? Should I *really* give up on poetry?"

She didn't respond, but I could've sworn I noticed her head nod just slightly. She turned and left the room, her high heels clacking on the tile, fading farther and farther away. I walked to the doorway, notebook clutched to my chest, and watched those blonde ringlets bounce against her shoulders, her jeans dark and tight, her t-shirt baggy and pastel orange—everything disappeared around the corner before I found the ability to move my feet again.

"Yes, Ma'am," I mumbled sadly. "Loud and clear."

THE GAMES WE PLAY

# Acknowledgments

I'd like to thank my boyfriend, Joshua, for being there for me during the countless nights of crying over my notebook and staying up late, trying to get through the worst cases of writer's block. He has urged me to continue writing and to never give up no matter how difficult the journey may seem. He has been a true inspiration and support system.

I'd also like to thank my parents, Rich and Kim, for their unconditional love and for opening up their home to me while I was going through school, working, and trying to save money so I could create my own editing business and travel to different states to gather information for potential future novels. And most importantly, I'd like to thank them for being there for me while my heart was broken over and over again thanks to boys, lost friends, and exhausting schoolwork.

Lastly, I'd like to thank three girls that had, at one time, been my best friends—girls who inspired me to write this book even though we haven't seen one another in years. Candice, Nicole and Dana, thank you for showing me what it was like to have such great friends. You guys helped me grow up, grow out of my shell, and learn how to trust people in a way I was afraid didn't actually exist. You girls were my rock for an entire year, and I don't know if I would have survived all of the drama without you there by my side.

# About The Author

Jacquelyn Phillips is a graduate of San Diego State University, having attended Sonoma State University for the first two years of her undergraduate English Program. She then continued her school journey in grad school, obtaining her Master of Fine Arts in Fiction writing in 2016 at San Diego State University. She was the editor-in-chief of literary journal, pacificREVIEW, the "Strangely Ever After" edition in 2014, had her short story, *Cinderella*, published in literary journal Aztec Literary Review in 2013, and then had her short story, *Power Surge*, published in pacificREVIEW in 2016. She was the editor and co-writer of Amazon Best-Seller, *ORCAstration*, with former killer whale trainer, Rich Phillips. She writes many dark fairy tales and hopes to create a novel out of them one day, but she currently is working on *The Games We Play* series, which she began writing in 2011. She lives in San Diego and believes that such a great city should be put on the map in literature. Her cat, Gatsby, is her loyal pet, named after one of her favorite characters in literary history. She currently bartends and waitresses at a brewery, continuing to pursue her dream of becoming the next great author, hoping to inspire those who read to follow their dreams and never be afraid to fall in love.

Made in the USA
Columbia, SC
14 June 2021